I0545777

Caitlin's Duke

Christine Young

Published by Rogue Phoenix Press, LLP
Copyright © 2019

ISBN: 978-1-62420-477-7

Credits
Cover Artist: Designs by Ms G
Editor: Christie L. Kraemer

She played a fiddle in an Irish pub
And she fell in love with an English Lord.

Chapter One

For the third evening in a row, Richard Oakes Crandoll Leighton, the Duke of Ravenwood, known to his friends as Roc, relaxed in the Rose & Thorn pub watching the fiddler dance around the room, her long black hair flowing beautifully around her shoulders and down her back with each motion, her eyes sparkling with enjoyment and raw passion.

Caitlin O'Shea intoxicated him with her beauty. She was the most beautiful woman he'd ever seen; jaw dropping beautiful. Every night for the last two weeks after she finished work, she shared a shepard's pie and a pint of Guinness with him. Tonight, he meant to walk her home and perhaps steal a kiss and if lucky, two. It seemed every time he took two steps forward with her, she immediately sent him one step back.

He didn't know how she played the fiddle while she danced and twirled around the room, but she did and she was amazing. She finished the last song of the night, sitting flirtatiously on his lap, drawing the final note with her bow. Then she graced him with the smile that sent his heart surging.

Unable to resist this new side to Caitlin, he set his hands on her waist, touching her, enjoying the feeling of her body so close to his while imagining her naked next to him. So far, she had eluded him and this simple gesture surprised him. It seemed to Roc she flirted with him tonight, another first. He intended to appreciate every second.

"Cat, do you mean to tease? It might not be wise." He loved spanning her tiny waist with his hands. If things went the way he hoped, she'd return to London with him when it was time for him to go home. To accomplish that he had his work cut out, because she seemed man shy.

She didn't answer right away but set her bow and fiddle on the table then, "Don't know how to tease a man. If that's what I'm doing, my sincere apologies or if you like it, I won't apologize." She nodded to her da who stood behind the bar. "Another pie?" she asked.

He let his inhibitions out and roared with laughter. She had a way of switching subjects without blinking. "Another pint too."

She stood, leaving him to go to the bar for the food and drink. When she returned, he'd set her instruments in their case.

He leaned back, watching her as he sipped the pint. "Do you want to stay here the rest of your life, here in Portrush? Or would you like to see another part of this vast world?" He'd take her anywhere she wanted to go as long as she would consent.

"Didn't realize there was a choice," she said with her mouth full. "Don't have the means to go anywhere. Don't know where I'd go if I did have the money." Swallowing, she drank her beer then set it on the table, looking thoughtful. "Perhaps I'd go to Africa and take a safari."

"You could go to London or Paris. Switzerland is always fun as is Germany. Safaris are dangerous." He drummed his fingers on the table. Didn't know why he was nervous, but she touched a part of him he thought long dead and he wasn't sure how to react to this slip of a woman who seemed so different from anyone he'd ever known.

She leaned forward, both hands on the table. "Now why would I want to do that? And what would I do there, in London or Paris or those other places you mentioned? Everyone would take one look at me and know I don't belong."

Shrugging, he held his breath thinking about the wisdom of what he was about to say then changed his mind and said something innocuous. "Just curious if those are some places you'd like to see."

"You live in London don't you, Roc? It might be fun but like I said, I don't have the money to travel. Might go to Belfast for a day or two but don't know why I would do that either. The fact is, I don't want to be beholdin' to any man. If you took me somewhere, well then, you'd want something from me."

He tried to ignore her last comment about wanting something from her because it was true. "I could help you with that, the money that is. If it's something you want to do." The first night he saw her in the pub, he'd gone home and wrote a message to his solicitor asking him to purchase a townhouse close to his. He knew it was more than presumptive but he didn't mean to return home without her. He also didn't know how to convince her that going with him was the best choice for her.

"Nothing's for free." She continued eating and studying him. "Just what would you ask in return? I know you'd want something. You're a man, after all."

He choked, not expecting the straightforwardness of her question. She challenged him, putting him on the defensive. "Only what you're willing to give."

"Now, I know you're a lord of some sort. Heard the rumors running through the town, but I'm a commoner and the only thing I can think you might want me to give you is my body. After all, I've nothing else." She pushed the half eaten food to the middle of the table as if it was no longer palatable. For a few uncertain seconds, she stared at her drink twirling the dark amber liquid in her glass before downing a few gulps. "I'll be no man's mistress."

"I'm not asking," he said, but eventually he would and at this moment he didn't like the direction of his thoughts. All he understood was that he craved her, needed her by his side. It had been years since he felt that kind of elemental and primitive desire. Five years ago he lost the woman he envisioned would remain by his side for the rest of his life. She died in a fire in Tuscany. He put that memory out of his mind for the moment, concentrating on the delicate and very beautiful female sitting in front of him.

"You're not? Well, I'll believe you for now, but I know that you want me by the look in your eyes. Raw desire, that's what I see and I'll not be givin' myself to you."

He slowly finished the last of his drink then setting his glass on the table, "Just because a man wants a woman doesn't mean he intends to make her his mistress. That's an entirely different proposition," he said, trying to defend himself and found there really was no defense when she spoke such blatant truth, seeming to read his thoughts.

"So you say."

"It's the truth," he told her but not in this case. "You're an amazing fiddler. Don't see how you can dance while you play. What can't you do?" He chose to change the subject instead of drowning in the last one.

Closing her eyes for a second or two and seeming to think, she said, "I'm a terrible house keeper. I spend the mornings cleaning the pub, the evenings playing my fiddle and the last thing I want to do when I get home is clean house. So many times there is dust on the tables and dishes in the sink. It seems I drop my clothes wherever I take them off."

He threw his head back, roaring with laughter, thinking if she were his mistress, she'd have people to do that for her. "I don't like to clean house either, but I suppose I've never really been tested. The chore has never been expected of me."

"What do you want out of life?" She smiled as if she understood the diversion when she asked the question.

"A little peace and quiet," he said quickly, realizing how true that was. He'd travelled most of Europe undertaking different missions directed by the English government. Now all he wanted was to do as he pleased for at least a year, perhaps more. Most of all, he didn't want to feel the need to sleep with one eye open.

"Is that all? I'd think someone of your status would want more, perhaps fame and fortune, perhaps..."

"I've more money than I can spend in a lifetime and because my father was not a wastrel, he was able to pass my title on to me. So no, I need to spend time at White's, find a willing woman who is not afraid of pleasure and perhaps in a few years find a woman I might want to wed and have children with."

"You want to marry." Her face turned a ghostly shade of white.

He couldn't help but wonder why the change in color. "In a few years," he told her, "And you? Do you want to marry?"

"Never," she grit out, turning her face away, seeming to hide from him.

He wanted to see the flicker of emotions over her face, needed to see why she was so adamant in her denial of marital bliss. Perhaps in time she'd tell him. "I thought women wanted to marry and have children. Find someone to take care of them."

She nodded to a well-dressed man at the bar, "See the drunk over

4

there? Da promised him my hand in marriage. He's a mean drunk. His name is Blair O'Connell. I told Da I wouldn't marry him even though he's an Irish lord, but my da insists. Says if I don't he'll kick me out."

Roc felt a moment of anger, which quickly turned to rage as he watched the man, kick a stray dog that had entered the pub. Roc's fists tightened. 'He'll kick you out of where?"

She shrugged her tiny shoulders, shoulders that shouldn't have to bear such a heavy burden. "He owns the small cottage I live in. I pay rent to him so I can be out of his house and by myself. I do value that small bit of independence and it's nice Da allows it. He doesn't have to, you know."

"Is there anywhere else you can go?" *Besides my new townhouse in London.* He knew he was getting ahead of himself. "Can I help?"

"No." She paused, thinking, yet the smile forming on her face gave him a chance to believe he might be part of her thoughts. "I can't afford anything else. He wouldn't ever fire me from the band, but I need to clean the pub if I'm going to pay all my bills."

"I could purchase a cottage and you could pay me rent," he blurted before he realized this was counter to his purposes. Convincing her to come with him in a few days was his priority, not buying a place for her to live in so she could stay in Ireland.

"That is a thought, but I'm sure I'd have to refuse. Everyone would believe the wrong things about me and if I have anything, it's my reputation. Without that there is nothing for me."

Grateful she refused, "I understand." Deep in his heart he was ecstatic she turned him down, but he still needed to find a way to make her life easier.

"Look, I need to walk home. It's late and I crave sleep." She stood then picked up her fiddle case.

"May I?" He took it from her. "Walk you home, that is? A girl shouldn't be out at night alone."

"Chivalry," she murmured, then smiling, "I have to walk home alone every night. I try to leave before the lord O'Connell leaves. I don't want him anywhere near me. He makes my skin crawl and sometimes I think he follows me, watches me in the house."

"So?" He waited patiently for an answer. "May I accompany you home?" he prompted.

"Yes," she smiled at him again, sucking her bottom lip between her teeth, "I think I'd like that, but you have to know that's all. Just a walk home, nothing more."

"I wouldn't have it any other way." He opened the door for Caitlin, stepping out into the cold night air. It was early spring and one never knew what the weather would be like here. Tonight is was cold, nearly frigid because the sky was clear, with stars dotting the blackness.

"Wait." She rushed into the pub then came out with a shawl. "I forgot my wrap. It's a bit chilly. The breeze reminded me." She looked a bit ashamed at her forgetfulness.

"I forget things too." He grinned at her. "Are you warm enough now?" he asked, shifting the case to his other hand before wrapping an arm around her to draw her closer for warmth.

She didn't push away from him and neither did she answer his question. Inwardly he smiled, enjoying the feel of her soft curves next to him. They walked in silence. He knew exactly where she lived. The last three nights and from a distance he made sure she made it to her home safely then set off for his lodgings.

She didn't have to tell him about O'Connell. He'd known the first time he watched the man ogling her there was something more to their relationship, none of it good. Now that he understood what her da had done, he meant to change things. As soon as possible he'd have a long chat with her da as well as Lord O'Connell.

"Here we are." She turned, stepping slightly away from him but now his hand rested at her waist.

He didn't want to let her go, needed to understand her thoughts where he was concerned. "It's dark inside. Do you want me to wait here?" He wondered at the expression flitting across her face. "Are you always afraid to step inside your home when you return at night?"

She was shaking her head even while she stepped closer to him. Next to him, he felt the fine trembling of her body.

"Was that a yes or a no? I'm a bit confused." He didn't want to laugh. Her fear was real and tangible, and without asking he was pretty sure the terror had something to with O'Connell.

6

"Both. Yes, when Blair has left before me. I can't know where he is or if he's waiting for me, and no, when he's still in the pub. If he's still in the tavern, he usually sleeps it off on the floor. Da wakes him up in the morning and sends him home."

"My little cat, you shouldn't ever be afraid." He tenderly brushed her flyaway hair behind her ears. The feel was silken and it seemed to be on fire. He wanted to feel the heat surround him and he needed more than anything to run his fingers through the length.

"Believe me, I don't like the feelings." In his arms, she shuddered as if the fear surrounded her.

"May I come in?" he asked, understanding he might very well be overstepping his bounds.

Cat didn't answer but she pulled a key from a pocket in her skirt and fumbled for a few minutes at the door. "I can't seem to..."

"Let me help." He didn't understand the trembling of her hands and he hoped she wasn't afraid of him. He took the key from her.

Seconds later, they stood inside her house. She scurried around the room, sending light into the small cottage. "Would you like a drink? I've tea. Not much else."

He hesitated a moment, unsure of the right answer. He detested tea. "Of course, that would be fine."

She seemed to sense his aversion to tea. "I've whiskey if that's what you would prefer." She stood by the cupboards in the kitchen.

"Whiskey would be nice," he told her and reminded himself he should gift her with a bottle simply because he intended to walk her home every night until they left for London, and he didn't want to deplete her meager supply.

She poured them both a glass, bringing it to him, "Would you like to sit down? I'm not sure what to do, never asked a man into my home before." She fiddled with the glass as if she didn't know whether she should drink it or play with it.

He smiled at her before sitting on the sofa. It was threadbare but must have been nice in another time. She deserved more than this. "I see what you mean about your housekeeping. Doubt if I would make a fuss if no one ever entered where I lived."

With one hand she held the glass and the other she plucked at her skirts, her eyes cast downward. Then she looked up, "Is the whiskey to your liking?"

For some reason he needed to be honest, "I've had better." He laughed. "As I'm sure you guessed."

"Thank you for being truthful. Da gives me the whiskey that no one will order. I'm not sure why."

"He wants you to have something for the man he promised you to if he comes calling." This thought ate at him. He didn't want to think about what that man could do to her in a drunken rage. Men like that were known to beat anyone who disagreed with them.

"I won't let him in," she shot back. "He's not welcome here. Da can promise him the moon but when it comes to me, he has no rights. I'll make decisions that are true for me."

Roc wasn't at all sure how Caitlin would keep the man out if he wanted in and that thought terrified him. Now more than ever, with this added knowledge, he needed to convince her that her best shot at a better life was in London with him.

"You might not be able to stop him. He's a lot stronger than you."

"I know." She ran her tongue around her lips before downing the drink. "Would you like another?" She stood and striding to the bottle of whiskey she poured herself more then seemed to wait for his answer.

He held his glass out and she poured more, setting the bottle on a nearby table. "Why would your father sell you to this man who is nothing more than the town drunk?"

She looked clearly shocked by his expression. "He's not really my father, and the man has money, owns property. Da says he wants more for me than playing my fiddle in the pub."

The answer was short and to the point, "Not your father? Who is he?" now he had many more questions than answers about this young woman he cared for more than he'd cared for anyone his entire adult life.

"I call him my da but he's really my uncle." She closed her eyes then downed the whiskey before pouring another.

"You probably shouldn't have any more."

"Of course, you're right. I have to wake up before six so I can go to the pub." But she sipped again, clearly distraught by their conversation.

"What happened to your mother and father?" The questions surrounding his Cat grew.

She lifted her delicate shoulders slightly, looking at him with tear filled eyes. "My mother died in childbirth and father...some duke or earl...some English lord who didn't care what happened to mother or me. I don't know who he is and neither do I care."

A wave of revulsion at the man who sired Cat swept through him. "Bloody hell," he gritted out unable to think of anything else to say. She was sired by a lord and now groveled in a small hut with nothing to her name.

"It's the god's honest truth. I don't know who my father is but I think Da does, but he won't tell me because I think deep down he hates me for taking his sister's life. And he might be afraid I'd try to find him."

"Then he's not much of a man," Roc said, reevaluating his desires where Cat was concerned as well as his previous behaviors. He'd always taken precautions when he had sex. As far as he knew, there were no bastards, no women he abandoned when he was tired of them. Good God, his mother, The Duchess would have killed him if he did anything like that.

"So you say," she said, standing, swaying a bit then steadying herself by placing a hand on the table. "Not used to drinking whiskey. Or so much."

"Perhaps you should have a hot cup of tea before I leave." He found himself in front of the sink not knowing what to do. Bloody eyes, it couldn't be that hard to make a cup of tea.

She was laughing and the sound warmed his heart even though he understood she was laughing at him. "I'll just have a glass of water. I'm not drunk, just exhausted and a wee bit tipsy. I'll probably sleep like a babe tonight thanks to you."

"Then I should be leaving so you can get some sleep." He held her hands in his, feeling the callouses on her fingers and wishing he could do something to convince her she would allow him to take her to London. She shouldn't have to work to keep food on her table when he could provide for her.

Yet after the conversations they'd had, he was pretty sure he understood why she told him she'd never be any man's mistress. He vowed though she'd change her mind. He would find a way.

"I like your company," she told him, moving closer to him, her chin tilted upward so he was looking into her blue violet eyes. Tonight, they were more violet than blue.

"But you don't want me to stay the night." He watched her expression turn to something he'd never seen before.

"Perhaps what I want is not what I can do." She touched her hand to his cheek, her eyes speaking of desire and passion.

"Just one kiss then I'll go." He rested his hand on hers, feeling the fine trembling, understanding fear had changed to hunger as well as a desperate passion. "I won't hurt you and nothing we do here, tonight, will damage your reputation."

"Promise?"

He saw the rise of her breasts and felt the pounding of her heartbeat in the pulse at her wrist. "Promise."

She moistened her lips as if in anticipation. "Roc?"

"No time for questions."

His lips met hers, the warmth and softness reached deep into his soul. He needed more yet refused to act on his desires. She opened her mouth, maybe to say something, maybe not, but her tongue swept across his lips, reached inside his mouth.

Her tiny gasp helped him realize she acted on instinct not knowledge. She had no idea what she had done, what she initiated when her tongue met his. But he wasn't about to let this opportunity pass. He deepened the kiss, pulling her closer, exploring every part of her she allowed. His hands held her face so he could have better access while his lips and tongue engaged in a sensual dance with hers.

Minutes later, when he pulled away, her lips were swollen slightly, tempting him even more to pursue this to the natural end. But she'd never forgive him if that was what he did. He didn't want regrets ever in this fledgling relationship.

"Are you working tomorrow?" he asked, hoping she would finally have a day off and he could spend some time alone with her.

"Just cleaning the pub in the morning. I'll be finished by noon.

Why?" She moved back from him, holding her hand on her chest as if she tried to slow her breathing.

"Good, then I'll pick you up here at one o'clock, if that's alright. We'll go for a carriage ride and perhaps I'll bring a basket of food. Would you like that? And some wine." He craved time alone with her, private time but also understood that for now, he would have to keep his courting to kisses. He laughed to himself, remembering his mother's teaching. "When you are out with a lady, you best think with your head and not your cock." He would have a devil of a time doing that with his Caitlin.

Her hands were under her chin, her eyes bright, "I'd like that, a carriage ride, food and some wine. I've never done anything like that before or been alone with a man."

At her innocent words, Roc's breath caught in his throat. "Goodnight, my little Cat, sleep well and I'll see you tomorrow." Roc left Cat's house, whistling and thinking to himself of ways to help this woman without her knowing. That's all he wanted, to help her and make her life easier. Well, that was not quite all, he wanted her in his bed.

When he stepped inside the home he rented, he sat down, writing another letter to his solicitor and to his mother, The Duchess. What he put in motion, he meant for it to answer the questions to Cat's parentage.

The first letter was destined for his solicitor inquiring as to the progress in purchasing the townhouse. The second one was to his mother.

Mother,

I've met a woman with a very interesting story. She is about eighteen years of age and the most beautiful woman I've ever met. Just looking at her steals my breath. This evening she told me her father was an English lord but she didn't know his name and her mother died in childbirth. I'm guessing the mother ran away from the man because Caitlin ended up here in Ireland. This isn't a lot of information to go on, but I will be forever in your debt if you can inquire into her possible parentage. By the way, she's the most beautiful woman I've ever set eyes on.

Love, your son
Roc

~ * ~

11

Caitlin watched Roc walk down the road then she slowly closed the door behind her. With the door shut tight, she leaned against it, her back resting on the wood. She touched a fingertip to her lips, recalling the sweetness of his kiss and longing for more.

The only other time she'd been kissed was when Blair caught her behind the pub. He'd pressed her hard against the side of the tavern demanding a response she couldn't give him. She shuddered, her skin seeming to crawl.

Turning quickly, she locked the door. Sometimes when he wasn't too drunk, Blair turned up after she went home, banging on the door until he gave up and left. Before she put her nightdress on, she blew out the lanterns and the candles.

Darkness surrounded her when she finally pulled back the covers to the bed and slipped beneath the quilt. She turned over, pounding the pillow as if that would help her sleep, but thoughts of Roc's kisses kept her awake.

Too bad Roc was an English lord. Why couldn't he be a commoner like her, someone she could let herself fall in love with? He was handsome, his broad shoulders narrowing to lean hips. His well-muscled legs long, but it was his dark brown eyes that drew her to him, beckoning her and making her feel so hot she wanted to take off all her clothes. But tonight she relished his lips pressed against hers, the intensity and the strange longing he drew from her. They were full and warm, soft too, probably the only soft part of him.

Hours later it seemed she drifted off to an uneasy slumber, dreams of Roc and his kisses haunting her as she pulled and tugged at the bedding. When the clock finally chimed six times, the covers were wrapped around her legs and her body was sweat sheened.

Rubbing her eyes, she quickly rose and padding to the small kitchen, she took a loaf of bread and cheese from the cupboard then heated water on the stove for tea. While she waited for the water to boil, she dressed in a well-worn day dress suitable for cleaning the bar before pulling her hair back and winding it into a tight chignon.

She ate quickly, eager to get the cleaning finished and return to her cottage. They were going for a carriage ride and her fingers shook at the idea of sitting next to him and watching the scenery go by. She wanted another kiss and meant to figure out how to convince him of that. Perhaps she could initiate the kiss. Would he like that or would that be too forward of her?

Winding her fingers around the hot cup, she let the heat warm her hands while she sipped the tea and ate a few bites. She felt a little nauseous, nerves rattling while she thought about spending some special time with Roc.

When she left, she locked the door behind her even though nothing ever happened in the small town of Portrush. She was wary of Blair and what he might do when he had too much to drink and when he discovered she'd let Roc walk her home last night, she didn't know what he might do.

She hoped her da had not let him sleep in the tavern and that she wouldn't find him residing in some dark corner. Waking him so she could clean did not bode well for her. He would ask her about last night because she didn't doubt he saw her walk out of the pub with Roc. It would surprise her if he hadn't followed them.

The tavern was quiet and empty when she stepped through the door. She pulled the curtains apart to let the light of the day inside. No one slept in a corner on the floor. Her breathing seemed to even out as she let the breath she'd been holding from her lungs. Her wishes had been granted.

Grabbing a damp cloth from the back room, she cleaned the tables then put the chairs on top of them so she could mop the floors.

A few hours later she finished her chores and was taking off her apron when a noise in the back caught here attention. She peaked around the corner, "Da? Is that you?"

"It's me, Caitlin. You about finished," he asked walking through the kitchen to meet her and give her a quick hug. "You got a few minutes? I'd like to speak with you about last night." He rubbed his neck, a gesture he used when his nerves were on edge.

Inhaling a long deep breath, she braced herself for a lecture about Roc and why he wasn't good for her and that she shouldn't let him walk her home. She took a quick look at the clock, "I've about thirty minutes."

"Good, put two chairs down for us to sit on." He walked into the main room with two cups of coffee and some freshly made tarts from Ida's place.

"I know what you're going to say, Da." She reached out accepting the hot cup and sipping gingerly.

"I don't think you do." He drank seeming to study her before he bit into the lemon tart.

"Yes, I can already hear you telling me that he's a lord and he's going back to England. All he wants from me is one thing." Her fury escalated as she thought about what she said about herself. Surely, she had something more to offer a man than just her body.

Her da was shaking his head, his expression grim. "No, don't need to tell you something you know. Rest assured this is different and it's coming from my heart because I love you."

"Then what?" Impatiently, she ran her finger along the rim of her cup, her mind still on the outing this afternoon with Roc. "Da, I love you too but we rarely agree anymore."

"Your mother." He leaned back in the chair, crossing his well-muscled arms over his chest and tucking his hands under his armpits.

"Mother? You've never said much about her. Why now? Because you think I'm on the verge of making the biggest mistake of my live?"

He leaned forward, bracing his forearms on the table. "Your mother, Fiona, she loved an adventure. It seemed to me she always wanted what she couldn't have. She flitted back and forth from here to Belfast. One day she didn't come home. I got a message from her months later that she was in London and she'd met a man, a marquise, she said or maybe an earl."

"I've heard some of this," she said yet she never tired of stories about the mother she never met. "Nothing you say about my mother can be compared to me. I'm satisfied here in Portrush even though..." She moistened her lips reminding herself Roc was not for her. "There is no one here for me. I'm fine with that."

"I know, bear with me. She returned about a year after she ran off and about ten months after I got the letter from her."

"I'm not going to let that happen. I'm no man's mistress, never will be. If I've learned anything from the stories about Mother, I know what I don't want." Anger simmered deep inside and she understood the simple

14

facts about this. If she didn't know her mother's story, she'd most likely do the same thing. Roc could seduce her if she allowed him to, but that scenario would never come to fruition. She would not allow it to happen.

"So you say. I just want you to be careful." He reached for her hands and for a short time he held them in his. "A man such as your lord can be very persuasive to a naïve young woman such as yourself."

"I promise. This," she gestured around the room, "is all I need." But it wasn't. She craved a wonderful man to call husband. There was no one in Portrush and for a moment she understood her mother's need to leave the small village. The move had been necessary for happiness, but it resulted in her death.

"I've pushed you toward Blair because he is a lord, an Irish one. He can take care of you. He has an estate and despite his penchant for drink, is well taken care of."

"He's a drunk and a lecher." She rubbed her arms, wishing her da would find something else to speak of. "The thought of kissing him or lying in bed with him sends chills up my spine."

"While he's a sloppy drunk, he'll never break your heart." It seemed he gave one last effort to convince her that marrying Blair would be good for her.

"You can't break anything you don't possess. I despise the man and you know as well as I do that he's a mean drunk."

"I don't think he would hurt you." Her da tried to defend Blair to her, but it wasn't going to work.

"He kicked a dog just last night because the poor animal wanted food. You feed the strays leftovers; the animal was just eager." Her words grew more heated and she became more determined as she spoke of Blair and the cruelty that lay just below the surface.

"He would never hurt a woman," he repeated, "especially you. He thinks himself in love with you.

She stood too quickly, knocking over her chair, "He won't hurt me because I don't plan on giving the odious man a chance. A title is not the worth of a man or a woman. Unless you have something else to say, it's time for me to leave. This is discussion is finished."

"What's your hurry? Sit a moment and relax." He reached out again this time to stop her. "You're not working tonight so you've got time."

She didn't want to lie to him, but she didn't see any other recourse. Perhaps leaving out something wasn't a lie. If she didn't come in early this morning the question would have never come up. "I'm tired. I didn't sleep well last night. I need to go home and this discussion with you is exhausting."

"Did your lord stay the night?" His voice turned angry, perhaps accusatory while he glared at her.

"Of course not. Don't you believe me when I tell you I'm not going to sleep with the man. He will not be in my bed because I understand he could never marry a commoner, and I won't be his mistress or his whore." She was very nearly screaming while the frustration of the morning and the lost sleep took over her senses and emotions.

"I'm sorry, dear. I do believe you. It's just that I can no longer protect you and I know that for a fact. I wanted you to have a good man, but it doesn't seem to be happening." He motioned for her to leave. "Go on, get some sleep. I apologize for making you angry."

"Blair O'Connell is not a good man. You need to tell him that you take back what you offered months ago. I'm not ever going to be that man's wife. So tell him I'm unpromised to him."

Her da cleared his throat. "I'll try but it seems he's given me a loan that I would have to pay back if you don't wed him."

She had been on her way out the door, but with those words she whirled on him, fists clenched at her sides. "You sold me? Was the O'Connell the highest bidder? How dare you do such a thing."

With that said she was out the door, slamming it shut behind her. She muttered as she raced to her cottage, needing a hot bath to get the filth of this conversation with the man she'd always trusted to have her best interests at heart off her body. She didn't think she could scrub enough.

Inside she set the pots to boiling then pumped water into buckets to partially fill the tub. Gazing at the clock, she realized she'd have to settle for a tepid bath. Once the water was in the small tub, she tore off her clothes, letting them fall on the floor then slipped into the water.

She only had fifteen minutes to bathe and dress. Soaping and rinsing she managed to wash all of her, including her hair. When she stood, she wrapped a bath sheet around her and stepped behind the curtain separating her bed from the main room.

The knocking on the door caught her attention. She turned to look just as Roc opened the door and looked inside.

"Cat, you ready? I know I'm a little early but I wanted to see you." He stepped inside when she didn't answer right away.

She gasped, moving backward and stumbling over the bucket she used to rinse the soap. "No."

"I brought you something..."

A dog appeared out of nowhere and jumped on her, licking her face and wagging its huge tale. Desperately, she tried to keep her towel in place. "An Irish Wolf Hound?" She tried to stand but the puppy kept her firmly on the floor.

Roc strode around the corner. "You don't have to take him if you don't..." Quickly he backed from the room. "Sorry, didn't realize you didn't have any clothes on."

She was sure she heard a hint of laughter and maybe a touch of appreciation, and she realized she wasn't very embarrassed. She didn't think he'd seen much except her legs sticking out from beneath the bath towel.

"Just wait out there and take this little guy or he'll never let me get dressed." She laughed as the dog licked her nose again. "Go on, go to your master. Shew."

"You're his master and I can't get him unless I come where you are." He was really laughing now, and if she wasn't completely naked underneath this simple covering, she'd laugh too.

She saw his booted feet, perfectly shined Hessians, below the curtain. "Come get him but close your eyes."

"Don't think that will work. Don't want to fall into your tub or onto you. I'll try to keep from looking at you but it's going to be hard."

"Very well." She let out a long breath of air. "Do your best. I suppose my legs aren't anything you haven't seen before." A sudden and unexpected wave of jealousy washed through her at her very own words.

He stepped around the curtain, and she knew he wasn't looking at her but the dog was practically sitting on her lap. If he were to retrieve the animal, he'd have no recourse but to take a quick look. She pulled the towel higher but as the dog wiggled on her lap, one edge slipped dangerously low. She tugged again.

"There, got him." He now held the squirming puppy in his arms and backed from the room with a devilish grin that set her heart spinning and her mind whirling with so many scenarios she didn't know what direction to take.

"I'll be right out." She dropped the bath sheet before putting on the clothing she'd carefully laid out just a few minutes ago.

"Better be or this little guy is going to be around that corner again. Can't hold this squirming bundle of energy forever."

"Done." She stepped around the curtain, grinning at him, just as the dog wiggled from Roc's arms and made a mad dash for the doorway.

"Oh no," Roc said, racing to take the dog outside but it was too late. The dog stopped and spread legs was doing just what they feared.

"He peed on my floor." She started laughing then laughed harder when Roc joined her, tears sliding down her cheeks.

"I'll clean it up," he volunteered, still laughing. He looked around the room and she pointed to a place by the sink where he found a sponge and soap.

"Tell me why the dog and why do you want to give him to me? Is it one of Ida's dogs?"

In the middle of cleaning up the spill, the dog pranced around him, seeming to think this was some type of game. "Yes, I picked up a basket of food from Ida and she told me the puppies were ready to leave their mama. Thought you could use a good dog for protection."

"I do love dogs and perhaps that's not a bad idea," she told him, scooping the puppy into her arms. Thoughtfully, she rubbed its ears, but he didn't want anything to do with petting. He managed to get out of her arms then found one of her wool socks, worrying it and shaking it as if he meant to kill it. "Now he's got my sock, little rascal."

On hands and knees, Rock grabbed the animal, retrieving the sock without letting the dog put a hole in it. "Got it." He held the sock in the air as if it was a prized possession.

"What am I going to do with him? I can't keep him outside. I've nowhere to put the little devil."

"Let's build a place where you can store him when you're gone. It won't hold him for long, but at least we can go on our outing. Then we can think of something else." He looked for pieces of furniture he could put together to make a pen. "There." He brushed his hands together then picked up the dog, setting him in the new pen. Then he put a bowl of water where the dog could get to it. "You're going to have to think of a name."

She walked toward him, trying to put her damp hair into a manageable do. "I have no idea what to call that beast and in a less than a year, he's going to eat me out of house and home."

"Let me help you with your hair. Can't help you with anything else." She turned her back to him, setting the needed pins on a nearby table. In a matter of seconds, he secured her hair.

"How do you know how to do that? Never mind, I probably don't want to know," she murmured, the same wave of jealousy she felt earlier surfaced. "Do you think he'll still be there when we get back?"

He lifted his shoulders in a gesture that said he didn't know. "I've picked up some of the things you left on the floor just in case he makes a jail break."

"Thank you." She didn't know why she was thanking him. He brought a little adorable nuisance into her home, one she could only feed if Da helped her out with scraps from the pub.

"Do you want a shawl," he asked as he grabbed one from the coat stand as well as her fiddle case. "It appears it might rain a bit."

Outside a breeze ruffled her air and made the leaves on the trees shimmer. A mountain of white clouds billowed on the horizon, but the carriage caught her attention.

"It's huge," she whispered totally in awe.

He let his head fall back, roaring with laughter. "It has nearly all the comforts of home. When I sail on one my ships, I always bring it with me. Come take a look. I had it custom made." He held out his arm for her.

She didn't understand why he laughed at her comment, but she did like laughter; much preferred it over anger and some of the other more depressing emotions. Didn't even care if he laughed at her, she'd try to find a way to laugh with him.

"I would like to see inside."

"Then you shall," he told her, gallantly opening the door and helping her inside.

The interior was plush and the seats wide enough to sit three across. "It's beautiful," she said, awestruck, looking to see if he laughed. "Is it as comfortable?"

"Not as much as your sofa at home, and when the carriage is moving one can't get rid of the potholes and rocks on the road but otherwise, yes. It has storage beneath the seats where I keep blankets and other items I've found I like to have handy on trips."

"Did Ida make the basket of food for you?" She sat down, running her hands along the fabric of the seats, soaking in the luxury, thinking if she had something like this to ride in she might like to take a trip to Belfast or perhaps farther to Dublin.

"For us." He corrected then sat across from her. "For long trips I had the man who made this carriage put in pullouts, see." He showed her. "I can sleep, well perhaps relax a bit more than normal."

"Potholes and rocks." She wondered if he ever slept with a woman here.

"No, I haven't," he said grinning again.

"Haven't what?" He couldn't possibly know what she'd been thinking. Why would his mind go there as well unless he was thinking about doing that with her?

"I haven't slept with any woman in this carriage or any other one I own," he told her, holding her hand in his.

"How many do you own?" She didn't understand why she was prying into his life. In a week or so he would leave. He'd told her as much and she'd never see him again.

"Two carriages and four ships." Letting go of her hand he leaned back, spreading his arms across the back of the seat, a smug expression on his handsome and too debonair features. Confidence exuded from him.

"You're very wealthy. What do you see in me?" She wanted to slap herself for asking the question. Didn't she know what he saw in her, an easy conquest and his next mistress? She meant to stay ahead of his game. She wasn't going to be an easy conquest.

20

"Does that bother you?" He tapped on the roof signaling the driver to start. "And I see a lot in you. You're a beautiful and intelligent woman. I could listen to you play your fiddle all day long."

"He does know where we are going?" She needed to change the subject before she put her foot in her mouth again.

"I certainly hope so," he said, leaning forward and reaching for her hands. "You need to try and relax. You're as stiff as a broomstick. I don't want to make you nervous. This is supposed to an enjoyable outing for you."

"It's just hard when you're so handsome and all I can think about is the kiss last night." She wished she hadn't said that.

His grin sent her heart spinning. "You liked the kiss, does that mean you want another one?" He suddenly drew her to his side of the carriage, settling her on his lap while his lips found hers.

~ * ~

"You've betrayed me," Blair O'Connell, Earl of Glenwild, glared at Sean O'Shea, Caitlin's da, over his pint of Guinness.

Sean pushed the money he borrowed from Blair toward the man, "I didn't mean to betray anyone. The lass doesn't want to marry you. Says she won't."

"You should have done more," Blair insisted, his glare still firmly planted on Sean. "Should have insisted."

"Did all I could do. If you didn't get drunk every night and right in front of Caitlin, you might have stood a better chance."

"Don't want your money back," Blair pushed it back toward Sean.

"You and I both know you only gave it to me because you thought she'd be your wife. Get it through your thick skull, it's not going to happen." Sean understood most of why Caitlin wanted nothing to do with this man.

"I'm going to find a way to make her say yes." He drank down the beer then pushed the glass toward Sean asking for more.

Sean felt a sick feeling fill his gut. His first thought went to revenge and he recalled Caitlin's words. If he could kick a dog, he could certainly do the same to a woman.

"You'll keep your distance where she is concerned," Sean gritted out, his fists tight.

"Or you'll do what? Do you forget who I am? I could have you arrested on some trumped up charge if I wanted to get rid of you."

"You could do that but no matter how smart you think you are or how much power you think you have, the man who is even now courting Caitlin can squish you with his thumb." Sean felt good that he'd done his research on the Duke of Ravenswood. The family was powerful and while the duke had not been present in London for years, it seemed his mother wielded more power than anyone but the prince regent.

"Just why do you think to have such an absurd idea. Who is this man, Roc Leighton, I believe."

"Perhaps I should allow you to find out the hard way by crossing him." Sean liked that idea and the more he thought about it, the better it became. For a time, he'd truly harbored the idea of a wedding between Blair and Caitlin, now he sensed what she felt all along. He was a despicable man.

"I'm the most powerful man all the way to Belfast. No one gainsays me." He puffed up a bit with those words.

"Ever heard of The Duchess?" Sean let the question hang for a few seconds while he waited for an answer.

"Never," Blair said but his usually ruddy complexion turned sallow.

Sean knew, just as everyone in these parts knew, who The Duchess was. "The Duchess is Roc's mother, but of course I see you've realized that meager fact. Roc is the Duke of Ravenswood and he commands all the power now."

"Well..." Blair sputtered. "He won't marry her like I would have. No, he'll take her virginity which was mine to take then he'll turn her into his mistress instead of his wife."

"It was only yours if Caitlin wished to grant it to the likes of you. Now the object of your obsession is out of your reach. I wouldn't even protest if Caitlin chose to become his mistress over becoming your wife." Sean watched for more reactions to the stunning news as well as his insinuations.

22

"You're just a bitter man because you never found a wife for yourself. You had to take solace in raising Fiona's girl," Blair shot out as if trying to anger him.

He never wanted a wife because he preferred men. He'd always kept a low profile where his desires were concerned. No one in this small village knew of his preference except Ida and of course Blair. She had become his confidant.

"Never had the desire for a wife because I stayed busy with Caitlin. Don't regret one tiny second either." He wiped his hands on the apron he wore. "Clients are starting to come into the pub. I've got work. If you know what's good for you, stay away from Caitlin. It's not a threat from me but one from the duke to you through me."

Blair sauntered to a table after ordering food. He seemed contrite, nursing his beer and staring out the window, his eyes glazed over. Sean had the feeling Blair would be sleeping on the floor tonight unless he could summon one of his servants to bring him home.

He'd be so drunk he wouldn't bother Caitlin, at least Sean prayed that would be the case.

Chapter Two

Caitlin sat on his lap in the carriage, her lips pressed softly and intimately against his. She touched his mouth with her tongue and he opened for her, trying to absorb all that she was into him. Her tiny mew from the back of her throat gave him her consent and he explored, touched, teased in a raw primal and urgent dance of passion.

He understood if he didn't end the sweet kiss, she might well have regrets so he pulled back, touching her face with a fingertip and tracing a path down her neck to settle at her pulse, which was beating rapidly. He smiled adoring his effect on her, craving her more than he ever thought possible.

With wide innocent eyes, she gazed at him, "Why did you stop? I like your kisses."

He drew in a breath of air, holding it for a few seconds in his lungs. Her sweet innocence as well as the honesty unraveled his soul. "I didn't want to take more than you were willing to give."

"And what would that be, more than I'm willing to give?" Her head tilted slightly as if she was trying to figure that out herself.

"Do you want the short version or a more descriptive tale of what continuing that kiss in the privacy of my carriage where no one could see what we do might be?" he asked as he set her across from him. The distance was needed, and control was necessary.

"Perhaps the short version would be the best. But I do like to kiss you and would have liked to feel you inside me for a little longer."

With her words his jaw clenched tightly and he couldn't stifle the groan he felt rumbling up from his belly. Inside her, that was what he craved, but she didn't understand what she said. "Suffice it to say, I would have done things that would have had you telling me no."

"I can't imagine what that would be," she told him, straitening her skirts, something she seemed to do when she was nervous. "You're such a gentleman, I doubt you would try to take something I wasn't willing to reciprocate.

Somehow, he couldn't help himself and the words were meant only to tease, "Would you like me to show you?" Now he couldn't take them back. In the silence of the carriage he feared she would say yes, and at the same time the thought sent a wave of desire vibrating through him so intense the sensation made his hands shake and his breath catch in his throat.

For a moment she looked out the window then back to him, "Perhaps I should trust your judgment. I'm just curious and I like the feel of your arms around me and your lips, well...I suppose unless I want to be your mistress, which I don't, I'm going to have to remain uninformed."

He laughed again while she looked outside then holding her hands in his, "I'm not laughing at you, if that's what you might be thinking. It's just that you never fail to surprise me with your innocence and pure heart. Those traits are not ones I'm used to seeing in anyone, let alone a woman. The world I come from is jaded to the very center of its heart. The women I've known want me for what I can give them not who I am. You're different." He brought her hands to his lips and kissed the back of them before he turned them over and one at a time kissed the heart of her palm. "We will be there soon."

"And where is there?" she asked, smiling at him, her usual good humor seemingly restored.

"I've located a place where there is a copse of trees. We can park the carriage for shelter if it does rain and there's a nearby abandoned home and barn where Winston, my driver, can take the horses to rest and eat. You see, I did want privacy today. I crave to have you all to myself."

"Is it a place I would recognize?" she asked, turning her attention to the scenery out the window as if attempting to answer her question.

"Most likely. The ledge overlooks the ocean and if the elements behave themselves, I'm hoping to watch the sun set on the ocean while we enjoy a glass of wine and I hold you in my arms."

"That actually sounds romantic. Is that how you woo all the women you like?" she asked.

"It is supposed to be romantic, and I've never done anything like this before," he told her, realizing just how out of character a romantic rendezvous watching the sun go down was to him. He always took the women he was interested in to bed and that was that. Then he would leave before morning light. He couldn't imagine leaving this woman in the middle of the night. He found he desired waking up beside her every morning. Eventually, he planned to have his way with her.

"Then what do you do?" she asked, looking inside the basket of food sitting next to her then quickly closing the lid seeming to realize he was watching her. Then, needing to admit to a simple fact, "I'm famished. Is there anything we can snack on while we are still in the carriage?"

"Pick out anything you like." He wanted to indulge her in every way. If this simple request for food was something she sought, she certainly could have it?

"Really? I'm not used to just eating for eating's sake. But I didn't have time to get a bite before you arrived with the puppy..." She paused, seeming to forget the food.

"What is it?" He had a pretty good hunch he knew what she was going to say and he'd hoped all along she wouldn't think of it. At least an hour had passed and she hadn't said a word.

When she looked at him, "I can't accept the dog."

There it was. "Why not?" She would have to make a damn good point in order for him to retrieve the beast and keep him for himself. She needed the animal to safeguard her and despite the protests he knew were coming, she had to do what was right for her and damn what other people might say or whisper behind her back.

"People will think—" she began but he cut her off.

Waving his hand in the air, "Bloody hell." He tried to control his anger but where this particular conversation was headed, he was finding it increasingly difficult. "I don't care what people think or say. It's a gift from the heart, with no expectations on my part. I'm not asking for anything in return as payment for the gift."

He needed to pace, vent his escalating emotions. Confined in the carriage, he felt as if he was near exploding. One look at Cat and his fury deflated. She appeared near to crying, and he didn't like that either. This wasn't supposed to be controversial.

"Didn't mean to make you angry. It's just that it's my reputation that will be the brunt of the gossip, not yours. Makes no difference how you feel." She seemed to square her shoulders and sit up straighter, guarding herself against what he might say next. "My decisions are just that, mine. You have no say where I'm concerned."

"Trying to understand what you would go through. I never wanted to visit gossip on our very simple and so far platonic relationship. I understand people would look at you differently." He touched the tiny tear drop slipping down her cheek, wishing he'd never caused her the pain but determined to make her see reason where the little beast was concerned.

"You can't comprehend because you're not a woman. Try all you want but no one will stare at you as if you're a pariah. Instead, they'll slap you on the back and praise your manly prowess." She stared out the window again. "I have to live in this community and you, by your own admission, are leaving."

He needed to look into her eyes, but he wasn't going to force her. "You're right, of course. Keep in mind, however, I'm going to have to leave sooner than later. If I'm not in the vicinity, no one will think you're my mistress. And the plain truth is that you are not my mistress and you haven't slept with me."

She turned to him, her hand now resting on his leg. Her gentle touch sent a myriad of emotions through his already aroused body. "They will still believe I gave you something in return for the dog. How much did he cost?"

He cleared his throat, trying not to frown because he certainly wasn't about to tell her the truth. "You're not supposed to ask the cost of a gift." The expenditure was nothing to him, but to her the amount would be enormous, probably unthinkable, astronomical.

She blushed, placing her hands on her cheeks. "I just thought it would help if you didn't spend very much on him. I'm sorry. I'm not usually a person to pry, but I know the cost of dogs and unless Ida let you underpay her, I've a pretty good idea what you spent."

27

"No need to apologize. Look, we must be here. The carriage is slowing." The change of scenery should accommodate a shift in conversation. He didn't want to defend himself or his actions. Her safety was paramount in his eyes. He would make sure she understood how well meaning he was. O'Connell would always be a threat to her, and he needed to know that in his absence, she would have some protection.

When the vehicle came to a stop, he helped her down. His hands on her waist, he lifted her then set her on the ground. She was small and delicate, easy prey for any man who wanted to take advantage.

"This is one of my favorite places." She walked to the edge of the cliff, where she could watch the waves braking on the boulders below them. Holding out her arms, "I love the way the wind blows harder here. Wouldn't it be fun if we could fly like the birds and hover over the breakers?"

"I supposed you must have been here at some time. Didn't know it was a preferred place." He stood beside her, his hands behind his back, watching her ever-changing expressions and relishing the thoughts she spoke of. "I thought it beautiful and a perfect place for a picnic with you. You'd like to fly?"

"Wouldn't you?" she asked, the smile on her face dazzling him.

"Perhaps someday I'll take you up in a hot air balloon. It's not the way the sea gulls are flying, but you can look down on the land below. Everything seems so small and insignificant."

"You would do that? You can do something like that." She looked stunned, amazed.

"Yes, and yes, but it would be easier to rent a balloon at Vauxhall Gardens in London. Another reason why you should come with me, so you can fly like the birds." He watched her stiffen but didn't regret the words, tempting her with things she wanted would be the only way he could succeed.

Winston approached, clearing his throat to let them know he was behind them. "Don't mean to interrupt. Shall I take the horses now?"

"Please and you can return after sunset. Unless there is a dire emergency, I want to be alone with Cat all afternoon."

"Will any messages come to me?" Winston asked.

"All, Ida takes them for me when I'm away and she knows where you'll be." Roc watched as his man led the horse away but left the carriage as planned. Roc feared the possibility of a short rainstorm, and he wanted to make sure there was a dry place for them to wait out any tempest that might blow their way.

He turned on a polished boot heel, "We're alone. Are you alright with that, my sweet Cat?"

"I always believed that to be your plan." She looked down a moment as another hint of color touched her cheeks. "I wouldn't have accepted your invitation if I didn't want to be with you, alone." After she looked up, "I trust you with my life as well as my heart."

"Perhaps you should be more afraid of my intentions today than what people will say about my innocent gift to you." He laughed softly as she looked at him, with her eyebrows drawn together in a scowl.

"I'm not afraid of your intentions. You won't do anything I don't want you to do. You've told that to me over and over, and I've no reason to doubt your word." She spoke with a determination in her voice.

"You know me so well, but what you don't know is that if I had a mind to seduce you, you probably wouldn't think to tell me no." She was untried in the art of love and sex. She wouldn't understand what he was doing and to what ends until it was too late.

She moistened her lips several times, seeming to mull over his words. "That's what happened to my mother, I'm sure of it. Do you think my father cared about her or just wanted what he could get from her?"

"I've no idea," he said, again wishing for a change of subject, one that was more suitable for an enjoyable afternoon. He didn't want to dwell on her mother's past, one that seemed to have shaped her feelings as well as her life. "Shall we walk or would you like to eat?"

"Let's walk. If I remember correctly, there's a trail over there that leads to a small beach below. The tide is out, so we can walk there, too, scrunch our toes in the sand." She set off in the direction of the path.

He caught up with her and offered her his arm, wanting to keep her close to him. "Why in such a hurry?"

"I like the beach, enjoy the feel of the salt spray on my face and the sand between my toes." She wrapped her hand around his upper arm, slowing her pace while she leaned into him.

"And I love watching the joy of simple things on your face. Your smile sends my heart in a tailspin." It did too but more than that it made him want to see her smile after he gave her a woman's pleasure, needed to see the sparkle of raw passion in her eyes. At this point in time, he didn't think that would happen anytime soon, and he tried to keep his mind off seducing her.

"You say things that confuse me," she told him as she stepped over a large rock, lifting her skirts high enough he could see more than just her ankles.

He recalled a short glimpse of her legs the other day when the dog knocked her over, but he'd uncharacteristically averted his gaze.

"If you were wise to the world, they wouldn't confuse you, but I like you just the way you are."

They stepped onto the sand, water whirling only a few feet away. She sat down on a rock, taking her shoes and stockings off. With her skirts lifted, she waded far enough for the water to cover her ankles and splash against her knees.

"Oooo, It's cold." Cat ran backwards away from the water then followed the tide out a ways. "You want to join me? Or are you too much of a coward to get your feet wet?"

The simple query gave him reason to pause. He was sure his grin spread from ear to ear. He couldn't remember the last time he played in the waves. It seemed his life over the last ten years had been a bit stoic even though he'd faced life-threatening danger more than once. "Like watching you better."

"Chicken," she said, kicking up the water so the spray filled the air around her. "You will get used to the cold." She turned toward him.

"Don't want to get used to numb feet or wet pants. If you don't watch yourself, you're going to get all wet." But he definitely didn't believe he'd ever get used to seeing her ankles. They were so slim, tiny and her feet were narrow as were the muscles of her legs. A ragged breath caught in his throat as he imagined seeing other parts of her. Bloody hell, he had to stop thinking this way. When he was with her and even when he was not, it seemed his body was in a constant state of arousal.

A large wave caught her by surprise, reaching past her knees. She turned to run but not before her dress was soaked nearly to her waist. He stepped into the receding water, heedless of his perfectly shined Hessians, drawing her into his arms and striding to dry ground.

She was laughing and the sound was contagious. He sat on a large boulder, holding her close, their laughter echoing in the small area.

"You're all wet?" He brushed her hair away from her face, taking the moment for a quick kiss.

"And your boots are most likely ruined." She laughed, touching his lips with a fingertip. "Do you care?"

"My boots are meant to protect my feet, and they did the job perfectly. But your dress..." He paused before committing to his next words. "You're going to have to take it off and let it dry or you most assuredly will catch cold. See, you're already shivering. I can give you my jacket."

"I can't take off all the layers, so I might as well leave the dress on," she told him, pushing slightly away as if she meant to see into his heart and soul.

If she did, she might find him lacking in too many ways to count. "I've an extra shirt and a pair of buckskins in the carriage. You can put those on while your dress and petticoats dry. I don't want to take you home before the sun slips below the ocean. I won't let a soaking wee dress ruin the day I planned for us."

"They will be huge on me. How will I keep the pants up?" She set her hands on his chest.

"I'm sure I've got something that can be used as a belt. Otherwise, you'll have to wear just the shirt and that won't keep you warm either. I'd rather not end this outing before we've watched the sunset," he repeated. Truly, there were too few alternatives here. He tugged on the leather thong holding his hair back.

"I'm really not cold."

"No, of course you're not. That's why your lips are blue and you're shivering so hard the quaking would wake the dead. If I didn't know better, I'd think it's an earthquake upon us." He wrapped the leather around her waist. "Plenty to spare so you can keep the pants from falling down."

"I am a bit cold," she tried to stand but he swept her into his arms and strode up the path to the carriage.

"I can walk."

"But I adore holding you."

Setting her inside, he rummaged through the compartments and pulled out an extra set of clothing then stepped outside. "Yell when you're done." He set the thin piece of leather on the seat.

He strode toward the edge of the cliff while shaking his head at the memories they just made together. He couldn't recall ever being with a woman who didn't care more about her appearance than having fun in the waves. If he could do it over, he might join her and frolic in the breakers. Playing in the waves during the summer would be nicer though than early spring. The ocean would still be cold, but the weather outside would be more tolerable.

"I'm finished." She poked her head outside just as a long bolt of lightning cut across the sky, jumping from one cloud to another.

When had the sky grown so dark and the wind picked up? Instead of helping her down, he entered the carriage, pulling the curtains down to ward off the rain that had just now began to pelt their small shelter.

"Are you still cold?" he asked, watching her rub her hands up and down her arms. "I'm sure the sudden tempest will pass soon and we'll still be able to enjoy the setting of the sun."

With teeth chattering, "Yes," she admitted which surprised him.

"Well, you've got your shawl." He wrapped it around her, realizing he could see the soft rounded curves of her breasts through the fabric of his shirt. The sight left very little to his imagination.

She pulled it close. "At least I'm not wet anymore." She'd spread her dress and a few underthings on the opposite seat.

"No, and I've blankets if you get even colder." Thunder rolled across the sky, shaking the carriage.

Her eyes wide she seemed to scoot closer to him. He wrapped an arm around her, letting her press against him, either for more warmth or, "Are you afraid of the storm or are you still cold?"

One hand resting on his chest as well as her head, "Not so much afraid but terrified. I understand it's just noise and light, but I can't help it.

And yes, I'm still a bit cold but getting warmer by the second."

"We can wait it out in here and eat, unless you want me to hold you until the tempest passes." He smoothed a hand up her back, realizing again she had very little on beneath the shirt, just her chemise which somehow escaped the drenching.

"I'm going to be brave." She pushed away from him, a determined look on her face. "This storm is not going to get the best of me and ruin this day with you. We should eat."

"Good girl." He watched her lean sideways and pull food from the basket, his shirt stretching provocatively across her breasts.

"Ham sandwich?" she asked, holding two in the air before handing one to Roc. Then she found a jar of pickles.

She handed the glass container to him and he opened it, holding it so she could take the first one. "These are Ida's pickles."

"I love pickles." She bit into it then her sandwich and smiled, a drop of pickle juice slipping down her chin.

He vanquished the drop with his fingertip. They ate in silence for a few minutes, listening to the rain and the thunder. She shivered with each loud boom, but she also seemed to stiffen her shoulders.

"A friend of my mother's owns two wineries, Logan Maxwell. He loves to indulge everyone with his very fine Bordeauxs and Chiantis. I don't leave home without a supply that will last me the duration of my trip." He pulled a bottle and two glasses from one of the compartments along with a corkscrew. Opening and pouring the wine, he handed a glass to Cat.

She sipped then looking over the rim, "It's very good." She ran a fingertip around the rim. "But then I really wouldn't know one wine from another."

"I'm glad you like it. Listen, do you hear anything?" he asked, pleased the storm passed so quickly. Without pause, he opened the curtain and was met with a ray of sunshine.

"The clouds have moved on too." She leaned over him to see out the window. Every curve seemed to press against his body, enticing, tempting, inviting him to explore.

"Would you like to take the wine outside with us? We can watch the sunset then head home."

"That would be nice."

He'd picked up her fiddle case and brought it with him. "Would you play for me?"

"A song for a glass of wine?" she laughed, picking up her fiddle. She began to play first a lively tune then a haunting melody. "See, you do want something from me."

"Thank you, you can play for me any time. As you well know, it's not the same thing. Come let's enjoy the rest of the evening."

Outside, sitting on a large boulder, the bottle of wine resting next to Roc on a flat surface of the rock that seemed to be made for them, he pulled out his pocket watch to look at the time.

"We've about fifteen minutes until the sun sinks below the horizon. You do know when that happens, you'll owe me a kiss," he told her, continuing to look over the ocean while wondering exactly what she was thinking.

"Maybe you'll owe me one," she said, leaning back, her hands resting on the boulder.

"Perhaps we should take advantage and kiss now then also when the sun is gone." Good lord, but he craved her, needed to draw the passion from her heart and soul.

"Perhaps we should," she agreed with him. "Is this the kiss I owe you or the one you owe me?" she asked, one hand resting on his chest her lips moist and nearly open, beguiling him.

"You choose." He lifted his shoulders in a slight shrug, trying to ease the tense muscles in his back.

~ * ~

"This is the one I owe you." She drew his head toward her. Placing her hand on either side, she gazed into his deep and oh so dark brown eyes, mesmerizing eyes. Then she whispered, "But you're going to have to help. I'm not real sure what to do."

She watched his tongue moisten his lips as if preparing for the kiss and felt an instant tightening of her body. She swallowed, nervously wondering if she would do this right.

"You're on your own," he whispered as their lips nearly met and she felt his breath flutter across her lips. "The kiss will be much more interesting if you don't get any coaching from me."

She touched his lips with her tongue then found as they met, she closed her eyes, savoring the warmth and softness of the one part of him that wasn't hard and well-muscled.

Cat felt as if she were drowning is a sea of longing for this man, heat swirling in parts of her she never before knew existed until she first kissed this man. With her tongue, she pushed forward as he opened for her. He turned slightly, setting his glass on the rocky shelf that held the wine bottle before he took her glass from her hand.

She waited for him to touch her, to show her the way but just like he told her, it seemed he wanted her to initiate everything. Shifting her hands, she explored him while she tried to remember what he did when he kissed her.

While she discovered his neck and shoulders, she relished everything about him. His scent of leather and spice intoxicated her. She let her hands drift down his neck then rest on his chest. His ragged breathing and the rapid beat of his heart surprised her, told her that somehow she affected him. Could she create a fire in this strong confidant man who seemed to lack for nothing?

He kept his hands to himself, which surprised her. They rested on his legs, his fingers curling then uncurling. She craved his touch, the way he always pulled her closer so her breasts pushed against him.

"I don't know what to do," she breathed when she pulled away. "Why don't you touch me?"

"If you knew any more..." Groaning, he didn't finish because his lips hungrily molded to hers once more and it seemed he assumed control of the kiss. His hands, starting at her waist slowly skimmed across her body, finding a resting place, cradling her face. They were large hands, warm hands with slightly work-roughened fingers.

Then, his hands were at the small of her back, drawing her closer just as she'd remembered. Yet this time he let his hands drift back to her waist then up to settle just below her breasts. She felt his thumbs touch the undersides, and a tiny mew of pleasure came from her, having never known how sensitive her body was.

He explored her further, his lips and teeth settling on her ear, his tongue touching inside, his teeth biting gently on the shell. She shivered in his embrace, her body tightening with each mercuric touch. He created a magical enchantment within her, which she never wanted to end. Her head fell back unconsciously giving him further access to her and telling him yes with every part of her body. And she understood how difficult it would be for her to ever tell him no.

"Roc..." Her voice faded away as she felt his touch to her nipples. "I..." she swallowed hard, wanting him to continue but instinctively understanding she tread on a narrow precipice. She did not want to fall. Even though the no word came to mind, she tamped it down, craving more of what he offered so sweetly.

When he lifted his head and his eyes gazed into hers, his smile was broad. "Next time it will be my turn," he told her, the promise implicit in the shine of his eyes. "You will have to tell me no if I take the kiss too far. Can you do that, my little cat?"

He handed her the glass of wine he'd taken from her, wrapping his arm around her, pulling her so her breast pushed against the side of his chest. Slowly she sipped, wondering what it was he intended when it was his turn to kiss her. Wasn't a kiss just a kiss? But just now he'd done more than ever before. He'd touched her places she never thought to be touched, let alone by a man.

"Look at the sky. That is why we are here. Drink up and I'll pour you another glass. It would be blasphemy not to finish the bottle."

"A myriad of brilliant colors stretched across the horizon." She tried for a topic that wouldn't have her wondering about things she shouldn't think about. Then she finished the sweet intoxicating liquid, holding the glass out for more.

He poured more wine for both of them. "Hmm..." For the longest time it seemed he didn't want to talk. "Oranges, pinks blend with the thin clouds and the ever-darkening sky. It's beautiful but not nearly as stunning as you, Cat."

She didn't know how to respond, having never thought of herself as beautiful let alone stunning. A strange feeling of discontent swept through her, "Liar," she whispered. "Promise me that whatever happens between us, you'll never lie to me."

He pulled back, his brows drawn together, his eyes growing dark and shuttered, "No, I'm not lying. Have you ever looked at yourself in a mirror? You're by far the most beautiful woman I've ever known."

"The sun is about to retire for the night," feeling uncomfortable she said, changing the topic of conversation to something she could understand or at least agree with him. Then she realized he would kiss her now and everything he said that she didn't understand would then come full circle.

He started the kiss with tiny forays up her neck. His teeth grazed then he sucked on her skin. She let her hands settle on his neck, running her fingers through his hair while he explored across her collarbone. Every part of her seemed to burn with desire for more, an inferno sweeping through her. This was how her mother fell from grace. She must be just like her.

Dear God, give me strength to say no before something happens that would change the course of my life forever. She tried to tell him no when his finger caressed her nipple and with his teeth, he pulled her shirt to the side, his mouth settling on her breast, his lips and teeth touching and nipping. She cried out, craving more yet knowing she should not.

Then with his teeth and tongue he opened her mouth, his tongue pushing inside, exploring all of her and she felt as if she melted inside. He cupped her breast in one hand, his thumb teasing the swollen tip.

She made a tiny sound in the back of her throat, needing him, yearning for this man and all the sensations more than she'd ever thought possible. She didn't want to tell him no, needed for him to do this forever.

She closed her eyes, still willing herself to tell him he should stop but the words wouldn't come. Instead, he drew away from her, gazing into her eyes. "While I'd like to keep going, I believe it's time I got you home." He pulled her shirt together, covering her.

"What just happened?" She rested her hand on his face, longing for something only he could give her.

"I gave you a small taste of lovemaking," he told her, looking pleased with himself and a bit smug, "a very small taste and if I'm not wrong, you enjoyed our lovemaking. I would teach you more."

She couldn't refute what he said. She did want more and she did enjoy it. In any case, she didn't want to lie. "I did, but...good lord, I couldn't think. I just wanted you to never stop."

He smiled at her, still touching her possessively, "I sensed that and when we do make love, you'll know and understand how I feel about you. You won't have any regrets. I promise," he said.

When she looked down, she realized the buds on her breasts were hard and swollen from his touch, no longer tiny. "You can see me, nearly all of me." Strangely, she realized she wasn't embarrassed. It all seemed normal and right.

"Come," he stood, holding his hand out to her. It didn't seem he wanted to address her comment. "Let's see if your dress is dry enough to put on."

"It will be late when we get back." She accepted his hand, wishing the night didn't have to end. If she returned to London with him and became his mistress, the nights wouldn't ever have to end. But they would, when he grew tired of her as all men grew tired of their mistresses. The only security was in marriage and he would never wed her.

"Do you have to clean the pub in the morning?" he asked her after he gathered the wine and glasses.

"I do but I can take a nap in the afternoon before the band has to play." He held her hand while they walked to the carriage.

Sometime when she wasn't looking Winston had arrived with the horses. Now he stood by the door, the horses hitched to the carriage, ready to go.

"Thank you, Winston," Roc told his man while he nodded. "Go straight to Caitlin's cottage."

Once inside, the carriage began to move then slowly picked up speed. "I should change back to my dress."

"Unless you want to be nearly naked in front of me, you should probably keep these on while we travel back. No one will see you, so no one can judge," he told her.

He pulled her close, her hand and head resting against his chest, warmth emanating from him. Pulling a blanket around them, he let his head fall back on the seat.

She slowly closed her eyes, listening to his breathing and the steady beat of his heart.

When she opened them again, it was too soft gentle kisses on her forehead and temples. "You're home," he whispered, his breath tickling her ear. "May I come in with you? Just for a moment. I've something I want to give you."

He took the key from her shaking hands, unlocking the door before the little beast greeted them with a raucous round of barking and whining from his pen.

"He needs to go outside, I'm sure." She ruffled the dog's head then picked him up. Before he could pee on her floor again, she let him outside. He ran around in circles finally settling on the perfect place. When finished he ran to her, tail wagging enthusiastically. "Good boy, did you miss us?" she praised then followed him inside.

Roc cleared his throat, his hands behind his back. "I have to leave for a few days, and I don't trust O'Connell. His presence around you doesn't bode well."

His words surprised her and it didn't seem she could focus on what he said about Blair. "I didn't think it would be so soon." He could have told her before he took her to see the sunset, but she understood the news would have put a decided damper on the day.

"It's just for a few days then I'll be back. You can't get rid of me so easily. While I'm gone, I would hope you will think about coming with me when I go home to London. You'll be safer there."

She was backing up and shaking her head, all her fears returning with a vengeance. She wanted him but she didn't want to give up her respect for herself. "I..."

"Just think," he told her, holding up his hands. "No commitments yet."

"You just don't understand."

"The reality I see is that if you stay here, Blair will find a way to make you his wife. Something you've told me repeatedly you don't want. Of course, I don't want that for you either."

"We can't be having this conversation again, Roc. I don't want to be your mistress either as I've told you repeatedly." If she was honest with herself, she would admit she'd rather be his mistress than Blair's wife. Why were both her options such horrible choices?

"Nevertheless, those are the facts of your situation. I don't trust that man and I fear for you. While the dog will protect you when he's older, at the moment he's a bit useless."

She laughed suddenly, seeing some humor in all these decisions she was forced to consider. "Did you hear that, Beast? He thinks you're useless but I think you're adorable."

"Only for the time being."

"You should go. I've got a lot to think about and very little time for sleep before six o'clock comes and I have to go to the pub."

"Two things before I leave." He pulled a small purse from his coat pocket. "This is for you. Like I said, I don't trust Blair. If something happens and you feel you have to leave quickly, this is enough money to book you passage on a ship and cab fare in London."

"I can't accept that." She pushed the hand holding the purse away from her. "Why can't you understand? I don't want your money or expensive gifts."

"You don't have a choice in this, and I'm going to leave it here whether you want me to or not. In this matter, I won't take no for an answer."

"There is always a choice and I choose no despite your words." She didn't mean to be so stubborn, but this gesture was one more step in the wrong direction.

"No, listen. No one but us knows. You're not required in any way to spend the money. It's just there in case of an emergency. Inside there is an address that isn't mine. It's my mother's. There is also a letter you can give her. I've asked her that she take care of you until I can catch up to you and make sure you are safe and protected."

This was so untoward. He gave her money to leave Ireland and run to his mother's house if she needed to get away. "Alright, I'm not so stubborn I can't see the benefits of accepting this." She placed it in a small bag in the corner of her room.

"What's the second thing?" She was pretty sure it was another kiss, which she wouldn't say no to simply because his kisses were turning into more than kisses and she loved the way they made her feel.

"Actually, there are three things."

"Three?" She smiled at him enjoying the wicked grin exposed on his face.

"My clothes," he told her, looking her up then down while she felt the same heat build inside that she did when he kissed her. She liked the way his appreciative gaze roamed her almost as if it was a caress.

He set her dress and petticoats in the corner before standing with his arms crossed in front of him.

"Do you expect me to disrobe in front of you? You wouldn't let me in the carriage. Why here?" Her words turned into a heavy Irish brogue.

"You can give them to me when I return in five days. While I'd love to watch you disrobe so I can feast my eyes on your nakedness, I believe that enjoyment is for some time in the not so distant future."

"What is the third thing then?" she asked stepping toward him.

"A kiss to send me on my way."

"Not one to keep you here," she challenged, while he wasted no time in sweeping her into his arms and kissing her soundly.

When he ended the kiss, "Take care of yourself and don't forget about the money. Use it if you need it." With that said he left.

Feeling bereft and lonely, she locked the door behind him. When had she fallen so hard for this man she could never have? Taking his clothes off and folding them neatly, she held them close, enjoying his scent, which lingered on the fabric.

In her nightdress and wool socks, she pulled the covers over her and in much the same way as the night before, she found sleep elusive.

The next day was cloudy and dreary, befitting her mood. She cleaned the pub and instead of napping before her evening's work, she walked to Ida's, meaning to talk to her about Beast then speak with Ida's daughter, probably her only friend in this small village.

Sybil was a quiet and, one might call, sickly girl. It seemed she had little strength to do the most mundane chores or activities. Caitlin put the leash Roc fashioned before he gave her the dog on Beast. He barked and grabbed the rope with his mouth, tugging on it as if asking what was taking her so long. She laughed.

Peeking inside Ida's home, "Good morning, Ida." Caitlin stepped through the front door. "The feast you sent our way yesterday was wonderful. No, it was fantastic."

"So, you had fun with your man?" Ida asked.

"He's not my man but yes, we had fun. Well, I think he did too." She handed Ida the basket.

"You didn't have to return that."

"While I can think of nothing I'd use it for, I'm sure you can put it to good use. Could you tell me what you charged Roc for the dog?" Caitlin sat down at the table.

"He told me you might ask." She puttered around her kitchen, putting dishes in the sink and drying some more.

"He was right, of course." She was pretty sure now that Roc would have told Ida not to reveal the cost.

"He also told me not to tell you and that the money meant nothing to him." She sounded perturbed. "Is he buying you gifts and what has he asked of you in return? Now I understand it's not anymore my business than what you want me to know about the dog but seeing you don't have a ma, I'm going to tell you what I think."

Caitlin grimaced, "It's not the way it looks. Beast is the only thing he's given me." She paused, except the emergency money, but Ida didn't need to know about that. "And..."

"It's for your protection, but he's giving you things and he's a man. Now you heed me, he thinks with a different part of his anatomy than a woman. Mark my words, he wants more from you than friendship."

"I know and it's all I can do when he kisses me to keep from succumbing to his immeasurable charms." As long as Roc was the nay sayer, she was safe.

Ida was wagging her finger at her, a stern expression on her matronly face, "Now you have to think and tell him no. If you say that one word, he won't take your innocence until he puts a ring on your finger."

"That's the problem, Ida. Roc has no intention of putting a ring on my finger and if he did, I'd say yes, but all he wants is for me to become his mistress when he goes home, back to London."

"Now you don't know that for sure."

Caitlin sat down, lifting her shoulders for a moment and trying not to relive all the times he told her the truth about what he wanted. "That's where you're wrong. He's asked me to be his mistress. So yes, I know for sure."

"Well, that picnic basket is the last nice thing I'm going to do for your young man. That is until he regains his senses. He loves you, you know, but like most men, he's just too damned stubborn to admit to it."

"Sadly, I doubt if he will. His mind is made up and I've a feeling once that happens, he rarely or ever changes his mind."

"You miss him and he's only been gone since last night." Ida set a loaf of bread that had been rising in the oven. "I just don't know what to say. I was sure the way he spoke of you, he's already fallen head over heels in love with you," Ida said.

"Love and lust are rarely the same thing." She wasn't sure what she was talking about here but she'd heard her da speak of love versus lust when he talked about her father.

"Now just what do you know about lust?" Ida set the dishtowel she'd been drying her hands with on the table.

"Nothing really." But last night when he touched her breast, she was sure that was lust.

"What has he done? You haven't..."

"I don't think so, no, but you really didn't finish your sentence," Caitlin said knowing now she didn't come to speak with Sybil but to talk with someone who knew a few things about men and women.

"Whew, you haven't then. Good girl, you told him no, did you? That's a good thing, you know. Every girl has to understand just how far they can let their man take advantage of her charms."

"I'm not following what you're saying." She stole an apple slice from the apple pie Ida was preparing.

"Just what did he do besides kiss you. Now, you don't have to be honest with me. It's your business after, all but I can't give you advice if I don't know the whole story. And I believe you came here looking for some."

"Sybil, you're home."

"I thought I heard your voice. Would you like me to walk your dog?" Sybil asked.

"You go right ahead, dear. Caitlin and I still have a few things to talk about. Then I'm sure the two of you might want to visit." She turned to Caitlin. "What time do you have to be at the pub?"

"Five. I probably won't have the time. Da likes me there early to help set up the tables and other things in the kitchen."

"What did the two of you do? I'm not going to let this go unless you tell me I'm an old busy body and to stop prying."

Caitlin fiddled with her dress while she felt the heat of Ida's gaze. "We kissed, a lot, and he touched me, my breast." She looked up, sucking her lips together. "I should have told him no, but I liked it."

"Anything else?" Ida, hands on hips and tapping her foot seemed to want to make this harder on her.

"Nothing else, but I wanted him, well, I didn't want him to stop."

"You told him no."

She was shaking her head again and lifting her shoulders, truly confused. "He stopped."

~ * ~

That night in the pub, Blair watched her, his hungry gaze resting on her breasts. She stole his breath and despite what her so called father told him, he didn't mean to ever let her go. He intended to find a way to bind her to him. If he got her pregnant, she wouldn't have a choice but to wed him. He wouldn't give her a choice, and he was also sure Sean would make sure she married him.

He knew from her da that she didn't want to travel the same path as her mother. If he forced the issue, she would say yes to him. He drank down the pint in front of him then motioned for another one.

"You think about what I told you the other day?" Sean asked after he set the pint in front of him.

"Thought a lot about your girl. Didn't change my mind though. She needs a man and children. I going to give that to her." He drummed his fingers on the bar, watching Caitlin as she danced around the room, playing a lively jig on her fiddle.

"Leave her alone," Sean warned.

"Or what?" Blair rose from the stool a bit unsteady so he sat down again. "There's nothing you can do about it. You know in this county I take what I want and I want the girl. No one gainsays me, not even her da."

When she danced by, he grabbed her around the waist and pulled her to him. He squeezed, enjoying her curves and wishing he dare explore other parts of her. Not in public though. He'd find a way to get past her front door.

"Let me go!" She tried to push away from him, but he held her tight with one hand, his other exploring her.

When he reached for his pint a knife slammed into the bar, resting so close to his hand, he shook. "What the bloody hell?" Blair stared into the furious eyes of Sean O'Shea.

"She said to let her go." Sean spoke with a determination and force Blair had never heard before. "Best you think long and hard about what you do next, and I'm not talking about this moment. She doesn't want anything to do with the likes of you, and I'd rather see her run off with the Englishman than become your wife."

Blair loosened his hold, letting Caitlin slip away. He decided he'd follow her home tonight, see if he could push his way inside before she locked the door. Tonight she would be his. Rubbing his hands together, delighted with his plan, he licked his lips.

Refocusing his attention on Sean, "You'll be dead if you try anything." Blair threatened back.

"Her life is worth more than mine. I understand you own the constables and you control the other parts of the government here. But you won't be around either to enjoy her."

"Maybe I should have you arrested now before you can bring any harm down around my head." He wasn't going to let this commoner get in the way of his plans. And now that he decided to act, a weight left his shoulders. It would not be long now.

Sean seemed to understand what he was thinking. "Even if you get her pregnant, she won't marry you. I've talked with her enough to know that. She'll stay single and keep the child. I'll help her everyway I can."

Sean's words gave him pause and good reason to think of a second

45

plan if this one failed. Maybe he could persuade her da to his side if he upped the taxes on the pub. He could squeeze her da so hard, Sean would beg her to marry him.

He grinned, thinking perhaps this would work better than forcing himself on her. She danced and played so well. The first time he saw her in the pub, he lost his heart and she'd detested him from the start.

He still meant to pay her a visit this evening. They could talk, share a glass of whiskey as she did with the English lord. And he'd steal a kiss before he left for home just like the Englishman. A bit of romance might not hurt his cause.

She was putting her fiddle away. So, she'd have a bite to eat and a pint of Guinness then she'd walk home. Since the Englishman left, Sean had been walking her to her little cottage.

He ordered another drink, feeling a bit sleepy. He drank it down quickly because he wanted to be able to follow her home when she left. He'd just tell Sean he didn't need to walk her tonight.

Finding he had to relieve himself, he looked to Caitlin who was just beginning to eat. He had the time. Leaving the pub and finding a secluded spot, he finished his business.

Looking up he watched as Sean strode from the direction of her home to go inside the pub. Furious with himself and the horrible timing, he fastened his pants and started for her house.

Darkness encapsulated the little cottage. He leaned against a tree, watching and waiting for an unforeseen opportunity.

Chapter Three

"Cat. Cat! Wake up. I want to show you something. I know it's late but you've just got to see this. Cat." Roc called, banging on her door eager to show her the shooting stars. He'd never seen so many sailing through the sky at one time. He looked in the window to see if he woke her.

"Roc?" She sat up, brushing her hair from her eyes. Swinging her legs over the side of her bed, she stumbled sleepily from the bed to the door. "You're back. Is that you?"

"Only an hour ago." He stepped inside the now open door. "Put your coat on and come. Never mind." Grabbing a quilt off the bed, he wrapped it around her. "You always sleep in wool socks?" he laughed, wondering if she would do the same when she slept in his bed.

"When it's cold, they keep my feet warm." She sounded miffed and defensive to him, but he didn't care. He was so happy to see her and have all his business deals wrapped up. He was going home in the morning and he hoped she'd go with him, but even if she didn't, he'd come back as soon as he shared all the details of his mission with his boss.

"I'd like to keep your feet warm," he blurted while he swept her into his arms and made his way down a path to a brick fence overlooking a field. "I saw these on my way home and knew you had to see this dazzling light show."

Beast woke up and danced around the couple barking and seeming to cry out, *Look I'm here. Pet me. Get me out of here.*

For a moment he set her aside to pick up the dog. "You best behave or I won't take you on another outing with your mistress," he told Beast, roughing his ears.

"What are you talking about?" She snuggled against him and he guessed it was for warmth more than anything. The night was a cold one but clear which made this meteor shower more impressive.

Beast followed them, prancing around Roc's feet then racing ahead only to return a few minutes later. He was so full of energy, Roc realized he must have spent most of his time in the pen.

Gently, he set his precious cargo on the stone fence before sitting down beside her. He pulled her close, making sure the blanket covered her. "Look in the sky and make a wish." He pointed heavenward.

"Why?" She sounded petulant as well as sleepy. She rubbed her eyes, staring into the night sky.

"It's a meteor shower. Most people call them shooting stars, but they aren't stars at all." He watched in awe as the show continued.

Beast stood on his hind legs, begging to be picked up but there was no room on his lap. "Lie down, Beast," he told the dog who didn't obey.

"What are they?" she asked, finally seeming interested in his excitement over rocks falling towards the earth.

Beast finally settled at his feet, his head resting on one foot. The dog would be loyal to her and possibly to both of them. He could only pray the animal wouldn't have to prove his loyalty.

"They are," he paused, thinking about Cat and all she meant to him, "what we call meteors, but they are really rocks falling through the earth's atmosphere. The heat so far above us sets them on fire. Now make a wish and it's sure to come true."

She looked for seconds upon seconds and he didn't know what she was thinking, perhaps she was wishing to come with him. Well, all she had to do was say the words and he'd have her on his ship in the morning, and they'd say goodbye to Portrush together.

"Did you make a wish?" she asked, finally smiling when she looked at him. "I did too."

"Good, are you warm enough?" He tucked her in closer to his side. "Tell me what you wished."

"My nose is cold." She laughed, what about yours? "Nope," she said when she touched his. "Can't tell a person your wish or it won't come true."

Holding her close and watching the stars shoot from the sky was the best thing, he'd done in a long time. Their visit to the beach five days ago had been fabulous, but sharing something that he was excited about with her was heaven in disguise. He needed to savor this moment with her, keeping it tucked inside his mind.

"Can't say I'm sorry I woke you but..." He didn't want to tell her he was leaving with the morning tide. Didn't think he stood one chance in hell of talking her into leaving with him, but he did need to know if anything happened during the week he'd been gone.

"I'm glad you woke me up. I was dreaming of you." She picked up his hand in hers.

Surprised by the simple gesture, he thought perhaps his cause was better today than when he left. He spread his fingers wide, measuring her hand with his. So tiny, exquisitely delicate and fragile, she didn't think of those as her characteristics, and she was too bricky for his taste. She'd take on the world alone with her fearlessness. Then he let his fingers entwine with hers, bringing their hands to his lips and kissing the back of hers.

"Does that mean you might change your mind about leaving with me?" He knew it was too soon to ask her, but he supposed the answer would be the same now as it would be an hour from now. They really only had a short time to figure this out.

"Honestly, I want to be with you but I can't become your mistress. The position is not one I would...I have to feel joy and happy about my choices. I would always regret that decision. I will miss you though." She leaned into him, her hands wrapping around him.

His heart fell for a few seconds. It wasn't what he wanted to hear but what he expected. "I'm leaving this morning on the tide, only a few hours from now. If you change your mind..." He could always hope. After all that was his wish, that she come with him.

Pushing away for a moment, he looked into her blue-violet eyes. She had the most unique and beautiful eyes, but when she leaned into him again, he felt the silent sobs of pain. "I understand. I'll never see you again. I suppose it always had to be this way."

"I will come back." That was a promise he intended to keep. After debriefing he would have little to nothing to do with his life. His shipping company as well as the farms they rented pretty much ran themselves. The men his mother had hired were among the most competent in all of England. He'd told Cat he wanted peace and quiet, but what he craved was her beside him, sharing his life.

"But not to stay, just to try to convince me of something I just can't bring myself to do." She brushed away the new tears that had fallen. "Let's not talk about this anymore."

As if Beast agreed with her, he stood and let out a low growl as if he sensed something was wrong.

"If you turn down this offer, you might find yourself wed to Blair. Ida told me some things before I left. I don't like what he has planned for you. It just doesn't bode well," he said, wishing he didn't have to resort to bad news to convince her what was best for her.

"I won't marry that man, ever," she said softly, so softly he had to bend closer to hear the words. "He's detestable and I know he'd hit me every time he got drunk, which is every night."

"If you stay here, you might not have a choice, He's a powerful man who is more than willing to wield that authority to get what he wants," he warned, wishing there was some other way to tell her that her options were limited.

"I think we've had this conversation before." She stood, "Come, Beast, we're going home," but it seemed she realized she wore only socks and no shoes and she sat back down.

Looking forlorn and a bit lost, she looked to him, more tears filling her eyes. She sighed heavily, her shoulders slumping. He wanted to kick himself for hurting her, but short of marrying her, there was nothing he could do.

When he first looked at her feet and realized her attempt to leave failed, he almost laughed at her expression but held it back, telling himself not to add insulting her to her misery. "I'll be pleased to carry you. That way I can hold you closer to me and your socks won't get wet."

"You don't have to do that."

"I want to carry you. Come, Beast."

Beast became more alert and looked at them when he heard his name and started homeward, leading the way as if he was the king and they were his ever-faithful followers. Once inside, Roc closed the door with his foot and let her slide to the ground against his body.

Beast growled at the partitioned room, but Roc ignored him, thinking the animal a little bit ornery for the late night. Still holding Cat, he opened the pen for Beast. "Go on, get inside and go back to sleep. This adventure is over." Beast trotted into the pen then lay down, closing his eyes.

Then turning his attention back to the woman in his arms, "*Mon petite chatte*," he murmured against her ear. In his arms she completed him, felt like heaven to his heart and soul.

Her quilt slowly slipped off her shoulders. His hands rested on her perfectly formed buttocks, unable to stop himself and needing to feel more of her than he'd allowed himself before, he wound the cloth of her nightdress in his hands until he could touch her, feel her silken flesh the way he'd wanted to for so many weeks now he couldn't remember.

His hands on her naked skin sent a bolt of raw desire rushing through him, and he knew only one thing would put out the inferno blazing within, but it was the one thing he couldn't take from her until she agreed to be his mistress. He ran his hands up her back, skin against skin until he reached her shoulders. He tried to memorize her shape and the feel of her against his hands. Groaning, he knew he was damned and also knew he would have to stop himself if she didn't say the words he needed to hear.

"Tell me no," he whispered in her ear while he trailed kisses down her neck then back to her mouth. Her flesh seared his lips with the heat of her passion and desire. He craved to feel all of her and to bury himself deep inside her. She was meant for him yet he failed to convince her of that fact.

The tiny sound in the back of her throat sounded more like a please than a no. "Roc..."

He needed help to end this. The feel of her against his hands was silken and smooth. She was so soft. He let his hand roam up her sides, feeling the beginning swell of her breasts. One small move and he could have her nightdress on the floor, another and they would be on her bed, naked and completing the lovemaking he just began.

"Tell me no. Just say the words."

Her fingernails dug into his skin, and it seemed she tried to bring herself closer. Once again, his hands settled on her derrière, squeezing, testing, wishing for so much more. She didn't really understand what she was doing, but she was offering herself to him, in the most elemental and primal ways. A swift mercuric heat swept through him and he hoped into her.

Bloody hell but she was his. He could take her with him, if he wanted. He could just kidnap her in the morning, not give her a choice. Why was she making this so bloody hard? He was tempted to bring her hand lower to feel him, and how much he wanted her. Beneath his perfectly fitted pants, his rod throbbed against the fabric.

"How are you so soft?" he murmured, returning his attention to her neck, then her lips and running his hands up the length of her back, until he groaned with unleashed passion rushing through him. "Are you soft everywhere?"

"I..." was all she could manage.

"Tell me no," he whispered again. "I don't know if I can stop unless you ask me. You have to tell me, Cat." He didn't want to beg her, but he knew his limitations and they were now at an end.

But she didn't say anything, only responded with hot little forays of her tiny pink tongue along his neck. He understood all too well he could take her now. She would never say no to him, not tonight. Yet he suddenly realized this was not what he wanted and he groaned. All his wayward thoughts of seduction would not come to fruition.

"I've kept you up too long, little cat, *mon petite chatte*. You have to go to bed and not with me as I would like." He let her nightdress fall to the floor, covering her once more from neck to foot.

She looked at him, her tongue briefly appearing and tempting him to continue what he started. "You don't want me? I thought for a moment. I'm embarrassed."

How had she ever gotten that idea? "More than you will ever understand. But I'm not going to leave here not knowing if what we did created a child. I can't do that to you or to me. You're too important and I've found I like having you in my life more than I ever thought possible." He could still hold her, could caress her nakedness again and nothing would turn out right.

"I don't want you to go," she whispered, pressing her hands against his body, clearly distressed. "I didn't say no because I didn't want you to stop. Roc, don't go tomorrow..."

There it was, the pain ran deeper than he could have ever imagined. "If I had a choice, I'd stay. The entire reason I've been in Ireland, the reason I met you, had nothing to do with pleasure and everything to do with work."

"What is it? What is that you do besides watch me play the fiddle and..." It seemed she couldn't finish the sentence.

"I can't say. The danger would come to you if you knew too much," he told her smoothing the tangle of hair away from her face.

"You speak in riddles I can't ever understand, and I believe you want it to be that way. But for now, I give up. I can't do this any longer and the morning will come and everything will be the way it was before I met you, before you found your way into my heart," she said angrily, turning her back on him for a moment.

His heart went out to her. Between them so many things had been left unsaid. They'd had too little time together to talk. "If you change your mind, be at my home by five and if you need to use the small purse I gave you, don't think twice. You have to trust your gut instincts," he warned her one more time and praying this last cautionary word would be heeded.

It seemed she forced a smile. He touched her lips, wishing he could stay. "As soon as I'm done in London, I promise I'll come back and try to change your mind." So many times he'd said the exact same words and just as many times she refuted them. "I'm going now."

He kissed her quickly, barely a hint of what they shared before. To Roc it was bittersweet, heartbreaking. He'd hoped for so much more this evening. When he left her behind, his gut rolled, understanding she was in trouble where the Earl of Glenwood, Blair O'Connell, was concerned.

As he walked, he didn't look back, couldn't bring himself to see her standing at the window, tears running down her cheeks. Moisture settled in the back of his throat. His fists tightened as fear for her swept through him. Something bad was about to happen and he was powerless to stop it. The fine hairs on the back of his neck stood on end.

The Duchess' home, the boarding house he stayed in, loomed in front of him. "Winston." He called out and wasn't surprised when the man appeared in the doorway dressed and seemingly ready to leave with the morning tide. The sooner they left the sooner he would be able to return. "Bring me a bottle of brandy and a glass."

The items were set beside him. Before he picked up pen and paper, he poured a glass. He was once more the master of his destiny. Well, he would be as soon as he was debriefed. He tossed back one glass then two, until he felt no more pain at leaving Cat to fend for herself.

He sat at his desk and slammed down the bottle then swore with a startling velocity before he tossed back his head, foregoing the glass and drank even more deeply from the bottle.

Damn Blair O'Connell, Damn the English government, Damn The Duchess, his mother, and damn the secret life he'd been coerced into living simply to rid himself of the boredom that had been such a part of his everyday life, he needed to roar his fury. Damn them all to one hundred thousand hells.

He fell silent then and leaned his head against the back of the chair. The brandy began to work its magic, erasing the pain and tension, the ache and the desire slowly from his constricted muscles. He closed his eyes, but he could not close his mind from the memories that were Cat nor could he cease to breathe in her scent to recall the silken softness of her flesh beneath his fingers beneath his lips.

He could not forget her hair, flying behind her as she danced with such wild abandon while playing her fiddle and tempting him to touch. He could not forget her promise to herself or how unique the deep violet-blue color of her eyes fascinated him with their depths and their ever-changing color.

He could not forget her form and more than anything else, he wanted to race back to her cottage and drag her here and into his bedroom and feel her beneath him on his bed this very night. Let the world be damned. Let any man stand between them and he would fight them to the bitter end.

He touched his lips, reminiscing about the sweet taste of her mouth and her flesh. This was not how he expected this mission to end. When he'd seen her in the pub, he'd thought sure she would be an easy conquest, would jump at the chance to leave this life behind her.

He'd been so very wrong about everything. Now he had to patch up his mistakes and make sure nothing happened to her before he could return. Perhaps he would be able to persuade her better if there was distance and time between them.

He would write a note to Ida, still fearing for Cat. Her life was indeed at stake even if she wouldn't admit that fact. She lived in an imaginary dream world where nothing was evil.

Caitlin just didn't understand the man who pursued her so diligently. Hell, of course she didn't comprehend to what ends an evil and desperate man would go to get what he wanted.

"What do you need?" Winston appeared in front of him. "You shouldn't drink the entire bottle. At least not until were on board the ship." He paused. "I suppose I don't need to tell you that."

The man was far too rigid for Roc's taste, but this characteristic had come in handy from time to time.

"I suppose you don't." Roc tipped the bottle back and drank again. It seemed the brandy did have a soothing affect.

"Sorry, sir, if I was too presumptive."

"Apology accepted," he said, reverting back to his usual efficiency. "First, when I finish this message, I want you to take it to Ida. She'll be awake soon, starting the new loaves of bread and fixing breakfast for her borders. If she isn't already." He picked up the pen that had been sitting in front of him, thinking of everything he needed to say, "Then I want you to visit the ship and make sure everything is set to go."

"Yes, sir."

"I'm impatient to get off." He paced the room, using the pent up energy sizzling inside before he strode back to his desk to pen the message to his friend.

Dear Ida,

Please check up on Caitlin. She is in trouble, as we both know. If you can find a way to keep her out of Blair's eyesight, then do whatever is necessary. He's stubborn when it comes to Caitlin. We both understand the man cannot be trusted. He's a pariah to everything that crosses his path.

I appreciate you're not completely thrilled with my intentions where Caitlin is concerned, but she will come to no harm with me and I will treat her with kindness and respect. You know I want her but rest assured I've almost been a perfect gentleman where she is concerned. You need not worry about her being with child. *Not that I wouldn't want one.*

We both have one major goal in mind. Keep Caitlin away from Blair. He is a mean drunk and I fear for her very life. Beast, her dog will provide no protection for her until he's grown. I hope you can help her train the animal. I fear without training, he'll rule his mistress.

I will return in a few weeks if everything goes as planned. Pray that it does. I'm not sure Caitlin has that long. The hairs on the back of my neck are even now standing on end with nervous apprehension.

Use the purse I gave you to send any messages to me you deem necessary. I have given Cat money to escape if need be. It's enough to book passage and purchase several cabs. I've also given her my mother's address. The Duchess will provide safe haven for Cat.

Yours truly,

Richard Oakes Crandall Leighton Duke of Ravenswood

Roc

He sealed the letter, stood and handed the note to Winston. "I'll be ready in an hour. See that you've returned by then. Are my bags packed and ready?"

"Everything is on board your ship."

Sitting down at his desk, he let his head fall into his hands. He closed his eyes, once again remembering the sweet kisses he shared with his Cat. Never before had he felt the way she made him feel.

The whining and scratching at his door caught his attention. "Beast?" he murmured, suddenly more terrified than he'd ever been.

He opened the door, intending to let the dog inside but the animal pawed at his leg then turned starting down the road. When Roc didn't immediately follow, Beast turned to run back up the walkway, repeating the process again.

Swearing beneath his breath, his heart pounding so rapidly he thought it would jump out of his chest, he followed.

~ * ~

It seemed to Blair, he'd been waiting an eternity for Caitlin to return. His stomach growled and he needed a drink. Thinking of the whiskey he watched them drink, he started for the cupboard when he heard the sound of a dog barking and two people chattering.

"Bloody hell." He swore, staring at the bottle, his cravings escalating. He needed a drink so he could think clearly, needed it so he'd know just the right words to make Caitlin want him.

The door suddenly swung open. From behind the dressing curtain, he witnessed everything. Caitlin was in his arms, wearing nothing but her nightdress and socks. It was all he could do hold back the groan when Roc pulled her nightdress up, caressing her butt. He saw all of her back and her long slim legs, watched them touch each other, watched while Roc explored her body.

The sight of her naked back left him aroused and in need of release. The show they put on was erotic and way too sensual. It was something even he had to admit was not meant to be seen by another human.

He'd watched whores have sex with their John's just to get aroused, and he guessed there might be those who watched him. That thought got him even harder. In an attempt to ease his arousal, he rubbed himself, thinking of Caitlin touching him there.

He closed his eyes and imagined his hands where Roc's were, imagined her hair wrapped around him while he caressed her intimately. For a moment he turned away, unable to keep from making a noise that would alert Roc to his whereabouts.

Anger built deep inside. Roc was taking what was his and she was giving it to him, more than eager. He had to decide if he still wanted her if she was used goods. She was the duke's whore and that didn't sit well with him.

In the parish there was no one else who would suit him, and he was thrilled when Roc left for the night before tossing her on the bed. For a few minutes, he'd thought Roc might have her wrap her legs around him and take her against the wall.

He wanted her no matter what the two had done, he realized, and he was going to have her despite her da's disapproval. She'd never really told him she didn't want him. After all, he was the best catch in Portrush and surrounding villages. What woman wouldn't want him?

He heard them say their goodbyes, heard more too. Before he left, he meant to retrieve the purse Roc gave her. She wasn't going to leave him.

Roc left her then with a quick kiss. She stood at the window watching him leave, tears slipping down her cheeks.

"He's not worth your tears." Blair stepped from behind the curtain, the dog growling. For a second he was taken aback until he realized the animal was penned in.

She whirled when he spoke, her eyes wide with what he could only call terror. How did you get in?" she asked, her voice shaking.

"The door was left open." In a few quick strides he was beside her even as she backed away, her hand outstretched as if she intended to keep him at bay.

"So, you invited yourself inside and you waited behind my curtain while Roc and I..." She gulped air, terrified now. "You should have said something. I thought you were a gentleman." Roc was too far away to call him back. He'd never hear her scream. She looked to the door thinking to run but he would be faster than her.

"I enjoyed your little mews of pleasure. And I'll relish them even more when you're in my arms."

"Never happen." She crossed her arms, wishing she could snap her fingers and vanish. This had been what Roc had warned her against. Now all his fears for her were coming to pass. She had not believed him, didn't think Blair would ever be so bold.

"Of course, it will." He tried to pull her into his arms, but she dodged away from him.

Her breaths ragged and short, "No, no," she said, understanding that one word would never stop him. "No. Go home, Blair. I don't want anything to do with you. Go away."

He was closing in on her again, and Beast was growling. "Playing hard to get? I like that. You can fight me if you want. I'll like that even better. Give me a challenge."

"I don't want you." Her heart in her throat, she managed to duck again, weaving closer to the wall, keeping a small measure of distance between them. She needed at least to head towards the door and the open space where she could run.

"I'm not leaving without a kiss. The sooner you give it to me the sooner I'll let you sleep. I know you have to get up in a few hours. We can always finish this tomorrow night. I'm a man of patience."

"I'd rather not sleep." She was running out of space to maneuver and the door was across the room, too far, way too far away. Desperately, her heart pounded.

"Of course you don't mean that. I promise, you'll love sleeping with me."

His words had changed from coaxing to demanding. She searched for a way to get rid of him but she was stranded. "Blair, you need to go home and sleep off the Guinness. You're not thinking straight. Everything will look different in the morning."

"All ready slept it off waiting for you to get back here with your lover." He wiped the back of his mouth with his hand. "Now I want to have a little of what you gave the duke.

"Roc is not my lover." She thought about telling him otherwise but decided the truth might serve her best. "I've turned him down just as I'm turning you down. Don't want either of you."

"He's felt most every part of you, hasn't he?" His sneer sent chills down her spine. "Don't try to convince me otherwise. I saw it with my own two eyes."

"No. No he hasn't." Once again, she was forced to dodge his outstretched arms.

"Don't lie to me. I watched him do just that."

"No, you're wrong." She was shaking her head, her back against

59

the wall. She no longer had anywhere to run.

Then he pulled her against him, his lips touching on her. She felt nausea roll in her stomach, smelled the whiskey on his breath as she struggled against him. Pushing at him, then beating on his back, she bit his lip hard.

"Damn you, you little bitch."

Suddenly she felt the full force of his fist against her head. She fell to the floor, unable to stop the whimper escaping her. It didn't seem he was finished with her. He pulled her from the floor, blood slipping down her face.

"No..." Her thin wail, slipped from her lips, understanding that everything she'd ever thought about him was true. "Please don't."

"I like it when you beg."

"Please." She couldn't help herself. "Blair, for the love of God let me go. You don't want to hurt me."

"Kiss me then." His hands on her shoulder, he shook her, his cold blue eyes searing into her. "Kiss me and I won't hurt you again." He licked his lips.

"No..." She was struggling against him, her head pounding, blood dripping from her nose. "I won't." She understood this would all get worse if she kept refusing him, but she didn't think he would stop if she swallowed her pride as well as her dislike for him and gave him the kiss he asked for.

"You're nothing but a little whore who thinks she can marry a duke. I'm an earl and you could have had me. You would have had a title and all the wealth anyone could wish for." He shook her again before pushing her away from him as if he now detested her. "I'll find a way to make you pay."

He already had. Her head throbbed and Roc was surely headed to his ship. He would be gone and Blair would be here. She had no way to defend herself against this man.

For a moment he turned his back on her but whirled again almost as if he read her thoughts. She'd been searching the room for a weapon she could use against him. Perhaps Roc should have given her a pistol instead of money and a puppy.

"And you're nothing but a pompous fool who happened to be born into a family with a title. If you had to work, you'd be fired on the first day and you'd probably starve." Her words would only provoke him more, but she was too angry to curb her thoughts. He would take whatever he wanted from her, but she would never say I do and she would never come to his bed a willing partner.

This time the slap to her face sent her reeling backward. The force wasn't nearly as strong as the first blow, but the room began to whirl and spin. She stopped her backward retreat, barely able to stand let alone move. Closing her eyes, she tried to control the sensations washing through her at such a rapid speed, she could barely breathe.

Slowly her knees crumpled and she found herself on the floor, her body open and vulnerable. She couldn't move, could barely see him. Starting to pull her legs to her chest in hopes of protecting herself, she was too late.

"Whore." He screamed and his booted foot claimed her ribs. Again and again he kicked her.

She stifled the moans then she couldn't help herself. Her mind closed just as her eyes did. She didn't know when he left, but the relief was palpable when she heard the closing of the door. Saving herself was paramount in her mind, but if Roc left before she could get to his house, she would have to find Ida.

That might well put Ida's life in jeopardy and Sybil's too. Blair was that ruthless.

Minutes ticked by while she tried to control the pain that encapsulated her. Trying to push from the floor, searing hot agony sent her back to the ground. *If you're going to escape, you have to put the pain to the back of your mind. Work through it, ignore it, do whatever you need to do. But get off the floor, pack a small bag and find Roc.*

Holding her breath, closing her eyes and after too many minutes passed, she was able to crawl to a chair. She made herself stand by willing her body to do as she commanded. The pain excruciating, she willed it away.

She sat then, breathing deeply. If she didn't move, her ribs didn't hurt so bad. The small cough nearly sent her to the floor again. Clinging to the chair's arms, she remained upright. She pressed a hand against her ribs, seeming to hold the pain inside.

Her satchel was on the other side of the room. The clock chimed four thirty. She had thirty minutes to get to his home. It was a walk that would normally take about five to ten minutes. She wasn't even sure if she could get that far.

She had few clothes to pack, but she knew she needed to put something in her bag before she left. The small purse was tucked in a pocket and she prayed Blair had not found it, but she was unwilling to take the time to check. It was either there or it was not.

More minutes passed but she was able to put two dresses a pair of shoes and some underclothes inside before she fastened it shut. She picked up her fiddle case understanding it wasn't prudent but unwilling to leave without her most valuable possession.

"One foot in front of the other," she whispered but by the time she reached Beast's pen, she was on all fours. She let the dog go and he bounded ahead, sniffing at the door.

"Get Roc. Bring him here. I don't know if I can make it to his house before he leaves." The animal seemed to understand. He raced outside through the door Blair had failed to shut in his haste to get away from her.

She tried to stand again and was met with some success. At the door she leaned against it inhaling huge gulps of air, commanding herself to move forward. She stepped outside and the cold air blasted her. She shivered, wrapping her arms around her but unwilling to waste steps to retrieve a covering.

Time seemed to stand still as she alternately crawled then walked toward the home Roc owned. Her nightdress as well as her socks were soaked through. Now the two-story building loomed in front of her, dark and huge. She pursed her lips together, trying to move forward, but the pain consumed her and she fell face first on the grass. Breathing hard, her pulse pounding out of control, she closed her eyes, trying to take a moment of recovery time. Her muscles just didn't seem to want to behave.

The grass was damp still, just as it had been when Roc brought her to see the shooting stars. Her body was wet, all of her freezing in the night air. She wriggled her toes, realizing she couldn't feel them they were so cold. Now her face throbbed, blood pulsing through her injuries. It was almost a welcome relief from the ever-present agony of her ribs.

"Don't give up now," she muttered but even the movement of her mouth hurt. "Death might be preferable to this." *No, don't think that way.*

Once again, she moved hand in front of the other, her knees seeming to follow along. Determinedly she drug her body across the cold ground.

Beast was with her now, licking her, whining. He raced around her, nudging her with his nose. She could see the house from where she collapsed again. "You're a good puppy. Did you find him? Of course you didn't. He's probably half way to England now."

Then she was picked up from the ground. A loud wail of anguish escaped her. Then, "No, leave me be."

"Not on your life, *mon petite chatte.*"

It was not Blair. It was Roc and he was still here. Beast brought him to her. She let her eyes fall shut, snuggling against his broad chest and allowed him to take her to his home.

She heard the sound of his boot pushing open the door. "Winston!"

"Yes, sir."

"Tell the first mate we'll be late. Then come right back."

"Yes sir."

Everything seemed to be happening to her while she remained in a daze. She tried not to move, but it seemed he set her in a chair.

"Cat? What happened?" He touched her face. "You're bleeding."

She wanted to laugh at the obvious but didn't dare create more pain. "Blair happened. Is my nose broken?" she asked and at the moment not really caring about the answer.

Gently he touched it, "No, it's fine but you're going to have one hell of a black eye. The black eye didn't keep you from walking. So, what left you face down on the grass?"

She tried not to breathe too deeply. "He kicked me."

"Damn him to hell," Roc cursed. "If it takes me my entire life, he'll pay for this. If you'll let me, I'll bind your ribs. It won't take away all the pain but it will help. Did you come here so you could go with me, for my protection? I can protect you from that man. He will be held accountable for what he did to you."

Trying not to move very much, slowly she nodded. "I need to go with you. I can't stay here. Understand what you were trying to tell me now."

"I'm glad you finally came to your senses." He smiled at her as if he wasn't an arrogant Englishman.

"I should have believed you."

"How did he get in the house? You didn't let him inside, did you?" He ran his hands up her arms. "Bloody eyes, you're freezing."

"Blair made me see the error of my ways." She grimaced as another wave of pain shot through her. "I never thought anything could hurt so much. My ribs hurt when I breathe."

"Cat, listen closely. If I'm going to bind your ribs, I need to take your nightdress off. Do you have underclothes you can put on?"

She inhaled. "Don't think I can do that, but there are some in the satchel." Despite all his gentlemanly ways, in a minute or two she'd be naked in front of him. She grimaced slightly.

After finding what she needed he came to her. "I promise I won't look."

If it wouldn't hurt so bad, she would have laughed. Instead, she tried to raise her hand to touch his face. "If you don't look, it might take forever and create more pain."

"Then..."

For the first time since she'd met him, Roc seemed to be at a loss for words. "I will close my eyes. That way I won't know you're looking at me." She felt a deep compassion for this man she was losing her heart to. Maybe Ida was right, perhaps he did love her but didn't understand that emotion.

He laughed. "You will close your eyes. Interesting. Are you sure?"

She nodded then grimaced in pain. "Just get it over with then we can put this moment behind us. I can sit or lie somewhere and not move."

"Always stoic. Unfortunately..."

It seemed he didn't want to finish the sentence, and she didn't want to hear the truth. "I'm ready."

"I'm going to unbutton the dress and slip it down your arms."

She didn't want to speak so she nodded her head, giving him the yes he needed. He undressed her quickly but getting her underclothes on was more difficult. The act seemed to take an eternity. Sweat beaded on her forehead while searing pain swept through her. She gritted her teeth, wishing it all away and all the while she couldn't stop remembering that he was indeed looking at her.

"Half my work is done. I'm going to wrap these cloths around you. Hopefully you can sit here and nothing will hurt, but I can't make any promises. I'll try not to touch you."

Slowly and with seemingly exquisite care, she felt the binding as he wrapped them around her ribs. When his knuckles grazed her, he apologized. Finally, he finished then settled her nightdress over her head.

"Can you put your arms into the sleeve?"

"Yes, but not without pain." Bravely she did what he asked.

He sat back on his haunches, smiling. "You've been very brave. Now are you ready to go with me or do you want me to take you back to your home?"

She laughed then immediately regretted it. "Your ship. I'm going to London with you if the offer still stands."

"Winston."

"Yes, sir." Winston stood in front of him, a slight smile on his usually stoic face.

"We're ready. Would you grab her satchel and fiddle case while I find a blanket to cover her? Don't want any more gossip surrounding us than there already is. Make sure Beast follows us and gets into the carriage."

"Sir, didn't think you cared about gossip, sir."

"Where I'm concerned I don't, but this involves Cat." He cleared his throat, "Caitlin and she does care and I'm sure her da does too."

"You're talking about me as if I'm not here." She tried to talk without moving any part of her but her mouth.

"Was anything I said wrong?" he asked, pulling her into his arms and grimacing at her cry of pain.

"No," she said.

"Everything is going to hurt for a while. I'm sorry. If I could have taken these blows for you, I would have."

"You would willingly bear the pain?" She had not thought anyone

65

would willingly accept this kind of agony.

"I had my ribs broken once a few years back. I'm sorry. I know this hurts but there is no other way." Carefully, he picked her up and striding to the carriage he set her inside.

"I'm really going to London," she murmured, closing her eyes but when the carriage started moving, all of her hurt again.

"Would you like me to hold you?" he asked. "My arms around you might help brace the jolting of the vehicle when it hits the potholes and rocks."

"I'm willing to try anything."

He smiled at her then picking her up, he set her beside him and wrapped an arm around her. His chest against her side did help the constant bumping.

She closed her eyes, holding as still as she could. Beast lay at her feet, his nose resting on them.

Before she realized, the carriage rolled up the gangplank and she found herself settled into his cabin and on his bed. The room was bigger than she would have expected, the bed large, seemingly made expressly for Roc.

"You need to rest." He rummaged through a trunk in the corner of the room and pulling out a pair of socks, he turned to her, a devilish grin on his face.

"What are you doing?"

"Your feet need to be warmed." He pulled her wet socks from her feet. When he touched her toes, "Bloody hell, Cat, they're like ice."

"I know. I can't seem to feel them."

"Where are you going to sleep?" she asked, looking around the room as he helped her under the covers.

"Not going to sleep anytime soon. For now, I'm going on deck while the ship heads out to sea."

~ * ~

Blair sat back in a comfortable chair in his library, thinking of Caitlin lying in the middle of the floor unable to move. The memory made him smile. He would see her tomorrow and she'd probably still be on the floor. She now understood what he would do when she told him no.

He left her curled up in agony. The brandy bottle at his lips, he took a long swig, laughter following.

The time would pass quickly. He set the bottle on the table not wanting to drink so much he fell asleep and lost the chance to visit with his soon to be wife.

"Would you like anything else?" his housekeeper asked.

He didn't recall her stepping into the room. She was such a mousy little person, always trying to hide from him.

"Just you." He couldn't think of a better way to spend the next few hours. Unlike Caitlin, she was always willing. Caitlin would learn how to please him in bed. The task might take him longer than he was used to, but she'd learn. "Come here." He patted his lap, feeling a full arousal sweeping inside.

"It's late, sir. I'd like to retire for the night." Instead of moving forward, she backed up a step.

"You have the look of a cornered rabbit." He patted his legs again, forgetting about his plans with Caitlin. "You need to obey me. As you well know, your job revolves around how much you please me."

"You were gone so long. I just thought..."

"Well, you thought wrong. Now, stop wasting my time." He watched her inhale a deep breath, her frail body seeming to shake.

She did his bidding. "I wouldn't want to do that."

He loved the dress he made her wear. It was so low cut he could see the tiny circle surrounding her nipples. One tug always brought it to her waist.

"I hate to disappoint, but if all goes well tomorrow, you'll have to share my time with another lady. Of course you wouldn't want to waste any time you might have with me."

"Share you?"

"You won't mind too terribly."

She was licking her lips, her hands on his shoulders. "No, I won't mind."

He was bending her over for better access to her breasts. Not wanting to bother with niceties, he tugged on the bodice. Her ample breasts burst free. His lips found the tips, sucking and biting until he heard her whimper.

"Do it the way I taught you," he said, turning his attention her other breast and sliding his hand beneath her dress.

"Yes, sir," she cried out.

He regarded her, "You can do better. Take my pants off."

Chapter Four

Roc leaned on the railing of the ship, watching as Portrush disappeared from view. He hated what happened to her but was fiercely pleased she was with him now. She would be under his protection and he wouldn't let anything happen to her. In time if all went as planned, she would be his and he wouldn't ever let her go.

"She all settled in?" Winston appeared by his side. "What happened, if you don't mind telling me? Even though I don't really know her, I've grown very fond of the lass."

"O'Connell happened and I wasn't there to help." Roc hit his fist against the wood railing. "I should have insisted she come with me."

"If you don't mind me saying so, you can't be everywhere. She chose not to follow you to London, and it's not in your nature to insist or force someone," Winston reminded him.

"I should have been more persuasive. As it is, Blair could have killed her, but I think he knows just when to stop." No threat to her existed now. All she had left was to heal.

"Rumor has it she isn't the first one to meet the brunt of his fist. She have a black eye?" Winston asked.

"Black eye, nearly broken nose and two broken ribs, some bruised as far as I can tell. I needed to get her bandaged up so I didn't look real close. If she'll let me, I'll take a better look when she wakes." He didn't want to ask her again, but examining her wounds was imperative.

Winston seemed to absorb all that Roc told him. Then, "What are you going to do if she won't let you?"

"I'll have to insist."

"And Blair?"

69

Winston's question rattled him. He understood the possibility of her refusal but he couldn't let that happen. "Not sure. In Ireland I'd have to walk softly. He's the power there and before I could call in any influence I have, I could be swinging from a tree. He doesn't have that power now."

"He'd have her then, sir. You don't want that," Winston said. "Good thing we're on the high seas headed for London. You think he'll be foolish enough to come after Caitlin?"

"Don't know for sure, but if he comes to London and I think he will, I'll have him. There won't be any recourse for him, nowhere for him to run." Roc had not seen the small purse he gave Cat when he pulled out her underclothes. And he'd seen her put the money in a tiny pocket in the satchel. He was sure Blair found it and the letter and address inside would send the man to The Duchess. He would be waiting.

"You'd set a trap then?" Winston asked, a smile on his face, the scar near his right eye turning white. "I'd be happy to be part of that ploy. No one should lay a hand on a woman."

The loud barking and whining coming from inside his cabin caught his attention. The dog had to be scratching on the door and Cat wouldn't be able to get up to let him out. "Guess Beast needs a walk on the deck. Going to have to teach him how to use the latrine." Roc had to laugh at that idea and was relieved with the change of subject. In a few strides, he let the animal out and directed him to the latrine. It seemed Beast caught on, at least this time and did his duty in the right place.

"Heck of a name for an animal, Beast," Winston said, scratching his jaw as if a bit puzzled. "While it's obvious why that dog has the name, couldn't you think of something better to call him?"

Roc remembered the look on her face when he gave her the dog. "She didn't really want the dog at first. And we kept calling him the little beast when he did something wrong, like trying to chew up one of her wool socks. Guess the name stuck. He answers to it now, seems like the moniker was meant for him."

Beast ran around the ship, seeming to make friends with the crew who tossed various items for him to retrieve. At first, he didn't want to bring the stuff back, but when he realized they would be tossed for him again, he delivered the objects quickly, wagging his tail and waiting for the game to continue.

He watched Beast for a few more seconds then, "I'm going to check on Cat. She's going to need help sitting up and if she's awake, she might be hungry." Whistling, he visited the ships galley, finding hot water and willow bark to make into a healing tea. Finding a sack, he heaped it with bread and cheese, some slices of bacon as well as a few other choice articles.

Winston walked with him, undoing the latch so he could push the door open. "Much obliged," Roc said.

"Anytime. If you need anything, just poke your head out the door and holler. I'll stay close by."

Roc nodded, entering the cabin to see Cat leaning against the backboard. "I see you were able to sit. Are you feeling better?" He could tell by her strained features she was still in a lot of pain.

"Wish I could say yes. They hurt every time I move even a hair." She tried to smile but it didn't really work. "Where's Beast?"

"Outside playing with the crew." He set the bag on the table and began to remove the items.

The first thing he did was prepare the tea and take it to her. "This is a little bitter but it will help with the pain. I added honey to make the brew more palatable."

She drank a small sip before frowning at him. "You sure this will help?"

"Promise. Drink it all and I'll give you something that tastes better." He watched as she drank the contents then set the cup on her lap.

He took the mug from her hands then filled it a quarter full with brandy. "You think to get me drunk?"

"The alcohol will dull the pain along with the willow bark. I'm only thinking of you. A quarter of the cup won't get you drunk."

"No, it won't but if it puts me to sleep for a few more hours and out of my misery, I'd be happy." She sighed then, closing her eyes, the cup resting on her lap.

His heart went out to her. He would do anything in his power to put her out of her misery, ease her pain but he was afraid he'd have to embarrass her again. Checking her wounds would cause more pain. "I need to check the bindings, and your wounds."

"Why." Her eyes wide, she looked frightened and apprehensive.

"I didn't check out your injuries this morning. We needed to get to the ship and I needed to ease some of the pain. If you have any broken ribs, and I suspect you have two, we need to take care they don't puncture your lung."

"I understand." She was staring at the cup in her lap while pursing her lips together. When she looked up, "Before you do that can I have at least two more of these? I don't think I'll care if you see me naked again, that is, if I'm half drunk on brandy."

He couldn't help himself. He roared with laughter. "Maybe you could close your eyes and you won't know I'm looking at you." He reminded her of her previous words.

When she looked up, she appeared a tad bit sheepish, "Did I really say that?" she asked. "I let you see all of me." A blush spread up her neck to her face. "And didn't even protest. Seems I don't remember much about what happened this morning."

"Wish I could say I didn't look, but truly I tried not to. And yes, you said those very words. Now I could examine you or I could get the ship's physician." He knew what she would say and it wasn't much of a choice by her standards, but it was all he could give her.

"The physician wouldn't happen to be female?" she asked, seeming to know the answer.

Surprised, he didn't expect that question. "I'm sure you can guess that he isn't. Finish that and I'll pour you some more. Then no more excuses. You can't put it off forever."

Pouring himself a glass, he sat at his desk, waiting for her. When she finished, he did as promised and refilled the cup this time half way.

"I see you brought food. Are you going offer some to me or keep it all to yourself?" she asked again seeming to put off the inevitable. She held up one hand, grimacing at the pain, "I know I'm just trying to take up time."

"Can't put it off forever."

"I understand. Really, I do, but..." she said.

"As to eating, didn't know if your stomach would let you put food in it," he said as he placed bread, cheese and bacon on a cloth. "Here," he said, deciding to give in to her ploys. It would only give her a few minutes reprieve.

She looked at it for a moment before breaking off a small chunk of bread then pairing it with a bite of cheese. "You were right. Could be the brandy..."

"But it's probably the pain, which has a way of doing that to a person. Nature's way of healing the body. You'll be able to keep the food down when you're feeling better."

"The room seems to be spinning a little." She let her head fall back and closed her eyes.

"Good, the brandy's working. Are you ready?"

She opened her eyes, "For what?" Before he could reply, "Oh...I remember now."

"I'm going to do this as quickly as possible and with as little pain to you as is necessary." He unbuttoned the nightdress, trying to understand the level of embarrassment she was encountering. He slipped it off her shoulders, attempting to look only at the strips of cloth he was unwinding from around her slender torso.

"You're looking at me," she whispered, staring downward at herself and his hands as he touched her ribs. Then she cried out.

"Sorry, bad news, I was right, two are broken and you're bruised in more places than I noticed last night." *The bastard.* He wanted Blair to feel pain such as this, needed him to suffer.

As quickly as he could he bound her ribs again and dressed her. "As to looking at you..." he sat back on the bed, "I tried not, really I did," He inhaled a swift breath of air. "But you're so beautiful."

Surprised when she gifted him with what he could only describe as a cheeky smile, "Then I should get to see you naked too. That's only fair don't you think?"

If she meant to tease him, she was doing it the wrong way. He didn't have a single issue with disrobing in front of her. Well, one; it would probably embarrass her more than him.

"If that's what you want." He stood, his hands on the fastening of his pants, grinning at her.

"That's alright. I meant your shirt anyway. I could look at your chest. That would be fair." She retracted her earlier statement.

"It doesn't look anything like yours." He lifted his shirt over his head then stepped in front of her.

Her eyes grew wide and she moistened her lips. "You are beautiful. I could look at you all day."

"Men aren't beautiful." He quickly put his shirt back on, intense feelings surfacing, sensations he couldn't act on. "Now do you need to sleep or would you like to talk?"

"I would...I have to..." She looked damned uncomfortable.

"You need to relieve yourself?" he asked, trying not to embarrass her further than he already had.

She nodded, seemingly unable to say the words.

"You need help?"

"No! yes," she said, "Just to get there, wherever that is. I'm not sure I can walk that far."

A day of embarrassment for her and this was no better, but he knew all this would happen today. He'd been an invalid himself, recovering once from a gunshot to his leg and another time broken ribs.

"Come." He picked her up in his arms, grimacing at the tiny cry of pain and strode to the door in the back of the cabin. He set her down before opening the door.

She looked at him as if she wanted him to vanish, "Close the door behind you. I'm not going anywhere. When you're finished, I'll take you back to the bed." He tried to smooth the way and hoped the rest of the afternoon would be different for her.

She was nodding her head yes so many times he was sure she might get dizzy, but he stepped back and she closed the door.

Emerging a few minutes later, "I'm done. Let me try to walk back to the bed. The brandy and willow bark have helped the pain, but I think the brandy has made me a wee bit wobbly." She graced him with an angelic smile.

"Would you like to lean on me?" The formality of his words surprised him. He was doing everything in his power to keep her from turning that brilliant shade of red again.

"That would be nice."

74

"Smart woman." He held her close and let her set the pace. It seemed to take an eternity, but in time they made it to the bed. Over the next few days she would progressively get better and need his help less and less.

"I don't know if I can get my legs up." She told him. "I hate being so needy."

He helped, "There, now have you had enough excitement for this morning or would you like me to stay here with you?"

She stifled a yawn with the back of her hand. "Would it be too much to ask if you stayed here until I fell asleep?"

"I'll do whatever you ask." He sat down beside her, taking her hand in his then slowly bringing it to his lips, he kissed the back, garnering a smile from her.

"Always the romantic," she sighed, closing her eyes for a second.

"I've never been called that before." It seemed he took what was offered from women. He never forced or hurt any lady. They flocked to him and he always understood it was for the money and the title. There had never been a woman who he felt was with him because she cared, until Cat.

"What have you been called?" She seemed curious to know a little more about him.

"Nothing I could say in front of a lady," he told herm, laughing.

"That bad?"

"And you, do you have any nicknames? Besides Cat." He relished holding her hand, no sexual ploy, nothing but the warmth and camaraderie between them.

"You're the only person who has ever called me that." Her expression turned whimsical then changed to a blank look. "I don't like to think of some of the other names I've been called. Maybe we should change the subject."

For some reason he couldn't name he wanted to pursue the question. "If you say the names, some of the pain will go away." He didn't know why he said that, but in his life, he'd found talking about things always helped.

"Really, you can promise something like that?" She looked at him with solemn eyes with a hint of anguish. Then she seemed to change, tilting her head and blinking slowly.

He didn't believe she knew how he would perceive her actions. "Tell me one name and I'll tell you something about myself you don't know."

"Something that embarrassed you?" she asked.

He rubbed the back of his neck taking a moment to think. "Don't think anything has ever embarrassed me. No wait, I've got it. I'll go first.

"On second thought..."

"You have to tell me," she persisted.

"Even if it embarrasses you? Because it won't embarrass me now."

"Let me think." She closed her eyes for only about two seconds. "Don't care. Tell me. I've already sat through the worst embarrassment of my life. This couldn't be worse."

"Remember, you asked," he said. "Thinking back over the years, I was about fifteen."

"So old." She grinned at him, laughing then grimaced from the pain shooting from her bruises.

"Don't interrupt, or I'll never finish the story." He sat beside her on the bed. Holding her hand and relishing this moment with her, he brought her hand to his lips, kissing the back.

"What if I have questions?"

"I'm sure you will. Don't' interrupt." He repeated with a grin. "To continue, I knew this girl whose family worked for my father. Don't recall what exactly he did. She was a few years older than me." He smiled, remembering her fondly. "She was my first, well, except the woman..."

"Your first what?" she interrupted. "I really can't follow the story unless you fill in the details. I can't read your mind."

"Except for the woman my father brought me to for my lessons, she was the first woman I had sex with." He knew a question would be forthcoming. He watched her as she seemed to think over what he said.

"Lessons, women aren't usually hired as tutors, are they? What did she teach you?" she asked turning toward him.

"You sure you want to know?" He waited patiently for an answer, unable to keep the grin from his face. Her inquisitiveness intrigued him to no end.

She looked ready to hit him, "You've gone this far and now you have me curious. Of course I want you to finish your story."

"My father hired a trusted woman to teach me how to make love and give a woman pleasure." He spoke softly, his voice changing as he said the words unable to keep thoughts of making love to his *petite chatte* from entering his mind. The feat was impossible, his mind recalling the beauty of her curves and his very real need to have a complete relationship with her.

"You had lessons in love making?" She sounded awed or confused perhaps a little of both. "I've never heard of such a thing."

"It's common among the people I know. But that really isn't my story. That wasn't embarrassing at all. It was quite arousing, satisfying."

"I have no idea what you're talking about," she said, indignant. "You talk in riddles that I can't quite comprehend."

"And you won't until you let me have my wicked way with you." He leaned over her and lightly kissed her on the tip of her nose. "Now let me finish and you can tell me what people have called you."

"That most likely isn't going to happen. You're finishing," she said, trying to change positions but finding the sharp pain when she moved nearly unbearable.

"Finishing my story or having my wicked way?" he asked, thoroughly enjoying these moments with her.

"Both."

"I refuse to believe that. I can be very persuasive when I crave something and I do hunger for you."

She cleared her throat, seeming to be reluctant to address his last comment. "Back to your embarrassing moment and I'm not going to answer your question. I'll keep my mouth shut."

"If you insist." He waited for a response and waited some more, wondering if she'd fallen asleep. "You awake?"

"I told you I wasn't going to say anything. You can finish your story," she told him primly.

He couldn't stop the rumble of laughter. "All right, I'll finish. Where was I?"

"After all that, how could I remember. It seems you don't really want to tell me," but she paused, "You were fifteen and the woman was older."

"Yes, that's true. I think she seduced me though. Anyway, we enjoyed each other's company and one thing led to another."

"Well, that's a good story."

He slanted her what he hoped was I knew you couldn't keep your mouth shut grin then went on, "I was making love to her. We were in this really secluded corner of our estate, when I heard, 'My god it's Richard.'"

"Richard? Sorry, who's Richard?"

"Me." He was laughing now and he couldn't stop. She was so beautifully innocent and naïve. He shouldn't have to explain any of this to her and that was one thing that made her so special. Cat was untouched by the jaded part of society. And her innocence was a shining spot in her character.

"I thought your name was Roc." She crossed her arms over her chest and immediately cried out, whimpering for a moment until the pain subsided.

"My friends call me Roc and my mother calls me Richard. Sometimes now that father passed, she calls me William. Roc stands for all three of my names. Richard Oakes Crandall."

"My head hurts, but I still want to know what embarrassed you. Nothing you've told me so far could possibly be embarrassing for anyone. You need to finish quickly because my eyelids are starting to droop."

"The young lady I was with was amazing. She could do things... Well, mother and father caught me buck-naked making love with this girl. We thought it was a private spot. Turns out Mother and Father used it for the same thing. When you're fifteen, your mother shouldn't see you in the most intimate of acts."

"I'm sure she was just as embarrassed. Should anyone see you in an intimate act?"

"No, and I don't know if she was embarrassed. Father got her out of there so fast it could make your head spin. Because of what he saw, I got my first lectures on not having sex with the hired help, how to keep from getting a girl with child and the pox."

"You just made me dizzy with more questions."

"Sorry, sir, but he wanted inside." Winston cracked the door but Beast pushed through, bounding inside and onto the bed.

Roc blocked the puppy from hitting Cat then grabbed him and held him tight, petting his head. "Now you wouldn't want to hurt your mistress, would you?"

Beast licked his face and let his head fall against her shoulder.

~ * ~

Roc and Cat stood at the railing as the ship docked in London. She admired the way Roc looked all decked out in fancy clothes she'd never seen him wear. It sent the point home to her, that there could never be anything between them. They were far too different as were the lives they were accustomed to living.

"Where are we going? I have the right to know." She wondered if he would take her to his mother's home. She wouldn't stay at his place, couldn't. Throughout the trip, he avoided her questions about where she would stay. Time and again, she asked for help in finding a small cottage she could afford and a job playing her fiddle.

He deflected every question with a query of his own, seeming to put off answering. Even now when there was no more time left, he seemed reluctant to give her a definitive answer.

"It's a surprise," he told her, squeezing her arm as if he meant to reassure. "Just be patient. You will find out very soon."

The action didn't give her any assurances that he didn't still intend to treat her like his mistress. "I don't like surprises," she told him, inhaling a long deep breath, keeping her gaze focused on the scene in front of her.

"Not even at Christmas?" With the gangplank lowered, he led her to the waiting carriage, helping her inside.

"Not since I was a little girl." she told him. When she compared her clothing to his, she was lacking. In Portrush there had never been a time when she thought less of herself. Now she was self-conscious, her dress very nearly threadbare and most likely out of fashion. Until this moment she'd never really thought about fashion. If she stayed with him, she would be an embarrassment to him.

"I plan to change that for you. I promise someday you'll come to love surprises." He seemed to watch her, his dark brown eyes impossible to read. "You will wait in anticipation every time I come to visit."

She wanted to blurt out, *I won't be your mistress*, but she hoped he understood without her having to say so. "Surprises scare me. They usually bring bad luck or just bad things. In my life, good surprises don't exist. I don't remember one surprise that was good."

At her words, his brows drew together, his eyes darkening. He sat back against the plush cushions in his elegant carriage, his hands folded in his lap. When she first saw this vehicle that seemed to have been created just for him, she'd been so impressed. Now she more clearly understood the extravagance that was his life style and the fact she didn't belong in it.

"There are going to be no more bad things in your life." His tone was matter of fact as well as convincing. "I'm going to see to that, and every surprise you have will be a good one."

"You can't make a promise like that. I've got to find a place to live and a job so I can pay my bills. Right now, I've no idea how to go about that if you won't help me." Once again, she watched his brows furrow together and his lips thin. He appeared angry to her and she didn't understand the reasons. He'd told her when they were in Portrush he didn't like her working. Since then she didn't broach the subject.

He leaned forward, taking her hands in his, "I don't want you to work and I think you know that. I'm going to provide for you."

There it was. If she didn't work, she wouldn't have a roof over her head or food to eat and even clothes to wear. At the moment all she possessed were two dresses and a few underthings. The surprise waiting for her wasn't going to be good. She didn't mean to owe him anything and she would never pay him with her body. She thought he understood.

Withdrawing her hands from his, "Work is not a choice nor is your seeming need to provide for me. I'm sure there are plenty of pubs in London that need a fiddler. You can't dictate to me what I can and can't do."

His expression turned to a scowl. "None of those taverns are safe for a woman. I don't want you hurt ever again. You must know I'll take care of you."

There it was again, the mistress insinuation. "I'm not afraid of hard work. If pubs aren't safe, I can keep house for any of the fine gentry in the city, but I'd rather play my fiddle."

"Maybe that can be arranged," he told her, his voice soft, drawing her into something she wasn't sure she could get out of.

The sound of his voice mesmerized and enchanted, made her think of the few kisses they shared. "Work in a pub or cleaning house?" she asked, anxious about his possible answer and what he was really thinking.

"Neither, playing the fiddle for me. I'd be happy to pay you enough for rent and food."

"That doesn't make sense. You just want me to play my fiddle, nothing more. People would still talk." She inhaled a deep breath, vowing she would stay strong because it was obvious he meant to do everything in his power to sway her to his wishes.

"Of course it makes sense. It's perfectly logical from my point of view. I don't want to share you with London. We're here."

She looked out the window at a row of townhouses all three stories tall and opulent. "Is this where The Duchess lives?" A fine trembling took over her body, understanding this probably was not his mother's home.

"Why would you think that?" He helped her down from the carriage, seemingly nonchalant, keeping her close.

She stiffened in his arms and pushed away when he thought to hold her a second too long. "You told me the address in my purse was that of your mother's. I assumed you might bring me there. Am I wrong?"

He didn't answer but took her hand in his, leading her to the porch before pulling a key from his pocket and unlocking the door. "This is not my mother's home. It isn't mine either."

"Then whose?" She really didn't believe he'd take her to his home. Now, her worst fears about his intentions were coming home to settle in her head.

They stepped inside. The rooms she could see were furnished, but the home seemed to echo with silence. She looked at him, her heart in her throat, afraid to ask again because she didn't know what to say.

"It's yours." He let go her hand and stepping back he smiled, seemingly pleased with himself. "I hope you like it. I had my solicitor purchase it when we were still in Portrush and it's in your name. No one can take it away from you, ever." He stopped for a moment then looked closely at her. "Well, do you like it?"

"No." Her Irish temper escalated. She was tongue tied even when his actions really didn't surprise her.

"You don't like it?" He acted astounded, wounded, even while she'd made it perfectly clear to the pig headed man she would not let him buy her favors.

"Of course, it's beautiful but I don't want it. You had no right to purchase this for me when I told you in no uncertain terms I would never owe you. I won't accept your lavish generosity that will give you permission to seduce me. There is no way for me to pay you for this." So angry she was shaking, she wanted to throw something at him.

"Stay here tonight and think on it. Maybe you'll change your mind by morning. Come, let me show you around the house." Without looking over his shoulder to see if she followed, he started for the kitchen.

"That's just it, Roc. I'm going to feel the same way in the morning that I feel now and I felt yesterday as I did last week. I've no intention of following in my mother's footsteps." She talked to his back as she trailed along behind. Stubborn, obstinate, inflexible man.

"This is the kitchen and the woman at the stove is Cook. She's amazing and her food is delicious. You'll enjoy everything she makes for you and us sometimes." He backed up a little then walked through the parlor, pointing out different things to her. "If you'd rather have different pieces of furniture, you're welcome to acquire anything you like."

"Roc." She hurried to catch up with him. "I can't accept any of this." She could think of no way to convince the stubborn man. "You're not listening to me."

"I'll pay attention when you say something I want to hear." He started up the steps. Her inquisitive nature kept her going. She followed, confused and upset but also wanting to see what was upstairs. Her heart told her she could stay here and he wouldn't demand anything, but her head spoke differently. She would always feel as if she owed him something and all she had to give was her body.

"You're acting crazy," she told him, unable to keep her mind riveted to her convictions while she admired the stylishness and beauty of the home.

He opened a door. "This is your bedroom."

She stopped, her mouth dropping when she absorbed the elegance. This home was nothing like she'd ever seen before. Then common sense found her brain while reality set it. "Roc, no."

"Adara," he called out, ignoring her adamant no.

A young woman, about her age stepped through an adjoining door. "Yes, sir. What can I do for you?"

"This is Adara. Caitlin, this is your lady's maid. She's here for you in any capacity you choose."

Her heart sunk and she found herself backing up, shaking her head over and over before she ran from the room, thoroughly humiliated, frustrated and completely annoyed. Tears ran down her cheeks and she would have fled through the front door but she had nowhere to go. Letting her pride get in the way of the practical at least for the night was not her way. She could weather any storm. She would stay here only until she could find a small home she could afford.

She closed her eyes, hoping when she opened them this was a dream and not a nightmare. But what had she expected?

He continued as if he didn't realize her heart was breaking, as if he'd never cared about her feelings. "I've bought you a few things, but I've given you credit at the dressmakers. Adara has arranged everything in the armoire and she will help you dress and undress."

"What? And you're not going to help me undress?" she asked bitterly sarcastic, praying this would all vanish and she'd find herself at home in Portrush with no problems.

His eyes darkened and his features seemed to shut out her questions. "Only if you want me to undress you." His voice was hard and nothing like the man she thought she knew.

"I'd like you to go now," she said, her voice shaking just as hard as her body. Anger engulfed her. Drowning in a sea of misunderstandings she ran from the room then down the stairs. The front door stopped her mad dash from the man she loved, the man who wanted her for his mistress and nothing more. If she were honest with herself, she wanted him probably more than he wanted her.

Roc passed her in the foyer. And as if there were no misunderstandings between them went on to say, "I'll be back later this evening to see if you have everything you need. I'd stay but I've unfinished business to attend to. Winston will remain here to help out with anything you might need. He is willing to run any errands for you."

He waited as if he expected a polite goodbye or possibly a kiss but that wasn't going to happen. Her hands clasped tightly in front of her, she needed to see him walk down the front steps while she put her new plans into action.

Even if she couldn't pay him what all this was worth, she would make payments as she could and keep track of them as well. The first order of business was to fire the two employees she couldn't afford.

Stepping into the kitchen, she cleared her throat, "Cook."

"Yes." The woman looked up.

Good lord whatever she was fixing smelled heavenly. Her mouth watered. Second thoughts assailed her. She'd never done anything like this before. "Cook, I'm sorry but I can't pay you. I don't have the funds. You can't keep this job."

"No worries, Miss Caitlin. My wages are paid for by the duke." She continued to stir whatever it was on the stove.

"That's just the thing. I have to pay him back. I'm not going to be beholden to him. And I can't afford you. You have to go."

"Miss Caitlin, I respect your wishes and I think I understand where you're coming from, but I'll stay as long as the duke wants to pay me. I've three little children to feed and I need the work."

Alright then, "Wouldn't want to take food from the mouths of babes." Her heavy sigh seemed to echo in the room.

"If it's any consolation, I've known the duke for years and years. He's never done anything like this before. He loves you, just hasn't figured it out yet. You keep your back straight and keep telling him how you feel. Eventually, he'll hear the words."

"If that were only true. I suppose he has the same hold over Adara." His power was all encompassing and there was nothing she could do to defeat him or overpower him, or even win this battle she was trying to fight, but she could stay true to herself. She would find a job.

"He does. Adara has an ailing father and mother. She pays the medical bills through her salary. If she lost this job, they would both assuredly die."

"What is there to do then?" she asked sitting on a chair in the kitchen while Cook set a cup of tea in front of her.

"Fight him in a different way." Cook sat down next to her and was unexpectedly joined by Winston who graciously accepted tea then poured a jigger of whiskey into the hot liquid.

"If it's any consolation, I've never seen Roc act this way either." Winston gingerly sipped the steaming tea.

"It's not," then, "I assume you know London well." She wasn't sure if it was a question or a statement.

"I do. What are you thinking? Nothing that's going to make Roc mad and wild with jealousy?" He roared with laughter.

"Mad, yes, but I doubt if he would be jealous."

"You don't understand your hold over him then. What is it you're thinking?" Winston seemed intrigued.

"I want a job. The only thing I do well is play my fiddle. Perhaps you can help me with that."

"And?" Winston asked, seeming to anticipate her next question. "He'll be angry with me."

"Probably," she said. "Are you willing to risk the duke's wrath?"

"I've disagreed with him before and he's still my friend and employer. I happen to think what you're doing is brave and the right thing to do. You realize he's never in his life been denied something or someone he wants. My dear, you have captivated his heart."

"I appreciate that. You know the taverns and pubs here in London. Take me to one you think would be safe. Perhaps you can even help me get an audition." She held her breath while she waited.

"Roc will be furious."

"Do you care?" she asked even though he pretty much told her he didn't just a minute ago.

"I do, lass, but I care about your feelings as well. I know just the place and the proprietor is a friend. With my help, I'm pretty sure he'll hire you. You are fabulous after all."

She stood, bumping the table, tea sloshing from the cups. "Thank you." She gave him a huge hug. "Can we go now?"

"It's a bit early in the day but perfect for the owner to check out your talents, your fiddling talents," he amended. "Before we go, you might want to go upstairs and sort through those gowns he purchased for you. While this one worked in Portrush, it's not going to be what you want here. Get Adara to help you. Something simple would do you well."

"At this point, I'm not sure Roc knows simple, but I'll do as you say and Adara might have a good eye for what dress if any is appropriate."

With Adara's help, she was decked out in the simplest gown they could find, her hair pinned neatly on the top of her head and a bit of makeup on her face. "I'm ready. How do I look?" Holding her breath, she stood in front of Winston, hoping his answer would build some confidence.

"Like a lady who means business," he told her. "Roc left a carriage for your use if you were to need it. And," he paused, "we will put it to good use." Gallantly, he offered his arm and they proceeded with their mission.

The pub was quiet and clean when they entered. The bartender and Winston hugged then slapped backs in greeting. She stood behind Winston, waiting for her future to be determined. This was her one and only chance. She had to make the best of it.

"Miss O'Shea is amazing. Not only is she a brilliant fiddler but she dances while she plays. Your customers will love her," Winston spoke her praise while she held her breath.

"Don't have the funds to employ a fiddler." The man said, seemingly disinterested.

"Give Cat a chance. Just listen and watch. I promise it will be worth your time and she will bring in more than you pay her."

The man shrugged his shoulders before rubbing his neck as if stress encompassed him. "As long as I can work and watch at the same time."

"Of course," Winston nodded to her.

Her fiddle raised she played a lively jig, dancing around the room while the notes flew into the air, the few patrons in the tavern mesmerized.

For several minutes she continued, dancing from one customer to another, drawing them into the magical web she wove with her tunes.

Men seeming to hear the music from outside swept into the tavern, ordering drinks while she played. She changed from the lively tune to one more haunting. More people entered.

She played longer and the tavern filled with patrons. Finally, Caitlin stopped, breathing hard yet feeling the exhilaration of performing. The clapping filled the room and cheers of *more* reverberated in the small chamber.

Winston stepped forward, arms crossed in front of his chest. His expression seeming to demand the man hire her. "What do you think? Her playing has doubled your customers in less than ten minutes. The fiddle and her dancing will fill your coffers to overflowing."

The man paused a few minutes. "It seems her talent is very good for business. Let me write up a contract for her and we'll be set."

"My approval of said contract is necessary," Winston warned while Cat drank from the pint Winston handed her then began to play again.

The exhilaration gave her confidence and she relished the clapping and approval from those who observed.

Winston tapped her on the shoulder. "Do you have any terms? He's writing up your contract as we speak."

"I want a meal when I'm done and whatever wages you think are appropriate. Perhaps a box of something to take home for the next morning." She drew her bow across her fiddle and all the talking seemed to cease. She smiled as she twirled then began an Irish jig.

"The minutes ticked by before Winston stopped her again. "He needs your signature on the contract."

Blood drained from her face, seeming to pool in her feet. "Winston, I can't read or write."

"No worries, lass. I've read the contract and approve of it. You are committed for a week, no more but have the option of continuing week by week. If that's to your liking?"

She nodded saying, "Yes," at the same time.

"Then all you need do is put an X on the line. I will write your name after it so there is no doubt about who he is to pay."

"Da taught me how to sign my name." she said, realizing she had a job and could pay Roc back one tiny coin at a time. She didn't have to give him her body in payment for lodgings. "Thank you, Winston. He's going to be angry with you. I'm genuinely sorry for that but ever so thankful you helped me out."

"Nothing I can't handle, child. I'm enjoying helping you. Now, go sign your name then you've a job to finish. I'll stay here and take you home when you're through tonight. By the way, I told him your favorite dinner is a Shepard's pie and a pint of Guinness if he has it."

~ * ~

Winston knew the fury of his boss and needed to avoid it at all cost. When Caitlin went back to work, he quickly penned a letter to Roc telling him where they were and what she was doing.

Roc,

You instructed me to do whatever I needed to keep your beautiful Caitlin happy, not an easy task after the way you left her this afternoon. If I might be so bold, she was distraught and beside herself with worry.

She wants a job. Doesn't want to owe you anything. Know you won't take my advice but you need to give Caitlin a little space. She's been yanked away from the only life she's ever known and now you expect her to understand the glittering life of money and power you've known all your life.

I digress. Caitlin does have a job now and she's drawing the crowds. People are pouring into the Boar's Head Pub to watch her. If you were thinking straight, you would be proud of her and respect her wishes.

I'll stay here with her and see her home at ten o'clock. But I've a feeling you'll be doing that job. Expect to see you as soon as your urgent business is taken care of. Give my regards to Drake Montgomerie since I'm sure that's who you're off to see in such a rush.

Winston

He folded the paper and sealed it. Seeking out a possible messenger, he found the tavern owner's son and gave him a coin to deliver the missive as quickly as possible. Winston gave him a couple more coins to hire a cab to take him to the address written on the outside of the letter.

He ordered a pint and a plate of fish and chips then sat back to watch the show. Caitlin's dancing was fairy-like and her fiddling was beyond anything Winston had ever heard before. She entertained and enthralled the patrons for another fifteen minutes before taking a break.

When she sat down at the table with Winston, she was grinning and so unpretentious. He thought she was the most beautiful woman he'd ever seen. "Are you happy, lass?" he asked, understanding the smile on her face told the whole story. "Would you like something to drink?"

"My throat is so dry, one would think I was singing too," she laughed, "I would, yes, please."

Winston raised a hand, signaling for a waitress and asked for a pint for Caitlin.

"I never thought I would miss this so much. Playing and dancing is my heart and soul. Without it I feel as if I'm half a person."

"Good, good, it's nice to see you enjoying yourself and earning a living all at the same time." He didn't have high hopes she'd be doing this for very long. When Roc found out what she was up to, he'd be here in record speed to put an end to her employment.

"Which brings up another issue. How am I going to get here tomorrow and the next day? I don't have any illusions where Roc is concerned."

"I'll do my best to help you convince Roc that you need this as much as you need to breathe."

She laughed, sipping the Guinness that was set in front of her. "The tavern owner told me he was going to raise my pay. Seems he's busier tonight than he's ever been. Maybe I can hire my own cab with the extra money."

"That's always a possibility." He needed to tell her before Roc strode inside and hauled her off. Bloody hell, he hoped the duke would have enough sense to wait until the end of the evening. "Got to tell you something, lass."

"What?" Smiling as if she trusted him with her life, she looked at him over the rim of her glass.

If he were twenty years younger...no, she'd still be Roc's. "I wrote a letter to Roc explaining your whereabouts and why. It's probably been delivered by now. Just thought you should know."

She made a noise in the back of her throat. "Thank you for telling me. Think I'd best get back to playing. Looks like the crowds are getting restless."

He stopped her, "I had to. He would have torn the town apart if he arrived at the townhouse and you weren't there."

"Adara might have told him. Cook left for home before we set out for the pub."

"I will try to waylay him before he does something he might come to regret."

"Hopefully before he embarrasses me."

Chapter Five

Roc stood in the doorway of the Montgomerie townhouse about to step outside, seconds away from leaving in his waiting carriage when the boy ran up the stairs. Roc's hand went to the pistol he carried.

"Duke of Ravenswood?" the boy asked. Breathless, he was inhaling large gulps of air. "Hurried as fast as I could."

"Yes," he replied, wondering what was happening. A sinking feeling settled in the pit of his stomach while he accepted the letter the boy handed over to him. Reaching into his purse he pulled out a coin and handed it to the boy who returned to the cab that had delivered the young man and the message.

The boy had to be sent by Winston. No one else knew where he was. Fumbling with the seal, he stopped breathing as he began to read. Roc...it began.

"Bloody hell," he murmured. This can't be true. Deep in his heart he understood Cat would do as she pleased and to keep her from getting into too much trouble, Winston would follow her. His man probably offered to help her. The Boar's Head tavern was respected. Caitlin would have never been able to find a reputable tavern so quickly.

Determinedly striding down the steps, he crumpled the paper into his fist, swearing with each footstep. "Boar's Head Tavern," he told the driver. "You can't get there fast enough," he said, the crumpled paper falling to the floor.

He was amazed when the driver drew to a stop ten minutes later. "Stay here. Don't know when I'll be back, but I want my carriage ready to go at a moment's notice."

If he had any sense at all he'd find Winston and wait for her to finish

91

the gig. But his emotions were turbulent and stormy, his logic reeling. What he really wanted was to find her, haul her over his shoulder and march out of the pub, but that would create too great a scandal. Cat didn't need more rumors circling in the ton to denigrate her.

He tried to school his features, meaning to listen to her reasons but he already knew them, had them memorized weeks ago. When he entered the pub, the room was brim full. He heard her fiddle immediately but couldn't see her. It took him a few minutes to find Winston and sit down.

"See you've been busy," he grit out losing the composure he'd fought for the last few minutes during the drive from Montgomerie's. "Did you even think to waylay her until I could get home to stop this nonsense.

"She was going to do it with or without me." Winston lifted his shoulders as if confirming he didn't have a choice. "You gave me explicit orders to keep her out of harm's way."

"If you didn't bring Cat here, it would have taken her a few days to find this place." Roc was boiling for a fight and this argument wasn't going to take the edge off. He needed to hit something. A good round of boxing might do the trick, but that wasn't going to be possible anytime soon.

"If she did find it." Winston brushed an imaginary piece of dust from his waistcoat. "And that's a huge if."

Roc didn't want to admit to Winston's good points. She could have ended up in a tavern on the waterfront. His gut churned again. He ordered a drink, still looking for Cat, impatient to find her. Then what...? He drew in a large breath before letting it slowly escape from his lungs.

Suddenly, she danced in front of him. Their gazes met, seeming to lock, her eyes wide with what he wasn't sure. He didn't want to believe the sight of him sent fear through her. His heart pounding in his chest, he fought the urge to abscond with his delicate lady.

"It's alright, sir. She only has an hour to go. You've got to let her have her dinner though before you take her home." The owner of the tavern stood in front of him. "She's good for business, you know."

"Dinner. She wheedled that out of the owner, did she?" Roc couldn't help the hint of a smile. "Just like at home, she's working for her dinner. Is she making any money?"

"A tidy sum," Winston said with a huge grin plastered on his smug face. "Owner upped her pay when the customers started pouring inside. She signed a contract for a week. So, keep in mind Caitlin's going to feel a certain obligation to return. Are you going to be able to deal with that?"

"She's not coming back here," Roc forced the words out, sweat beading on his forehead, control minimal at this point. "I already decided against my better judgment that I'd let her finish the evening, but she's not going to entertain men every night for a week."

"Well," Winston paused momentarily before taking a sip. "you're going to have a fight on your hands. This is what she wants to do and she's also determined to pay you what she thinks she owes you. She can't do that if you won't let her work. Unless you detain her forcibly, she now has the money to hire a cab."

"I want to give her everything. She doesn't need to work." He clenched and unclenched his fists when a man reached out and touched her butt. "I'm going to deck him." He stood, anger boiling over.

"You don't want to start a fight." Winston reached out to stop him. "And, Roc, best you learn right now your definition of everything she wants or needs is far different from Caitlin's. She doesn't want things. She just wants you, all of you."

"She's got that," he said unable to take his gaze from her, and it seemed she refused to look at him.

"Does she?" Winston asked, "Have all of you?"

"Of course she does." But Winston's question penetrated his darkest thoughts. She didn't know she had all of him. He tried to show her with his actions. If she'd let him, he'd give her the moon and the stars, all the planets in the universe.

"I'm afraid she won't agree with you, but it's none of my business." Winston smiled, seeming to be pleased.

Roc sat back, nursing the drink while keeping his attention focused on Cat as well as the men reaching out to her. Mulling over his conversation with Winston, he had to acknowledge some of what his friend said was true.

He didn't know if he could give her the freedom and independence she needed. Every night she spent at the tavern, he'd be in fear of her life. Telling her no and sticking by the command would be even more difficult.

But seeing terror in her eyes would be unbearable. Nothing good would come of her working here, except perhaps her pride.

"You going to come with her every night I can't?" Roc asked Winston, knowing if he couldn't be here the odds were against Winston accompanying Cat. "She needs a bodyguard."

"You know that's impossible." Winston ran his hands through his hair. "What would she do then?"

"You need ask?" Roc sounded incredulous and very nearly needed to shake a bit of sense into both Winston and Cat.

"No, sir. I know just as well as you do. She'd hire a cab and come here herself. Nothing would stop her. If you hire a man to protect her, she would feel duty bound to pay for that also."

"I'm glad you're finally seeing the whole picture." Roc leaned back, stretching his legs and crossing them. He tried to relax, but the environment made remaining calm impossible. That wouldn't happen until he got Cat home where he knew she'd be safe.

Winston cleared his throat. "Now, I'm not saying coming here nightly is something she should be doing. But it sounds to me you want to coddle her. She's only nineteen and she needs to explore who she is."

"When did you get so philosophical?"

"Just saying things how they appear to me," Winston said, nodding in her direction. "Her smile is the loveliest damn thing I've ever seen. You know," he paused, "she's the most beautiful woman I've ever seen."

"Caitlin's dinner." The waitress set the bowl of Shepard's pie on the table. "And a box for her to take home for tomorrow."

Roc felt the same way about Caitlin and maybe that's why she first drew his attention, but now that he knew her better, the beauty was more than skin deep. "Then she's done for the night." Roc wanted to take the bowl and let her eat in the carriage but resisted the temptation.

She sat down without looking at him, her hands in her lap. Breathing heavily from her exertion, there was a fine sheen of moisture on her face. She was breathtakingly lovely.

"You need to eat," Roc said, pushing the bowl in her direction. "When you're finished, I'll take you home."

Winston stood, smiling at Caitlin then turning his attention to Roc,

94

"I'm going to leave. I'll see you tomorrow. Where should I meet you?"

"Caitlin's place," he muttered, realizing he would most likely spend the night on her couch.

"That wise?" Winston asked.

Roc wasn't about to answer his friend's question. He knew he was compounding one bad action with another. She would hear the rumors if he could ever let himself bring her to the tavern to play. It would not be long before the stories whispering through the ton would speak her name with his in a derogatory manner.

He remembered how she dug into her food when she played in the pub in Portrush. Now she was spooning tiny amounts into her mouth, clearly nervous, perhaps apprehensive about his reaction to this work she was determined to do. The owner brought a small purse, setting it on the table next to her. He'd created this damn need for her to work and there was no remedy that he could see.

"Are you ready to go home?" He leaned forward, wishing he dared take her hands in his. This morning he'd been an obstinate bastard, avoiding her questions and pretending he didn't remember all their conversations about her mistress status. Now he would have to make her understand his feelings, but he wasn't at all sure what they were himself.

"Perhaps, if you're not going to be angry with me." She pushed the food away before picking up her fiddle as well as the box meant for tomorrow's breakfast. "I'll let you take me to the place you want me to call home."

"I'm never angry with you, just some of the things you believe you can do. Like this." He waved his hand around the room. "I hope you wouldn't try to come to work without Winston or myself accompanying you."

It seemed she meant to ignore him and his questions. Stiff backed, she picked up her fiddle case and strode through the patrons and outside.

Cold air nipped at his face. He wished she'd thought to bring a warmer wrap with her. The shawl she covered her shoulders with would never keep the wind at bay. He whistled for his driver, who appeared with the carriage in the front of the pub. In silence, they drove home.

Once inside the parlor, Cat stopped, opening the purse she earned and taking out all the coins but two. "This is yours. I'll keep track of what I owe you."

"You don't need..." He stopped, seeing the frown lines forming on her face. "Very well, if that's what you want."

"Do you remember anything I told you this morning?" she asked, placing the coins in his hand and closing his fingers over them. "I don't want to owe you anything, money or unlimited use of my body."

"I don't agree with most of what you said, but I do remember." Just because he provided a home for her to live in didn't automatically mean she was his mistress or that he'd collect anything.

"Good, then we have some common ground." She removed her wrap, hanging it on the rack near the door.

"Do you remember what we did after I walked you home when we were both in Portrush?" he asked, hoping to diffuse some of the anger and frustration they were both feeling.

A wave of color washed over her cheeks. "Yes... How could I forget?"

He felt sure she was thinking of the kisses and not the whiskey. The blush gave him a feeling of Deja vu. "Would you like to repeat the evening?" He didn't give her a chance to tell him no. So much time had passed since they shared any intimacy. Even though they slept on the same bed in the ship, he had kept his hands to himself even when her ribs no longer hurt and her black eye vanished.

"I've wanted to do this all day. Most of the time, I couldn't think of anything else." With his hands on the sides of her face, he slowly met her lips with his. He craved her sweet taste, the essence of her that was slowly becoming a part of him he couldn't deny.

A tiny sound of pleasure as her tongue met his, the sensations primal and magical. A mercuric heat swept through him and the fantasy life he imagined with her taking shape in reality. Sifting his hands through her hair, pins flew in all directions. His body hardened as he tried to deepen the kiss more, understanding what he yearned for would not be his tonight. Yet he would hold memories of this kiss close to his heart while he longed for more.

He gazed at her. Violet blue eyes were shimmering with passion and desire, a thirst for him that was unquestionable was evident in her eyes. "Maybe we should have the whiskey now." His voice turned husky.

"I don't know where it is. I always pour." She looked around the room. Then smiling, "We should always stick to tradition."

"Tradition is good. Over there on the sideboard." He pointed, needing distance between them. "The glasses too."

Her movements were graceful. Strange he'd never realized that before. Silence seemed to tick by while he watched her move elegantly around the room. She sat down on the sofa in the parlor before handing him his glass.

"Can we talk about something other than what I did today?" she asked, staring at him over the rim of her glass. "I don't know what that could be, but surely you must have an idea or two."

"What would you like to talk about?" he asked, studying her, trying to see inside her head. Yet he couldn't keep from touching her. He ran a fingertip down her neck then across the top of her bodice, relishing the small shiver of pleasure his touch elicited.

"I have no idea." Then after a pause, she looked at him, "What did you do this afternoon. Where did you go that you were away for so long?"

"Just business as usual." She would not accept that simple answer that explained nothing. He had no doubts.

"You're too elusive by far. I'm curious what you do that you have so much wealth you can spend it anyway you choose and you still have more money than you seem to know what to do with." She turned away for a moment. "I'm sorry, that's not my business. I'm afraid I can be a bit nosy."

He placed her hand in his, "Where my wealth comes from is no secret. It was derived the same place as my title. I was born into a family where money seemed to grow on trees. Yet in reality it was from good investments over the generations and there seemed to be no wastrels in the family tree to lose the hard-earned funds."

"You were just lucky then," she laughed. "I feel as if perhaps for a few minutes, you're the Roc I met in Portrush, not the autocratic lord you became when we set foot on English soil."

"I would hear you laugh more often." They both finished their drink. "Would you like another?"

"Yes, if it means you'll stay and talk to me. You know I tried to fire Cook and Adara this afternoon."

He poured a bit more than usual. "You didn't meet with success." Cook would have told her about her children and enlighten her about Adara's plight as well. After that, she was too kind hearted to keep them from the money they needed.

"No, but I'm going to pay you their wages too." Her voice took on a stubborn tone.

"I thought we weren't going to talk about that tonight," he said, trying for a neutral topic of conversation and finding nothing.

"You won't tell me about your business then tell me about your family. Why is your mother called The Duchess, and why do people cower in her wake?"

He let his head fall back and roared with laughter. "I hope when you meet her, she is not on a mission to fulfill some cause. Let me see, when my father passed away, all the family responsibilities were automatically delivered to her. I wasn't old enough or wise enough to take on everything all at once, nor did I want to. Our holdings are vast and aren't limited to England."

"You own the house in Portrush. What does Ida have to do with your family?" she asked.

"You're asking more questions and I haven't finished the first one. We'll go back to cowering in her wake." He touched her cheek. "I'd really rather kiss you. Ah well, my father had so many people working for him, spying really, that he knew secrets about most of the lords and ladies of the ton. He shared them with mother and when he passed, she continued in the same vein. If she needs help with anything, she always has a favor or two she can call in. Literally, she owns the aristocracy in this city."

"I'm shocked, amazed, totally confused. Why would she want to know secrets about others?"

"Power. That's the simple answer, but when one has their own secrets or need help with something, it's easier to get that assistance if you have a truth to hold over another's head."

"And the favor requires silence from your mother," she said, seeming to understand the process.

"Mother knows about most everyone's secret rendezvous, their mistress and lovers. All of their indiscretions are recorded and kept in a secure spot. When mother needs something, she has more power than anyone should have."

"You have that same power." She downed her glass then poured another one. "Your mother will know you're keeping me as your mistress." Her face paled to a ghostly shade. "Will she hold that over me someday?"

His mother was one factor he had not thought on when he bought the home for her. If she kept tabs on anyone, it was him. "The truth?"

"Yes."

"She will know by tomorrow morning, and she will also know about your work at the pub. If you had not gone there this evening, it might have taken her a few more days to discover what I've done. What I've set in motion." Where Cat was concerned, he would have to run interference with his mother. If he could find a way, she wouldn't come here and embarrass Caitlin.

"I can expect a visit then." She closed her eyes and seeming to need more from him than words, she leaned into him. "Hold me. Make me forget this horrible nightmare."

He wrapped his arms around her, reveling in the feeling of her body pressed close to his. "In a couple of days, I would suspect. I would pray this is a pleasant dream and no nightmare."

"I'm terrified. What will she do? Despite the fact I don't want you paying for all this, I don't want to be put on the streets before I can find a place to live. I pray she wouldn't do that."

Trying to give comfort, he massaged her back. "My mother would never put you on the street. In any case, she doesn't have that kind of power over me." No, he had more to fear from The Duchess than his Cat. "My mother would most likely endeavor to protect you from me."

"You don't know that, can't possibly read her mind. Why would she side with me over you?"

He chuckled, "I can read her mind. She would chastise me and take you in to her home. You will not like what she'll have planned for you if this comes about. I can guarantee that fact."

"Planned for me?" The words seemed to catch in her throat. "I won't let you take control of my life. Why would I let your mother?"

"She won't give you a choice."

"Like mother like son," she murmured.

Was he really as bad as his mother? No, never, and at the moment all he needed was his Cat. "Kiss me," he said, drawing her into his arms and hopefully one step further into securing her in his life.

"I can forget all my problems in your arms. The feel of your lips against mine is magical."

His lips met hers again, but this time he couldn't resist her. Through the fabric of her dress, he rubbed his thumb over her hardened nipple, took delight in her response as she pulled his head closer to her then ran her fingers through his hair.

He unfastened the buttons on the back of her dress. Something her ladies' maid would have to do but she wasn't here. When he hired her, he told her if they weren't home by eight o'clock, she could leave and return to her family. He told himself, he would have to help her from her clothes or she would have to sleep in them.

When the buttons were unfastened, his fingers slowly traced her spine until they met more clothing. Her corset was loosely laced so he finished, even while they kissed, touching tongue against tongue, melding their lives more closely together. He had one mission. He had to caress her as he did that night, when he almost said to hell with everything and made love to her.

"*Mon petite chatte*, what you do to me. I can barely breathe and my heart races so fast." He wanted to feel all of her, needed her beneath him. "You have to tell me no."

"When you hold me, all my fears vanish. I can't say no even though in the morning I'll wish I had."

That was enough said to give him incentive to stop. "Ah, Cat, I've failed you. Go to bed now. Your dress is unfastened and corset unlaced. Sleep well. If you need me, I'll be on your sofa."

"Your sofa," she corrected and, "are there no other beds in this house than mine? On second thought, why don't we share my bed, like we did on the ship? You would be more comfortable, I'm sure."

"No." He couldn't allow himself that pleasure. "You were hurting then, you're not now. Lying next to you knowing you would return my passion, there is no way I could ever sleep with you, without making love to you."

"Please Roc, don't leave me tonight."

~ * ~

Morning light filled the bedroom she and Roc had shared for the past week. He had been remarkable, allowing her to play at the Boar's Head tavern each night and sleeping beside her when they returned.

They kissed and shared intimacies and as much as possible he'd been a gentleman, taking nothing she didn't want to give with no regrets. That was the crux of their lovemaking, regrets.

Except for the fact he bought everything for her, paid for her every need, she was his mistress in name only. The few coins she gave him each night after work wouldn't pay one day's wages for either Adara or Cook let alone make a dent in the mortgage.

This morning he left her with a kiss and a promise to return early. The weather looked delightful, he told her, and he was going to take her to Vauxhall Gardens when he returned. They could walk through the park, buy food from the vendors while thoroughly enjoying the day and the promise of the night to come.

He told her he had a very special surprise waiting for her. But she told him again how much she hated surprises and he should call whatever he planned something else.

The scuffle coming from downstairs made her sit up in bed and grab the robe lying on the bedside. Her first thoughts were those of Blair. What if he found her and Roc wasn't here to defend her? Winston wasn't either. The man always accompanied Roc unless he was directed to stay with her. That left Adara and Cook the only people who could defend the castle so to speak.

Before she could set her feet on the floor, the door to her room burst open. "No." She clutched the robe to her chest.

"Get out of my way." The woman spoke to Adara, rudely pushing her aside. "This is too important. I need to speak with Caitlin immediately and alone."

"You've no right to intrude on milady," Adara said, yet she seemed unable to do anything about the older woman as she backed away.

"I've every right," she said but a slow smile grew on her features. "Give us some privacy, please."

"Who are you?" Caitlin asked. Beginning to guess the truth, she still needed to hear the words.

"You're savior. I'm going to take you away from this and make sure my son behaves properly where you're concerned. Did you know you're the most beautiful woman I've ever seen?" Then The Duchess paused, tapping her cane on the floor. "You remind me of someone, I can't think of exactly who at the moment. Well, I'll remember soon enough. I'm not getting any younger so I'd better start thinking.

"Adara, come back in. I know you're listening at the door. Help her dress. Preferably in something Richard didn't buy for her. Caitlin is coming to my home to live."

Caitlin pushed herself against the headboard. "I don't want to." How had this roared out of her control in such a short time? She'd only lived in London one week.

"Do you want to marry my son or do you want to be called his mistress for the rest of your life? You know he's like all other men. He doesn't have the God given sense to see what's right in front of his face. Unless he's given no choices when it comes to what he wants, he'll keep everything just the way it is."

"I want to be with him." She was totally confused and felt as if a herd of stampeding horses just ran her over. "But you can't change his mind by insisting I live in your home."

"Pshaw," The Duchess waved a hand in the air. "I suppose you'll have to trust me with this endeavor. I do know what I'm about. Go on, get dressed. I'll wait for you in the parlor, but if you're not downstairs in ten minutes, I'll be right back up to see what's taking you so long."

Caitlin swallowed, fear of the unknown pooling in her throat. Frozen to the bed she couldn't move.

Adara stood in front of her, grinning happily. "This is what you want, isn't it? Now Roc will have to treat you the way you deserve, like a real lady. If he doesn't get to sleep with you every night, he is sure to marry you."

"You think so?" Caitlin wasn't all that sure about anything. "I'm certain he could defy his mother and make sure I'm back here this very evening."

"We'll put you in that dress you arrived in. It's threadbare and old, but Roc didn't give it to you. You can't wear those other clothes until the two of you are married." Adara found the clothes then the small satchel she arrived with, setting them on the bed.

"I'm positive The Duchess will be humiliated when she sees me." Caitlin clenched her jaw, thinking she was jumping into a blazing fire that might burn hotter than Roc. The two were so much alike the thought left her breathless.

"Of course she won't." Adara finished the laces on Caitlin's corset then the fastenings. "Here are your shoes. I'll take the bag downstairs. Where is your fiddle?"

"Downstairs. I'll only be a minute." Caitlin watched as Adara left, depression and confusion sweeping through her.

At the mirror in her room, she patted her hair in place, lose strands falling unflattering around her face. Roc could fix it, his fingers nimble with the pins. A bit of jealousy landed in her heart. His experiences were far more than hers. He'd been with women, most likely lots of them. He'd actually had someone to teach him about lovemaking. What did she have?

Right now he wanted her. That was all. Love and want were two different things. Who would he want tomorrow or a year from now? Perhaps going with The Duchess was the best decision for her.

"In for a penny, in for a pound," she muttered as she made her way down the steps, her small suitcase in hand.

In the parlor she found The Duchess and Adara waiting for her while sipping what appeared to be tea. A plate of lemon bars sat on the nearby table. When The Duchess saw her, she held the plate up, offering her a delicacy.

"No thank you. Couldn't possibly eat a thing. I'm ready for whatever it is you have planned." She certainly didn't feel ready for this or for Roc's anger when he discovered she went missing again. "I should really leave Roc a message but I can't write. Could you do it?" That fact had to be another strike against her in his mother's eyes.

The Duchess stood. "I already have. I left one on the stand here by the door, and I sent a messenger to find him with another note. He should know as soon as possible so he won't worry about you. When he gets the note, he'll come straight to my home and create havoc. I wouldn't have it any other way. The boy must learn how to treat the woman who's going to be his wife." Her smile seemed almost angelic.

"Good." Then after swallowing the fear, "Thank you for that. Roc will be furious, you understand."

"I'm looking forward to chastising my boy and teaching him something I evidently overlooked during his formative years."

Caitlin followed The Duchess from the house, fiddle case in hand and Adara trailed behind her with the tiny satchel. Surprised, yet not so much, when Adara climbed in the carriage with them. She figured out the two new each other, just as The Duchess must have had some contact with Cook.

The Duchess leaned forward and patted her on the hand. "You will need a lady's maid at my home too. But this time I'll be paying for her, not Roc. I'll buy whatever you need."

"Oh, you can't do that. I don't...well there is no reason for you to take me in, at least that I can see."

"Don't you fret over any of this. I've taken in ten of my nieces, or was it nine, and found each of them a husband. They are all good men. I intend to do exactly that. Now it's not the season, but there are still a few balls around town and I intend to present you at the next one. The Marquis of Rushingham is hosting a ball in celebration of his new marriage." She snapped her fingers, "That's it, I've got it now. Rushingham and his mistress, I'll think of her name. Eyes just like yours," she mumbled as if talking to herself.

Got what? "I can't possibly go to a ball, I've nothing to wear." Pushed and shoved by both mother and son, she held her breath, waiting for the next shock to splinter her life in a different direction.

"My dear, I'll take you shopping tomorrow. I do love to go the dressmakers with my nieces. It will be just as much fun with you. By the way, please feel free to call me Charlotte." The Duchess gazed out the window then.

"Charlotte, I've no money to spend on dresses, particularly ones that are specially made for me and ones I've no need for. I'm not going to any balls. I wouldn't know how to act or what to do."

"I will pay and no, you won't owe me a thing. I've enough money to last me several lifetimes, so don't worry about funds. It will be fun." The Duchess cackled happily.

"I have no say in any of this?" Overwhelmed, she decided to keep her mouth shut. No one listened to her anyway. Mother and son were far too much alike. They did what they pleased and damn anyone who gets in their way.

"Not while I'm your chaperone. Here we are. I can't wait to introduce you to David, my new husband. He plays the bagpipes."

"You found her." A small woman with greying hair met them at the door. "Good, good, she's just as lovely as the rumors have it. Indeed, my old eyes are telling me she's the most beautiful woman I've ever seen. No wonder your son fell head over heels in love with her."

"Yes, Scarlett, we did find Caitlin. Please fetch some lemon bars and tea. You can take Caitlin's bag to her room and show Adara to her quarters. I'd like to believe the woman my son falls in love with is more than just a pretty face."

When Scarlett reached for her fiddle, Caitlin held it close to her chest, shaking her head at the woman. "No. I want to keep it with me. Don't want to lose it, you know."

"Very well," Scarlett smiled. "This one's a real keeper. Hope you teach some sense to that young man who's your son."

Caitlin wandered into the parlor, gazing around the room. Fiddle case in hand she sat down with it on her lap. "I'm really not sure what I'm doing here."

"Why don't you play for us, dear? Perhaps that will ease some of the nerves that seem to envelope you. Your whole body is shaking like a leaf blowing in the wind. Of course you don't have to play if you don't want to."

Hesitating a moment, she decided to get out her fiddle. The Duchess was right, playing would settle her nerves and her stomach. She tuned the strings then started a lively version of an Irish jig. Unable to help herself, she stood then and danced around the room, caught up in the magic of the music.

"What have we here?"

"Why, David, I didn't expect you home so soon." The Duchess sat while David placed a chaste kiss on her forehead. "Heard you were up to something and I wanted to find out what it was." He held up a hand, "Wait a moment and I'll get my pipes from the study."

Caitlin sat, waiting for David to return. They decided on a tune and as they played, the sound of their instruments seemed to blend as one. Moving from one song to the next the pair played so well together. Now Charlotte joined them with the lyrics of the song, her voice sweet and clear.

Finally, Caitlin set the fiddle down, needing to stop for rest. When the music ceased, a loud clapping echoed from the front of the room. Scarlett stood by Blair O'Connell. Caitlin's heart caught in her throat and the nerves that had been soothed by music returned full force.

"That was very nice, Caitlin. I see you found a chaperone. Where is Roc?" Blair asked.

"See the man out," The Duchess said, waving her hand in the air. "I don't believe the Earl of Glenwood is welcome in this home."

David set his pipes on the floor, striding toward the man. "Best you leave now. The Duchess has a way of making a man's life miserable if her directives are not followed."

"No." Blair stood his ground. "Caitlin is my fiancée. Her Da promised her to me, and I'm not leaving without her."

"I am not!" She stood, forcing herself to look at the man. "You nearly killed me. Even if I was your fiancée once, I'd never marry you now after you gifted me with a black eye and two broken ribs."

"David, see that he leaves now," Charlotte said, clearly distraught, her usual stern voice wavering for a moment before she regained control.

"The old man doesn't have that ability," Blair laughed. "Caitlin was promised to me and I mean to keep her."

Caitlin didn't think Blair saw the blow coming. He was flat on the ground and pushed from the house before he could retaliate. Roc stood over him. "Don't come back."

"I'll have you prosecuted." Blair wiped blood from his nose but he was slowly sitting then standing.

"You can try." Roc closed the door behind him and to Scarlet and the rest of them, "That man is not welcome here or anywhere near Caitlin. If he comes here again, don't open the door for him."

"What is this about nearly killing Caitlin?" The Duchess didn't look at her but addressed her question to Roc.

"The morning we left, O'Connell paid a visit to Caitlin. He hit her twice in the face giving her a black eye and sending her to the ground where he proceeded to kick her in the ribs and the back. She crawled along the damp earth to my home so she could escape him. If I had departed ten minutes sooner, she would have been left to fend for herself. He even took the coin I gave her so she would have the necessary funds to leave if she needed."

"You had to protect her," Charlotte said, turning her attention now to Caitlin. "Why didn't you tell me, child?"

Caitlin didn't know what to say, couldn't think. "You didn't ask." She inhaled a shaky breath that did very little to calm her. "And it seemed such a long time ago."

"Come now, Cat, we're going home." Roc picked up her fiddle and began to pack it away in her case. "Where is Adara? Did she come with you?"

"In her quarters," The Duchess said, her voice penetrating the room with its force. "Caitlin is staying here."

"You just saw why she cannot remain here where she has no one to safeguard her," Roc protested vehemently.

"It's not your choice," Caitlin's voice wavered. "It's mine."

"I've made it my business to keep you alive and well. With Blair in town things have changed. You need my protection."

"I'm perfectly capable of that very thing," The Duchess spoke up. "I'll bring in some men to guard the house and when we go to the dressmakers tomorrow, I'll take them with me. I'll send a message to Drake Montgomerie. He'll make sure everything is taken care of."

"If she stays here, so do I." Roc sat down beside her, possessively wrapping an arm around her. "In the same bed."

"Are you trying to rattle my feathers?" The Duchess asked. "You can't do that. You must court her properly."

"Why now?" He negligently shrugged his shoulders. "There has never been anything proper about our relationship. I don't plan on starting when her life is in danger."

She felt as if she were a small child in a corner of the room where everyone was making decisions about her life and talking around her but she had no say. She wanted to speak up and assert herself, but she had no clue how to do that. The two didn't listen to each other and had never heard a word she said, so what difference did it make?

It seemed Roc just noticed what she wore. "Why are you dressed in that? It's going to fall apart any second now, and you'll be left naked for everyone in the world to stare at."

"As I told you, I'm taking her to the dressmaker's tomorrow." The Duchess spoke up again.

"Not without me," he said, "Now, I promised you an evening in Vauxhall Gardens. If we return to your house and put you in another dress, one that won't fall apart with a gust of wind, we can still enjoy the evening." Then he turned to his mother. "It's not what I envisioned, but if you and David want, you can play chaperone. I won't object. Is that proper enough?"

"I was looking forward to the outing." Caitlin wasn't sure if she should say anything. Didn't want to make life harder for her.

"Good then it's settled." He held out his hand. Then he spoke to his mother. "In the meantime. you can arrange for a couple of guards, and if you like you can attend with us."

"Vauxhall might be settled but Caitlin's reputation will be torn even farther if you insist on staying here and in her room as well. Is that what you want, Richard Oakes Crandall?" Charlotte asked.

"Her life is more important than her reputation. Enough of this argument, Cat and I are going to have some much-needed fun. You decide what you want to do."

In Roc's elaborate carriage, Cat took a moment to close her eyes and feel a moment's peace. "You said when you got home all you wanted was some much-needed peace and quiet."

"I did, didn't I?" he spoke softly. "I'm sorry you got caught up in my life but...I'm also glad you are with me and part of that life."

She stopped him, "It's more like you got caught up in mine. I was surprised Blair came to London for me."

"I'm not but in this time where I can think instead of react, mother is right about your reputation. It's what you've been telling me all along and I tried not to hear you."

"You don't want to court me."

"I don't want anyone else to either." He kissed the back of her hand. "I need to know where you are every minute of every day. I need to lie beside you at night even if nothing happens between us."

"That's ridiculous," she smiled, watching him and knowing she needed the same thing.

"I know. Come here where you can sit on my lap. I need to kiss you all the way to the house."

She was more than willing to oblige. The peace she felt in his arms was something she'd never known before meeting him.

The dress changed, the carriage ride to the gardens finished, hand in hand they crossed the bridge. He steered her down several different paths then stopped as once promised at a vendor, buying them food and drink.

A band played while she tapped her foot and wished she could play with them. "You played a fiddle in an Irish pub." He held her close, her back against his front as they watched the musicians.

And I fell in love with an English lord.

When they finished, he led her farther along the paths, finally stopping. He bent close to her ear, "See over there."

"Hot air balloons." Excited, she turned, his lips brushing hers. "Can we go for a ride?"

"Just like I promised. Now," he paused grinning. "You don't care if I pay for it do you?"

She pulled back, regarding him thoughtfully, "No, if it's part of courting. I don't know anything about that."

"The man always pays. It's a good thing. Come." He took her hand

and they strode quickly to the balloons.

Money changed hands and before she knew it, she was inside the basket as it sailed upward.

"Don't look over the side, that could tip it," he told her, "Look straight out. See over there."

She clapped her hands together, feeling the smile growing as they ascended into the heavens. The sun was beginning to set and the colors painted the sky beautifully.

"Everything looks so tiny. Are those people down there? Look, I see Charlotte and David."

"I believe you're right and they don't know where we've gone." He laughed, seeming pleased with himself. "As a child I was never able to escape her watchful eye. I did better as I grew older."

"Now you're back in her clutches. Da never paid much attention to me. I came and went as I pleased. Now I feel as if I'm in prison. But not up here," she told him quickly. "This is freedom. I so wish I could fly."

He drew her closer, "I thought this would help make you feel a bit more freedom. I'm sorry you've been unhappy. That was never my intention."

"You make me happy." She looked into his deep brown eyes, sad eyes tonight. She needed to see him happy again.

"I don't want to sleep without you by my side, and I'm not sure how far I can push mother. Keep remembering, she wants what's best for you and she understands the vagaries of the ton better than most."

"We're coming down." She moved closer to him, enjoying the warmth of his body and knowing how much she'd miss him. Sleep without him would be elusive at best tonight, and the following ones. "How long am I going to have to stay at your mother's home?"

He ran his fingers through his hair, "Until you find a suitable husband."

"No, I don't want a husband."

"There you two are. I wondered what happened, but David saw the direction you headed."

"I eluded you for a few minutes."

"I figured out who you reminded me of. Fiona. You remind me of a woman named Fiona who had the most unique and beautiful violet blue eyes. Just like yours. Until now she was the most beautiful woman I'd ever seen."

~ * ~

Blair settled into a chair in a back corner of the Boar's Head tavern, nursing a beer and watching. Tonight of all nights he didn't want to drink too much. He listened to the patrons talk about the beautiful lady who played the fiddle and danced. She was magical, her haunting violet blue eyes mesmerizing everyone who saw them.

He drummed his fingers on the table, staring at the woman who sat next to him. She was nothing like his Caitlin. He needed to find a way to get rid of Roc and drag his intended back to Portrush. This lady, Addie someone, was going to help him.

All his inquiries about the Duke of Ravenswood and his mother, known in most circles as The Duchess, brought him to the conclusion Roc was untouchable. He discovered no vulnerabilities. He had limited power and money at his disposal, making his quest nearly impossible, but he meant to find a way.

"I could make you feel better if you let me." The woman named Addie ran a finger along his arm. She wouldn't tell him her last name, said it didn't matter. All he needed to know was Addie.

"You know what I needed from you and you failed me. I've paid you a lot of coin for information." She was supposed to get something to hold over the duke's head.

She shrugged her shoulders, sending him a strange expression. "Can't find something that isn't there. They are all either saints or they've been able to keep their secrets."

"Ravenswood is no saint. He was in Ireland, his business questionable. I heard he's a spy and looking into the different rebellions and who led them for the crown."

"That cannot be proved, and you can't smear his name with that lie. He will be able to refute any gossip you might have heard. My sources told me he was there buying property. These people you want to defame are above the law, at least they make it appear that way."

He withdrew his hand and called for another beer. *What the hell, nothing's going to happen tonight. Might as well drink as much as I like.* "You must keep looking. I know there has got to be something."

"The only rumors that have a basis in truth is the fact your Caitlin O'Shea is the duke's mistress. Now she's staying with The Duchess, dispelling that gossip. You need to face the truth. This family is an honest and even hard-working family despite their enormous wealth. Your Caitlin is not going to be coming to your side any time soon. Gossip also has it there will be a wedding soon between these two."

"I can have him arrested for hitting me." He spoke petulantly. "The man gave me a bloody nose."

The woman laughed at him, eyeing him as if he were dirt. "I will keep looking as long as you're paying me. You don't have a case either. He will figure out a reason or he will procure witnesses who say the opposite."

"Fine," he said, handing a bag of gold coin to her. "But nothing else unless you have something I can use."

"I'll meet you here tomorrow." Addie flounced out the door to meet Hamilton Winthrop down the street.

"What did you find out?" Hamilton offered her his arm as they strolled down the street.

"Blair O'Connell is not going to give up. He's going to trump up something on Roc, probably false. I thought it interesting there really is nothing on that family that can be held against them," Addie said, thinking O'Connell was a weasel of a man.

"Where Blair O'Connell is concerned you need to take care. He's ruthless and Roc told me he hit Caitlin, giving her a black eye as well as broken ribs."

"Montgomerie and Leighton should be apprised of what he's up to. Do you believe the gossip?" Addie asked.

"What? That Roc has taken Caitlin for his mistress." He paused, thinking. "Yes and no. I barely know the man. He's been all over Europe just as we have. Strange that our paths never crossed."

"From what I've heard about Caitlin, she is undeniably the most beautiful woman anyone has ever seen. She's jaw dropping beautiful," Addie said, looking to Hamilton for a reaction.

"In my eyes, no one is as beautiful as you."

"Good answer," she laughed, "In any case tomorrow is another day and we're going to have to appear to work for that man so we know what he's planning. I'm seeing him tomorrow at the tavern. Maybe we can make up something that has a thread of truth to it so I can stay in his good graces.

Chapter Six

Two weeks later, The Duke of Ravenswood, Roc, stood at the entrance to the ball given by the marquis of Rushingham. As Roc was announced, he searched for Cat and The Duchess, discovering them in a far corner of the room. He laughed softly to himself, realizing his Cat was hiding. She would feel uncomfortable and awkward. He wasn't sure what his mother had been thinking.

Quick strides brought him to Cat's side. "How are you?" He whispered close to her ear. "You're beautiful tonight, like always. Try to relax. I know this is all new to you."

"Are you trying to tell me you like to do this? This ball stuff?" She allowed him to take her gloved hand and kiss the back.

"No, I detest these affairs. But I've never attended one with you. Would you like to dance?" He almost laughed at the way her eyes widened with the look of shock. "Is that a no?"

"I don't know how to dance," she said, sounding terrified. "If you want your feet intact when we finish, best we don't try to dance."

"You of all people telling me you can't dance. I watched you play the fiddle and dance as if you floated on air. It was magic, you were magical, enchanting, captivating." He was beginning to understand though. She danced alone and in any way she wanted. There was a significant freedom to her dancing. Here she would have to follow designated steps of the dance, which of course she'd never been taught.

"You don't know what you're asking." She seemed to shy away from him, her hands folded tightly in front of her.

"Just give it a try." He held out his arms, expecting her to walk to him and take his hands. "I'll lead the way and make sure you don't fall."

"Really, I don't know what you want me to do." Hesitating, she stood as if she meant to try.

He smiled, recognizing this wasn't going to work. She was out of her element and totally reluctant. "Take my hand, like this." He showed her then, "Put your other hand on my shoulder." He settled his hand on her back. "Now just move with me."

She stumbled and did attempt the steps, but it truly was of no use. He watched a tear slide down her cheek. He brushed the moisture away with his thumb, regretting his decision to pressure her. "I'm so sorry." He let go of her and with her hand in his, strolled to the balcony.

"Thank you for not forcing me." She let him hold her close, her head resting on his shoulder, one hand on his chest.

The closeness was heavenly and he craved the intimacies. "I will get you dance lessons." He laughed, then amending his statement. "If that's what you'd like. We could practice together."

"Why? How many balls would I find myself going to? No one besides you is going to court me, and how long are you going to be there for me? When you get tired of me, what then?" There was a slight sound of distress in her voice.

Had he done that to her? Caused her distress? Her point was one he'd never thought of before. He'd be courting her forever if he didn't make a change in this crazy relationship his mother forced on them. And was this what he wanted for his life? "In the scope of things, I suppose lessons are not important."

"Good, whoever taught me would soon learn I've two left feet. It would be an impossible task." Her heavy sigh caught his attention.

He pulled her around so she faced him, "You know what these dark corners on balconies are good for?" He needed to kiss her, feel her tongue inside his mouth, trace her lips with his tongue. This was the perfect place to show her he wasn't going anywhere and that he'd always be a steadying hand a solid part of her life.

"You know I don't." She moistened her lips, and he was sure she knew he was going to kiss her. "What are these dark corners good for? Something nefarious I'm guessing?"

"Only if kissing you is nefarious," he whispered and he drew closer to her lips.

"A kiss, what if someone finds us?"

"Don't worry so much. If someone comes back here, it's to do the same thing."

"Roc..." but he cut her off.

"Ah..." her lips were sweet and soft. She opened for him, accepting all he craved to give her. He pulled her closer, knowing she felt his arousal against her and wondering if she understood how much more he wanted to give her, experience with her. He would be the man to teach her everything.

Not if he didn't marry her.

Moonlight highlighted her, yet the darkness kept him from seeing into her eyes. He felt her pulse at the base of her neck, pressing his lips against the spot that throbbed with her life's blood.

She ran her hands up his chest then wound her fingers around his neck. Her breasts pushed against him, begging for him to touch. The night would end and once again they would sleep chastely together. The situation was untenable and it was going to end. As soon as the time was right, he meant to ask her to marry him.

Lightness entered his heart at his sudden decision.

Perhaps when they returned home tonight, he could ask her or maybe something more romantic. He would take her to the small lake that was part of the Leighton's summer home, a picnic with some of her favorite foods, a bottle of Chianti from Logan Maxwell's vineyard, and a ring. He'd procure one first thing in the morning and weather permitting, he would ask her tomorrow afternoon. At his sudden but very practical decision, peace settled around him.

His mother would love planning the wedding with her. Charlotte seemed to take great delight in wedding planning, although most of the weddings she organized ended up in disaster.

He kissed her then kissed her again, one hand sliding up to cup her breast, relishing the softness as well as the way she filled his hand. He kissed her eyes, her cheeks, the corners of her mouth. Nipping on the sensitive skin, playing chase with her tongue, he kissed her hard and deep and she answered with the raw passion he loved. This was the woman who would make him happy for the rest of his life. He only prayed he could do the same for her.

The hard wrapping on his back surprised him. His mother was known for keeping young suitors in line with her cane, but she always maintained that kisses were fine.

"Go away, mother," he said, while he slowly turned, setting Cat behind him. "Stay put," he told Caitlin.

"Unhand my daughter," The Marquis of Rushingham said, his cane held high over his head as if he meant to strike Roc square in the face. "You've no right to her without my permission."

Roc tried to make sense of the marquis' words. As far as Roc knew, the marquis had two sons who died last year in a carriage accident. It was a foolish tragedy that left the poor man distraught for months. "What makes you believe Cat is your daughter? Her da lives in Portrush." But the few discussions he'd had with Caitlin let him to believe this man could very well be her father.

The Duchess and David appeared on the balcony as if needing to give a helping hand. Mother might know something about this unfounded claim. "Why would the marquis think Caitlin is his daughter and her mother has passed?"

"She looks just like my long-lost Fiona. Has the same violet blue eyes, the face, the way she carries herself. This woman is my lost daughter."

Roc felt Cat's hands grip his waist tighter. He'd heard her mother's name was Fiona but he had no reply at the moment, tongue tied for the first time in so many years he couldn't count.

"Perhaps you should pay attention to your wife instead of dreaming up false claims," The Duchess said. "She's waiting for you and I'm sure she'd like some companionship."

"What happened to Fiona?" Roc asked, hoping for more information from the man.

"She vanished. One day she was in her home and the next she was nowhere to be found. I searched all over London and England. Sent a man to Ireland, but I couldn't find her. After a year I gave up and returned home."

"Why did Fiona vanish?" Cat asked stepping from behind Roc,

seeming to need to take part in this conversation. It appeared she needed to hear the marquis admit how much he abused his relationship with her mother.

"That was between Fiona and myself. We had a disagreement." The marquis inhaled a sharp breath, his scowl deepening the lines across his forehead. "You're coming with me. This is your home now, and I'm going to help you chart your future."

"No," Cat said so quietly yet so firmly her one word set the hair on the back of Roc's neck on end. "I've no reason to believe you're my father. My home is with Charlotte and David. Charlotte is my chaperone. Surely you cannot object to that."

"I will arrange for a chaperone for my daughter," he insisted. "Her wellbeing is my duty now that I've found her."

Despite the glower on the marquis face, Roc wrapped an arm around Cat in hope of reassuring her. "Prove you are Caitlin's father and we will further discuss this, perhaps tomorrow afternoon if it fits into my mother's schedule. As for now, Caitlin and I are leaving. You have no power here." He turned to his mother and David, "And you?"

"We will all leave in my son's carriage as is appropriate. If you wish to discuss this civilly, stop by tomorrow afternoon. David and I will both be present but don't bother if you don't have proof," The Duchess said.

On the way home, Roc waited for his mother to tell him what she knew, but the woman remained abnormally silent. Cat sat next to him, her hand on his leg. Once inside the house, his mother seemed to come alive again, directing everyone, as did Beast. The puppy jumped on Cat, licking her while he squealed with delight.

"Sit," Roc commanded.

Beast looked his way before he settled down and obeyed, lying down at Cat's feet.

"Scarlett, please pour us each a glass of brandy and bring out some of those strawberry tarts we had for afternoon tea and the, lemon bars of course. Everyone else into the parlor. We've a lot to talk over and some important decisions to be made."

Roc suspected the marquis told the truth and Cat just found the father who kept her mother as mistress until she carried his child then he must have said something that sent her back to Portrush. "What is it you think you know, Mother?"

He accepted a glass of brandy from Scarlet before sitting down on the sofa with Cat next to him. He needed to keep her close. She was shaking so hard, he feared she'd fall off the couch.

Charlotte took a long drink of her brandy then, "I remember Fiona O'Shea very well. Just as your Caitlin is the most beautiful woman I can remember seeing, her mother was the most beautiful woman in London twenty years ago."

Cat started to speak then stopped when Roc squeezed her shoulder. It seemed she was unsure of herself and too hesitant, but the story had to come out and Cat would have to learn she was so beautiful people would continue to remark about that fact for the rest of her life.

"So, the marquis really is her father," Roc began then stopped himself. "All we know is that the marquis knew Fiona and we assume he kept her as his mistress. Cat's father could be anyone."

"Probably not. As I recall Fiona was indeed his mistress and loyal to him. I believe she loved him very much and didn't feel that her love was returned. One day she vanished just as he told us. I'm pretty sure everything he's said is true," Charlotte told them.

"He didn't even ask about Fiona," Cat said. "He kept her, used her then did nothing to reassure that he would take care of her and the child she carried. He's a despicable man. Once I thought I wanted a father, needed to learn who he was and meet him as well. Now that I have one, I think Da is the real father to me. He's the only one I've ever known."

"This is all fine but the fact he is the father and there are other people who will remember the circumstances. The man has an undeniable hold on you, dear. We have to find a way to thwart that power he has over your life." Charlotte tapped her cane on the floor, seeming to think.

Roc was sure his mother knew exactly what she was going to say. She had a plan and if he knew his mother, The Duchess, what she desired would most likely come to pass.

"How? Don't I have a say in any of this? I'm not going with that man, not living in his home. I'd rather be put out on the street."

"You could run from him as your mother did," Charlotte said, "but

I've a much better solution."

Roc sipped his drink, having no idea what his mother was going to say, but he was sure the solution would be viable and most likely the best way to tie the marquis' hands where Cat was concerned.

"You've peaked my interest, Mother. How do you propose to stop him from claiming his daughter and forcing her hand?" Roc sat back, relaxed and waiting for the announcement.

Charlotte tapped her cane on the floor, commanding everyone's attention as her smile grew. "The two of you will wed tomorrow."

Roc looked to Cat for some response to his mother's words. Her face had drained of all color. If he could guess, she planned to refuse his hand in marriage. There were several ways he could try to convince her to marry him but the one she needed most he couldn't do. He couldn't tell her he loved her when he didn't understand that emotion or exactly what the word meant. There were things he could tell her and promise though.

Finally, Cat gave the answer he expected her to instantly blurt out. "No, I can't make him marry me. He doesn't want to."

Beast must have understood the distress in her voice. He sat up then paws on her knees, he tried to lick her face. Cat rubbed his ears, looking at him with the most wistful expression on her beautiful face.

"Where you're concerned, you've no idea what I want, Cat. Mother, I believe you've a splendid idea but why so soon? If it's tomorrow afternoon, you won't have time to plan much of a wedding."

"He holds more power than we do at least where your Caitlin is concerned. The sooner the two of you are wed, the fewer claims he has on her as well as her future. Tomorrow will do fine, early afternoon or even late morning better. I'll start the plans this evening and call in a few favors."

"Scarlett, go to the dressmakers first thing in the morning. She'll be up and about before six. See if she has something suitable for a wedding gown and bring her and the garment here so she can fit the dress to Caitlin. Her dress is the most important part of the wedding besides the bride and the groom."

"I haven't agreed to anything," Caitlin said, her voice wavering as she gazed at him, her eyes seeming to fill with moisture. "How can everyone just think Roc is willing and if he isn't neither am I?"

Beast jumped onto the sofa, laying his head in her lap while she stroked his head.

"Doesn't she have to agree?" Roc asked, chuckling softly. If he could have done this his way, Cat would be more than agreeable. Now he had to convince her he was not being forced and that he made plans to ask her to marry him just this evening. Indeed, no one forced him to do anything, not even his mother. He was his own man and made his decisions accordingly.

"My dear," Charlotte began, her patient voice, Roc noted, taking precedence, "unless you want to live with the marquis and be under his control, you have no choice in this matter. We must take care of this little problem before the marquis asserts his fatherly duties over you. If my elderly wisdom means anything, I believe you care about my son and might even be in love with him."

"There is always a choice," Caitlin maintained, her shoulders slumping slightly as if she understood the unavoidable truth here.

"Yes, there is and in this case, you have two. Is Roc so deplorable that you would not want to marry him? Does he have nothing you might want in a husband?" Charlotte asked.

"No, of course not, I..." It seemed she couldn't think of anything more to say.

"I promise I will treat you fairly, even give you pin money." He wanted to sweep her into his arms and take her upstairs so he could have a more private and convincing conversation with her.

"I don't want your money," Caitlin continued to protest.

"Do you want me?" Roc asked, hoping the answer was the one he needed to hear. "Be honest now."

Blood rushed to her cheeks. "Can we discuss this somewhere else?"

Roc looked to his mother for her reaction. "Do you mind? I believe I have some explaining to do."

She waved her hands in the air, an expression on her matronly face Roc had never seen before, "Go on with you. Take your fiancée upstairs, but don't rush the wedding night. I need your promise, Roc."

He cleared his throat then dragging a huge breath of air into his lungs, "I've waited this long, at her wishes, not yours, I'm not going to

121

make love with her tonight. Waiting until the wedding night has a nice sound to it."

"Dear," Charlotte stopped them for a moment, "are you protestant or catholic?"

"Not really anything. Da wasn't much for going to church and he didn't make me. Know that's probably not what you want to hear."

"Just needing to know what kind of minister to procure for the service tomorrow. We can always have two ceremonies if you don't want to be wed by a protestant minister."

"Whatever Roc wants," she mumbled. "A priest or a minister, it's not important to me."

"Come on, let them plan the wedding while I convince you it's what I want and what you'll want too." Roc said, his arm around her, whispering close to her ear and delighting in the little shiver rippling through her body.

"Perhaps you should stay a few more minutes then I'll let you two go. Caitlin must have her beauty sleep, but I do want the two of you to have a few things to your liking tomorrow."

They sat down again, but Roc kept her close, feeling if he let her get too far away from him, she'd vanish just like her mother did twenty years ago. He might never find her because she'd never return to Portrush where Blair O'Connell lived.

"Just a few things," Charlotte said.

"Like what?" Suddenly he was anxious to leave and frustrated with everything that had been taken out of his control. Beast seemed to feel the same. He'd moved to the stairs, sitting still but obviously waiting.

Charlotte let a huge sigh escape. "Flowers, cake, guests, food, and so much more."

"What's your favorite flower, dear," Charlotte addressed her question to Caitlin.

"I like violets and lilacs. Would any of those work?"

"Yes, yes, it would be easier if we didn't have to procure everything by tomorrow but I'll try. Now what kind of cake would you like?"

"Anything but chocolate." Roc cut in then turned to Caitlin who didn't seem to care about that either. She was despondent and out of sorts when she should be happy. He had to fix that before the wedding tomorrow.

"I'm sorry this all seems so strange to me. How about something filled with lemon. A white cake maybe and a nice filling, I didn't know planning a wedding was so... was so..."

"Complicated?" Roc laughed. "Usually people take months to plan their nuptials and the reception. We have one evening, but I'm sure mother will do a splendid job. I put all my faith in her magnificent abilities to organize at a moment's notice."

"The guests are important and some won't come because of the timing. Do you have any requests?" This time she looked to Roc for information.

"I've been away for so long, I haven't kept track of my childhood friends. I'd like Drake and Ella Montgomerie to attend if they want and maybe Addie and Hamilton Winthrop. It would be nice to have people who can take care of any unexpected issues that might arise. I've heard Addie is a wicked marksman." He'd heard stories of another wedding where Addie shot a man, a serial killer, in the head who was trying to kidnap one of the brides.

Charlotte gave a little shudder at his words. "Drake and Ella are fine as are Addie and Hamilton. I'll make sure to let them know what is happening. I believe they'll both be here if they don't have any other pressing obligations."

"I know someone, she's my lady's maid, but she's really the only friend I have here. Can Adara attend as my guest?" Caitlin asked. "I've no idea what is proper and what is not."

"She will be here. Adara can be your maid of honor. Who would you like as best man, Roc?" Charlotte asked.

"Suppose Drake should be the best man if he can come, but if that's not possible, I'd like David to stand up for me." Roc looked at the older man who'd made his mother so happy. His heart went out to him, the man who gave a new meaning to her life.

"I'd be honored," David said. "Perhaps Caitlin and I can play at her reception. She doesn't like formal dancing, but she's amazing when she has her fiddle.

"Is that all?" Roc asked, hoping to take his new fiancée upstairs but she seemed to be more amenable to the marriage now. He might not have to do a lot of convincing after all.

"Guess we're done here. Have a good evening and keep your word tonight." Charlotte let them go with a nod.

In her bedroom, he let her put on her nightdress in privacy and waited until she settled on the bed, a whimsical expression on her face.

"You do know we've things to discuss," he told her, watching the expressions flitting across her face and hoping in the end she'd agree to this wedding. Beast had followed and now was on the opposite side of the bed. He probably wondered if he'd have a place to sleep when they were finally man and wife.

"Roc." She took his hand in his, placing it on her heart. "I do want to marry you. I've wanted it for months now, but I don't want my circumstances to force you to do anything that isn't right for you. I'm sure there is another way out of my predicament. There is always another way."

"You can accept the marquis as your father and go live with him," he said not, meaning to sound quite so harsh. "If this had not happened, I was planning on asking for your hand tomorrow after I purchased a ring."

"Why would you do that when you've been adverse to marriage since I met you, since I first kissed you."

"I realized something."

"So simple, what was it you comprehended so suddenly?" It seemed she couldn't help herself, she smiled.

"Something that was obvious if I took a moment to think about it. I've been a bloody fool where you're concerned."

"Really," she said, leaning into him, her unrestrained curves pressing against him, enticing, arousing until he needed to force enchanting carnal thoughts from his head.

"Yes, I don't want to spend the rest of my life courting you, lying next to you on this bed without making love to you. I want you for the rest of my life, in my bed and my home, next to me through good times and bad. There is so much more. But I decided tonight when we were at the ball that I was going to ask you to marry me. I meant to take you to the lake on the Leighton summer estate, with a bottle of wine and some of your favorite foods. I needed to buy a ring but I meant to do that in the morning. By tomorrow afternoon you would have been, hopefully, my fiancée. The marquis simply speeded up the process."

"You mean that? You don't love me, so why?"

"Love is just a word. What I feel for you will last a lifetime. Please say yes."

She nodded, catching her lower lip between her teeth then, "I believe you."

"Is that a yes?" he asked, having a difficult time restraining himself.

Before she could answer, his lips found hers in a long drugging kiss. He groaned as he pulled her closer, deepening the kiss and yearning to take this farther. There were promises that needed keeping.

"Damn the promises, damn them all to hell."

~ * ~

When Caitlin opened her eyes the next morning, brilliant sunlight streamed in the open window and a soft breeze made the curtains move. The chatter in her private space gave her a start. She sat up, pushing her hair from her eyes. Charlotte and Adara were busy with the water for her bath and the scent of violets filled the air.

"Where's Roc?" She swung her feet over the bed. She missed him and wished he was with her now when she felt so unsure of herself. "This is really happening isn't it?" Different emptions rolled through her as she clutched her stomach.

"He's with David, getting ready for your wedding. It's not going to take him as long so I'm sure they'll be drinking some of Logan's fine Bordeaux or enjoying a glass of whiskey."

"I thought maybe he changed his mind and left. I thought he would be here with me when I woke up." This wasn't a very good start of her day, one that would change her life forever. He always woke her with a kiss and a smile.

"He didn't sleep here last night. I made sure of it. For some reason I didn't completely trust him to keep his word. Besides, it's bad luck to see the bride before the wedding." Charlotte laughed. "Now Adara and I are going to leave you to your bath. We'll be back in ten minutes with your wedding dress and the seamstress to make sure it fits like a glove along with some *pain au chocolate.*"

The door closed and Caitlin was alone with her thoughts. They left a tray of food and drink resting on the tub, but she didn't see how she was going to take a bath and eat too. Looking at the chocolate croissants made her stomach roll. She sipped the wine and the liquid rolled down her throat and seemed to ease the nerves controlling her stomach.

Trying to make light of what was just about to happen, she hummed a lively jig, wishing she had her fiddle with her, then remembered Adara and Charlotte would be back soon and if she didn't hurry, they would find her still in the tub and very naked.

Quickly, she finished her bath and wrapping a huge bath sheet around her, she waited for them to return. With a piece of bacon in hand, she walked around the room before stopping to look out the window.

Everything was the same, so why did she feel so different? She wasn't even married yet. The wedding night was yet to come, and she didn't know what to expect. A shiver of apprehension and strange eagerness swept through her. Fear of the unknown was an integral part of her thoughts, but she guessed Roc would make everything right. It seemed he always had a way of doing just that.

If her mother had lived, would she talk to her about tonight? Charlotte might but she didn't have the nerve to ask. Adara wasn't wed and, well...she didn't know if she even had a beau.

"Are you finished, dear?" Charlotte poked her head inside the room, "I've brought everything you need and Ella is here as well. I hope it's all right if she comes in with us. I thought you might want someone close to your age to confide in. I'm sure she will be happy to answer any questions."

It seemed Charlotte read her mind. "The more the merrier," Caitlin said, turning away from the window.

"I've two dresses here, one for you and one for Adara to wear," Charlotte said, holding them up for inspection.

"And we have two seamstresses. I'm Ella Montgomerie, Drake's wife. I'm so happy to meet you and astounded as well that Roc has finally decided to settle down. My God, you're the most beautiful woman I've ever seen. You make my toes curl, you're so gorgeous."

Caitlin felt blood rush to her face, truly overwhelmed by Ella's words. "I'm sure you're just being nice."

"No, it's the truth and I'm certain this is not the first time you've heard the words. Am I right?" Ella asked, tapping her toe impatiently.

"You're right but it doesn't make sense. I'm just common. There is nothing unusual or amazing about the way I look," Caitlin said, feeling uncomfortable at the attention and wondering why people thought she was so beautiful.

"Pshaw, there is nothing common about you, dear. If that were so, Richard would probably not have seen a future wife in you, and I'm alluding to more than just your beautiful face," Charlotte said, shaking out the wedding dress before handing the gown back to the dressmaker. "Now we brought you underclothes that go with your dress as well."

The seamstress hung the gown on a hanger. It was a beautiful pale lavender gauze over a white slip. It seemed to Caitlin that it was cut very low in the front and over the shoulders. She'd never worn anything quite so revealing or so expensive or beautiful. Charlotte must have spent so much money. Honestly, she wished people would stop spending money on her she'd never in her lifetime be able to pay back.

A few minutes later, she emerged from the dressing room with the appropriate underclothes all decorated with lace and embroidered with delicate purple flowers. The ribbon's holding up her stockings were lavender. Even her corset was laced with lavender ribbons.

"I guess I'm ready." She held her breath, smoothing her skirls and not sure what she was supposed to do.

"Now, hold your arms up," the dressmaker said. "And we'll make sure it's absolutely perfect."

She did and the gown slipped down around her and was fastened. "My, my, it nearly fits her exactly as is," the dressmaker said. "With just a few nips and tucks, we'll have this fitted to you in no time at all." Humming, she began to work.

Caitlin had never had a fitting and she didn't think she could stand still this long. Her legs itched and she needed to stretch every muscle. She wanted to groan but held it back, knowing this was something she would have to get used to doing.

"Almost done," the seamstress said an hour later, "and it's so beautiful. "You are practically sewn into this. You'll have to make sure Adara is there to get you out of this. Don't leave it up to the eager groom. He would most likely rip it in his haste."

"Then her groom could not get it off her without ruining the garment," Ella agreed, as she waltzed around the room, clearly delighted with the events of the day. "I will have to give you some advice when the others leave. It was not too long ago I was newly wed, but as everyone here knows, I was not a virgin. Drake made sure of that before the wedding day. So, for me there were no surprises."

"I think I'd like that. I've no idea," she turned to Ella, dragging in a long breath of air. "You can tell me what's going to happen? I've never had a mother. I've never..."

Adara stepped into the room, wearing her new dress. "We must do your hair first. The wedding will start in less than an hour."

"Before noon? I didn't expect that," Caitlin said.

"The minister was able to be here at eleven thirty," Charlotte said, "and we need to get this done before the marquis decides to pay us a visit. We don't want him waltzing in and objecting to the wedding. My lands, he couldn't have picked a more qualified husband for his daughter. What on earth is he objecting to anyway?"

"We certainly don't want anyone's objection," Ella said, grinning. "We just won't let him in the door until everything is final. I'm sure my husband will never allow anything to happen here. He brought men to guard each entrance, and I'm also certain they have orders to keep unwanted guests out."

"We have gifts for you. Now there are traditional gifts. You must have something borrowed," Charlotte began.

"Something blue, something old and something new," Adara finished, smiling. "We want only good luck for you and your duke."

Charlotte opened a small box. "Here are some amethyst earrings. They are to be your borrowed gift. My William gifted me with these on the day Roc was born. Someday they will be yours, but I'm not ready to give them up quite yet, besides Roc bought something new for you."

"When did he have time?"

"This morning when he purchased your ring. He saw this and could

128

not resist, telling me I must give it to you to wear today. It matches your gown splendidly."

"First, let me see the earrings," Caitlin said, opening the box and unable to stifle the tiny gasp at the site. "They are beautiful. I'll wear them with pride."

"Here is Richard's gift," Charlotte handed her a much larger box.

When she opened it, she was unable to speak. She looked to Charlotte, "Is this really mine?" The necklace was made of several rows of diamond and amethyst stones.

"He knew your favorite color is lavender. I've never seen a man so smitten," Charlotte said. "Except maybe my William, Roc's father."

"So, we have something borrowed and something new. What is old?" Adara asked.

"I have something old," Ella spoke up. "It's a handkerchief that Drake's mother wore when she married his father. Drake and his mother are not really close so it holds no sentimental value to him. But it is old and he'd like you to keep it with you."

Caitlin accepted it. "I don't know what to do with it. Am I just supposed to carry it in my hand?"

"No, my dear," Charlotte said. "You put it here for modesty." She placed it in the deep V of her dress.

"Now we're going to leave, all except Ella. You have ten minutes then the two of you need to be downstairs. I trust you will help her with all her questions," Charlotte spoke to Ella.

"Of course, Aunt Charlotte, everything she wants to know and perhaps a little bit more."

Seconds ticked by as the room was cleared. Ella turned to Caitlin, taking her hands. "You're worried about the wedding night. Are you a virgin? Now I've a bit of trouble believing Roc remained celibate all this time given his reputation, It can only tell you how much he respects your wishes and cares about you."

"I don't know what to say. My mother was a mistress to a man who didn't respect her. She died having me. He knew I didn't want to follow in her footsteps, so to speak."

"He listened to you. Now I can't say it was clear to you. I never thought Drake was listening to me, but as it turns out he did. Our circumstances aren't anything the same, but Roc loves you. It's obvious to everyone but you, I'm sure."

"That's what Charlotte and Adara have told me. I just don't want to force him into something he doesn't want, like marrying me when all he wanted was for me to become his mistress." Caitlin had so many second thoughts about this wedding and how Roc would feel about her afterwards.

"That's just the thing. Men like Drake and your Roc can't be forced into anything. Now I've some advice."

Caitlin sat down while Ella poured her a glass of wine. "Advice I need more than anything."

"First off, don't worry about tonight. Roc will teach you everything you need to know. He has your best interest at heart and he's made that perfectly obvious for months now. What you need to do is trust him and try to relax."

"Well, that's easier said than done." Caitlin wasn't sure she couldn't do what Ella advised, but she would certainly try.

"Second, I've another gift for you and Roc. When the two of you are finally alone, open the package. Until he sees this, he'll want to take all your wedding finery off. Just let him unfasten your dress and unlace your corset. Promise me you'll put this on for him. It will help both of you relax."

"Adara is charged with helping me out of the gown," Cas said.

"Just the buttons, it will be excellent foreplay for the evening, but make sure Adara tackles the corset then."

"Do you think Roc needs to relax also?" Her mouth was so dry, she could barely swallow.

"Yes, he'll be nervous that he makes everything right for you tonight. What's in the package will help with all that. I promise."

"I trust you and I will do everything I can, but Roc is..."

"Persistent and knows what he wants." Ella finished for her, laughing. "Just like my Drake and we wouldn't want our men any other way, would we?"

"I don't know. He's the only man to kiss me." She didn't want to fear tonight but still she did.

"Now the last piece of advice is the most fun and the first time it will totally shock Roc."

"I don't think that's possible." Caitlin even relaxed her guard enough to laugh.

"So, whenever the mood strikes or you want to surprise him, and trust me, they love this, you follow my instructions."

Ella piqued her interest. "What would have that kind of effect on Roc? He so reserved, even stoic at times, and nothing seems to surprise him."

"Well," Ella leaned in close, "don't wear your underclothes but don't tell him. Let him find out for himself. Then you can tease them with thoughts of lovemaking in dangerous or well-populated space. They like the intrigue. Men like Roc and Drake live for the danger, and they don't get much of it these days."

"I don't...well, I don't know if I could do something like that."

"Of course you can, and you won't regret anything. After tonight it will be easier. Just think about how discovering you naked beneath your dress will make him feel."

Caitlin nodded but what Ella told her was scandalous and intriguing as well. "Is it time then?" She inhaled a long draught of air feeling as if she was going to her funeral not her wedding.

"I believe you're about to take your last steps as a single woman," Ella smiled as she spoke the words.

They stopped at the top of the stairs, David magically appearing by her side. "May I walk you down the aisle? I know I'm not your da, but I'd like to do this." He whispered as Ella walked down the steps to find a seat in the parlor.

"Of course, I'd be honored," she said.

The music started and Adara handed her a bouquet of violets and lilacs then walked ahead of her. Everything passed in a blur. Before she could blink, it seemed she was saying I do and Roc was putting a ring on her finger. Then he kissed her and she felt as if she would melt.

"To the bride and groom." Charlotte poured glasses of champagne for everyone. They toasted. Roc swept her into his arms and carried her up the steps to the ballroom on the third floor.

When he set her down, "Are you happy, Mrs. Leighton, Duchess of

Ravenswood?" She was staring into his deep brown eyes that seemed to hold so much passion she nearly swooned.

"Yes, I think so I mean I'm happy, just a bit nervous. In my wildest thoughts, I would have never believed I would be wed to someone like you."

"No need for nerves. I'm not going to ask you to dance without your fiddle. David has his bagpipes ready. Do you want to play for us? Your fiddle is over there." Roc nodded toward David.

"I always want to play, thank you."

The music was lively and Caitlin let herself be one with the songs. They played until everyone stopped dancing unable to catch a breath. Roc took the fiddle from her and placed it in its case.

"Time to cut the cake then we are going to be alone with each other. I want you all to myself." He drew her into his arms for a long breathtaking kiss, one that was greeted with applause from their guests.

"What is this? You dare a wedding without my permission?" The marquis stepped into the ballroom, stopping the celebration.

Drake moved between them, cutting off the marquis' path to Caitlin. "They are married as of two hours ago. Unless you want to celebrate the nuptials, I suggest you leave."

"She can't marry without my consent," the marquis insisted.

"Caitlin has wed and everything is in order, all the papers are signed as well. There is nothing you can do, especially since you have no proof that you are Caitlin's father. Again, unless you want to celebrate with us, you will leave."

Two of Drake's men appeared as if from nowhere by his side ready to escort him from the premises. He shook their hands off his arms before leaving. "You won't get away with this."

"Can we go now?" she asked, feeling as if the wedding suddenly turned somber.

"Not until we cut the cake," Roc insisted. "I want my bride to have everything with no disappointments or regrets. Do you realize I'm your husband now?" he whispered to her. "You can have your wicked way with me any time you like, and I'll never protest. I promise you I'll let you do whatever you want with my body."

She was a bit startled by his statement, not knowing what he was speaking of but trying to guess. "Yes, but I truly don't know what all that entails. All I understand is that I won't have a bastard if we do have children."

"Well, it means a whole lot more, and I intend to teach you some of it tonight. I promise, you'll have no misgivings when you give me my man's pleasure."

Man's pleasure? Well, of course you ninny, he would want pleasure too. But she didn't have any idea how to go about it. She thought things just happened. Changing the subject so she could think a bit more on what he said, "Ella gave us something. She made me promise to wear it tonight." She was looking into his eyes, wishing they were alone and that she didn't have to pretend.

"Us?" One eyebrow rose a fraction. "So, it's something for you to wear and for me to appreciate before taking it off. I can't think of anything more delightful. Shall we go now so we can see just what this gift is?"

"I suppose. She told me you'd know what to do. So, I guess I'll rely on your more educated self." She was rambling, she knew, but she was so beyond anything she understood as well as the not so subtle innuendos people were saying.

"You can't leave without the rice," Adara said as she and Ella passed little bags out to everyone there. "It's supposed to get in your hair and your dress," she laughed. "So Roc can have fun trying to get rid of it."

All assembled on the stairway. Roc looked at his Cat, and taking her hand, they started down the steps, laughing and holding their hands in front of their faces to ward off the rice which seemed to fall everywhere.

Roc's fancy carriage waited for them in front of the townhouse and after helping her inside, he settled her on his lap. His arms were around her while he whispered in her ear. "Have no worries about tonight. Try to relax." He trailed loving kisses down her neck and across her bodice.

She shivered even while an inferno seemed to grow inside her. "Roc," she let her head fall back enjoying the attention he gave her.

"What is it, Cat?"

"What is a man's pleasure and how do I have my wicked way with you? I really want to know everything." She sat up a little straighter, placing a hand on his cheek. "If it's something you want, well..." She ran her tongue across her lips, trying to make it easier for her to talk. "I'd like to do it for you. I want to give you everything you've ever wanted."

"You already have. I didn't have any idea what it was I craved several months ago but just sitting here with me, you give me untold delight. I like looking at your smile and seeing the passion in your eyes."

"That really doesn't help me," she said, thinking maybe if she kissed him that would be a start. With her hands on either side of his face, she drew him to her. He complied but made no move to kiss her as he usually did. She touched her lips to his then traced the seam with her tongue. She heard him groan deep in the back of his throat as he opened for her and her tongue slowly glided inside.

His hands on her waist tightened and moved higher until he cupped her breasts. She felt deep longing in parts of her she'd never realized existed until Roc started kissing her that first time not so long ago.

She needed to make this right for him. Mimicking him she trailed kisses along his jawbone, kissed the corners of his mouth then along his neck. She remembered how it felt when his bare hands rested on her naked back. Never had she felt so much desire.

Through the fabric of her gown, his thumbs flicked across her nipples. Then taking care not to rip the delicate gauze, he lowered the bodice. "My god." He breathed, lowering his mouth to draw a nipple into his mouth, his teeth grazing the bud and gently nipping. "I'm hard pressed to make it home." Quickly he pulled the gown up to cover her.

"Until we have more privacy, you need to tell me no." He breathed in a long gulp of air.

"You know I've never been able to do that. It has always been you who has stopped. I think I would have let you do anything you wanted." That fact was true and it was no different now, yet she was relieved he never made her his mistress. If he had, she was sure he would have never married her.

The carriage rolled to a stop and the door was opened, "We have arrived and now you can do whatever you want with me."

~ * ~

Blair O'Connell sat in the pub, downing pint after pint and chasing each one back with a shot of whiskey. Plans were made, details taken care of and the first chance he could find, he meant to whisk Caitlin away. The duke and his supposed power be damned.

He would take her to Gretna Green where he would wed and bed her. Never mind she was married to the duke of Ravenswood already. No one would have to know that. Once he had the new marriage certificates in hand, he would take her back to Portrush where the two of them belonged. If she was nice to him, he might even let her play her fiddle in the Rose and Thorn pub her da owned.

In Portrush where he had power, he could dispute the legality of her marriage here in London and take advantage of the judges he could buy. She would come to cherish all he gave her and if she held back, he'd show her who dictated and enforced the rules.

He waved his hand in the air, "Another one and bring me your special. Don't care what it is." As long as he had his beer and whiskey, food didn't matter to him. Sometimes the food seemed a bit tasteless, but he knew he had to keep his strength in order to carry out his plans.

Downing the drinks and the food he studied a map, plotting out the route they would take and the inns where they would stop. It would take them days to get there, but he would enjoy the time with Caitlin. He would make love to her every night. In his dreams she would call out his name, begging for more and he would give her everything she asked for. She would understand his generosity as well as his needs.

He smiled at the thought of seeing her naked, remembering how her butt had filled the duke's hands that evening. Needing to feel her silken flesh beneath his hands, he groaned. Perhaps he should find a willing woman to ease the ache he felt between his legs.

"Care if I join you?" With a smile and a wink, Addie sat down across the table from him, a large intimidating man standing behind her. "We have certain important things to talk about."

"You're a disloyal bitch," he said through gritted teeth, remembering the scene at Roc and Caitlin's wedding. "You owe me what I paid you. I'll take it all back or I'll find a way to make you sorry."

Addie pushed the coin across the table saying, "See that you leave town tomorrow. Tonight would be better, but that might put undue hardship on you. Poor thing." She laughed then, her smile sending chills down his spine. This was one dangerous lady.

He wasn't about to back down to a woman. "I'll leave when it pleases me," he told her, accepting the coin and pocketing it.

"Tomorrow or Hamilton will hire men to put you on whatever ship is leaving port. You could end up anywhere in the world. Certainly not Portrush or anywhere in Ireland." She smiled at him while Hamilton squeezed her shoulders in seeming approval.

"You wouldn't dare shanghai an earl." He muttered, sputtering saliva then stood. He meant to leave the tavern and leave town before these two could set any plans in motion, but it all deepened on Caitlin and how soon the duke would allow her out of their bed. If he were the bridegroom, it would be at least a week before either one of them saw the light of day.

"Of course we wouldn't do anything against the law. We'd pay your passage and you'd have the best quarters on the ship besides the captain's cabin. You'd sail in luxury." Hamilton moved away from Addie far enough so he stood eye to eye with Blair.

"That has to be illegal," he said, looking from one to the other, afraid they might do that very thing tonight.

"Maybe yes, maybe no." Hamilton lifted his shoulder slightly. "You would have to prove we put you on the ship against your will, and it would be our word against yours and the captain of the ship." He paused. "I'm sure they would be more than willing, for a tidy sum, to side with us. Indeed, most of the ships that sail into this port are friends of mine or the duke."

"You're despicable," Blair said, his body shaking with the anger boiling up inside. He didn't like that this man backed him into a corner and that a woman bested him. If he dared, he'd show her how a real man treated an uppity woman.

"No, just creative. I doubt if your purpose here is legitimate, and I wouldn't have anything happen to the new duchess of Ravenswood. She is treasured by all who know her," Addie said, her voice soft but years of practice helped make the sound threatening.

"I second that," Hamilton grinned.

"As soon as my business here is finished, I'll leave and you won't see me again. I find I'm not particularly fond of London. Is that good enough?" He would leave when he could find Caitlin alone and not a moment sooner.

"No, tomorrow is your deadline and before that you can leave by your means," Addie paused.

"Or ours," Hamilton finished for her.

Chapter Seven

Roc swept Cat into his arms, carrying her into the house then up the steps to the master room. When he kicked the door shut, he drew her close and kissed her deep. His huge body enveloping her as the need to protect at all cost consumed him. With a look and smile, she turned his life upside down and he didn't care. He embraced the sensations and emotions that set his life spinning out of control.

He tried to think only of tonight and his new wife, her needs as well as her fears. Putting a smile on her lips was the only thing he should be thinking about this evening. When she asked how she could have her wicked way with him, he nearly roared with laughter. He planned to teach her everything she needed to know to do just that.

He lifted his head and regarded her slightly swollen lips and passion filled violet blue eyes beckoning to him. Candlelight shimmering around the room reflected off her hair. "I believe the gift Ella gave you is sitting on the bed. Should I help you with the fastenings of this beautiful gown?" Truly he wasn't sure they would get as far as the gift if he saw the slender curve of her spine or the tender swell of her derriere.

"It's Adara." She poked her head through the door. "My eyes are closed. Hope everyone is still dressed."

The knock on the door left Roc groaning yet also understanding this was important to their wedding night. "Come in. Do what you need to do. Quickly, please."

"Ella told me I'm supposed to help Caitlin with taking off her dress. Don't think she wants you to rip it, and she especially wants Caitlin to dress in her gift." Adara slipped into the room, smiling. "Cook is on her way up with something for the two of to eat and drink this evening."

Roc stepped back, his arms crossed over his chest, watching as Ella grabbed the gift and with Adara following walked into the dressing room.

Before he turned away, Cat turned, looking over her shoulder smiling. "I'll be back soon."

"You better be," he whispered.

Then he took the time to open the door for the servants bringing food to come inside before he lit the fire.

He watched it for a few seconds as the flames leapt and danced, warming the room. If she was donning something he couldn't resist, he decided he was overdressed. Sitting down on the bed, he pulled off his boots and tugged his shirt lose from his trousers before unfastening the buttons.

He poured a small glass of brandy and watched as the food was delivered; smoked salmon and cheeses, several different pastries and two different bottles of wine. Sitting in a chair so he could have full view of his Cat when she stepped through the doorway, he sipped the brandy, letting the warmth settle in his stomach.

Adara stepped through first and with a little curtsy, she said, "She's truly beautiful but she's very nervous."

The door closing behind Adara seemed to be Cat's cue to step forward. She stood, framed in the doorway, her hands in front of her, dark hair falling around her shoulders.

His breath caught in his throat, "My God, Cat, you should see yourself." Maybe she shouldn't. She might run the other direction.

"Do you like it?" she asked, the hesitant smile knifing straight to his heart. "I can change if you don't."

For a moment he thought he'd died and gone to heaven. "Ella knew exactly what to give you. The lingerie is beautiful, you are absolutely gorgeous, and, no, I don't want you to change what you're wearing. Never change anything about yourself, for me or anyone else." Slowly, he walked toward her. She seemed to know what he wanted when she extended her hand to meet his.

"Are you sure?" she asked, seeming to need some reassurances. "You wouldn't lie to me, would you?"

"This is the perfect gift for you, for me, just like she told you. It was quite thoughtful." He didn't need to take it off to see her. Every curve Cat possessed, he could see, including the dark triangle of her woman's mound and the rosy pink buds that were her nipples. His body hardened with need for the woman he cared for more everyday he knew her.

"I feel exposed," she whispered, plucking at the fabric of the gown. "Can you see through the fabric?

Not wishing to answer her question, he led her to a white fur rug in front of the fire. She looked at him as if she wanted him to tell her what to do. He swallowed before he said, "You're supposed to look a little exposed. The husband is supposed to see his wife, all of her and this is just a way to ease you as well as any fears you might have. The fabric covering you gives the illusion of nakedness when indeed you are wearing two articles of clothing. Sit, please. No worries, you are completely dressed."

He busied himself pouring wine and filling a plate of food for both of them. She stared into the fire for the longest time before she spoke.

Then, "If you can see all of me, it's only fair that I get to see all of you. Don't you think? I've never seen any of you unclothed."

He watched as she let out a long breath of air from her lungs. "You're right." Quickly, he shrugged out of his shirt. Sitting beside her, he took her hand in his, placing the palm on his chest. "You can even touch me." He knew he was risking the loss of control, but she deserved to do whatever she wanted, and he could teach her what he liked because he meant to learn everything she liked.

"You're so hard and muscled. I'm nothing like that," she murmured while she brought the glass of wine to her lips and drank. Then, "I don't think I can eat anything."

"Let's watch the fire burn," he said, drawing her against him, her back resting on his chest, his arms circling her. His need to feel her beneath him so strong he groaned. What he needed right now was hardly relevant.

"I like the way you feel." She ran her hands along his arms. "I know you're different from me in other ways."

"And you know this how?" he queried while he moved her hair from the back of her neck and kissed the nape. He loved the tiny shiver of pleasure and the feminine mew of desire his kisses elicited.

"Everyone's seen paintings and statues," she told him, pushing into him, allowing his fingers to roam.

He choked, understanding that was a far cry from seeing a man fully aroused and he was closing in on that state of full arousal right now. "Of course, everyone has. How are you feeling? Still nervous?"

"A little." He set their glasses on a side table and turning her, he kissed her again, their tongues dueling. In this he'd taught her well. She explored and tasted then tested him, her fingers digging into his shoulders, her breath melding with his.

Running her hands down his chest they settled on his nipples, touching them hesitantly at first. He couldn't stop the groan of desire emanating from him. He understood he needed to move slowly and when her roving hands settled on his waistband and began to unfasten his pants, he stopped her. He could not let her innocent exploration get in the way of the enjoyment he meant to give her tonight.

"Not yet," he told her, wishing he didn't have to stop her. "Let me give you pleasure first. After we've made love, you can touch me anywhere and I won't object."

"You give me pleasure when you kiss me. Is there more?" She gazed into his eyes as he slowly slipped her robe from her shoulders.

He feasted his eyes on her breasts then threw the fabric of her gown bent to draw a nipple into his mouth while he cupped her other breast in his hand. Her hips moved and arched against him. She was wild with need, nearly spinning away from him, and he'd just begun. He needed to inhale the essence that was hers and slow this down.

Cat moaned softly, her fingers winding into his hair. Her nails bit into his shoulders before running her hands up and down his arms. He found her mouth again and molded it to his, opening it with his tongue then pushing forward with an ancient primal rhythm that was raw and enchanting at the same time.

She responded sweetly and with so much passion, desire emanating from her. Continuing to kiss her, he slid his hand along one leg and while he retraced his path, he pulled the fabric higher with his fingers. The length of her legs was well muscled and sleek, but the flesh was silken.

He continued until he reached her hipbone then sliding his palm across the flat of her belly, he did the same on the other leg. He felt the shudder of desire pass through her. With his teeth, he delicately undid the ties holding the fine gown to her shoulders and watched as the fabric slid to pool around her waist.

Her breasts were large and firm, the nipples surrounded with a rosy blush. They were tight buds begging for his attention. Instead, he swept her into his arms, letting the gown fall to the ground then proceeded to the bed.

With her legs spread, he came down on top of her, resting with his forearms braced on either side of her. God, how he wanted, no craved to make everything right this evening.

"Tell me what you like," he whispered, tracing the small shell of her ear then continuing with more kisses to every place he could find. He explored and touched every part of her while her body continued to arch, writhing against him and her breathy little sounds gave him reason to believe she was well pleased.

"Everything," she breathed, her hands resting on the fastening of his pants once more.

He allowed her to undo them, but when his fingers explored the soft and swollen feminine folds that waited for him, she gave a startled little cry. "Roc."

"Do you like this?" he asked, giving attention to the tiny bud nestled in her most private part and would eventually give her so much pleasure she wouldn't be able to move for a few seconds.

"Roc..." she breathed again. "What are you doing to me?" Her hips bucked against his hand. "I've never felt like this before."

Thank God. "What you're going to do to me in a few minutes. It's pleasure, that's all." He laughed inside, enjoying this passionate side of his wife. They would have years together and he meant to enjoy every moment of their lives.

"I can't, can't breathe." Her body suddenly shuddered and bucked, spasm after spasm taking over while she cried out. If he had been naked, he would not have been able to stop himself. He 'd be deep inside her. Now she was beginning to calm. He tried to soothe her, kissing her forehead before running his hands along her arms and letting her come down slowly.

"Did you like that?" he asked, eager to hear the answer even though he knew he pleased her.

"I can't move. I feel as if I'm very nearly without bones." She set her hand upon his cheek. "Do I get to do the same to you? Will you be totally unraveled when I give you a man's pleasure?"

"Don't ever doubt your power over me. I will be unraveled, without bones. I'm very nearly there just watching you climax." He kissed her again, trailed kisses down her legs then back up, stopping to taste her and give attention to her. Without much stimulation she was moving again.

He slid up the length of her body, stopping at her breasts to give them his devotion then her lips. When he kissed her again, he sat back. Pushing his trousers to his knees he moved enough to kick them to the floor. He was hard and fully aroused, ready to finally make Cat his in every way.

She gasped; her eyes wide yet he saw no fear. "You don't look like the statues and paintings."

He wanted to roar with laughter but heard the slight catch to her voice. Instead, "I'm aroused and in need of you. The artwork you speak of is the way a man appears in his normal state, not arousal and ready to make love."

"Oh." It seemed she thought over all he told her. "I didn't know."

He knew she was wet, slick with her cream and her body was ready to accept him. Slowly he slid inside until he touched the tiny barrier he would have to break despite his aversion to giving her pain. He didn't know if he should warn her of the pain, but he'd feel the cad if he surprised her.

"A small thing Cat," he said, watching her eyes widen as he continued to stimulate her.

"I'll feel a tiny bit of pain." She told him, her voice wavering.

"How did you know?"

"Ella told me a few things, but she said not to worry. You'll make everything right and other stuff. It would be over soon and after that there would be only pleasure." She paused, staring at him, "You're so big."

At that he lost all logical reasoning, realizing he'd never been with a virgin or even a woman who was a little bit innocent before. All the women he'd had relationships with were experienced and most of them more than a little bit jaded, losing their virginity long before they were with him.

"My size is not why it will hurt a little and only for a short time."

He wanted to say *are you ready* but stopped himself, realizing those words did not fit the situation. Perhaps he shouldn't have told her.

"I trust you." She touched his forehead as he slowly moved inside her. "I want to get the pain over with so there will only be pleasure. That's what Ella told me, only pleasure once the pain vanished."

He'd never felt this nervous before. Pain was not something he purposely brought on another person. When he broke through the barrier, he felt the quick reflex of agony shoot through her. She stiffened and a tear slipped down her cheek, yet she didn't cry out, didn't make a sound, yet her body suddenly turned rigid.

"I'm sorry," he whispered. "Making love with me will never hurt again. This was the only time and there was no way to get around it." If there had been, he would have done everything possible to make that happen.

When he felt her hips move to accept him, he filled her completely and when he felt the climax build within her and the fierce spasms sweep through her again, he drove deep inside her tight velvet walls and emptied himself within.

For several second, he propped himself above her. Cat's flesh shone with a fine layer of perspiration. He felt her heart race then slow as her breathing shifted from the rapid pace to an even slow one.

"Did I give you pleasure," she asked as he rolled off her, bringing her close.

"More than any man deserves." He wound her silken hair through his fingers, knowing this was not enough but for a while she might need to think on what they did.

"I'm parched," she said, resting her head on his chest and idly running her ringers along his chest and around his nipples. "Can we have some of that wine now? I might just be able to eat something." She pulled the covers up to cover her breasts.

He would allow her that for now. In the future, he hoped she would relax enough to remain naked in front of him. "You're no longer nervous?" he asked, standing. He heard the swift intake of breath when her gaze rested on him.

"You're perfect," she murmured, reaching out a second as if she meant to touch him, then quickly withdrawing her hand.

"Hardly." He strode around the bed and refilled the glasses, handing one to her before he brought the two plates of uneaten food to the bed.

"What should we talk about?" she asked him, still staring at him. It seemed the moment turned a little anxious.

In truth he could barely keep his gaze from remaining on her. "Anything you want and you can ask me any questions that come to mind." He fed a piece of cheese to her, letting her tongue touch his fingers. If he wasn't careful, this next seduction would happen before she ate.

"What do you think about the marquis? He seemed a bit strange to me. I'm thinking there were more reasons than one my mother ran from him." She followed his lead, feeding him a slice of cheese.

He sucked one finger into his mouth then holding her hand, he sucked and nibbled each fingertip. He loved the little mew of pleasure she gifted him with. "I agree with you. He overreacted to the fact I married you. Any other marquis in England would have reveled in the fact a duke married his daughter, a man who was not a wastrel or cad, one who could give his daughter everything she ever dreamed of."

She ate half a strawberry before feeding it to him, seeming to need a change of subject. "Ella told me some other interesting things, scandalous things to do for you. She says her husband loves her to be scandalous. Would you like that also?"

"I've never known Ella Montgomerie to do anything inappropriate. What is it she does? I'm curious." He put a slice of ham on a piece of bread before piling it with cheese.

"You would never know she's doing it, only Drake," Cat said seeming to realize she'd said too much and he didn't want to stop asking questions until she told him what he needed to know.

He held the mini sandwich up so she could take a bite. Then he finished and made another one, watching her sip the wine. "That's even more intriguing. Only Drake would know..."

"I shouldn't have said anything." She sipped more of the wine he poured, closing her eyes, seeming to enjoy the taste as it slid down her throat.

For a moment he thought she might fall asleep but she opened her eyes, her sooty lashes framing them. "Do you think Blair will just go home and leave me be?"

"I pray that he does. I don't have an easy feeling about the marquis or O'Connell. There is something off about both men." He knew he couldn't relax until O'Connell left for Ireland and the marquis stopped the creepy inquiries about Cat. "I'll have guards assigned to you whenever you leave the home."

"Where am I going to go?" she asked, turning to him and lifting her slim delicate shoulder in a shrug. "It's not like I know anyone here. I've more clothes than I need."

"You know Ella and my mother, Addie as well." He didn't want her to feel confined to this house or lonely. She needed someone besides Adara to talk to. He would have to think of some way to remedy this. "Would you like to ride out to the summer home? We can go tomorrow or the next day. Mother hasn't lived there in years, and she would be pleased if you redecorated. At the moment all the furniture is covered in sheets. We could make love in every room of the house."

"Are you certain? I wouldn't want to impose. Charlotte has been so nice to me," she said, sitting up.

The covers slipped to her waist and she started to pull them up. "Don't," he reached out to touch her. "I like to look at you."

She pursed her lips, gazing at him with a strained expression, seeming to think his words over. "I don't know if I can do that." Her face turned a beautiful shade of red.

"I've already touched and kissed I believe almost every inch of you. You shouldn't be shy."

"It's different when you're touching me. Most of the time I have my eyes closed," she said, holding the sheet up as if she thought he might rip it from her, her fingers clutching it tightly.

"You could eat with your eyes closed then I could look at you and you wouldn't be embarrassed," he said, laughing.

"Is that like...like the time you wrapped my ribs? I closed my eyes so I wouldn't see you looking at me." She smiled at him. "I'm trying to get used to this and I want to give you everything you ask for, but I'm not sure I can relax if I get rid of the covers."

146

He pulled her into his arms, kissing her soundly and uncovering a breast then cupping it in his hand. It would take more than one night of lovemaking to sweep the shyness away, but he would work on that. He realized she effectively changed the subject from Ella and her scandalous actions.

He would wait until Cat did the same and he was sure he'd be delighted with anything she did that was outrageous as long as he was the recipient of that scandalous behavior.

When he pulled back, her lips were slightly swollen and her breasts were uncovered to his gaze. Lightly, he touched each nipple with a fingertip and watched them harden instantly.

"Please," he said, his gaze lingering on the milk white globes, "let me look at you. I don't think I can ever get my fill."

She touched his chest, her eyes shining with passion. "Will you let me give you your man's pleasure now? I'm not sure what to do, but I've a feeling it's something different than when you came inside," she paused for a second. "Am I pregnant?"

He was surprised then not so surprised by her question given her mother's situation. "Probably not but you could be. Would that be alright with you if you carried my child?"

"I don't want to die, but I don't want you to stop loving me either."

That thought stopped him from pursuing his pleasure but he didn't care. He wasn't sure if she was ready for lovemaking that was so different. He would have to introduce her to different ways to make love and pleasure each other before she gave him his.

"The circumstances of your mother's death..." he paused, thinking of all the ways a woman could die in childbirth. "Do you know anything more than the fact she died?"

"Only Da said there was an infection. He had to deliver me and he didn't know anything. The midwife was somewhere else at the time, and I guess I wasn't waiting for anyone to get there and help out."

"Infections can be prevented. Your mother should not have died. Your hips are wide enough to bear children. You shouldn't have any difficulties, but there are no guarantees. For the future there are ways I can keep you from conceiving, if that's what you want."

"I think it's something to talk about. I know you must want children. It's just the fear of the unknown that makes me nervous, nothing more."

"We will have the best midwife in the city," he tried to reassure. "I promise and I've delivered a few babies myself."

"I do want your children. Make love to me and vanquish my fears. Trust is too important to forget."

~ * ~

Another day and night passed before the newly married couple emerged from their honeymoon chambers. When Caitlin woke up, Roc was gone from the room, a message on the tray with the hot chocolate and croissants she liked. Staring at the message and wishing she could read it, she nibbled on the pastry and sipped the cocoa. Winston knew, but she never told Rock she couldn't read or write.

Adara walked in. Cat inhaled a swift breath of air, hoping her maid could read. "Adara?"

"What is it?"

"Can you read?" Cat looked down for a moment then, "I can't." She held out the missive.

Adara accepted the note, "Most words. Have trouble with the really big ones." Then she began, hesitating when she came to a word she wasn't sure of.

Cat,

I miss you already. It seems if you're not around me, if I can't see you, I miss you.

Be ready in an hour and we'll explore Ravenswood estate. I'd like to make this home our main place of residence. That way I'll have you all to myself. Sharing you with anyone right now is not an option. The trunk filled with the clothes I bought you is now loaded and ready to follow us. I'll let you and Adara decide what you should wear today and pack the rest of the clothing mother purchased for you.

I can hardly wait to see what we can do with the

home. As the summer warms maybe we can swim naked in the nearby lake. In any case, I digress. Meet me downstairs in an hour.

Yours truly,
Roc

Adara stammered a few times and blushed when she read the part about swimming naked in the lake but didn't say anything. Beast darted in, jumping on the bed to greet his mistress. "My goodness, I didn't expect the two of you to emerge from the bedroom so soon. Now I hear we're leaving town for Ravenswood."

"We are. Roc must have grown restless." Caitlin wrapped her arms around Beast, giving him a hug before she smoothed the bed sheets, remembering all that had transpired since they were married.

"Well, it's a very good morning, I guess there are a few things that need to be tended to before we can go. I've called for a bath for you. Is there anything else I can get you?"

"Yes." Caitlin sat up, keeping the covers pulled high and pushing her hair away from her face before tying it behind her head. "I need you to find a day dress that fastens in the front. Go ahead and pack everything else. I'm not wearing anything beneath the gown." With those words and watching the horror on Adara's, face she felt a rush of heat cover her entire body.

"Are you sure?" Adara asked, gazing at her as if she was truly insane. "What will the duke think?"

"Positive, and I'm hoping once he discovers it, he will enjoy what comes next," Caitlin said, grinning before laughing softly. "When you find someone to marry, we can have a little sit down about these things. Ella Montgomerie gave me a long list of things to do to keep my husband interested in only me. I plan on trying all of them including swimming naked with him even though I can't swim."

"I'll trust your judgment on this idea. You need to know that I'm coming with you to Ravenswood. Winston will be driving you and the duke. I'll be in another carriage with Cook. I think Roc has sent other servants ahead of us to prepare the home. I'll leave while you take your bath. Ring when you're finished and I'll help you dress." She paused. "Do you need help? You won't have anything to lace up or..."

"I will need help slipping the dress over my head. Other than that, no. I'll summon you when I need you. Are you all packed?"

"Yes, milady. The duke told us early this morning when he strolled down the steps with the widest grin on his handsome face that I've ever seen."

Adara left and with the bath filled, Caitlin slipped into the warmth of the water. Roc's words of swimming naked in the lake sent a wave of trepidation simmering through her. She didn't know how to swim. Lakes and rivers frightened her. Why she felt at ease in the ocean left her confused, but perhaps it was because she never let the water rise higher than her knees.

Beast settled his head on the rim of the tub, silently asking her to pet him. Doing his bidding, she continued to think about the events to come.

Ah, but she could do that in a river or a lake too. Well, best she hurry. Roc told her she should be ready in an hour. She didn't know how Roc would know when an hour was up, but she didn't doubt he would.

She held her nose before she ducked under the water. Soaping her hair, she tried not to think about Roc's reaction to her plans. She prayed it would be on the scope of what Ella told her. But Roc wasn't Drake. He was a man, though, and Ella told her they think with their cock not their head and this crazy plan of hers would have Roc doing just that if the last two nights were any indication.

She finished the bath and wrapping a large bath sheet around her, she called for Adara. Only a few seconds passed before her lady's maid opened the door.

"You're ready to dress? Well, almost dress. Are you sure this is something you want to do?" Adara asked, eyeing the dress hanging nearby. "You can always change your mind." She stopped, "Why, the bodice is very nearly see through."

"Positive and I won't change my mind." Caitlin let the towel slip to the floor then holding her arms over her head, she let Adara help her.

"I just don't understand why you would do this." Adara fastened all the buttons before stepping back with a little gasp. "I can see your nipples through the fabric. You can't possibly want that. What will your duke say?"

Caitlin grinned. "That's exactly what I want. Roc loves to see my breasts and touch me, but I don't want him to know right away. I set a small jacket aside that I believe will cover me just enough so that when I move certain ways and if he's paying attention, he'll get a glimpse of what I'm offering." She had not realized until now that the fabric of this gown was almost as sheer as the lavender lingerie Ella gave her for a wedding night gift.

"I don't understand why you want to parade around half naked. The gossip will be horrible, and you'll end up a pariah. The ton will never cease their rabid talk. And you, just newly married. The scandal." Adara stood in front of her, ringing her hands, a gloomy expression on her face.

"That's just the thing, no one but my husband and of course you will see me. No one will gossip or spread rumors about something they know nothing about. You're not going to spread gossip, are you?" Tapping a toe, Caitlin waited for a response.

"No, of course not. I'd never say anything," Adara said with a little sob, "You must believe me."

"Good, then there is no problem, is there? Of course I believe you and trust you. Now, I might see you later tonight, but given the circumstances of my clothing, I won't need your help to undress, besides Roc like to undress me more than anything."

Together they walked down the stairs, Beast following. Roc stood at the bottom, a huge grin on his handsome face. "You're on time and you look more beautiful than I've ever seen you."

"You gave me an hour. I didn't need more than that," she said trying for a prim air but even in her own mind she knew she didn't succeed.

He held out an arm for her. She wound her hand around his upper arm, enjoying the play of his muscles as they walked. Her nerves seemed to be stretched parchment thin, her heart racing.

"Are you eager to be somewhere other than our bedroom?" he asked as he helped her into his carriage. "I know I am, although I loved the scenery there and I don't think I can ever get enough."

"I'm eager to be anywhere with you." She looked out the window at Adara who's expression was sorrowful; perhaps it was more worried.

"I'm going to be just fine," she said to the young woman who'd been through so much with her.

Adara nodded as the carriage drew away from the townhouse.

Catlin sat back, smiling and letting the tiny jacket that barely covered her tempt Roc. "Do you have any old friends or just people you know who you might want to visit us?" She moved slowly, hoping he would get a glimpse of what she tried to reveal.

"Do you like to surround yourself with people?" he asked, touching her chin and turning her to look at him.

"I don't know anything about parties and entertaining, but I want to please you." She didn't wait for an answer. "I know I please you in bed, but I mean in other ways. You understand I know nothing of the aristocracy and their ways. I attended one ball that was a disaster. I've never gone to the opera or a play, but I'm willing to learn whatever you want to teach me."

"I'm not much for the opera or plays and the entertaining I do would just be friends and family. I appreciate your offering though." He kissed her, running his hands along her arms before winding his fingers through her hair, the pins holding it in place flying through the air.

"I mean it, Roc." She pushed away the jacket slipping slightly. His eyes riveted on her. Inside, she smiled but she wasn't ready to end this conversation. "I don't want you to find me lacking in the future when you grow tired of making love to me."

"I'll never grow tired of you or your body." It seemed he didn't see what she revealed or he was playing games with her also.

But she didn't think he was capable of ignoring her when she was so blatantly offering herself to him. "Roc, I want to be the perfect wife. Who can we invite for dinner?" She paused, touching his chest. "Besides Ella and Addie and their collective spouses? They are the only people I know."

He sat back, gazing at her with a strange expression. "There are the Maxwell's, Logan and Eveleen. Logan provides all that wonderful wine we drink. They ended up with a winery in Tuscany that I won in a game of chance. I gifted my mother with it, and she sold it to Eveleen for a tiny amount so she would have something to give Logan for Christmas."

"We should do that, invite them. Does anyone else live close by, any cousins of Ella's?"

"No, but maybe we could host a reunion of sorts. It's been a couple of years since they've all been together. Mother would love something like that," he said, settling one hand on her shoulder.

"You could help me plan and your mother will help too? Maybe in August." She shuddered as he slipped the jacket from her shoulders. "W..." She swallowed hard, suddenly realizing her plans were about to be revealed. "We should write the cousins in America."

"What have we here?" He bent. His lips closed over her lightly veiled nipple. She let her head fall back as she sucked in a deep breath of air. Between his fingers he rolled the other nipple while his teeth bit gently. When he looked up, "You couldn't wait until this evening? This is very naughty, and I love the scandalous idea of yours. Is this one of Ella's ideas? The one you were talking about on our wedding night?"

"Couldn't wait and yes." She breathed in a gulp of air, her raspy breaths causing her to close her eyes. "Didn't want to...Ella." She sighed with the pleasure he created so easily within her.

"Do you have any other surprises?" He molded his lips to hers, their tongues dueling, playing chase.

She wound her fingers through his hair, her nails biting into his scalp. "Don't know what you're talking about."

"You have barely anything on up here, where I can see the curve of your breasts and your nipples. Do you have anything on beneath your dress? Should I find out?" he asked, his voice husky with the desire she loved so much.

"Only if you want to find out." She could barely breathe. Air seemed to be nonexistent.

"Would I disappoint you if I didn't explore beneath your skirts? You've shocked me, you know? I'm not sure I can keep from swooning at the very idea."

She laughed at his words. "I can't imagine you ever swooning. And you don't need to explore anywhere you don't want to discover."

He pulled her onto his lap as she let out a gasp of surprise. "You know me better than most," he whispered as his tongue traced the shell of her ear and his hand settled on one leg. "Should I find out what isn't beneath your skirt?" His voice seemed to shake with passion and desire.

She liked what she did to him with just the suggestion of nothing on. How would he react when he discovered the truth? "You almost always do what you want..." she tried for a seductive tone but understood that wasn't in her repertoire.

"But not with you." He bit gently on her earlobe. Yet his hand now rested at the top of her stockings.

Surely, he must feel the naked skin above. "I won't stop you if that's what you're asking."

"Stop what?" he asked as his hand moved higher, fingers kneading and caressing naked flesh.

Her body was fully aroused, had been since she first put the dress on and thought about him deep inside her. He would know she wore nothing beneath her skirt. She couldn't think. He could do that to her, make her boneless and mindless all at the same time. "I don't know."

Unconsciously, she moved her legs, giving him access to her core. "Aw, *mon petite chatte*, you are very naughty." He slipped a finger inside her and with his thumb gave his attention to the small nub nestled inside her feminine folds.

He teased her and excited her, but he didn't bring her to climax. She moaned, needing her release. "Roc, please."

"We are almost there, home. Just as I have to wait, so do you. I wouldn't want to shock Winston." He withdrew his hand, letting it rest on her naked belly.

"I need..."

"I understand. As soon as we have more privacy, I'll see to our needs. We will find the first room to make love in." He stole a quick kiss then lowered his hand once more, keeping her arousal intact but not bringing her to climax. She clung to him, her nails raking down his chest. She needed to feel him, but he kept her from pulling his shirt from his waist band.

"I don't think Winston can be shocked," she said, closing her eyes while inhaling a deep breath, wishing they were in their bedroom.

"You'd be surprised." He continued to tease and withdraw then tease again. "Winston has always been shocked where I'm concerned."

She tried to squirm off his lap, needing to touch his arousal she felt pulsing against her, but he wouldn't allow it.

"Roc, I'm sorry..." She couldn't breathe. "I...I won't ever do this again," she told him.

"Do this whenever you want. This is so surprising and intriguing, exciting. I'll always be wondering what you wear beneath your dresses. Don't put any underclothing on ever again and I will die a happy, contented man."

"Just do this. I don't think I can wait any longer..." she moaned softly. "I didn't know exactly how intense this would be, what I've set in motion."

He had an image of her and where this would lead, something he dreamt of the night before and he was going to do this his way. Keeping her stimulated and ready was his to do but he didn't like making her wait for her release.

"You can wait. Your climax will be even sweeter when it's prolonged." It seemed she would not have to wait too much longer.

"Only a few more minutes. See, we've stopped." He withdrew his hand and smoothed her skirts then adjusted her jacket to more fully cover her.

Before Winston opened the door, Roc jumped from the carriage. "Wait outside for a few minutes. I want some privacy with my wife."

She didn't know what Winston said, could only assume he agreed. Unable to move, she was thrilled when Roc reached into the carriage and swept her into his arms.

"I'm going to carry you over the threshold of our second home. Don't want any bad luck. Then I'm going to help you to your release. Is that alright?"

She couldn't do anything but nod, so aroused she needed relief this instant. "I'm fine."

"Little liar, you're wet and more than ready for me, but it's a sweet lie and I appreciate it." He swept her into his arms striding swiftly into the home. When they were inside, he let her feet touch the ground. "Wrap your legs around my waist."

"Do what." She could barely comprehend what he said. "Do..."

He helped her, pulling her legs around him. "Keep your legs around my waist."

"I..." Yet she clung to him as he strode through the house.

"I always wanted to do this."

His pants were down and he was on her back, his fingers inside her then he was inside her deep and penetrating. He drove deep. She felt as if he must indeed touch that part of her that would create his child. "Roc!" She cried out. "Roc."

His groan was deep and guttural, the moment so intense she knew they would never again create what they shared this second, mercuric and primal all of her seemed to sweep into him as he released himself inside her. For those few moments they were as one and perhaps in those moment they made a child.

"Roc."

The sound penetrated her foggy mind. She stiffened beneath him.

"Everything is fine, Winston. I told you to give us a few minutes. Go away before I fire you."

"Yes, sir. Sorry, sir, didn't see anything."

The sound of their breathing was all that could be heard. She had done this to them. This didn't compare to the lovemaking in their bedroom. There was something about the elemental danger of being seen that made the moments so intense and enduring.

"Are you alright?" Roc asked, brushing hair from her face.

She felt the dampness of her hair pressed against her face. "I'll never be the same again."

"I promise you we are going to make love in every room of this house." Roc stood back, gazing at her as if he was seeing her in a very different light.

"Can we do that? How many rooms are there?" She wasn't at all certain she had the endurance for something so intense, feeling boneless and spineless at this moment. She didn't think she could walk.

"Not today," he laughed, pulling her to a sitting position and adjusting her clothing as well as his, "but perhaps in the next few days or weeks. As soon as you think you're ready, we can take a look at the house."

She smoothed her skirts then with a tiny grin, "Thank God, I would have never been able to stay alive if you wanted to have sex in every room today."

He held out his arm to her after he lifted her from the table and set her down. "Shall we explore? You're going to have to keep in mind I know what you're not wearing and that is exactly where my thoughts are going to be."

"Should I go upstairs and put on more clothing?" she asked, afraid she might have unleashed a monster in both of them.

"Absolutely not. I want to enjoy thinking about the next place we'll make love. While I told you not every room today, that doesn't mean I'm not going to let you enjoy my charms a few more times before we retire for the night."

The sharp breath she inhaled gave her some fortification for the rest of the day. "Alright then, what room do you want to look at next?" she asked, prepared for whatever developed.

"The kitchen, I believe. Cook is going to need all of the latest appliances. We will have to restore that area first or she will have a fit and quite possibly leave. I know you can't cook and neither can I. Everything is old and needs replacing." He led the way.

"I don't have any idea what she might need. Don't you think you should let Cook make a list and you can buy her what she asks for?"

"Heavens, I'm surprised a bonny lass such as you doesn't know how to cook," he laughed.

She hit him on the arm. "You know all I ever had was a woodstove. I boiled water for tea and that was just about all. And," she paused, "you also know I ate all my meals at the pub."

"I don't need a wife who can cook and you know that fact as well." He proceeded through the dining room to a small kitchen. "Yes, we must purchase a new stove and fix up the scullery too. I do believe I'll send Winston into town with Cook so she can pick out the very best. Now, would you like to have sex in the kitchen or the scullery?"

Beast barked, seeming to enjoy himself.

~ * ~

The marquis of Rushingham crossed his arms over his chest and regarded the newly remodeled small upstairs room. He remembered Fiona fondly. She refused to become his mistress so he kidnapped her and kept her in this room, making love with her most every night despite her protests. She didn't really mean to protest; it was just a game to get him more excited. He was a marquis after all.

He gave her everything she could have ever wanted, including himself. But she still left him. He never figured out how she got out a locked door. She'd had to have help but his staff was loyal. At least he thought they were.

In any case, he would have never believed she could get back to Ireland without funds. He searched the ports and the roads leading out of London, finding no trace of her.

"Sir?"

"What?" He turned to see his upstairs maid.

"You wanted me to clean the room," she told him. "I've finished with that. Is there anything else?"

"Yes, new curtains and bedding to add to the new furniture I bought. I'll purchase clothing for our new arrival. We're going to have a visitor."

"Has Fiona returned? If so, what will you tell your wife?"

"No, but a very lovely lady will occupy this room. Perhaps this time she'll stay with me. And," he paused, "if you're concerned about my wife, there is no need. She doesn't need to know anything."

"Yes sir, I'll make sure everything is ready. Does she have a name?" the maid asked. "I need to know what to call her."

"Caitlin, and she's to be allowed to play her fiddle anytime she likes. She's really quite good," he said, remembering his first love Fiona. She played the fiddle too but nothing like Caitlin.

He needed Fiona desperately, but Caitlin would have to do. His body hardened with need as he remembered his Fiona. She had fought him though, at least until he subdued her.

He rubbed his head, it hurt to think of her and that she left him. Caitlin was his now. She would have to take Fiona's place in his heart. No one but him would have her.

He turned, striding down the steps to the first floor, putting his plan of abduction into action. Damn Ravenswood for making this harder than it should be. The man moved her out to his summer home, so far from the city and more difficult to get Caitlin alone.

Determined though, he'd find a way.

"Darling, where have you been?" His wife sat in the parlor, sipping tea.

It seemed to the marquis that was all she ever did. Compared to Fiona, she was a mouse of a woman. He needed children, an heir or two having lost his sons to a freak accident. His first wife died of grief, so he wed again.

"Making plans for our anniversary." He bent and kissed her cheek before walking to the sideboard and pouring a glass of whiskey.

"Do you have something exciting in mind? I love it when you surprise me." She smiled at him and all he could see was Fiona.

"Very exciting." He'd have to find some way to rid himself of his wife. Fiona would give him another child. But he'd wait until Fiona was upstairs secured in her old room.

"I'm so pleased. You've been inattentive of late, and I was afraid you were growing tired of me."

"Never that, my darling." He pulled her into his arms, kissing her before lifting her skirts.

My Fiona.

Chapter Eight

"I've barely seen you the last week and a half," Roc bent to kiss her, a chaste kiss but heavenly just the same when she turned in his arms to accept him.

"Liar," she laughed, "we've made love in five rooms and you've kept me awake every night. I'm going to need my sleep, a full night of it soon. Perhaps you should go into town."

"That much of you is not enough of you and I've no pending business in town." He swept her off her feet, twirling in a circle. "Cook packed a basket for us. Why don't we take a ride this afternoon and enjoy the sunshine, watch the sunset?" Truly, he didn't want to let her go. "You can't say no."

"I don't want to say no but you also understand I can't ride a horse. Should I run along beside you?" she asked indignantly, petite hands on her shapely hips.

"No, of course not, but don't you think it's about time you learned to ride? It is something every lass should know how to do." He studied the expression on her face, waiting for an answer. She could tell him she didn't want to learn and he'd let it go for today. Holding her in his arms while they rode to the lake would be just as pleasant, possibly more.

"I'm afraid of horses," she said, wiping her hands on her dress. "Won't they know?"

"I'm really a very good teacher, but if you don't want to learn..." He needed to challenge her to overcome her terror of an animal that could be a friend if ever in need. He was still worried about O'Connell and the marquis. He'd not seen either of them in days. Addie and Hamilton promised him they would take care of O'Connell, but as of yet, they had not left a message.

"I'll try if you insist," she said with a heavy sigh. "Just because I believe you're right about learning."

"I insist," he said, wishing she hadn't let that one word be part of the bargain. "Go change. Ask Adara to bring out the riding habit I bought for you." He paused briefly. "It wouldn't be prudent to go without underclothing. I want you to ride astride, sidesaddle is useless in an emergency." Good lord, but she'd surprised him several times, and now all he could think about when he was with her was what she didn't have on beneath her dress.

She nodded, "Kiss me first for courage then I'll change my clothes and be down here as soon as possible."

The kiss was short and very sweet. He was tempted to put everything aside and find another room in the house to make love to her in, but the lake would do for today. "Go, I'll be waiting for you right here."

He watched her as she left then, "Winston." He had several errands for his man to arrange for him.

The man appeared as if he'd been waiting for the summons. "Sir, what can I do for you?"

"I want you and three other men to follow behind the duchess and myself. Stand guard at the lake but far enough away we can have privacy. We will be swimming. And," he paused a second in thought, "send someone to the Winthrop estate and bade them come to Ravenswood."

"Naked, I presume," Winston said with just a hint of disapproval. "You make that lass do things..."

Roc waved his hand in the air dismissing Winston's words. "It's not your concern and I don't make her do anything. She's a willing, no, more than willing participant in our escapades." For a moment he almost told him about Cat's part in their lovemaking and the way she teased him, but thankfully he held his tongue."

"Of course it isn't sir, but I had to mention what all the servants are talking about. Perhaps you...never mind. I'll do as you asked." He turned quickly, leaving to do his bidding.

"The servants should not have loose tongues. They needn't talk about Cat and myself. Let them know if I hear any more gossip, the perpetrators will be dismissed."

"Yes, sir."

In the kitchen, "Cook, what have you packed? I'm sure it's amazingly delicious," he poked through the basket unwilling to wait for her to tell him.

"Fried chicken, smoked salmon, some tomatoes and cucumbers and array of berry tarts for afterwards. Two kinds of wine picked from those Logan sent you for a house warming."

"Looks delectable. Do you like the new kitchen and scullery?" he asked, sampling one of the tarts.

"Don't you eat all of this before the missus can have some. She's a wee little thing. You make her eat more. And yes, the kitchen is wonderful. Perfect in every way."

"Good, if there's anything else I can get you let me or Caitlin know." He left with the basket in hand, whistling one of the tunes Cat played most often.

When he entered the parlor, Cat was waiting for him. "You're late," she said, smiling. "Am I dressed right? Adara assured me this was a riding habit, but if it's something else, I wouldn't know." She lifted her shoulder in a tiny shrug while she grinned at him.

He offered an arm, "You're perfect. Shall we get our first riding lesson?" he asked, grinning as he thought of her very first riding lesson, which involved him not a horse.

"You do understand, I'm terrified." She held back a moment but stiffening her spine, she walked forward. "I can do this."

"Of course you can. Any girl who can crawl a quarter mile to my house with broken ribs in the middle of the night can learn to ride a horse. This is so much easier."

She remained silent as they made their way to the stables. Her hands shook, but he was determined she learn and it seemed his Cat was just as single-minded as he was.

He stopped in front of a light brown mare, "This is your horse. She's docile and if we had children, I would teach them with her. I call her Sweety because that's her nature. Here." He handed her a few pieces of apple he pulled from the basket. "She loves apples."

162

"Like this," she asked, holding out her quivering hand. "Will she bite?"

"No, not Sweety. Put it on the palm of your hand then hold still." He crossed his arms in front of him, watching her and admiring her determination.

She laughed when Sweety took the piece of apple from her, "Her tongue tickles." Then she wiped her hand on her skirt.

"See, nothing to be alarmed over." He stroked the mare and nodded for Cat to do the same. "You want her to like you and be eager to see you when you walk into the stables even if it's only because she wants an apple."

Thirty minutes later they left the stables on the way to the lake. His guards fell into place a discreet distance behind them.

"You're a natural," he told her. "You're born to ride just as you play the fiddle."

"This doesn't feel natural at all," she grit out. "And my backside hurts."

"Good thing we're not going very far." He told her, laughing inside at her refreshing honesty. He'd never been with a woman who would blurt out the truth or wear nothing under her dress. That thought gave him reason to smile.

"It certainly is a good thing. I might not be able to walk if I have to ride her much farther."

"Don't tense up, try to relax. Sweety's not going to go any faster than she is right now. You're doing fine and we'll be there in another five minutes" This outing was exactly what he needed with his Cat with the added benefit of a riding and swimming lesson.

"Easier said than done," she told him, but she was moving with the horse, seeming to understand they could be one with each other. "I believe I'm catching the hang of it."

He pointed to a spot in front of them. "Right over that hill and you'll see the most beautiful lake in the world. We can swim or eat. Then we'll stay here until the sun has set."

"Did I tell you I don't know how to swim?" She paused for a few seconds. "Did you bring something to wear in the water?"

"Did you?" He rode close to her, "I plan on making love to you in the lake. Don't need clothing for that. Indeed, it would get in the way, don't you think?" He watched as color rose to her face. "Nothing to be embarrassed about. I've seen every beautiful inch of you, tasted and touched as well."

"What if someone..." she hesitated. "I don't care if you see me. I adore the way your eyes shine with passion when I'm naked in front of you. But..."

"They won't. No one would dare interrupt our tryst. Besides, we have guards with specific instructions." He pulled her onto his lap, enjoying the feel of her in his arms, knowing he'd never stop wanting her.

"What kind of instructions and what if the guards... They won't see us, will they?" She sounded indignant. "And why did you do that? I was riding just fine."

"Do what?" His lips molded against hers. She tasted of mint as he inhaled her breath into him, felt her tongue glide against his.

It seemed she no longer needed an answer. Despite the fact his horse had no direction, the stallion knew where to go, and her little mare followed closely behind, Beast trotting behind Sweety. With her in his arms he slid to the ground. He didn't want to let her go. With a sigh, he set her on her feet.

"Let's walk." She stroked his cheek, smiling at him. "I need to stretch my legs and make sure they can really move."

"You want to walk?" He had other plans, but he decided he'd humor her.

"Yes, and talk."

"About what?" He was suddenly curious.

"I'm not really sure if you can answer my questions, you being a man and all, but I don't have anyone else to ask. If your mother were here or Ella I'd ask them..." She let her voice trail off, looking at him with a strange expression, one he'd never seen before.

"I'll try to tell you everything I know." He felt intrigued as well as concerned. His Cat rarely asked questions that seemed personal. "What do you want to know?"

"I..." She sucked her lip into her mouth then, "Never mind," She skipped ahead of him.

He inhaled a sharp breath following her then falling in step with her. "You can't say something like that then leave me wondering what is on your mind. You wouldn't have begun this conversation if it wasn't important to you."

"It's just that." He watched her swallow, clearly apprehensive. She turned away from him but he needed to see into her eyes.

"It's just what?" He held her by her shoulders so she had to look at him. "Ask the question. I promise I won't judge if that's what you're afraid of."

"There is so much I don't know or understand about us, about you. We said we were going to talk about it but we haven't." He watched her eyes close as her body shook.

"Whatever question is on your mind can't be so bad." Trying to be patient, he waited.

"Not bad, at least I hope not but like I said, we didn't talk about it and I don't know what you want or how you will feel and there is nothing I can do about it now." She tried to walk away but he held her, wrapping an arm around her.

Confused, he didn't know where or how to proceed in this conversation that didn't seem to lead anywhere. "Cat..."

"How do I know if I'm pregnant?" she suddenly blurted out, a lone tear slipping from her eye. "I don't want you to be angry with me if I am and I don't know if I am. Do you even want children? It's just that..." She was rambling and it was endearing.

His heart soared at the thought of a child, his child, a child with his Cat who meant more to him than life. At one time, not so long ago, he believed he'd never be so lucky. "I'm ecstatic. Why are you asking?" He needed a few simple facts before he jumped to conclusions.

She looked away, a soft flush caressing her cheeks. "It's not something I've ever talked about. Ida helped me when I first started but after that..."

Once again, she wasn't able to finish the sentence. "What did you first start?" He now had a pretty good idea where this conversation was headed but he didn't want to embarrass her more.

"Never mind, let's try that swimming stuff. It's probably time for all that."

"You can't swim," he reminded her. "But the naked stuff you're pretty good at. I'll teach you but one lesson will not be enough to have you knifing through the water."

"Maybe we could eat first." She changed her mind while she stared blankly at the water rippling and reflecting the sunlight. Beast bounded into the lake, splashing and barking.

"Seems he doesn't need a swimming lesson." Roc laughed at the big dog's antics.

"Too bad I can't just jump in and know what I'm doing. This swimming thing would be so much easier."

"We'll eat first, only if you really ask me that question you teased me with earlier." She'd not had her woman's time since they were married. And he tried to calculate the days since they were married. It was going on three weeks. Inwardly, he smiled but he had to find a way to broach the subject to make her more at ease. He needed to have her speak openly with him and not be afraid or embarrassed.

"I really don't want to talk about it right now and I'm hungry." She sat down on the blanket he'd spread a second ago. "I think I could eat a horse."

"Better not let Sweety hear that," he laughed. "She might not let you ride her again and you'll have to walk home."

She looked to her mare, "Sorry."

He decided to play along with her. He'd know for sure soon enough. "What is your pleasure?" He pulled out the wine first. Uncorking the bottle, he poured them both a glass.

"Anything, I really am hungry and I'm sure everything Cook packed I'll enjoy," She sipped the wine then gazed at him over the rim.

Roc knew not to press her for questions or talk. They finished eating. He leaned against a boulder, watching her. "Do you want to try swimming now?" he asked while he unlaced his shirt and drew it over his head. Next he kicked off his perfectly shined Hessian boots.

It seemed Beast didn't want to swim. He lay down beside her, his big head resting on his paws, drooling.

"I suppose so. Are you sure no one will find us?" she asked as he turned his attention to unfastening her riding habit, letting his fingers whisk across tender skin.

A few minutes later and they were both naked. His body responded to the sight of hers. Full breasts, slender waist and long supple legs beckoned to him. With a groan of unsatisfied desire, he swept her into his arms and carried her to the lake, telling himself now was not the time. Swimming lesson first then a touch of heaven with the liquid caressing them.

Wading into the water he waited until they were waist deep to set her down. "You can touch here." He needed to help her feel confident and safe. "I bet if you tried to go underwater you couldn't."

"That's one bet I'm not going to take you up on," she told him, holding on to him even though her feet were solidly on the ground.

"Maybe another time."

She stood, the water just below her breasts. Slowly he reached out to touch one nipple with the tip of his finger, amazed at its rapid transformation. There was so much more for them to enjoy with each other and today he wanted this to be about her.

Beast suddenly bounded into the water, splashing them. She moved closer to him, shielding her face from the water droplets filling the space around them.

"Beast, no!" he said forcefully, but the dog didn't mind. He swam next to them, pressing his nose into Caitlin's back as if he encouraged her to try and swim.

"Beast," Caitlin said. "Can you get him to leave?"

"Probably not. When he gets tired of being ignored, he'll probably give us a moments reprieve." And true to form a few minutes later, Beast paddled back to shore.

"Guess he does mind better than I thought."

"Should we try this again?" he asked unable to keep his hands from roaming to her breasts.

"The water's a little chilly and should you touch me like that? I thought you were going to teach me something first." With each passing moment, she seemed to cling to him tighter. "Let's get out."

"Not until you've at least tried to float. One step at a time, turn around and you can float on your back." He did want her to learn to swim and he needed to take this seriously, but he just wasn't sure he could when she was naked.

"Just like that?" She appeared skeptical. "I'm not going to take my feet off the ground."

"I'll help. Tilt your head back," he told her while he placed one hand near the small of her back and the other beneath her head. "Now all you have to do is relax and the water and your natural buoyancy will do the rest."

She hesitated then looking over her shoulder, "You won't let go? Promise?"

"Only if you're floating by yourself." He encouraged, pushing on her back to make her float, watching as her legs glided to the surface. "There."

Her eyes were closed but her body rested on the surface. He moved so he stood beside her, still supporting her back, but he couldn't resist her breasts. Slowly he lowered his head, letting his mouth close over one puckered nipple then the other.

"Roc!" She sat up flailing, her feet kicking, fighting the water to find the ground.

"I couldn't stop myself. Hope you don't mind too much. You were floating very well."

"This isn't going to work if you keep taking advantage of me." She swiped wet hair from her face. "I should at least wear some undergarments and you wouldn't be so tempted."

"That would probably be even more erotic and tempting. Hold onto my shoulders and let your body float to the surface. Don't let go of me." He swam with her then. Their bodies erotically brushed against each other with each sure stroke.

"Even in this cold water, you make me hot," she whispered, her nails biting into his shoulders. Am I doing this right?"

He stopped where only he could touch down. "Perfect," he murmured. "Wrap your legs around me, *mon petite chatte*. I need to feel your skin against mine, with only the gentle slide of water between us."

168

She did and he was rewarded, his rod pulsing against her core. "You should make love to me now," her words a throaty whisper against his neck while she bit gently.

Water sliding between them enhanced every movement, each sweetly hot caress until they both cried out with the pleasure created between them. Her head fell against him as she clung to his body.

"You are mine, only mine." He soothed her, caressing her back until her body finally relaxed against his.

Slowly he swam back to shore and carried her from the water, stopping at the blanket where the food had been set out and pulled out the huge towel that he managed to stuff into the basket. He dried her off, taking the time to caress all of her then he helped her with her clothing, wishing they dared remain naked to take in all the glorious colors of the setting sun that were about to be displayed in front of them.

When he finished dressing Cat, she sat down, finding her glass of wine, "I'm going to enjoy watching you until all your clothes cover you." She told him, her gaze riveted on him.

He let his head fall back, roaring with delight, "And I want you to drink your fill of me and the wine." Hard to control his arousal while she watched him, he was determined, knowing it would only have to be for a short time.

Dressed, he sat down and pulled her against him, his legs spread to accommodate her body. He fed her a berry tart then one for himself. The sun still above the horizon, it would be at least thirty minutes before the sun would actually disappear.

"Sir, sir," Winston rode over the hill, his horse skidding to a stop when he noticed them.

"What is it," Roc asked irritated. "This better be important." Yet he knew Winston would never interrupt a tryst if the message could wait.

"You've company, the Winthrops and they say they have news of O'Connell," Winston said as he tried to catch his breath.

"Good, see that they are fed and give them lots of wine. Make them comfortable. Take them to the gazebo and they can make good use of their time before we return. Tell them forty-five minutes or so. It will take us a while to ride back, and we're not returning before we see what we rode out here to see."

"I will, sir." Winston left.

"Shouldn't you find out their news?" She placed a hand on his arm, her brows drawn together in seeming concern.

"We will in good time." One hand cupped her breast, teased and aroused as the sun slowly made its downward path. "This is our time and I'm not going to have it ruined. We are still newlywed." He sipped his wine, enjoying her body flush against his while her tantalizing curves called to him.

"Sometimes I think of Da," she said, her body responding to him. "Do you think we could send him a message that I'm fine and that we're married?"

"I've sent several messages to him, including one telling him we are wed." He nuzzled her neck, licking and biting, his lips feathering across her skin.

"Thank you." She sighed softly, relaxing into him.

"What was that question you were going to ask before we swam?" Perhaps with a glass of wine relaxing her, she would finally get to the point.

"Hmm...I don't remember."

Perhaps this was too relaxed. "You wanted to know how you would know if you carried a child. I assume my child. Then you spoke in riddles about when you first started something."

"I know..."

Against his body he felt her shaky breath, and beneath his fingertips the rapid beat of her pulse. "Just ask." A muscle in his jaw twitched and he tried to do what he asked of her. Relax.

Suddenly, she blurted, "My woman's time. I'm late."

"And you're concerned because..." He tried to prompt her. He could ease her embarrassment, but for their future she needed to be able to come to him with anything.

"Does that mean..."

Once again, she left the sentence unfinished. "You tell me what you think it means. I'm only a man who never presumes anything where women folk are concerned."

"Am I pregnant? Are you angry?"

"Finally. Was that so hard? Never mind, it obviously was very hard." He paused, contemplating the best way to answer. "Does that mean you're pregnant?" he repeated her question. "Possibly and probably, are you always on time?"

"Yes, always." She smoothed the fabric of her skirt, keeping her gaze averted from his.

"Then you most likely are carrying my child. Your second question, am I angry? Not at al. I'm thrilled, excited even overjoyed. Need to feel the babe kick inside you and so much more."

She moistened her lips, turning into him a smile on her face. "I think the sun is setting."

It seemed she wanted to change the subject but this was the reason they rode to the lake, to watch the sun dip beneath the horizon and paint the sky with gorgeous colors. He inhaled the scent of her, violets. She always smelled of violets.

Now, colors lined the sky, horizontal patterns of varying shades of peaches and oranges enhanced by the few clouds that dotted the scenery.

He rose and pulled her to her feet, kissing her soundly as the sun slowly disappeared from the sky.

Then, "We need to see to our guests and uncover what they know. I want to be home before it's dark."

~ * ~

Fifteen minutes later Roc helped Cat from Sweety, handing the reins over to the stable boy and giving instructions. Beast was ahead of them, racing to the house then around the perimeter as if the walk to the lake and back was not enough exercise for the hound who seemed to be growing at an astronomical pace.

"We should learn O'Connell's fate in a few minutes then we'll have to find another room to make love in." He laughed at the face Cat made as he drew her against him. "Are you tired?" he asked, "I'm now concerned not just for you but for our child. I will have to take tender concern and make sure I treat you like the duchess you are."

"Just saying that man's name gives me the chills. I don't ever want to see him again. I hope they sent him home with a strong enough message he'll never bother me again." She was ager for good news but afraid Addie and Hamilton met with too great an opposition in the earl of Glenwood.

Inside, Winston greeted them. "If you're looking for the Winthrop's they're in the gazebo as you suggested, watching the sunset and probably doing what the two of you would be doing if you were out there alone. Probably should give them a bit of warning that you're nearby."

"Didn't know you could see the sunset from the gazebo. We'll have to try that tomorrow," Roc said, laughing as he led the way to the backyard the scent of roses redolent.

"Tomorrow I'm going to cut some of these for the house. I'll have to figure out where all the vases are." She inhaled the fragrance, realizing she loved roses almost as much as violets. Perhaps she could have asked for roses at their wedding.

"You should do that. I have to go into town on business. I won't return until dinner if everything goes as planned. You can surprise me with what you don't have on beneath your dress then we can find a room we've never been in." He stole a quick kiss just before they reached the gazebo.

"Hamilton," he called out. "You two decent?"

"Just give us a minute," Hamilton answered with a chuckle. "Got some rearranging to do."

"Hamilton!" Addie's voice was clearly angry. "You could have left it at *give us a minute.*"

"She's dressed," Hamilton said, "Come on, we've got lots of good news. You don't have to worry one more second about O'Connell."

When they stepped around the corner, Addie's face was flushed, and while her gown seemed fastened properly, her hair was in disarray. Why was it the woman always paid for indiscretions with the way they looked afterwards and the men did not?

"Good evening. Has Cook provided you with food?" Caitlin asked.

"Food and some of Maxwell's best Chianti." Hamilton said. "Come sit with us and we'll tell you a little tale you'll appreciate over the years." Hamilton pulled out two more glasses, "Cook foresaw your finding us here and provided the crystal. Bordeaux or Chianti?"

"Either will do, what about you?" Roc turned to Cat.

"Neither, when we return, I'd prefer tea. Wine just doesn't sound too good to me right now." She sat down next to Roc, expectant and eager to hear what these two had to say.

Roc placed her hand in his. His strength ebbed through her, giving her reason to believe in her future as well as all the possibilities. "Tell us everything. Don't leave out a single detail."

"After you tell me he won't threaten me again," Caitlin said. "Then you can make the story as long or as short as you want."

Addie leaned forward, setting her hand on Caitlin's arm. "I know how worried you are. Be assured, that for at least a year or more he won't be anywhere near. After that, if necessary, we'll find another place for him to visit."

"Then he's not going to Portrush." Roc said, "Tell us the long story. I want to know exactly what happened and where he is headed. I assume aboard some ship. Need to understand what we can expect for our future."

"About a week ago," Addie began, her voice taking on a strange tone, "we gave Blair O'Connell an ultimatum, go home and never threaten Caitlin again."

"I'm assuming there was an *or else*." Roc seemed to enjoy the story.

"Of course," Addie said with a slight lift of her shoulders. "One never gets anywhere with their adversary if they don't have an or else, subtle or otherwise, implied in the text of one's conversation. You do know the earl is a deplorable man."

"So..." Caitlin prompted, feeling more at ease where Blair O'Connell was concerned.

"He didn't leave," Hamilton told them with no embellishments. "At least not of his own accord. We had to give him a little push in the right direction before he'd comply to our wishes. I guess one could say he accepted the or else part of the bargain as his option."

"You didn't give him a choice?" Caitlin asked in disbelief. "You didn't shanghai him. You could be prosecuted for that."

"He had a choice and refused so we bought him first class passage on a ship to India. He should love it there with all the wonderful sights to see," Addie said, grinning. "Why, Hamilton, now that I think on it, I'd love to visit India. Not this week or even next month but in the future."

"It was passage for only one way," Hamilton added, downing what was left of the wine in his glass. "When we travel there, we could see the Taj Mahal and maybe see a tiger. Of course, a safari in Africa could be enjoyable. We could hike to the top of Kilimanjaro."

"Enough darling, we've digressed and forgotten just what our purpose here is," Addie said.

"He has enough funds to purchase his way home. He is a rich man as he has never ceased to tell people," Roc said, wondering where this was leading.

"Here's the thing, he didn't have time to pack before the ship left. All he had with him was the clothing he was wearing." Addie finished her wine, a pert expression on her beautiful face.

"No purse?" Caitlin asked, understanding booking passage would cost him something and if he had no money, he wouldn't know what to do.

"He can wire for the money, but of course that would take time. Double the time it took to sail to India." Hamilton said. "In any case, if he chose not to wire for the money, he would have to work on board ship to pay for his trip home," Hamilton filled in some of the empty spaces, "and that would take some time too."

"Or he would have to work in India to earn the funds. Either way he will have to do a good day's labor for several months," Roc said, seeming to appreciate the conversation and where it was going.

"He should have a different appreciation of life when he's not rich," Addie said. "Any other questions?"

It seemed to Caitlin the pair were finished and ready to move on to their next adventure.

"Not right now," Caitlin said, "except maybe about the marquis. He makes my skin crawl and he doesn't seem quite right in the head. When he stares at me, it seems he's seeing someone else."

"Would you like us to concentrate our attentions on the marquis and his comings and goings?" Addie sent the question Hamilton's way. "It would keep us out of trouble for a few days anyway."

"Whatever you want, my tender dove. I wouldn't want to see you in trouble and this espionage is always so much fun without putting our lives on the line like we used to do," Hamilton said.

Caitlin watched these two who were so different from everyone she knew. They seemed to enjoy intrigue and conspiracy, even baiting each other. "I'd appreciate your help," Caitlin said, wishing she could be more like Addie who seemed so self-assured and confidant.

"Then you have it," Addie said with a huge grin. "We will keep you apprised of everything we learn."

Hamilton stood, holding out his hand to Addie. "We should leave the newlyweds to do whatever newlyweds do. It's been so long it seems I've forgotten what we're supposed to do."

Addie hit him in the arm, "You certainly have not forgotten. We were being newlyweds in this very gazebo less than thirty minutes ago. Lying doesn't become you, Hamilton."

"Was I acting like a newlywed? Never. Curb your tongue, woman." He picked up the basket and wrapping his arm around Addie before drawing her close, sauntered to the duke's house.

Caitlin and Roc watched them walk away. "Are you feeling better now?" Roc asked her.

"Where O'Connell is concerned, yes, but the marquis seems infinitely more evil and dangerous," Caitlin said, understanding that as long as no one comprehended what the marquis planned for her, she was at risk.

"We're lucky to have friends such as Addie and Hamilton," Roc said, "Shall we return home and see what Cook has prepared for dinner?"

"You go ahead. I find I tire much more easily now days and I'm not hungry. We ate a lot this afternoon." Caitlin could think only of her bed and a night of sleep. As much as she loved Roc's attention, she needed to sleep to regain her strength, but she didn't want to tell him no to his attentions.

"I'm going to try to do everything I can to make life easier for you. It is getting late. Would you like me to bring you anything from the kitchen?" Roc asked, drawing her close.

His strength gave her comfort and she appreciated all he did for her. "I won't wait up for you, but feel free to wake me up when you come to bed."

"You need your beauty sleep. Perhaps I should sleep in another room tonight since I've a horrible time keeping my hands off your beautiful body," Roc said with a manly chuckle.

"You don't need to do that," she told him, wishing things were different and she had more energy.

"I do. Remember I told you I had business in the city. Just to give you some peace and quiet, I'm going to take Winston and drive into town tonight. That way I can be home sooner tomorrow. You take this time to sleep and relax. Now that we believe there is a child on the way, you're going to have to take more time for yourself. If you don't take care of yourself first, you won't be able to take care of anyone else, meaning me."

"The last few days my stomach has been rolling in the mornings. I thought I was getting sick, but that isn't true is it?" She guessed nausea was something that went along with pregnancy. In the pub she heard men talking about their wives and the sicknesses they endured, some less than others, and it was another indication of pregnancy.

"No, nausea in the mornings is a normal occurrence during pregnancy, a consequence I suppose. At least that's what I've heard. You should talk with Ella. I'll make sure she comes over in a couple of days."

"Thank you, I'd like that. Could I use one of your men to send the message? Maybe she can come tomorrow if she's not busy. I've so many questions and at times I'm terrified then worried for my life. Even though the only woman I know of who died in childbirth is my mother."

"There is no reason to be afraid, and of course you can send one of my men any time. They are here to serve you, so you needn't ask. Talk to the man who stands guard at the door. There are several but whoever is there, will obey your wishes just as they would mine."

"Will you walk me to our room," she asked, hoping to feel his arms around her before she went to bed and he left for town. She was having misgivings about him leaving. Without him next to her during the night, she wasn't sure she could sleep. She'd grown used to the warmth and security he brought to her every night.

"I'd be honored." They walked in silence until the door loomed in front of them. Inside, he drew her into his embrace for a long drugging kiss. "Sleep well, *mon petite chatte.*"

She moaned, knowing he would leave yet right now with him kissing her, she needed him to make love to her. Then he could go. She ran her fingers through his hair, pulling him closer.

"Don't leave yet. I need you once more then I can sleep." Her fingers desperately fumbled with the fastening of his pants.

"Whatever you want, *petite chatte*. I'll stay as long as you need me. All you ever need to do is ask."

"I want you. Now." She pushed his shirt over his head, desperate to feel the security he always brought with his lovemaking, frantic to feel his body tight against hers.

He nearly ripped her dress as he fought the seemingly anxious need emanating from her. "You can have whatever it is you need. Just tell me what it is," Roc said as he came down upon her on the bed.

Later, much later, Caitlin watched Roc leave. She needed to sleep but she missed him. What had she been thinking to send him away? Lying back on the bed, she concentrated on the image of him. His broad shoulders narrowing to a slim waist, strong legs...he was everything she'd ever dreamed of and he was hers.

Many hours later sunlight slanted through the window. The clock chimed eleven times. Caitlin sat up, brushing hair from her face. She felt refreshed and ready for the day for the first time in a couple of weeks. Having hidden the sickness she felt every morning, it was ironic that he was gone and she felt fine.

Suddenly, she didn't feel so fine. Rushing to the chamber pot, she emptied the contents of her stomach.

"No," she murmured. Then used the chamber pot again. "I thought I was going to be fine." She rang for Adara.

"You're finally up. What's happening?" Adara asked, stepping forward, concern etched across her usually happy features.

Caitlin smiled wanly. "I'm pregnant, nothing to be alarmed about. Roc told me this is normal."

"Well, of course it is, but there are things I can get you to make it easier and by the way, congratulations. How far along are you?" Adara asked.

"Not very far, and I'm not really sure. Perhaps we should keep it to ourselves," she said.

"Of course, milady. I'll bring you a cup of tea that will ease the sickness. Cook has lots of remedies and she'll keep your secret until you're ready to tell the world that the duke and duchess of Ravenswood are pregnant."

"I'm sure it's not prudent yet. I'm only guessing I'm pregnant," Caitlin said, wishing no one knew about this expect Roc and of course herself.

"How far along do you think you are?" Adara tidied the room and called for a bath and food, including the tea that would help ease her sickness.

"I've no idea. Maybe three weeks," Caitlin said, shrugging her shoulders to put emphasis on her doubt.

"Then you absolutely should say nothing. It's still possible to lose the child in the early stages. Wait a few months and keep this wonderful news between you and the duke," Adara advised.

"I've already asked to see Ella to ask her some questions. Should I..." More waves of self-doubt washed through her.

"Of course, ask her, find out what you need to know and swear her to silence. I'm sure she'll understand. She has two children and she's been through all of this herself."

"Thank you. I want to talk to someone who has experienced what I'm about to. Roc is helpful and while he knows more than I do, he still can't answer all my questions."

"Are you happy?" Adara asked.

"Terrified, ecstatic, worried, hopeful, I can't tell you how many conflicting emotions I have," Caitlin said, smoothing the fabric of her nightdress.

"Ah, your bath is here and the tea will be here soon. You'll feel better after you've bathed and eaten. What did you have planned today?" Adara asked.

"Not much, just rest and cut some roses. Could you help me find some vases to put them in?"

"I'd be honored to help. Cook too. Will the duke return today?" Adara asked.

"He left last night so he could be here before dinner. It's almost noon so I would think sooner than later I'll see him." Caitlin missed him even though he'd only been away for a short time.

"I'm glad to hear that. The duke's men have doubled in size just in the last two hours. Is there something we should be aware of? Now there are two men at each door."

"Not that I know of." Caitlin thought of O'Connell then the marquis before her focus returned full circle to the marquis. "My husband is involved in matters I've no idea about, things he keeps secret. Perhaps we should all be careful if he's increased the guards."

"Do you still want to cut roses? It might be prudent to remain inside," Adara asked as Cook entered the room with the much needed tea as well as the water for her bath following.

"I do. I'm not going to let some evil person or threat of danger stop me from doing what I want to do. I don't intend to live my life in fear." She sipped the tea then set it down, ignoring the meager food she set on her plate.

Tea drunk, bath finished, Caitlin finally made it outside to enjoy the sunshine of a day that was not too hot. Roses filled the basket she carried and she eagerly awaited Roc's return. She sat down in the gazebo to rest. Before she knew it, she was waking up to a loud noise.

Carrying the basket of flowers, she stepped from the gazebo and walked a few steps. "Roc?" she asked, looking around and trying to see him.

A beefy arm wrapped around her neck, a cloth over her mouth and nose. She couldn't fight, her body falling limp.

When she woke, she sat on a bed in a small room. The furniture was sparse and one window allowed a meager amount of light inside. She was alone. "Roc? Where are you?" Her head spun and she didn't think she could walk. For a few seconds she closed her eyes, trying to regain her equilibrium.

Fear enveloped her as her body shook and she felt the sudden and very rapid increase of her heartbeat. "Roc?" She stood, slowly walking around the room, helping herself and steadying her quivering legs by placing her hands on the furniture. When she looked out the window, she saw what she thought was London. But she didn't recognize any landmarks.

She didn't have to ask though. She knew what had happened. Despite their best efforts, "The marquis, happened." Where was Roc and the Winthrops? They promised to keep her safe.

This was not what she expected. Pulling out a drawer of the nightstand near the bed, she discovered a small hair comb. When she turned it over in her hands, she wondered if it once a long time ago it belonged to her mother.

"Were you imprisoned in this room, Fiona? Did you find a way to escape? If you did, I will too. I promise you, Roc. He won't keep me here forever." She clutched the black comb in her hand. How long had she been here and had Roc returned to their home and found her missing? Too many unanswered questions whirled in her head.

She sat down on the bed, feeling bereft and confused. The lock on the door moved and a woman stepped inside.

"Fiona?" the woman asked as she stepped toward her. "You're not Fiona. The marquis told me she returned. What on earth was he thinking? Who are you?"

"No, I'm Caitlin." She pushed herself back on the bed, hitting the backrest. "Fiona is my mother and she's dead. He knows it too. Why would the marquis lie about this?"

"Hush, child, just humor him and pretend you are the woman he thinks you are. Your life will be much easier if you let him imagine you are the woman he's infatuated with and has been for the last twenty years. He will treat you gently. I promise."

"No." She found herself shaking her head in protest, even while she shook with terror, sweat beading on her forehead, her body shaking uncontrollably. "I can't. I can't pretend anything, and I won't let him touch me. I won't do it. Besides, unlike my mother, I have a husband who will search for me. He won't leave one home in London untouched."

"You have to go along with his wishes to a certain point. Pretend, lass, just as your mother did for too long until I could finally get her out of this room without either of us being discovered. I'm going to help you, but I need time to put a plan in action."

"Just send a message to my husband, the Duke of Ravenswood. He will come for me." What was this woman waiting for? "If you do this Roc won't let anything happen to you, if that's what you're worried about."

"I can't do that. I value my life as well as yours. I promise you I'll help you, but you have to help yourself by doing as I say. I don't want to die either and if you give me away or don't follow my instruction, we'll both meet an untimely end. Now, hush, he'll be here soon and don't let on about what I've told you. Remember that you are Fiona O'Sheay, not Caitlin O'Sheay."

"But I'm not and if he touches me, I'll scream and fight him with every breath in my body."

"For the most part do what he says. He wants you, so say whatever you can to waylay him from his sexual needs. Perhaps you should keep reminding the marquis you are Caitlin, not Fiona. Tell him you're married. The only woman he's ever cared about is Fiona, but not enough to wed her, just to imprison her. Tell him you're pregnant with another man's child. That might give him reason to let you go."

"I won't let him defile me," Caitlin said shaking her head and pushing against the bed board as if he was in the room with her. "How did you know I'm pregnant?"

"Assumed as much and now you've confirmed the fact."

"I won't let him touch me."

"That's not what I'm advising. Just make him believe you're not Fiona and use every idea you can think of to keep him from taking you against your will. As far as I know, the marquis has never forced anyone."

The door creaked open and the marquis stepped inside the room. For a few seconds, he seemed to study her, his eyes narrowing as if he found her lacking in some way.

"Fiona, I've missed you. I'm so glad you came home." The marquis opened his arms to her as if he expected her to step into them.

"I'm not Fiona and I despise you, father."

~ * ~

Addie and Hamilton spoke quietly to Roc about the marquis who had been exhibiting strange behavior for the last twenty years, escalating now that Caitlin had been presented at the ball weeks ago.

"He's deranged and totally unpredictable. He doesn't talk to anyone save a few people and is making strange decisions. He's set papers in motion to divorce his wife of only a few months," Hamilton told Roc, wishing he had better news.

"Caitlin looks just like her mother I've been told. The resemblance is more than remarkable," Addie said. "Rumor has it he was so smitten with Fiona that he was willing to give her just about anything."

"Except his name," Roc gritted out.

"She was a commoner and, in his mind, marriage just couldn't happen between them and he never understood why she didn't want to be his mistress," Hamilton said grinning wickedly. "You would have become my mistress if I asked you, wouldn't you Addie?"

"Of course, my dear then I would have killed you in your sleep," Addie said sweetly, sending Hamilton sputtering ale on the table with his laughter.

"We have to take care of the marquis, convince him Caitlin is not Fiona. Otherwise I've no idea what he'll resort to."

"We can't treat him as we did O'Connell and send him on a ship to another country," Addie put in her opinion.

"All we can do is keep the marquis away from Cat, but that's physically impossible. If he's patient, he'll find a way to get to Cat," Roc said, tapping his fingers on the table.

"Hamilton and I have talked a lot about all of this. There is another option, but I don't know if we can prove the marquis is insane," Addie said.

"We could have him committed to Bedlam," Hamilton finished for her. "With a few statements from some of his peers, he could be railroaded into the hospital for the insane."

"Only if he does something we can prove is the product of an insane man, one who needs psychiatric care," Addie said.

"So, you're telling me we can't commit him unless he does something to Caitlin that shows he's insane," Roc said, leaning back in his chairs then crossing his arms over his chest seemingly thoughtful.

"That's what we're saying, but short of sending him off on a ship, we've nothing else we can do. He's well known in London," Hamilton said.

Roc sat forward and in Addie's mind he was clearly tense. "Find out if any of his servants were employed twenty years ago when Fiona was allegedly held prisoner in that home. I want to talk to them immediately."

"Have inquired already and we found one lady who is still a servant for the marquis. We haven't had the chance to talk with her though. She's pretty illusive and we've had a difficult time cornering her to have any kind of conversation," Hamilton said.

"Do you know where she lives or is she housed in the servants' quarters upstairs in the marquis' townhouse?" Roc asked, running his hands through his hair. "She must go outside sometime, run errands or just visit family."

"That's just the thing. The lady in question lives in a separate home or townhouse about two blocks from the marquis. Rumor has it that was the home where he kept Fiona until she escaped."

"How did she get away from him if he kept her locked in?" Roc asked, clearly intrigued.

"We think Fiona had help but..."

"I think," Addie said, "the servant is protecting herself from the marquis. If he ever found out she aided Fiona, he would have killed her. Fiona would have had to purchase her passage back to Ireland."

"The lady would need help getting Fiona out of London unless she has some type of connections at the wharf. Make some inquiries there and get back to me. I plan on spending more time with Caitlin. When I get home, I'm not going to let her out of my sight."

Addie watched Roc stride quickly from the room, praying it wasn't already too late. She had a sinking feeling in her gut.

"We need to stake out that townhouse. Nothing has happened that we know of, but everything we've heard points to the fact the marquis is planning something," Addie said. "I didn't want to say anything more to worry the duke, but I also heard the marquis has purchased certain things and they weren't for his wife," Addie said as she studied her husband, waiting for a reaction.

Chapter Nine

Roc ran several more errands, speaking to some of the people who knew the marquis and his history better than he did. He'd been just eight years old when Fiona had been held captive. His last stop was at his mother's then he would return home.

His gut feelings warned him to go home now, yet he also understood the importance of speaking with Charlotte. When he strode up the steps and into his mother's home, he felt another wave of fear sweep through him, the hair on the back of his neck standing on end.

Rubbing the back of his neck he realized he was sweating and for the first time he could remember his hands shook. "Mother," he called out. "Scarlett, anyone home."

The impatience he felt was tangible and he fought to push the pique to the back of his mind and concentrate on what he came here to discover. If anyone could shed some light on the marquis strange proclivities, mother could, and he was sure she still had favors to call in. Not everyone who she held secrets over their heads had passed away. Knowing his mother, she would have kept track of the younger generation as well.

"Why, master Richard, what do we owe this visit? Is little Caitlin fine? Is she with you? I'll fetch you a glass of brandy. Do make yourself comfortable. I'll tell Charlotte you're here. She's in the library doing something. Not sure what." Scarlett bustled around the room, filling a crystal glass with brandy and giving it to him before disappearing.

Roc sat down but apprehensively shifted in the chair, his unease growing. He rose when his mother entered, giving her a hug. "I need whatever information you have as well as advice." He sat down.

"About the marquis?"

"You've heard things." He wasn't going to like the answer of that he was sure. "But I'm more interested in what happened twenty or so years ago. I'm sure there was gossip."

"Not a lot." Charlotte poured herself a drink then sat down. "But what I am sure of is that Fiona had a lot of help, not by just one person but several. I doubt the marquis gave her any money, so she would have been penniless."

"And do you know who these people were and if they're still alive." He understood she liked to drag these things out, loved the drama but this wasn't something he had time for right now.

"I'll put out feelers. The thing is, I've new contacts and it's quite easy to find things to hold over people's heads. For example," she paused, a delighted smile appearing on her weathered features. "The marquis' new wife seems to love women. She's married the man simply for the title and the wealth that goes along with it. What she didn't know was that the marquis has spent twenty years trying to find a woman who was dead. He's spent a fortune on that quest. I'm not at all sure there is anything to inherit."

"All that is interesting, but what I need to have is proof the man is insane. I'm looking to have him committed to Bedlam."

"Finding proof should not be too difficult. From the time I've known him, he's done strange things. He has one servant, a woman, who is rumored to be loyal to him. Has said she would take a bullet for him. But..." she paused.

"But?" He tapped his fingers on his legs then downed the brandy in one gulp.

"I've proof this woman was crucial to Fiona's sudden departure. I do have your best interest at heart, William. While you've been playing the newlywed game, I've done my research.

"Richard," he reminded her.

"Oh yes, well, when you're in this mode, you remind me so much of your father. Sometimes I can't help but call you by his name."

"What have you discovered? I need to get home to Cat. I'm worried about her. There's an unusual rolling of my stomach. Do you have the name of the servant?"

Shaking her head, "No, but she's recently moved to the old

185

townhouse that the marquis reportedly gave to Fiona. The thing was, once Fiona entered that home no one ever saw her again. He was infatuated with her and didn't want anyone to see her for fear she would leave him. He kept her locked away from everyone."

"So, if I visit the townhouse, I can talk to this woman?" he asked.

"Probably not, she keeps quiet, trying to protect her life. I discovered her and what some believe she did quite by accident. Her safety depends on her true identity and how she might have helped Fiona remaining unknown to the marquis."

"I wouldn't do anything to jeopardize this woman's identity or her safety." Roc felt the sudden rise of anger, understanding his mother and that he'd have to wait until she was ready to reveal the name if she ever was.

"Of course you would. The only woman you care about is Caitlin. You would jeopardize anyone who got in your way. At the moment there doesn't seem to be any danger for Caitlin. The marquis has been remodeling the home and purchasing new garments, mostly lingerie in preparation, but he hasn't made a move to kidnap her."

"And you would tell me when he's ready. There is no predicting a man who is insane. He could work with logic leading his way or he might randomly decide he couldn't wait any longer to possess this woman who has eluded him for twenty years."

"I'm sorry Roc, but the only recourse you have right now is to post men watching this townhouse. I've already put a man on the street to help you out. I've heard Addie and Hamilton are helping you also."

"Does nothing get past you?" Roc asked, stunned by all his mother revealed.

"I hope not but I'd never be so presumptive to say nothing gets past me. I've a feeling this won't be over anytime soon. In his insanity he's a monster but he seems more intelligent and sly. The past twenty years he's been a model citizen. All it took to set him on edge was seeing the picture of his Fiona in Caitlin. He doesn't seem to understand Caitlin is his daughter, not the woman he's coveted for so very long."

"That doesn't make me feel any better," Roc murmured, downing a second glass of brandy as he stood.

"Go home to your wife," Charlotte said. "If you've been gone all day, she's sure to be missing you."

"Not just today, I left last night," he said, realizing his absence might have played into the crazy man's plans.

"Best you get home now if you've been gone that long. What on earth possessed you in the light of what is happening to leave your wife? I thought you were smarter than that, Richard."

"So, now I don't remind you of your late husband. I've been asking myself the same thing all day. But there were things I had to discover. Mother, this is not something we're positive about, yet I'm not sure enough to say something to you. We're pregnant."

"Then all the more reason to get yourself home and hold her in your arms. She's is sure to be terrified of her condition and fearful of the unknown. Your Cat is such an innocent and with no mother, you are the only one she has to tell her things she should know already." She waved her hand in the air, "Get yourself home to your wife and the baby in her womb. If she needs someone to talk to, I'm here for her."

But Roc had one more place he needed to visit before he returned to his wife. Surveillance of the townhouse where Fiona was supposed to have lived seemed imperative as well as prudent.

He needed to see if anyone lived there, and he wanted to talk to the man his mother put outside to watch for any movement. Riding past the marquis' townhouse, he continued another two blocks until he drew to a stop. Dismounting and tying the reins of his horse to a post, he strode to the door.

In the foyer the lights were off or turned low. Picking up the knocker he banged on the door. No one came to greet or toss him out. He looked into the windows but sheets covered the furniture.

This didn't appear to be a home anyone lived in or was meant to live in soon. He strode around the perimeter of the home. In the back and on the top floor one light shone through the window.

His breath caught in his throat when a curtain was opened briefly then fell shut. He'd seen a face and now he wanted to know more. At the back door, he knocked before he finally opened the screen and tried the latch. The door was locked tight.

His heart thundered as he thought to break the lock.

"You probably shouldn't do that." Addie's voice behind him effectively stopped his foolhardy action. "Truly, it would not be wise to be caught breaking and entering."

"How long have you been here?" Roc asked, turning his full attention to Addie and Hamilton.

"Long enough to know that no one has entered through the back or the front. You should go home to your wife. She'll be missing you." Hamilton stood behind his wife and he seemed to enjoy taking second place to her first in their dealings. It seemed Hamilton knew what he was thinking, "Addie is much more intelligent than I am. I have to have her back though. Even if she is the best damn shot in the country, as you might have noticed she has no brawn."

If the situation had been lighter, Roc might have laughed. Hamilton was one of the most intelligent men he had known. "Who was looking out that window?" Roc wasn't ready to let anything go.

"We believe it's the servant we spoke of at our meeting early this afternoon," Addie said. "We will keep watch and if she goes out, we'll have a few words with her. Leave this in our care."

"Bloody hell, but I just want to be left in peace and quiet with my wife." He remembered telling her that after the work he'd been doing for the government, all he wanted was a little peace and quiet. "Best not to wish for anything," he muttered.

"Wish for anything?" Hamilton asked. "Don't understand."

"Before I left Ireland with Cat, I told her all I wanted for the next few months was a little peace and quiet."

"Perhaps you'll get that when the marquis is in Bedlam," Addie said, grimacing. "I hear that's a horrible place."

"If he does anything to harm Cat, it's better than he deserves," Roc said as he turned to stride back to his horse, Addie and Hamilton following them.

"You're serious about that?" Hamilton asked, "Not sure we'll be able to force that issue. Putting the bastard in Newgate would be easier."

"That works for me. Makes more sense than a hospital." Roc mounted his horse then looking down the street, "Is that one of my mother's men?"

"Yes, and he's been there for a few hours. Someone else will take his place soon. Addie and I are going home until tomorrow. If you need anything, send a message," Hamilton said. "We'd like to spend a few minutes with our beautiful child who is growing up way to fast."

The thought of their child brought him back full circle to his child who was barely a thought, yet he desperately needed to hang on to that memory. He had a long wait and making sure Cat had everything she needed to stay healthy was first on his agenda.

"Hopefully I won't see either of you until tomorrow. I'll have Winston check in with yours and my mother's men. I don't plan on leaving Cat's side once I'm at home."

"Good, that's what she needs, of course, to keep her safe and healthy," Addie said.

Giving his stallion a nudge, he started toward his home in a brisk trot, slowing the horse as they entered a congested road then urging him faster when the road cleared.

The sun was still fairly high in the sky when he dismounted and handed his stable boy the reigns. Once again, a feeling of ill being swept through him and when he strode through the front door, his heart lodged in his throat.

"Sir." Winston greeted him amidst the chaos in the small room. "Glad your back, sir," he said.

"Cat?" he started for the steps, but Winston held out a hand to stop him.

"She's not up there." Winston's voice sounded odd.

"Where is she?" His hands on his hips he was in no mood for guessing games.

"That's just the thing, sir. No one knows." Winston ran a finger around his shirt collar while sweat beaded on his forehead.

"You were supposed to keep track of her. She was going to cut flowers but that was this morning." He strode toward the gardens.

"She's not there. Just the flowers she cut," Adara said. "I left her for a moment to talk to Cook, and when I returned the roses were all over the ground and she was no where to be seen. I called for her and searched the grounds along with Winston but she's not here."

Earlier in the day he'd felt the fear as well as her terror. That light in the third floor room could be on for Cat. She might be there and he let Addie and Hamilton talk him out of breaking and entering.

He didn't think it had been Cat who looked out the window though. She would have made sure he saw her. Then it had to be the servant who might be a friend or it could have been the marquis and he'd know they were looking for Catlin.

If the marquis moved her from the townhouse, he might never find Caitlin. He paced, thinking, unsure of what he should do or how he should proceed. His instincts told him to march in there and take her.

He understood both his mother and the Winthrops would advise against that plan but Bloody hell, he couldn't leave Cat at the mercy of a crazy person who thought she was someone else.

Sitting at his desk and trying to think more clearly, he penned a message to Hamilton and Drake as well, asking for their help and explaining the situation. Striding up the stairs to the bedchamber he shared with Cat, he quickly changed clothing. When he emerged, he wore all black and had painted his face with charcoal, the charcoal left over from his espionage days.

The ride into town took what seemed to Roc like hours. Tying his horse a block from the townhouse and keeping to the shadows, he made his way to the home where he was sure Cat was imprisoned.

He managed to put his vested interest in the back of his mind, needing to focus on the task at hand, not on what he could lose if this all failed. He saw the guard at the front of the house as well as the one at the back.

Meaning to enter the home from the back door, he spoke to that guard. "Join the man at the front of the house. I'll whistle if I need anything. Don't come inside unless you hear the whistle."

The light in the upstairs bedroom was no longer on which disturbed him. At the back door, he pulled out the tools needed to pick the lock. Focused on the task in front of him, he stole a breath from the night and began working.

With the last click of the latch, he slowly pushed the door open, cringing at what seemed a loud creak. The servant's stairway must be located somewhere in the scullery or the kitchen.

Finding the door, he slipped inside then let the door silently close behind him. The old stairs creaked, groaning with each step of his foot. Between each, he waited and listened. The house was silent, too silent. He needed to hear her voice.

His heartbeats thundered in his chest. Each breath seemed raspy and in the dark silence, he understood Cat would not be imprisoned here. In the few hours that had passed since her abduction, she must have found a way to escape the townhouse as well as the marquis. This old place with too many tales to tell stood empty.

He never doubted her courage, only her strength. She would do anything to flee the marquis. She told him as much. On the third floor he listened at the door for any sounds. All he heard was the silence of the night. The darkness seemed to encapsulate him while he held his breath.

Three doors opened to this hallway. The room the light shone from earlier in the day looked over the back of the house. Keeping his back to the wall, he stealthily made his way to the room.

When he touched the door, it swung open. A woman lay on the bed, but it wasn't Cat. Otherwise the room was empty and only a soft echo of a summer breeze floated through the open window.

"Cat...where are you? What happened that you left this place and you didn't wait for me?"

The low moan from the woman on the bed refocused his attention. Kneeling beside the woman, "Where is Caitlin?"

"She..." The woman touched his face. "Are you the duke of Ravenswood?" Her hand fell to her side and the groan of pain sent a shiver of Roc's spine.

"Yes, I ask you again. Where is Cat?" He had never felt such fear, never been so terrified. When she didn't answer, "Did the marquis take her somewhere?"

"No, I helped her leave. I told her to go to your mother's home. Thought it would be safe there." The woman's voice was growing weaker, her hand had the feel of ice.

Torn between rushing to his mother's house and helping this

woman, he stood at the window and whistled. "What happened to you?"

"The marquis discovered what I did and how I helped Fiona twenty years ago. He shot me. Tried to kill me, he did. He's looking for Caitlin too. Still believes she's Fiona."

In the darkness, Roc finally found the entry. "You're going to be fine," he told her, wadding up the woman's apron to place on the wound to stop the bleeding.

"What is it?" The two guards appeared behind him.

"This woman has been shot and she needs medical attention. When Hamilton gets here, tell him I've gone after Caitlin. She's supposed to be at mother's home. He'll know where that is."

Roc didn't have time or patience to wait for a reply. Heading down the main stairs, he raced out the door. Minutes flew by as he made his way to his mother's townhouse.

Through the doors, "Cat! Cat where are you." All he craved right now was his wife to be in his arms.

"What on earth, Richard," Charlotte and David appeared from the parlor. "What is all this commotion?"

"Where is Cat?" he asked, frustration eating at him. He'd expected to see his wife sitting in the parlor, sipping brandy or tea or whatever and maybe having a lemon bar with his mother.

"What are you talking about?" Charlotte asked, David standing beside her. "Why would Caitlin be here without you?"

"Don't play with me, mother. I'm not in the mood." Roc turned, running his fingers through his hair, frustration eating at him. If Cat wasn't here, where was she?

"I'm not," she said more forcibly than she usually would have protested. "You're clearly distraught. Sit down and tell me what has you so worried so I can help."

"Don't have time to sit. I've got to find her." But Roc strode into the parlor then poured himself a whiskey and downed it in one gulp.

"I'm guessing you were sure she was here so now, what would be your next best guess?"

He poured another drink before sitting down. "Where is she?" Moisture pooled in his eyes. The thought of losing her devastated him. His gut churned, sickness taking over all emotions. "The marquis is looking for her. What if he finds her before I do?"

"He won't. I'll send men out to search all the streets between here and that old place of his. She's got to be someplace familiar," It seemed Charlotte tried to soothe him, but it wasn't working.

"Send men to my house, the townhouse I set up for her when I thought she would be my mistress." A wave of guilt swept through him at that thought and his astronomical ego.

"I'm going to the pub. If she found herself unable to pay for a cab, she might go to the only place where she could earn the fare, and it's not far from the home where the marquis imprisoned her."

~ * ~

With the help of the servant who befriended her, Caitlin dressed in a gown that must have been Fiona's. She followed the woman down the servant's stairway to the back door.

"Thank you." She hugged the woman, understanding the risks the lady had taken for her. "Take care and I pray nothing will happen to you. The marquis is crazy. Stay as far away from him as you can." Caitlin rubbed her arms, chills sweeping through her at the thought of his touch. Thank God, he didn't force her. At least she could be grateful for that.

"You go straight to The Duchess' house. If your duke comes for you, I'll tell him where I sent you. Now go. Don't waste any time." She shooed her away with her hands. "Hurry now. If the marquis comes back here, I won't tell him anything."

"Shouldn't you leave too?"

"I'm not in danger but as soon as I can, I'm going to my sister's home," she said.

"Good, I don't want to see you hurt because of me."

Without another word, Caitlin set off in the direction the woman told her. She wove her way through the back pathways behind the house. When she started, the sun still cast some light through the trees, but now it was growing darker and she wasn't sure where she was.

Night animals began to send their voices to each other. A croak of a frog and the hoot of an animal sent an eerie chill down her spine. She wanted to get out of these woods before she started running in a blind panic.

Her feet seemed glued to the ground and winded, she had to rest. Leaning against a tree, she inhaled a few sharp breaths of air. Her hand on her belly, she directed a quick prayer heavenward for the child in her womb. A low whine caught her attention then a cold nose pushed against her hand, begging for a caress.

"Beast, how did you find me?" She knelt, rubbing his ears and letting him lick her face, relieved to finally have a friend with her. "You can't possibly know how good you make me feel. The only other one I'd rather see is Roc. Come on, let's get out of here." Beast's presence gave her hope. If her dog could find her, so could her husband.

A few more minutes passed before she stepped from the darkness onto the busy London street. "The woman told me to turn left, or was it right." Caitlin had been so terrified the marquis would show up, she didn't listen very well. "In for a penny in for a pound," she murmured to Beast. "Which way should we go?"

She turned left, walking along the gas lit street until she recognized a few structures. The buildings she saw were not ones anywhere near Charlotte's home. She should have turned right.

"Should we retrace our steps?" she asked Beast who sat and stared at her with his huge brown eyes. "I wish you could talk. It would really help if I had someone who had a sense of direction leading the way."

Noticing the pub where she worked for a week, she decided that might be a place to start. If the owner would let her play, she could earn enough money for cab fare. Plus, the place was friendly and she needed to see someone who didn't mean her harm.

"Well, Beast, that might be a horrible idea. I don't have my fiddle. So, what can I play with?" She rubbed his ears, hoping that in any case the owner would remember her name and loan her the money. I could promise to play for him another time," she told her Beast.

At the door, she peered inside, hesitating. The place looked much the same as it did several months ago. She remembered how determined she'd been to pay Roc everything she owed him. Now that she had some idea the money he spent and the funds he had available to him, in a lifetime of work she could never have paid him back.

Keeping Beast close to her side, she walked through the tavern then stopped at the bar.

"Caitlin, how are you? Heard you married the duke of Ravenswood. What could you be doing here?" the man asked, seeming to beam with pleasure.

She sat down before placing her arms on the bar. She felt at home in pubs and was immediately reminded of her da. "I did marry him." But how could she tell this man the whole story and that now she didn't know where he was and that she desperately needed to find him.

"A pint of Guinness for the duchess," he said, hollering to one of the servers. "Don't dally, she looks parched. Perhaps some Shepard's pie too."

"You remembered but I can't," she said with a grimace and a slight lift to her shoulders. "I don't have any money with me."

"Shame on your duke. He shouldn't allow his wife to walk the streets of London alone with no money. The drink's on me and if I see your man, I'll collect. Who's this animal you got with you? Your protection?" he laughed.

"Roc bought him for me for that exact reason, but he's not really big enough yet, although he turned up out of the blue tonight, and while he didn't need to protect me, he's a friend for me when I'm feeling alone. His name's Beast and that's exactly what he'll look like by this time next year."

"Think you've got a story to share. Would you like that bite to eat while you wait? You can tell me your story over the food and a pint. Don't leave out anything and if I can help, I will," he told her, patting her hand as if he was her father.

She hesitated a moment. "I am hungry but I don't want charity and Roc isn't here. Even before I married, I paid my bills."

"I plan on collecting." He ordered shepherd's pie for her and a huge bone for Beast.

When she finished eating, she motioned him over, "If you've a fiddle around here somewhere, I'll play a few tunes. Then maybe you could give me fare to get home."

"Ah, lass, you don't have to work to pay for your meal and a cab fare, but I'd love to hear you play again. The sweetest sounds come from your fiddle and we're all in luck." He gestured to the crowds. "I'll let you play for my patrons. The duke won't get angry, will he?"

"I don't think so. He'll be pleased you helped me, I think. I haven't played in a week or two," she said realizing how preoccupied she'd been with Roc and all the new things she needed to learn in order to be a good wife and mother even though Roc only really cared about one thing.

The man disappeared into a back room and emerged with a fiddle and bow. "Here you go." He crossed his arm, a broad grin on his weathered face. "I can hardly wait."

Taking a few minutes to tune the fiddle, when she was satisfied, she began to play. Caught up in the music she danced around the room, stopping at various customers to smile and engage. It seemed she'd never stopped playing and entertaining. The music flowed through her into the pub's patrons.

From a lively Irish jig, she switched to a haunting melody that brought tears to the eyes of everyone. Just as before customers began to fill the space as the sounds drifted through the door and rumor that she was playing again spread along the waterfront.

Cat lost herself in the music that seemed to be part of her soul. She lost track of time as well as her surroundings. Hours slipped by until she finally stopped, winded and needing a moment of rest. The clapping in the pub thundered as the patrons showed their appreciation of her efforts.

Even when everyone stopped, one person continued the applause, clapping as he walked toward her. "Well done, Caitlin."

"Blair!" Her heart caught in her throat and she couldn't breathe. He was supposed to be on a ship to somewhere a long way away. What had happened and how had be bested the Winthrops?

"You surprised? Of course you are. Your friends thought to outsmart me. They didn't." He stepped closer, undeterred by Beast's threatening growl. "I always get what I want and you, my dear Caitlin, are what I want."

"You want me to toss him out," the bar tender asked. "I got a bouncer who can do just that."

"Yes, please if you don't mind." She could barely utter the words.

"He wants to take me back home despite I'm married to someone else. He gave me a black eye and a couple of broken ribs."

"No longer want to make you my wife," he sneered. "But I don't want to discuss my reasons in front of these fine people who seem to adore you, a used woman who is not fit to bear my children."

"If you don't want me, then why are you here? Go home and find yourself a woman who is suitable."

"I still want you, a commoner. What is a commoner good for?" His smile sent a chill down her spine.

"I'm not going with you." She meant to stand her ground. "You can't make me leave this tavern. All these people will stand in your way."

"You think that's what they're going to do, but..." He brushed imaginary dust off his shoulders. "I'll see your friends sent to prison for shanghaiing. They won't escape my wrath."

She wanted to argue with him but thought better. What she needed to do was stay in the pub and not set a foot outside. "They didn't do anything against the law. They booked you first class passage on a ship. That's all." Her heart raced though, knowing that the pair were a hair away from breaking the law.

He roared with laughter. "Is that what they told you? Luckily the ship's captain was willing to negotiate. I offered him a better deal."

"Yes." She tried for a meek demeanor. By watching Addie she'd learned a few tricks. Letting that man know she wasn't afraid of him would not be prudent. But she wasn't going to fear him, and she was going to do everything in her power to keep him from hurting her. All she needed was time and she did have help.

A cheer went up around the room. "Caitlin, Caitlin, Caitlin."

The patrons wanted her to play and she meant to oblige. Picking up her fiddle, she began another song. At least another hour passed before she was too winded to play longer. Her feet hurt as well as her fingers. "I'll play some more as soon as I catch my breath," she told them.

A pint appeared in front of her, "From that man over there," the owner told her, nodding to the left.

An older man with a few missing teeth grinned at her holding up his beer in salute. She nodded her thanks.

She was exhausted and unsure how much longer she could keep this up. Her hand on her belly, she tried to still the rising nausea. Thoughts of losing the shepherd's pie and the Guinness she ate and drank in Blair's lap gave her reason to grin.

"You're not looking so well. Think you should be getting yourself home. Want me to hail you a cab?" the bar owner asked. "I can try and keep that man away from you."

"I'd like that but I'm not sure where I should go." Not wanting to involve the pub owner in her troubles, she wasn't sure what to tell him. "I need to find Roc and I'm certain he's trying to find me, but if Blair gets me alone... Well, I don't want to find out, that's all."

"Well, you should be getting yourself back to your home of course." The man looked puzzled. "Your man will have protections in place."

"It's a long story, but I've got to make sure my guess as to where I'll find Roc is the right one. I'm tempted to stay here until he finds me, if that's all right with you." She didn't know if she could keep her eyes open for that long, but she prayed for the stamina as well as a miracle.

"You're in some kind of trouble, lass. Do you want me to call for the constables? Is this man a threat to you?"

At that thought, she panicked there could be something to Blair's threat to see her new friends jailed, and she didn't want to put Addie and Hamilton in danger even though she figured it wouldn't be the first time they were on the wrong side of the law.

A dire threat, but she didn't want to involve this man. "He's no friend," she told him, "but I don't think he'll show his hand as long as there are people around. Witnesses are not what he wants."

"There you are! Fiona." The marquis pushed his way through the patrons of the tavern. Waving a pistol in one hand and a stiletto in the other, the people moved away from him, creating a path straight to her.

"No." Caitlin pushed against the bar, trying to put distance between them but unable to do that. "I'm not going anywhere with you." Her breath caught in her throat. "You're an evil, crazy old man."

"I shot her, you know," the marquis said. "The lady who helped you betrayed me and I can't have that, Fiona. You've deceived me, too, but I'm going to give you another chance. Come with me now, and I'll be real nice to you. I'll even let you go for a walk in the sunshine every now and then. If you obey, you won't have to stay in your room." He paused, "but not until I can trust you again."

"You're insane," Caitlin said, "You know I'm not Fiona. She was my mother and she's dead. She died trying to get away from you." It was a part truth. Had she given birth in some other circumstances, she might have lived and she might have known a mother's love.

"Liar! That's not true!" he shouted, spittle flying from his mouth. "You're standing right in front of me, Fiona. Why would you lie? Why would you say you died?" His gun hand shook.

"I'm not lying," Caitlin said with a calm she didn't feel and trying once more to convince him. "I'm your daughter and when you stop to think about it, you'll realize I'm speaking the truth."

"Don't have a daughter. Fiona and I didn't have any children. Move away from the bar..." He motioned with the gun.

"Fiona was pregnant when she ran away from you. Bloody hell, but you locked her up. You're crazy, demented," she repeated, understanding her words would not get the desired effect.

"Come with me, or I'm going to shoot that animal sitting at your feet," the marquis threatened.

She looked to the dog then back to the marquis, deciding she should try to obey his commands even while stalling for time. Slowly stepping forward, "I'm coming. Don't shoot him. He's harmless, you know."

"Leave the lady alone. She says she doesn't want to come with you," one of the patrons said. "Why don't you just sit down and enjoy a pint and listen to her play her fiddle?"

"If you let her be, maybe she'll play us another song."

"Caitlin, Caitlin, Caitlin," The chant went up around the tavern again. "Play us a song."

More people entered, joining in with the chant.

"Give her a chance to tell us if she wants to leave with the likes of you," another called out. "We want her to stay and play."

Caitlin had no idea these people would defend her in front of a lord. Perhaps they didn't know who he was. Possibly they just wanted her to keep playing. In any case, she didn't care. They were creating the perfect situation for her and helping her stall for time.

"I'd be happy to play another song. Something lively perhaps." She picked up the fiddle.

"Don't think you can get my mind off what I need to have happen here. You're coming with me." He waved the gun again. "Put the damn violin down," he gritted out, watching her.

Defiantly, she drew her bow over the strings, but the marquis knocked the fiddle out of her hands. The instrument landed on the ground with a clatter just as the marquis grabbed her arm. He hauled her in front of him, but she kicked at his shins. His grip loosened and she pushed away from him.

The scuffle caused more confusion in the bar. A man shoved the marquis, stumbling, and trying to regain his balance, a shot rang out.

She felt the burning in her arm as she slowly crumpled to the ground. Except for the night that Blair gave her a black eye and broken ribs, she'd never felt such searing pain. She tried to keep the moan from escaping as the world turned upside down and the floor beneath her spun in dizzying circles.

Roc. She tried to call out for him, but she understood he couldn't help her. Beast licked her on the face, whining in his usual puppy voice that meant he was disturbed.

"Move away. Everyone move away from her." Blair's voice boomed above the noise and confusion.

"She's going with me." Blair picked her up. "I've no time to waste now that the marquis has shown his hand. She's not going with that man or her duke. She's mine."

Instead of escaping from the tavern with her, he was shaking his leg and yelling. "Get him off me. Get the damn dog off me."

"I'm going to shoot that bloody animal, Caitlin. Tell your dog to stay." Blair shook her by the shoulders seeming to need to emphasize his point, the pain in her arm escalating with the brutal shaking.

As long as Beast held to Blair's trousers, she wasn't going anywhere. "No," she whispered hardly able to speak, the pain enveloping her. "No, I won't tell him that."

He pointed his gun, "You know I don't make idol threats. Bloody hell, do you want me to shoot the damn dog?"

It seemed he managed to loosen the dog's hold on his leg enough to kick Beast and send the poor animal to the ground with a whine of pain. Once more though the animal gripped Blair's leg, seemingly undeterred by the man's brutality.

"Beast, stay," she whispered staring at him. "Let him go and stay."

He sat on his haunches, his eyes wide and seeming to question then Caitlin prayed he wouldn't take this moment to behave. She needed him to follow her, craved his companionship even though he couldn't help her.

"Everyone, stay where you are. I'm not going to hurt her. But she belongs to me, always has," Blair said his, voice harsh and demanding. "She was promised to me."

"Know a certain duke who'll argue that point with you." The owner of the bar spoke up. "He's going to come after you and when he does, you'll regret this moment because everyone here is witness to your perfidy."

Blair was backing from the tavern, brandishing his gun, an arm wrapped around Caitlin's neck, heedless of her wound. The patrons of the pub held the marquis by his arms. "Give him to the constables. They'll know what to do with that man. Someone go after Caitlin and see if you can keep track of where they go."

Cool evening air caressed her face. She closed her eyes, wishing for a miracle she knew wouldn't come her way. The world seemed to spin, and a growing nausea rose in her stomach. She swallowed hard, hoping Blair wouldn't get angry with her any time soon understanding how cruel he could be when provoked.

He tossed her in a carriage before sitting down across from her. Her arm was sticky with blood and he was doing nothing. If anything, he seemed oblivious to her. "You need to stop the bleeding," she told him. "That is if you want me to stay alive long enough for you to enjoy my company."

"Don't have anything to bandage your arm with," he mumbled, turning his head to stare out the window.

She didn't like the idea of his hands on her dress, but if she wanted the bleeding stopped, something needed to be done. "Rip up my petticoats and wrap the fabric around my arm. Maybe that will stop the blood," she said, leaning back and closing her eyes.

Terror swept through her when she felt his clammy hands against her legs, but she realized he was only tearing the fabric. He sat next to her before he bandaged the wound. She wondered if the ball was still embedded in her arm or if it passed through. No matter. Unless Roc found her, she'd probably die, if not from the wound then from Blair beating her because she would never willingly allow him to touch her intimately.

As the city lights dimmed and the road roughened, she dozed a few times, the ache in her arm became a dull throb. Perhaps she was getting used to the pain.

"Wake up," he shook her, his hand on her wounded arm.

She cried out at the pain and rude awakening. "Where are we?" She sat up trying to look out the window. "Are we stopping?"

"Just long enough to buy some food and whiskey. Need a new carriage with fresh horses. Can you walk?" he asked, "No, better stay out here. Don't want anyone to see you with me."

"I don't, Blair, I don't feel well." She tried not to say anything but he was asking things of her she couldn't do.

He helped her from the vehicle, setting her on a boulder near the side of the road. "Stay here until I get back. I don't want to have to chase after the likes of you."

She nodded, understanding if she tried to escape, she could only manage a few feet. She left all her hopes in Roc finding her before Blair hurt her again. A cool breeze chilled her and a full moon lit the earth. She wrapped her arms around herself, trying to ward off the chilly night.

"There you are. Thought I told you to stay put." He slapped her face, knocking her off the boulder.

Landing on her shoulder, she cried out again. "I didn't go anywhere." She knew the folly in protesting and was grateful the new carriage and horses rolled up before he could vent his anger on her again.

"Get in," he told her, standing beside the carriage with the door open for her. "I don't have all night to wait for you."

Pushing away from the ground, she tried to stand but fell back down. She tried again but didn't have the strength. "I can't move," she said.

"Liar, you're just trying to stall for time." But he picked her up and helped her inside.

She fell against the seat, "Where are we going?"

"Gretna Green. We're getting married as soon as possible."

~ * ~

The Duchess sent for the constables then Drake, while David set out to search all the places they might find Caitlin. Charlotte was worried sick for her son as well as Caitlin, his new wife.

She rarely paced but that was what she was doing now. Scarlett watched her wringing her hands while David tried to console her.

"Scarlett, I've known the marquis for over twenty years, and I would have never thought he was capable of something like this. He imprisoned that beautiful woman and got her pregnant, all the time labeling her as his mistress."

"Well, you must not have known him so well," Scarlett said bitterly. "He's not what a marquis should be." She set a new plate of lemon bars on a nearby table before pouring both of them a brandy.

"Richard is beside himself. He's so worried about Caitlin. I've never seen him like this."

"He's never been in love before," Scarlett said then added, "or a soon to be father. Caitlin has become his world, everything in it revolves around her."

"What can we do for them, besides sit and wait for news? At times like these, I'd rather be a man."

"They can go out and search. They can do something. We have to sit and wait. I do believe I need another lemon bar, you?" She handed the plate to Charlotte.

Charlotte bit into one but set in down. For some reason it was tasteless. The last time she'd been this worried, well she didn't remember the last time. Caitlin was so young and beautiful. While it didn't surprise her that men coveted her for her beauty, she knew the knowledge went over Caitlin's head.

"Did you see the look on your son's face when you told him Caitlin was not here waiting for him? He was horrified and I knew at that moment so many monstrous ideas were sweeping through his head."

"He was beside himself with fear for his wife and baby, don't forget the child growing in her womb," Charlotte said, her words spoken whisper thin her fear tangible. "The heir to all of this."

With all her charges she'd been through so much, but never such a direct threat on a woman's life. Of course Ella had been kidnapped, but she never found out about it until Ella rescued herself. And Christel's baby had been kidnapped and kept away from her, and she'd been instrumental in finding and recovering the child for Christel.

She thought back on all the years that had passed since William, Duke of Ravenswood, Richard's father, passed away. He had been the love of her life, but she'd found someone else, David McLellan. Life had been good for her, and now she prayed it would prove just as wonderful for Richard.

Oh, how she prayed the rest of her life would be blessed with peace and quiet, yet she acknowledged she might grow bored if there wasn't at least a tiny bit of excitement."

"And Fayth ran off to America with Jarrett. I feared for her but I truly didn't believe her life was ever in danger. Larena nearly got herself imprisoned for being too inquisitive."

"We've had quite the time, haven't we," Scarlett said laughing then brushing the tears from her eyes.

"We just have to get Caitlin back safe and sound," Charlotte said.

"What will tomorrow bring?" Scarlet asked.

Chapter Ten

Roc and Winston checked out all the houses, every last one where Caitlin might have found refuge from the marquis. Nothing. His heart in his throat, he raced to the tavern where Cat played when she tried to pay him her rent. She would feel protected there.

The tavern owner would do his best to keep her safe. He would send a message of her whereabouts, but he'd been so many places no messages could have reached him.

Almost before his stallion pulled to a stop in front of the establishment he was on foot, tying the reins to a post. A carriage swept past him, nearly barreling over him in its haste. He stared at the vehicle, his heart racing, a shadow passing through him. Then, in a few quick strides he entered the pub.

"Is she here?" He noticed the marquis and the men holding him. "What did you do with Caitlin?"

"Fiona you mean?" the marquis said in a tight whisper. "That man ran off with my Fiona."

"What man?" Roc asked, needing to shake the information from the odious marquis. The revulsion he felt seeing him and knowing what he'd done to Cat nearly undid him.

"The one your wife called, Blair," the tavern owner said. "She didn't want to go with him, but after she was shot, she didn't have the strength to fight him off and he kicked her poor dog."

"Shot!" Roc's heart leapt to his throat as he grabbed the marquis by the throat, ready to kill him. "What happened? Tell me everything and don't leave anything out."

"I stumbled and my pistol went off. Hit my Fiona in the shoulder.

Didn't mean to shoot her." Tears slipped from his eyes, clearly distraught by what he'd done.

"Does anyone know where or have any idea as to the direction O'Connell is taking Caitlin?" Roc asked needing to find her before anything else happened to her.

"Heard talk about marrying her even though she's your wife. Seems he thinks his marriage will overrule yours. Feel as if I'm surrounded by crazy men, but I suppose she is so beautiful she could drive a man insane," the pub owner said, wiping off the countertop as he spoke.

"Probably headed north to Scotland," someone behind him said. "Gretna Green is the closest and they don't ask any questions. Heard him say he didn't want to marry used goods, though. Don't think that man knows what he wants."

"Winston." Roc's voice held a note of panic. "We're headed north."

"Yes, sir," he said. "Ready anytime you are, sir."

"The closest inn is about eight miles from here. I'm going to assume O'Connell will want to change up horses there as will we."

"He won't stay very far ahead of us. He must be thinking we'll catch up to him," Winston said, following Roc out the door. "That is if he even believes you'll follow."

"Beast come," Roc said.

Mounted and with Beast on Roc's lap, the two men rode, a full moon casting much needed light on the road, while shadows left eerie sensations spilling down Roc's spine. Not knowing how Cat was undid Roc. He couldn't keep his mind from traveling to the worst-case scenario. She had to be all right. He made himself believe when he caught up to them she would be just like he saw her the day before.

Miles pounded beneath the horse's hooves and when they finally drew up in front of the inn, no carriage waited. They were still ahead of them.

"We need to make this exchange quickly. You take care of the horses and I'll check inside."

Roc dismounted, handing the reins of his stallion to a stable boy. "I want to purchase two more horses for me and two for my friend. Have them saddled and ready in five minutes."

206

Roc strode to the inn and Winston followed the stable boy. "Pack a satchel of food for three. Don't really care what it is. Whatever you've got ready."

"Yes, sir, we've ham and cheese. Wife just pulled a fresh loaf of bread from the oven."

"Did a man and a woman stop here a little while ago?" Roc asked, slapping his riding gloves on his leg, impatient for an answer.

"Just a man," the innkeeper said. "He purchased some food, changed the horses on his carriage and left. Didn't see a woman."

Roc turned to Winston who just returned from the stables, "He wouldn't leave her alone. He'd be afraid she'd try to escape." Roc didn't want to pursue his next thought.

"Don't like telling you this, sir. But Caitlin might not have been able to run away from him. She was shot, you know. Horses are ready any time you are."

"Either that or she knew we'd be following and she'd didn't want to risk further injury. We both know what that man is capable of when he's angry." They needed to hurry. O'Connell wouldn't stop for anything. Not as long as he didn't have to. He could just keep changing horses and drivers.

"Keep positive thoughts, I say. Caitlin won't give up as long as she knows you're coming for her. We both know she's got grit and the horses are faster than any carriage."

"I pray to God the wound is only a flesh wound. If that ball is lodged in her arm, infection could set in." When he finally caught up to Caitlin, he didn't know in what condition he'd find her.

"You prepared to take out the bullet?" Winston asked. "If you don't want to, you know I can do it."

Roc grit his teeth, "I can do it but let's still keep the best scenario in mind and hope it's a flesh wound, nothing more."

"Horses are ready." The stable boy poked his head inside the inn.

Roc paid the innkeeper and tipped the stable boy. Mounting one of the horses and with reins of the other horses in hand, both he and Winston headed north again.

Another hour passed before he saw a carriage in the distance. "You think that's them?" Winston asked. "Sure does look as if it could be."

"I pray it is. I need to see Cat." Roc urged his horse faster, wanting to be there now. He needed to see Cat, hold her and reassure she was safe with him, that everything would turn out.

"He's dangerous. Don't forget that when you stop the carriage. O'Connell could shoot us both," Winston said.

"You're not telling me anything I don't know already." Roc felt like a wild man with only one objective in his head. He spurred his horse faster, knowing he could regret the action but also understanding he couldn't wait.

"You got a plan?" Winston asked as he kept pace with Roc.

"Of course I do," Roc grinned, yet the plan was too simple by far and didn't come without risk.

Minutes later, Winston pulled aside the lead horse, bringing the carriage to a stop.

The driver didn't protest, instead he held up his hands. "I'm not armed. Don't shoot."

"Just get down and step aside. We're not highwaymen. I just want my wife back. The man inside kidnapped her." He sounded too calm even though his heart raced and his nerves seem to be unraveling.

With his pistol pointed toward the carriage, he opened the door. O'Connell held Caitlin in front of him as a shield.

"Shoot me and you could kill her," O'Connell said, his voice shaking.

"Let her go," Roc said, unwilling to take a shot that might hit Cat instead of O'Connell.

From outside, Beast growled, barring his teeth.

"Stay put," Roc ordered.

Winston opened the opposite door. "You're outnumbered, O'Connell. There's nowhere for you to go. While Roc won't shoot you, I don't have anyone blocking you from my bullet."

"Best you let Caitlin go then slowly place your gun on the floor," Roc said, watching him closely, his hand steadier than he thought possible.

"Put your hands up," Winston added with a low growl.

"Kick the gun outside," Roc ordered, watching for some movement that would indicate O'Connell wasn't about to comply.

O'Connell obeyed and when he lifted his hands in the air, Cat crumpled to the seat, her body limp.

"Cat!" he gasped, air pummeling from his lungs as he rushed to catch her in his arms before she hit the ground.

Her shallow breathing and tiny moan of pain left him wishing for a quick ride to the next inn. The next shelter was about twenty minutes by carriage and ten by horse. Without examining her, he didn't know if he could risk taking her by horse, yet her condition didn't give him a choice.

"Want me to get him out of the carriage, Sir?" Winston asked, motioning for the earl to vacate the vehicle before Roc could answer.

"No, I'm going to ride with Cat to the next inn. See if the driver has rope and tie him up. We'll send for a constable at the next place." Roc held Cat tenderly in his arms.

"I'll see you there," Roc said after Cat was safely astride the horse. He knew he could be making a huge mistake by aggravating the wound, but the time he was going to save could mean her life. Gut instinct told him hers was not a flesh wound.

"Ride with care. You've precious cargo," Winston called after him, "I'll be there soon."

Just as he calculated, he arrived at the inn in about ten minutes. Striding inside, he called out for the innkeeper. "My wife's badly injured. I want a room then clean bandages and hot water, soap and whiskey." He waited for the man to give him a key and a room number, explaining how his man would arrive soon with a prisoner and he was to call a constable.

Taking the steps two at a time, he stopped in front of the door, "Roc? You really came for me." She tried to reach out and touch, but it seemed the pain stopped her.

"Yes, of course, I'm glad to see you're awake. How does your arm feel?" He knew it must hurt terribly.

"Like I've been shot. Where's Blair? Where's Beast?"

"You don't need to worry about him and your dog stayed with Winston and will arrive with him in the carriage. Blair's not going to bother you again." He set her on a chair, relieved she was talking and seemingly alert. On the trip here, she barely moved.

"That's what Addie and Hamilton told me then he showed up in the pub. Roc!" she cried out when he touched her.

"I have to look at this. Fix it."

A knock on the door then, "Sir, I've the hot water and bandages, everything else you asked for. Anything else you need that you might not have thought of?"

"A second bottle of whiskey. Hurry." He unwrapped the makeshift bandage. Touching the wound, she flinched each time and tried not to let out sounds of pain.

"Roc, it hurts more now... Do you have to keep touching it?"

"I need to assess the damage, and I'm afraid it's going to hurt a hell of a lot more before I'm done. The ball is still in your arm, and it has to come out now then I'm going to have to stitch it."

"Here's the second bottle of whiskey you asked for." The errand boy stood at the door after handing over the bottle.

Roc ignored the boy for a moment before reaching into his pocket and tossing him a coin. "Thanks."

"Drink this." He held the bottle out to Cat.

Wide eyed, she was looking at him and shaking her head. "The baby...don't think it's good for him."

"Him? You sure?"

"No..."

"Well, this will help dull the pain and you're going to need it when I pour more of it on the wound before I dig the ball out of your arm. It's going to hurt like nothing you've never imagined."

"More than the broken ribs?"

He didn't want to frighten her but she should understand the truth. "More."

She reached out with her good arm and drank before she handed it back to him. "There."

"You need to drink more. I want you so drunk you won't comprehend what I'm doing and hopefully you won't feel a thing," he told her, knowing what he was about to do was still going to hurt no matter what he gave her to drink or how much.

She heaved a long deep sigh then drank. "Is that enough?" she asked after taking several long gulps.

"For now." He handed her a leather strap from his belt. "Bite down on this." He dreaded what he had to do next, but there was no way around it.

Her violet blue eyes wide with questions, she still did as he said. Once the strap was firmly in her mouth, "Bite down hard," he told her before he cut the sleeve of her gown away with his knife.

When he poured the whisky into the bullet hole, he thought she was going to jump from the chair. The tiny whimpering noises he heard broke his heart. He despised what he was forced to do and what he'd been unable to prevent.

"I'm sorry *mon petite chatte*. Truly I don't want to do this." With one finger he explored the wound, finally discovering the location of the ball. Two fingers inside the wound, he pulled the bullet out then held it up.

"Roc..." Her eyes closed and her body began to slump, the leather strap falling from her mouth.

He caught her mid-air then set her on the bed, still needing to stitch and bandage the wound. The fact she wasn't aware of any more pain was a godsend, but as soon as she woke not only would her arm throb but her head would pound from the half bottle of whiskey he had her drink.

"Sir," Winston opened the door. "Everything alright?"

"I had to take the ball out and bandage her arm again, need to stitch it first. Can you get me something? If there's no infection, she should be fine in a few days. O'Connell?"

"The village constable has him in custody. Don't think much of anything is going to happen to the man. All we can do is encourage him to go home when they let him go."

"He kidnapped Cat," Roc said, incredulous that nothing would happen to him. "He should be in prison, not returning to his life in Portrush."

"O'Connell tells a different story. He says he was trying to get help for her and that he and his driver were attacked by highwaymen who shot her," Winston said, regarding Roc thoughtfully. "You willing to go along with that?"

"So he tells one story and we tell another one. That all seems way too convenient but it doesn't surprise me." Roc paced, thinking and wishing he had more than one word against the other.

211

"Neither of us have proof of the tale," Winston said.

"But we have Cat and when she's well, she will tell them what he did and that he kidnapped her from the tavern." Roc understood all too well how these things would go.

"I've the room next door. What can I get you now? Something to eat for Caitlin?"

"Bring up tea and a bowl of soup for Cat. If she doesn't wake up soon on her own, I'm going to wake her up. See if they have willow bark tea. I'd like whatever they're serving for dinner and another bottle of wine. Also, anything that looks appealing."

Winston left and Roc returned to his vigil by Cat's side. He smoothed her hair away from her face. Bloody hell, but when O'Connell beat her, he swore she'd never feel pain again. His promise to her had not been kept.

Holding her hand, he closed his eyes, imagining the rest of their lives together. Good lord but all he'd wanted after his years working for the government was peace and quiet.

He needed that peace and quiet with his Cat. It would begin now, today as soon as he made sure her arm healed.

"Roc?"

Her voice was whisper thin. She opened her eyes and tried to lift her hand to touch him. He pulled it into his. It was so cold.

"How are you feeling?" he asked, kissing the back of her hand, smiling and trying to send encouragement her way.

"I don't know. My head is pounding and my arm throbs. It was the whiskey, wasn't it?"

"Most likely. Winston is bringing soup for you and other food if your stomach will accept it." He needed for her to eat and maybe some of the soup would be good for her.

"Blair?"

"For now, he's imprisoned. When you're well enough in a few days you can give testimony as to what he did." Roc said. "Then hopefully, he'll spend a long time in jail."

"I wish we could just let him go and forget any of this ever happened." She moistened her lips then and tried to clear her throat. "I don't have any ill will toward him, and I think the people of Portrush need him. He did provide for the poor sometimes."

"You're thirsty and I don't have anything for you to drink." Thinking about O'Connell giving anything away didn't ring true for him. If he did, it was to get something back in return.

"But you do, I've brought a couple of things you can choose from." Winston backed into the room with a platter of food. "I've the tea you wanted. Should I pour Caitlin a cup?" he asked cheerfully. "There is the soup, of course, whiskey and that bottle of wine I brought up earlier."

"A cup of tea would be nice," Caitlin said.

"It will also ease the pain," Roc told her, "But not like the whiskey. It won't make you drunk or hurt the baby in any way. So, no worries. Just relax and let me take care of you."

"Can you help me sit up?" she asked, pushing hair away from her face. She still had a few pins in her hair, and when she ran her hands through what was left of the chignon, they fell out.

Roc picked them up then fixed her hair, securing it in place before he helped her to sit. Winston stood in front of her with a steamy cup of tea. "Here you are. Finish this and I'll bring you a cup of soup."

Winston stayed for less than an hour while everyone ate. Roc was thrilled when Cat included bread and cheese in her meal of soup.

"I haven't eaten since yesterday," she told him. "My stomach is fine right now, so I should eat before you have to do something that will change that."

"How's your arm?" he asked, unwilling to tell her he would have to take a look at it in another hour then wake her several times during the night.

"Right now I feel a dull ache. I'm sure when the tea wears off, it's going to hurt like crazy, isn't it?" She plucked at her skirt.

"Is there any chance I could get something clean to wear and maybe a bath. My arm is sticky with blood, and I'm afraid this dress has been ruined. If I'm still wearing these clothes in the next hour, I think I'll scream."

"So sorry. I should have asked at the desk for clothes for you. There must be someone who could head me in the direction of a seamstress. For now, let's get you out of the gown and anything that's bloody. I'll get you a hot bath."

When the tub and the water arrived, Roc helped her from the dress, trying to salvage what he could of her underclothes so she'd have something clean to sleep in. He helped her into the tub.

"It's heavenly," she sighed softly, leaning her head on the rim and closing her eyes.

"Would you like me to wash your back?" he asked, knowing how that sounded but she would need help and for the second time since he met Cat and was confronted with her beautiful body, he was not aroused. All he wanted was to make this as easy a healing time as possible.

She gazed at him, questioning then seeming to see he was serious and concerned she nodded. "I think that would be nice."

He soaped the washrag before running it along her back. "Tell me if I hurt you, your arm."

"If you hurt me, I'll probably gasp or cry out. You'll know." She managed a small laugh.

"I do need to wash the blood from your arm. Some of it has dried. I didn't do a very good job when I was searching for the bullet." He remembered how her wound looked. O'Connell did little to help her after she was shot. All he managed was to wrap some cloth around her arm.

"Do whatever you need, but promise me you'll hold me tonight. I need your arms around me. It seems as if it's been years since you held me and in reality, it's only been one night."

"I'll do whatever you want," he said, wishing the bullet had gone into his arm instead of hers.

"You're so agreeable." She smiled seeming to enjoy his company. "I like that side of you."

"Where you're concerned, I'm always agreeable. I thought you knew that," Roc said, grinning and trying not to let on how serious her wound was. It had been left too long without care. In his experiences, he'd seen strong men die from this type of injury. She was fragile and delicate, he paused in thought, but strong enough to survive broken ribs.

~ * ~

214

Caitlin thrashed in the bed. Images of men shooting at her, tugging at her arms and legs, haunted her. They were more interested in what they wanted than what she needed. She pushed at the hand on her shoulder. "No, no..." she moaned, realizing tears slipped from her eyes, "Leave me alone."

"Cat, wake up please. I've got to check your arm then bandage it again. It needs a clean dressing. Don't be afraid of me. I'm only going to help," Roc shook her gently.

"Don't want you to touch me. No." She turned away, wishing he'd go away." All she wanted was to sleep in peace. "Don't need a new bandage."

"I have to, wake up little cat. After I check this, you can go back to sleep and I'll leave you be until dawn." He stroked her back. "I promise I'll let you sleep again."

She moved into his caress, loving the tender concern this touch elicited. "I thought you were going to hold me, not torment me," she told him. "I don't want you to check the bandage."

He laughed softly and the sound warmed her soul. "I'll hold you when I'm finished. I did keep you wrapped in my arms for several hours. Ah...you're waking up now. I think you had a bad dream."

"I don't want to wake up," she said petulantly, but she did. The nightmares were horrendous. Truth was she didn't want to go to sleep again if meant another bad dream.

"Good girl, now can you sit up by yourself?" he watched her, his soft brown eyes penetrating her soul.

"I'll try." She pushed against the bed, inching upward until her back finally rested alongside the wall. She smiled at him, needing to reach out and touch him, but she kept her hands in her lap.

"I'm going to unwind this dressing." Slowly he took the cloth off. His gaze focused on her arm. His sharp indrawn breath gave her reason to question what he must see.

"What is it?"

"Nothing," he said yet his brows were drawn together, crease lines marring his forehead and she knew he wasn't telling her the truth.

"Don't lie to me," she told him. "What is it that has you so concerned? You're terrifying me, and I know you don't want to do that." She needed the truth. "What's wrong with my arm?"

"There is some infection, a few red streaks. I'm going to rinse it out with more whiskey. It's going to sting." He waited for her reaction while he picked up the bottle.

"I can handle whatever you need to do. Just do it though. Don't make me wait. I want to get this over with." She held her breath, anticipating the pain that would come with the cure.

He handed her the leather strap she was becoming too familiar with. Slipping it between her teeth, she gasped as he poured the whiskey over the wound, yet the stinging didn't last very long.

"I shouldn't have to do this again. It really is much better," He wrapped cloth around her arm once more. "I'll check this in about six hours." He sat back, crossing his arms over his chest, appearing pleased with himself. "Now, what would you like to eat?"

She really didn't care but knew he wanted an answer. "Soup always tastes good and any fruit the inn might have. Are there still strawberries?" Just the thought of food in her stomach made it roll with nausea.

"I'll find out. You sleep and I'll be back in an hour or so," he told her, rising from the chair.

He was being too solicitous by far. "I don't want to sleep," she told him peevishly and feeling bored to tears. "That's all I've done for what seems like forever. I crave the feel of the sun on my face and the wind in my hair."

He cleared his throat as he turned on his way out the door. "You need to rest so your wound will heal cleanly. When you're strong enough, I'll take you for a short outing. Besides, it's still night so the sun isn't shining yet."

"A small walk out doors right now would cause more infection?" she asked sarcastically but she really didn't know and understood she should trust his judgment.

"Yes, your body needs to be strong enough to fight the infection. Now, I'll make a bargain with you. If there is no sign of infection when I redress the wound, we can take a stroll and explore the inn tonight. That should ease the boredom setting in."

216

"And maybe down the road a little ways in the morning?" She pushed him, but perhaps if she smiled and made other promises, he would see it her way. "We could make love."

He laughed from the belly before a look of tender concern washed over his features. "You're trying to bribe me. It would work if I weren't so worried about you. There is nothing more that I want than to make love to my lovely wife, but it's not going to happen today or even tomorrow."

"You don't have to laugh at me." She turned away from him, embarrassed yet realizing he was possibly right. Whenever the willow bark tea wore off, her arm throbbed and the pain nearly made her swoon.

"Ah, *mon petite chatte*, I'm not laughing at you. I'm laughing at how easily you can read my mind. More than anything I'd like you to seduce me then I'd love to give you everything your heart desires. For now, I'm going to check on a few things and see if I can find a dressmaker where I can purchase a few pieces of clothing for you." He bent over slightly and kissed her forehead. "I'll see you in a few hours, behave yourself."

When the door closed behind him, she pushed herself off the bed and tried to walk around the room. With the help of the furniture, she was able to navigate the perimeter. Perhaps he was right. She was too weak to walk very, far but she really needed a tiny bit of fresh air.

Pulling the curtain across the window, the sun was shining, the sky was nearly clear, and a few billowy white clouds dotted the horizon. She tugged open the window then inhaled the clean fresh air. People came and went from the inn. Winston sat on a log down the road smoking a cigar.

Tempted to lean out the window and wave to him, she sat back on a nearby chair instead. Winded, she closed her eyes, hoping that when a new day dawned, she would be stronger and she unwillingly accepted the fact that Roc was correct about the state of her health.

The tea beside her bed had grown tepid but she drank it anyway, hoping it would help her sleep if she didn't have as much pain. Instead of sleep though, when she closed her eyes, she imagined Roc's fingers dancing across her body. Could almost feel the caress of his tongue and teeth on her skin. She moaned softly, wishing he was lying beside her and holding her.

When she woke, her body was covered with a fine sheen of perspiration. Her body shuddered slightly when she touched her tender nipples. She was hot and wet, so ready for him she could almost feel him deep inside.

Sitting up, she brushed hair from her face then wrapped it around itself before tying it in a knot. Sunshine no longer filtered through the window. Instead, darkness seemed to envelope the countryside. Except for the moonlight the blackness would be all encompassing.

"Where are you, Roc?" she murmured, searching the room for him. "It couldn't take that long to find a dressmaker and purchase a few things." But she knew he had other errands to run, business to take care of, things he would never reveal to her.

"My arm doesn't hurt as much." She touched it to make sure she wasn't dreaming. The tenderness around the wound seemed to have vanished, and she wondered if that meant there was no more infection.

She broke off a piece of dry bread then picked at it, her stomach rumbling. If he didn't show up soon, she was going to have to figure out what was left of her clothing that would be decent if she dressed. She needed something more to eat than day old bread, knowing she would have to go downstairs to procure a meal.

The door opened and Roc's smiling face was the first thing she saw. "Hope I didn't take too long. Wanted to give you time to rest. Are you hungry?" He set a platter of food on the table and a bottle of wine.

"Famished," she told him. "Do you have a dress for me?" She sat down, peaking under the platter coverings. He brought roasted venison, berries and tomatoes along with cucumber slices.

"My mother, bless her heart, sent two dresses along with some underthings. It seems the tavern owner had a message delivered to her and an approximate direction we were headed."

From a wrapped package, he pulled out a stylish dark blue dress then all the underclothing she would need. "Do you like the dress?" he asked. "There's another one. It's a deep red."

"They are beautiful." Since before she'd been with Roc, she'd never seen or worn clothing like this. And these items were purchased on the spur of the moment.

"I'm glad you like them," he said as he dished up food then poured wine for both of them. "If your arm shows no infection, I'll take you for a walk tomorrow and if you continue in that vein, we'll drive home the next day."

"Can we go home tomorrow? I just want to leave this place and the thoughts that go with it behind me." She left her food untouched, waiting for an answer. Yet she was tempted to wrap her arms around him and kiss him, no bribery intended.

He was smiling at her but shaking his head. "I don't want to put you in more jeopardy. I've nearly lost you twice..."

"You're not going to lose me on a carriage ride to town. I'm not a delicate flower that needs to be coddled," she told him in a huff, setting her fork on the table. Unable to face this man who thought he had to treat her as if she were a fine porcelain, she stood. "I'm suddenly not hungry."

She strode to the window, leaning on the pane, tears slipping from her eyes. He was beside her, turning her so she was pressed against him. "I'm so sorry." His lips found hers in a long drugging kiss, one she learned to yearn for every moment she was awake.

He held her so close she heard his heartbeat, felt each breath of air he inhaled, and she longed for him. "I didn't mean to cry."

"No one ever means to shed tears," he told her, kissing the tiny drops of moisture on her face. "While I don't pretend to understand what you're feeling, I've been in a similar situation. It's not easy to sit still and wait to heal, but it's for the best," he told her.

"I'll bet you didn't sit still until some doctor told you that you could get up and move," she spoke softly yet waited for the denial.

"And you would be right," he told her. "I wish I could deny your accusation, but you have to understand, I'm not tiny and breakable. There's nothing fragile about me. I'm afraid if something happens, you'll break." He paused seeming to think, "That was a life or death situation. If I didn't leave the spot, I'd be dead now or in the hands of an enemy who inflict torture with glee."

"Please, Roc." His dark brown eyes shuttered and it seemed he closed himself to her for a moment. "None of that matters now."

"Eat and we'll talk later. One step at a time. I, too, would like to go home. I'm tired of the inn and long to share our bed. Come back to the table and find something that will sit well in your stomach."

She licked her dry lips and acknowledged to herself she'd like to eat. "One step at a time," she agreed, letting him hold her arm and escort her to the table.

"I like it when you're agreeable," he laughed, sipping his wine and seeming to watch her eat.

Artfully she lowered her lashes. "I'm always agreeable. At least I think I am."

He chuckled, "I'm not sure I completely concur, but in any case, I enjoy every side of you, the agreeable and the not so agreeable."

"You'd hate it if I always accepted your word as gospel," she told him.

An uneasy silence followed. She didn't know what he would say or if this was just a ploy to make her eat. In any case, she would have eaten. The wine tasted good and she indulged in a glass, feeling its effect almost as soon as the liquid hit her stomach.

The venison was a bit tough, but the fruit and vegetables were wonderful. She ate until she couldn't then set her fork on the plate. "We finished the first part of our bargain. What's the next step?" Caitlin asked.

Roc leaned back in the chair, looking too handsome and extremely confidant, but she acknowledged, he always appeared sure of himself and master of his small world, to which of course he was the ruler.

"If you're through eating, I'm going to take another look at the bullet hole in your arm." He stood, holding his hand out to her.

She placed hers in his, feeling the warmth soak through her. "After that?" She searched for a miracle to happen, longed for him to tell her if everything looked fine, he would take her home tonight, yet she understood it wasn't prudent to travel in the dead of night.

He set her on the bed and she wondered why he didn't keep her in the chair. She touched his cheek with the back of her hand then he placed his on top of hers. "I know, sweetheart. This hasn't been easy for either of us, but with a little patience, it's going to be over soon. Then we have the rest of our lives to look forward to."

"I'm afraid I'm all out of patience," she told him as he unwound the fabric.

He touched the wound in different places. For once she didn't flinch or feel more than a small tenderness. "Does this hurt?" he asked her watching her intently.

"No, not much." She wanted to hear then *we're going home* but he continued to look at her.

"You're telling me the truth," he said softly. "You wouldn't lie to me just to get your way."

She stiffened at his words even though she considered doing that very thing. "No, I didn't lie but I thought about it. The wound really hurts no more than expected."

He chuckled softly, "You can't lie, even if you tried. I'd bet you tell me the truth a moment after the falsehood was uttered."

"I just want out of this room. I feel as if the walls are closing in around me." She closed her eyes then, "Tomorrow we'll go for a walk and if I'm strong enough, we'll go home in that fancy carriage of yours."

"Ours," he corrected. "And yes, I want what you want as long as I don't think it'll put you in danger."

The next morning he woke her with a kiss and a smile. Once again, the weather was perfect with clear sunny skies. "Are you ready to try that walk?" He kissed her again.

"Can we eat first?" She smiled, pushing hair from her face. Her nightdress had slipped from her shoulder, revealing a breast, her nipple a tight bud. To her surprise he didn't blink, yet his brows drew together and crease lines formed on his forehead. Perhaps he'd not grown immune to her after all.

"There's porridge and bread, some honey and milk and I believe a platter of bacon was also delivered."

"Hot tea?" she asked, needing something hot to help her wake up this morning before she ate.

With a hint of reluctance in his eyes, he pulled her nightdress over her shoulders. "If we're home tonight..."

It seemed he wanted her to finish the sentence in her mind but, "I'll make love to you."

Deep in his throat he groaned but he checked the wound. "Just as good as yesterday. Now there's not even a hint of infection. What would you like to wear?"

"The dark blue dress. You'll have to help me with the corset and the fastenings. Everything is in the back." She laughed at his look of distress. He must believe she was getting her strength back and the sight of him, wanting her, gave her reason to look to their future.

"I'm not sure I can be responsible for my actions. Should I get someone who works here to help you?" He ran a finger around the collar of his shirt.

"I don't want anyone but you," she told him, her hand on his chest, her chin lifted so she gazed into his dark brown eyes.

"Not sure it's safe." He lowered his head, kissing her deeply before moving away from her. "If you hope to go home today, you should make this easier on me. I do believe you've learned the power you hold over my mind and body. Where you're concerned, I'm only a helpless man and if I see you naked..." he moistened his lips. "And healthy..."

"Fine, I'll go into the changing room, but when the corset needs to be laced, you won't have a choice." This was a side of her husband she'd never seen and she had to acknowledge to herself she liked it. "Since Adara is not here with us, you have to lace and fasten it or I'll be parading around naked because, now that I have your permission to leave, I'm not staying here."

"You would parade around naked? Somehow, I don't believe you. That kind of threat will never convince me to do your wishes. However, since I want to see a smile on your face, I'll do whatever you ask within reason."

After a few minutes of struggling with the clothes and thinking to ask him to help her sooner than the lacings, she emerged from the room. "I had trouble with everything."

"Your arm hurt?" He looked ready to put a stop to the walk.

"Just when I tried to pull things up. It was the position I had to twist my arm that hurt, otherwise my arm doesn't give me any problems at all." She tapped her foot, tilting her head to the side and watching him for any sign he might go back on his promise. She turned her back to him, looking over one shoulder.

His duties finished, he turned her and kissed her again. "Doesn't seem I can get enough of you. I need you in my arms like I need to breathe." He held out his arm for her. "Shall we?"

By the time they reached the outside of the inn, she was a little short of breath. He seemed to notice and stopped, allowing her a chance to breathe deeply several times.

She inhaled a long slow breath, enjoying the fresh summer air. "Thank you. I needed this. Feel stronger already."

"As soon as you're ready," he told her, patting her hand.

"I'm ready." They started down the lane, keeping off the road. The morning breeze was brisk but the air was warm. Just as the day before, a few billowy clouds gathered on the horizon.

They walked for about ten minutes. "We should turn around now," she told him, feeling a bit unsteady on her legs.

"Let's sit under that tree for a few minutes first. You can rest in the shade then we'll start back," he told her, spreading a blanket he'd thought to bring for just this time of occasion.

"Look, what's that?" she asked, pointing to a long line of wagons and carts of what appeared to be a caravan of naval men.

"I don't know but I'd like to find out. Can you stay here by yourself for a few minutes?"

She was nodding, finding it difficult to make out all of the shapes. "Are those prison carts?" she asked thinking of Blair and what that might mean for him. Truly, she wanted him punished but not sent to Australia or worse Tasmania.

"I believe they are." Roc set out at a fast pace, not looking back and seemingly intent on his destination.

She watched as he engaged two men in conversation then sauntered past the carts to the last one. He spoke to someone then turned on a heel, striding back to her.

When he was close, she rose, folding the blanket then draping it over her arm. "What is happening?" she asked, somehow knowing it concerned Blair.

Roc ran his hands through his hair then turned to watch the vanishing procession of prison carts. "It seems there was no need for your testimony after all. O'Connell has been encouraged to join the British navy. The choice was, as I'm sure you thought, a trip to Australia or serving the country for a few years as a sailor."

She weighed the horrible choices in her mind and would have come to the same conclusion. A few years of service to the country versus a lifetime and no possible release to Australia as his choices would have prompted the decision he made.

"He's gone then. Do you think he can escape this sentence?" she asked not really sure what she wanted except that he was out of her life forever.

"The only way he can escape is by death. He won't chance that, not with the possibility of returning home," Roc said, staring at the convoy as it slowly disappeared from view.

Chills swept through her and a feeling that finally her life was her own. She clung to Roc as if he were the source of her life. "I don't want Blair to die."

"And there's no reason to believe this will end in his death. Most seamen survive their enlistment." Roc said, trying to reassure her.

"I know that, at least my logical side tries to tell me he will be fine but Roc, I know him. He's arrogant and vain, and he won't work. He believes himself above and better than other people."

"And that could be his downfall. The other men won't let him shirk his duties and they will take matters into their hands if the captain doesn't."

"He won't survive, will he?"

"Probably not," Roc sighed then changing the subject, he pointed to the inn. "Our carriage is waiting for us. I believe Winston will have our meager belongings packed. We should be home by dark if everything goes as we planned."

~ * ~

O'Sheay watched as two government officials strode arrogantly into his pub. He was always weary of the English, particularly when they arrived in pairs.

"What can I do for you two fine Englishman," he spoke in the deepest Irish brogue he could manage. "A pint of Guinness?"

One of the men held out his hand in greeting, "Drake Montgomery and this is Hamilton Winthrop."

"As I said, what can I do for you?"

"We've news of your brother, Blair O'Connell," Montgomery said, "and news of Caitlin as well."

"Don't have a brother," he replied, pushing the freshly poured pints to the men. "Only child, if you know what I mean, but I'd like news of my niece. Is she well and prospering?"

Drake tapped his fingers on the bar, seeming to think. "Caitlin is doing well. She's married to the duke of Ravenswood, Roc as you probably know him." He drank again. "You're the legal Earl of Glenwood, the oldest brother, and we're here to see you put in your rightful place. Your brother, Blair O'Connell is a member of the English navy now. Seemed after kidnapping Caitlin and finding himself on the wrong side of the law, he chose to enlist rather than spend the rest of his life in Australia.

"He won't be seeing his beloved Portrush anytime soon." Hamilton continued the conversation. "Seeing many different ports will be exciting for him."

"Don't want the title. Didn't want it twenty years ago and don't want it now," O'Sheay said. "Don't like lording it over folks who have less. I'm sure the place would decay in front of everyone's eyes if I was in charge."

"The people and the English government need an Earl here who has the well-being of his people in mind and will support the English as well."

"Not sure I can support an establishment that takes advantage of the people who don't worship the same as the queen. Doesn't seem right to me." He continued to clean the counter while Montgomerie talked to him.

"I'm certain the people of this town would prefer you to your brother," Montgomerie insisted. "There is no one else. You are the heir apparent and you have an obligation to this parish."

"Don't have any obligations where the crown and titles are concerned," he persisted. "Told you, don't want the title."

"Comes with the ability to tax or not to tax the people who work on your land. Do you want to see them thrive? Your brother didn't. I'm sure you've noticed they don't have much to spend. Noticed too that your prices for a pint are cheap. You could charge a lot more." Drake smiled at him and O'Sheay grimaced.

He understood everything Montgomerie told him was solid truth and he understood if he accepted the title, he could make their lives easier. His chin rose a notch, "Very well, what do I have to do? But mind you now, I won't be usin' the name O'Connell."

"What name you use makes no difference to the crown. You'll rake over the responsibilities. While you don't need to live at the estate, you should at least visit then take a look at the books. Bring them home and see what your brother is doing."

"You're implying the books might have been changed to make them..."

"I'm not implying anything. For all we know," Drake glanced at Hamilton, "everything is in order, but what I'm advising is that you make sure what is written down is true."

"If I do this, what will happen when Blair returns?" He hated confrontation and conceded to his younger brother when Blair confronted him with the knowledge about his sexual preferences.

"That's between you and your brother. I'm sure when you discover the truths that we think your brother has been hiding, you'll know the answer to your question." Drake finished his pint. "We'll be staying at the home next to Ida's. I believe you know it as Roc's home if you have any questions. He's given us permission to stay there for a week if necessary."

"I'll take a look tonight after work." He watched them leave the tavern, wishing they never visited Portrush and gave him this information. He was pretty sure he'd find all sorts of inconsistencies in the books.

From everything the townspeople told him about their dealings with Blair, he understood Blair stole from them. He meant to pay them back every penny he could.

Later that night, O'Sheay used the key he'd kept in a black box beneath the counter in the pub. He guessed he knew the time would eventually come when his baby brother would get into so much trouble, he couldn't get out of it.

Opening the front door, he was met with of wave of memories.

Thoughts of his mother and father, standing at the door to greet him when he came home from school, assailed him.

Recalling the anger of his parents when they found him in the stables with a young man he knew from school. They beat him, telling him he was never to do anything like that again. After that he hid his dalliances better. His parents thought the beating reformed him. Even when they died, they went to their graves believing he no longer wanted to be with men.

Blair knew and with that knowledge he blackmailed him into giving up the title. After a while he did believe it for the best. Now he was back in the home that had left him scarred and in pain.

He could help the people of Portrush and he meant to do just that. And he'd have to find a way to tell Caitlin he wasn't her uncle, just a good friend of her mother's.

Chapter Eleven

The carriage stopped in front of the townhouse just as the sun was beginning to set. Winston rode ahead and lights shone through the windows, sending a welcome home to them. His home was cheery and at this moment heaven scent. It seemed an eternity since he'd been in either home, here or Ravenswood.

"We're here," Roc kissed Cat, waking her up and enjoying the sleepy-eyed look she regarded him with. "We're home and I'm going to carry you through the door just as I did that first night we were wed. Cook will have something delicious for dinner, and Adara will have a bath drawn for you. After that, our time is our own and we can do whatever we please."

"I finally feel as if I don't have a care in the world. At least for the moment, all our troubles are over," she told him, her voice finally without stress as Beast bounded through the door, jumping on her and nearly knocking her to the floor. "Beast, down!"

"Beast, sit, stay." Roc commanded, watching fascinated as the huge puppy did his bidding. He wanted to laugh at the sad expression on his face.

"Beast was just happy to see us." She seemed to protest the fact he expected the dog to behave.

"We have the child to think of. If this animal isn't well behaved, he could hurt the baby." He placed his hand on her belly, enjoying the tiny baby bump growing there. At one point in his life he'd never thought to have a child. Now in about seven months or so, God willing, he'd be a father.

"I'm going to try not to be terrified about what I know nothing about," she said, bending down to pat the puppy's head. "And where Beast is concerned, you seem to have a way with him. Perhaps in your spare time you should attempt to train him."

"I'll do everything I can think of to make the remaining time easier," he told her, sweeping her off her feet and striding up the stairs. She was light as a feather, and even though she didn't want to admit to the truth she was fragile and delicate. "Come, Beast," he called over his shoulder.

"You don't need to do this. I can walk," she said even while she clung to him. Then she whispered in his ear, her breath arousing him, "but I like it when you carry me."

He laughed when her teeth gently bit his ear, his body hardening instantly, "Ah, *mon petite chatte* you have sharp little teeth and claws but I'm not complaining. You can bite my ear anytime you want." He enjoyed the rush of blood to her cheeks. So charming she could try to seduce him but when he teased her about her deeds, she was embarrassed.

Stepping inside the door, he let her body slide against his. Enjoying her soft curves, his hand cupping her bottom while pulling her close enough he hoped she felt his arousal.

"Hmm...can we forego dinner and baths. Take me to the bedroom and we can explore this further," she murmured.

"You're eager to sleep with your husband?" he asked, chuckling. It seemed he'd been celibate for way too long and now that they were alone, he didn't want to wait a moment longer. "What more could a man ask for?"

The voice behind him made his immediate plans for the evening vanish, "You should wait to curb your base instincts."

Beast was wagging his tail but growling too. That was exactly the same feeling he had at the moment.

Then turning to confront the intruder, "In my own home, Mother," he told her, noticing the twinkle in her eyes, "my base needs are not your business." He set Cat on her feet. "Why are you here?"

"So sorry we intruded on your homecoming, but we brought news of your da. Things we believe you should know, things that could change your perspective." Ella stepped forward, smiling. "We can talk while eat. Cook has made all of Roc's favorites and Shepard's pie for Cat."

Cook stepped from the kitchen, grinning as if she was truly glad to see them. "I hope my pie lives up to your expectations, Lady Caitlin, and instead of Logan's fine wine, we've searched the city for some Guinness.

So, welcome home, milady."

"Would you like a bath before you eat?" Roc asked Caitlin, his first was concern was for her wellbeing, not news about her da no matter how important his mother thought it was.

"I've a nice hot bath waiting for you. The water is just being poured," Adara walked down the steps, a smile of greeting on her sweet face. "Welcome home, milady and milord."

"While I am famished, I'll enjoy the meal more if I have a bath first," Caitlin said. "I hope that's alright with the rest of you."

"If it's not they'll just have to enjoy the Guinness or the wine while they wait. I'm sure everyone knows you were shot a few days ago and your health is what is important," Roc said, his gaze resting softly on her. "I'll walk you upstairs." Then turning to Ella and his mother, "Please excuse us for a few minutes. I'm going to see if I can get a bath also."

"You make too much over the incident when we both know I'm completely recovered," Caitlin said as she followed Adara upstairs. "I don't want or need to be coddled."

Adara stopped a moment, "I believe Winston arranged for a bath for you too, sir. If you want one that is, you don't have to ask for hot water."

Addressing both Ella and his mother, "I'm going to take advantage of the hot bath. I'll be down as soon as possible, and the two of you can tell us whatever it is you think we should know then. After that, Cat and I will be happy to say goodnight."

Roc didn't wait for a response from the ladies. If they had anything to say that Cat shouldn't hear, it would have to wait. He decided then he would share everything with her. For her protection, she needed to understand the circumstances, whatever they might be. He prayed whatever information they possessed it would be good news.

Tempted to join Cat, he dismissed his urge and settled into the hot water provided for him. He heard Winston puttering around in the master chamber, most likely laying out clothing for this evening, an evening he'd planned to spend alone with Cat that had now been reduced to spending it with his mother and Ella Montgomerie.

"Will we ever have that peace and quiet we've sought," he murmured, washing himself. Finished in record time, naked, he walked into the dressing room. As he guessed, clothes were set out for him. He laughed at Winston's choice then chose a soft comfortable pair of buckskins and a white shirt that slipped over his head. He pulled his boots on and was ready to meet whatever information his mother had for them head on.

His mother had changed his nappies. He knew her well enough that clothing meant nothing to him. Tonight, he was going to dress for no one but himself and Cat.

Downstairs, Ella and his mother were engaged in a heated conversation. At least it seemed that way. When he stepped through the door, the excited chatter stopped.

"Mother, Ella." He poured a glass of whiskey then sat down across from his mother. "What are the two of you up too now?" He smiled as he sipped, slowly studying the two women.

"Nothing, nothing at all, what makes you think we are up to anything?" Charlotte asked, as if trying to avoid eye contact with him.

"I know you very well and while Ella is not well known to me, I can tell by the expressions on your faces." He sipped again. "The two of you were arguing about something and I'm sure it had to do with Cat."

"A lemon bar?" His mother tried to divert.

He laughed, "A desert before dinner? Not a chance. Where's David?" David always provided a welcome buffer between his mother and whatever mission she had on her mind. "Did he choose to let you bring damning information into my home?"

"Visiting Aidan. It seems she's pregnant again and she has this condition that keeps her severely nauseous through most of her pregnancy. He's there to help Blade with their other child, Evan."

"I thought one of her lady's maid has some kind of concoction that keeps her from being too sick," Ella said.

"She does, but David feels that fatherly need to protect his daughters as well as an excuse to see his grandchild. I understood when I wed David that Scotland would call to him often," Charlotte said. "After all, he has three of his four daughters living there."

"So," changing the subject, "was there something you wanted to tell me that you don't want Caitlin to hear?" Roc asked, sipping thoughtfully and waiting to discover the secret he didn't mean to keep from Cat.

231

"I just wanted to check with you first. There is news about her da that is life changing but not bad. Otherwise..." Charlotte paused.

"Life changing." He finished the whiskey then rose to pour another glass. He wandered around the room, glancing out the windows. Then he turned, "I want Caitlin to be apprised of everything that involves her. There will be no secrets about her life."

"Good then we'll wait until dinner and for Caitlin to join us," Charlotte said, smiling. "I do believe she'll be surprised, but when she mulls everything over, also pleased."

"What will I be pleased about?" Caitlin asked as she walked into the room. Her low-cut gown highlighting the delicate features of her face to perfection.

Bloody hell, but she was beautiful. He remembered purchasing the dress with Caitlin in mind. The evening gown was cut low and her breasts, while they'd been large before the child, nearly overflowed the bodice now. Yet the gown was still in good taste and didn't show too much. The lust he felt when they first walked through the front door returned with a vengeance.

He walked to her, offering his arm to escort into the parlor. "Should we go into dinner now or would you like something to drink first?" Then he whispered, "Or we could forego both and go straight to our bedchamber."

"Dinner would be nice," she said, gazing at him as if she'd never seen him before. "I'm hungry tonight, more so than in the last few days. I've never seen you dressed so casually, not even in Portrush. I like it."

In truth and in her presence, he'd probably never worn the casual attire. "Then dinner it is."

"Let me tell Cook we're ready. It might take a few minutes to get everything on the table," Charlotte said, disappearing though the dining room doors.

"I'd like tea then," Caitlin said, sitting down and nervously smoothing her skirts then rearranging them a second time.

Roc sat beside her, possessively draping his arm around her shoulder, toying with the tiny sleeves resting just off her shoulders and wishing they were alone and he could slide them down her arms. "Then tea it is."

Ella poured her a cup, handing it to her. "How do you feel? I know for me the first few months were exhausting. All I ever wanted to do was sleep and eat when my stomach would hold the food."

She shrugged, "Between the bullet wound and the baby, I don't know what is causing what, but today I feel so much better than I have since I was shot. Roc, since I'm healing nicely..." She turned toward him gracing him with a smile that knifed straight to his heart. "...perhaps we can do something outside tomorrow, even take a ride in a carriage."

"My wife does not like to be restrained to one spot even if it's best for her," Roc said.

"None of us do," Ella said, a tinge of outrage as well as indignation in her voice. "Drake would tie me to our bed every time I've been with child if he dared. For some reason men think women are fragile, but they've never given birth. Anyone who is delicate and fragile could not birth a child."

"Oh my." Caitlin's hand went to her chest. "We should talk sometime, openly please, but just the two of us. I'm terrified of what I don't know, and I want to hear about everything that is going to happen to me."

"I understand I've been indelicate but I'll answer any question you have." Ella said, shooting Roc a look that told him not to argue. "We should visit, just the two of us."

"The table is ready." Adara stood in the doorway then she stepped aside.

Cook and Adara, as a welcome home, had arranged a four-course dinner for Roc and Caitlin. The dinner while delicious was not a priority for Roc but feeling the need to make sure the women felt appreciated, he ate something of everything. He was more concerned about what Cat ate.

With desert served, he leaned back and to his mother, "What was the news that was so important for Cat to hear? It's growing late and I've other plans for the rest of the evening."

Primly his mother touched her napkin to her lips then set it on the table. "Drake, Ella's husband is in Portrush as we speak."

"Whatever for?" Caitlin asked. "There is nothing there, no reason for him to... My God does it have something to do with Blair?"

Roc placed a hand on hers, trying to help Cat remain calm. "I'm sure all is fine. I believe it is good news Mother has for you. Isn't it, Mother?"

"Well, the first part is not," The Duchess said, leaning forward a stern look on her face.

"Then perhaps I'd like a drink," Caitlin said.

"Wine?" Roc asked, rising to pour her a glass.

"That would be fine." She drank a large gulp before setting it down and looking at his mother. "Go on."

"First off, you do know that your da is not your father, but what you don't know is that he's not your uncle either." Charlotte paused then letting this bit of information settle into Cat's mind.

"Who is he then and why did he tell me something that's not true," Cat asked, drinking more wine as if it would help her digest the information Charlotte tossed at her.

"I believe he wanted to protect both you and your mother," Charlotte said. "And actually, he's Blair O'Connell's older brother and he's now the earl of Glenwild. When he met your mother, he was the heir apparent."

Roc watched her pale to a ghostly shade of white. He didn't want to press her for her feelings, but he needed to understand what she was thinking. Patience would be something to employ right now. Too bad he didn't have any.

"Both questions and answers are tied together," Charlotte said. "All for the good of Portrush and surrounding areas.

"So, you answered who and why but that's not the entire story, is it?" Caitlin asked.

"For some reason, and I don't have the answer for that, he relinquished his title to his younger brother. You might have a better idea as to the reason than the rest of us. Do you, dear? It's the last remaining piece of this puzzle."

Caitlin was shaking her head but the expression on her face told him she knew more than she was willing to tell. "Perhaps we should sleep on this. The reason might be something my da doesn't want people to know. I'm sure that neither you or Ella need to know the reason he gave up his heritage."

"I can only guess, but it was his secret to keep and it's obvious to me, he didn't want the world to know. Enough so, he was willing to let his brother assume the title. I'm not sure he even cared about the title," Roc said, musing softly. "He seemed content with his pub and his life.

"We can wait until the morning if there is nothing else," Charlotte said as if assuming Cat would change her mind and tell them more at a later date.

"The two of you will be back in the morning?" Roc asked skeptically, wishing his mother away. "Don't expect us to be up very early. I've other things in mind. Perhaps the two of you should consider returning in the afternoon, tomorrow night or even the next day."

"Pshaw," Charlotte waved her hand in the air. "The two of you are no longer newlyweds. You're not supposed to sleep away the day."

"Aunty," Ella set her hand on Charlotte's arm, "Drake and I are far from being newlyweds and when we have the chance, well..."

"Drake is insatiable where it comes to you. I don't expect that from my son. He has more control than your Drake." Charlotte sounded adamant.

Roc wanted to laugh at his mother, instead, he turned his attention to his wife. "You make me insatiable when I look at you." He kissed Cat's hand then brought it tenderly to his face.

Cat's eyes glimmered with the passion he'd come to expect from her. He smiled at her, knowing she wanted him just as much as he did her. "Will you come to bed with me, Cat? he asked.

"We should wait until your mother and Ella leave," Caitlin said, but to Roc she seemed to agree with him.

"Mother, the sooner the two of you leave, the sooner..." He let the sentence hang, unwilling to embarrass Cat any farther but needing to bring the point home. "The sooner we will send word that we would like to meet you."

"Of course we'll leave the two of you alone. The last few days must have been horrendous waiting for Caitlin to heal. I was shot before Drake and I were wed, and he barely left my side. Even when Aunty Charlotte insisted, he found a way to stay in the bedroom."

"You were shot too?" Caitlin asked.

"I was but I survived the ordeal just fine, even survived Drake's hovering," Ella laughed. She'd made her way to the door and was even now wrapping her shawl around her shoulders. "Aunty?"

"Yes, yes, I'm leaving too."

"Caitlin, don't forget that as long as you're carrying his child, he'll be ten times worse if not more so." Ella tied her bonnet. "He'll want to breathe for you, would do anything for you if he could."

"Thank you." Caitlin hugged both Ella and Charlotte. "I could spend hours asking you questions about what's happening to me."

Roc realized everything Ella said about him was true and he wouldn't change a thing. He didn't care if he hovered and protected Cat with his life. She meant everything to him. And it was true he would do anything to make life easier for her.

"Then we'll see the two of you in a couple of days?" Roc asked, understanding his mother would undoubtedly be here tomorrow afternoon. He doubted she would show up in the morning.

"Your mother is very sweet," Cat said watching them walk down the porch, leaning into him, his arm wrapped around her.

He tossed his head back and laughed. "Very few people if any have ever called The Duchess sweet."

Cat looked up, "The Duchess is never sweet. You're right. She has a reputation to uphold but your mother is sweet and has your best interest as well as her nieces at heart."

"Yours too." He swept her into his arms, carrying her up the steps to their bedroom. "We haven't spent much time here, just our wedding night and the next one after that."

"I've many fond memories of this room, with you," she said as he set her down. "Look," she pointed to the table beside the fireplace. "Cook has left us a midnight snack."

"Cook is a smart woman," Roc said as he set Cat on her feet. "Too bad you don't have that lingerie Ella gave you on our wedding night." He thought about the gown with longing. Her curves enticed and thrilled him and loved the illusion of seeing all of her while she wore clothing. That night she had never looked more beautiful to him. Now, however, she glowed, her beauty so much more than skin deep.

236

"You want to take it off me?" she asked, her hand on his chest as she gave him a gentle push. He sat down on the bed, a bit surprised by the aggressive behavior.

"More than anything."

"Perhaps you should have some wine first then you can take this gown off. It will be a simple task," she purred, wanting to seduce without telling him her secret.

Her flirtatious smile sent his mind spinning and his heart to his throat.

~ * ~

She had been delighted to see Charlotte and Ella, but they overstayed their welcome. Roc's righteous indignation was amusing and his attempts at politeness were strained at best. At his shuttered dark expressions, she'd wanted to laugh.

Now, they were finally alone, something they'd both wanted for several hours. Needing to give him pleasure and surprise him as well, she'd taken the opportunity her bath provided to dress just for him. Ironic that Ella had been the one who prompted her decision to amaze Roc, and she was now the one who was reluctant to leave. Her appearance in the parlor when they arrived home served as a reminder.

Cook brought the platter of food and bottle of wine to the room at her bequest and she hoped in some way to rediscover their wedding night, minus the see-through lingerie, which was at Ravenswood. But this surprise for Roc might be better. She could barely wait to see the expression on his face and the look in his eyes when he discovered her secret.

Cat took a moment to pour them each a glass of wine. One sip was enough for her, but she let him drink half his glass before she fed him a few berries, reveling in the touch of his tongue against her fingertips. That simple stroke sent an inferno pulsing through her.

"What are you up to," he asked seemingly unable to stop grinning, but he didn't wait for an answer. "Whatever your plans are I believe I approve and like even before you tell me what is making you smile so prettily. *Mon petite chatte*, I don't think I can wait much longer."

She traced his lips with a fingertip, "I mean to seduce you. You're my duke, you know. Caitlin's duke, I like the sound of that. Do you?" She took his glass from his hand, setting it on the table. Then she sat astride him, his hands on her waist. She let her head fall back, giving him access to her neck and shoulders while she held on to him.

"Cat." He moistened his lips, "You can seduce me any day or night you want. Whenever it suits you, will suit me just fine, my duchess, never doubt for a moment that you're mine." He groaned when she lifted his shirt over his head, her hands on his chest, soft fingertips raking across his nipples.

She arranged her skirts around them, waiting for his explorations to discover her nakedness beneath her gown. Leaning forward, her lips molded over his while her tongue pushed inside, her fingers now gliding through the soft length of his hair. He seemed content to let her take the lead, but she wasn't sure how to proceed now that he had his shirt off. It seemed she had not thought this out completely.

"What should I do now," she asked as she trailed kisses down his neck and across his collarbone. "You need to tell me. I'm new to this as you well know."

"You're doing just fine on your own," he murmured, gliding his hands up then down her ribcage, stopping just below her breasts. It seemed he wanted her to set the pace and seduce him as she said she planned. "If you did any better, I'd most likely burst into flames."

He touched the tiny sleeves, sliding them down her shoulders and following with tiny nipping kisses until, "Move your arms." She did. "Yes, like that." Her bodice settled around her waist; her breasts free of any restraint were his to gaze upon. "No corset?" he asked before his lips settled on a nipple and his fingers gave attention to the other one.

"No corset," she agreed, arching her back while he sucked and nipped. She moaned softly, tiny sounds of pleasure arising from her. Deep within she pulsed, craving him.

"What else don't you have on?" he asked as he ran a hand along her leg. She'd worn her silk stockings, and she knew the second he realized she wore nothing beneath her gown.

His fingers touched intimate places while she arched against his hand, needing more. She unfastened his buckskins, his arousal hard and pulsing beneath her fingers.

In the next moment he was deep inside. "Roc..." she cried out. Minutes later they both were stated for the time being. With her head resting on his chest, "You've no idea what you do to me."

"You're incredible, Cat, and so very beautiful you steal my breath every time I look at you," he told her, softly brushing tangled hair from her face. "You're everything to me. I can't live without you."

They sat on the bed, covers pulled to their waists. Her back was against his chest, sipping wine. "I'd like to visit Portrush and my da as soon as the baby can travel." All the people she'd ever cared about except for Roc lived in the little shipping town of Portrush.

"Then we will," he told her, enjoying this small moment of peace and quiet, something he'd coveted for so long now. "Sean O'Connell will love to see his granddaughter or grandson. It will be nice for you to see Ida and Sybil, I'm guessing."

"You're generous. Will you allow Da to be the grandfather of our child?" she asked, wishing she could talk to her da right now. He should know about the marquis and how he treated Fiona. Perhaps he did know, her mother would have confided in him.

"Yes, of course, he's the only father you've known your entire life and your real father doesn't merit the title of grandfather. Besides, he will be the only grandfather our child will know since my father is no longer with us."

She inhaled a long breath of air then sighed as she was thinking about her past. "I always wondered how he had what seemed like unlimited funds. Whenever something went wrong, he had the money to fix it. Onc year it rained so hard, the roof leaked. I thought we would have to tighten our belts and fix it with buckets beneath the leaks and dabs of mud to fill in the holes. It all makes sense now."

"But you didn't." Roc stroked her arm, pushing her hair to one side, placing soft enticing kisses on the back of her neck. She moved slightly to give him better access.

"No, within the week, everything was dry again, the roof no longer leaking. When I was older, I asked him about some of the things he paid for so easily but he always diverted my attention to something else." Now she had answers, yet she wasn't too sure she liked them. Didn't like the idea that Blair was related to him in any way let alone a brother.

"Do you know why he abdicated the title to his brother?" he asked, seducing her as he spoke, exploring places that made her shiver then moving on to more intimate spots. She opened for his exploration, determined to give him everything he asked for.

"No, not for certain. Roc, if you want answers to your questions, you need to stop what you're doing. I can't think let alone speak. I can't even breath, my heart is racing so hard," she said, his fingers roaming, arousing, and heating her body to a molten storm as she responded to his caress.

"Can't do that," he told her, bringing her to a climax with his caresses. "I like to look into your eyes when I bring you pleasure. Really, you should see the passion in your eyes and the raw energy emanating from you."

Her breathing torn and labored, she relaxed against him in a spineless bundle of ragged nerves. "Roc, you've got to stop doing this to me. At least give me time to recuperate."

He chuckled softly, "You don't want me to touch you here, and here?" he asked as he seemed to enjoy arousing her until she couldn't move.

"I do, don't stop, but I want to finish..." She couldn't think, all she could do was react to him and what he did to her body.

"Our conversation?" he asked. "Later, little cat. We've got all night and tomorrow. I can wait to finish whatever it was we were talking about. Hopefully, we can remember."

They made love to each other until she slept in his arms. He enjoyed the sweet moments afterward as much as the intense hot seconds of their climaxes. Everything they shared together was hot and sweet, intimate and relaxed. He wanted her forever and knew he'd never grow tired of her. "My duchess," he murmured softly, endearingly, understanding the perfection he obtained without looking.

Strange that he didn't feel tired but full of unspent energy. Instead, he anticipated his life with her, the good and the bad times and he prayed they had most of the bad times behind them and would look forward to the peace and quiet he longed for.

He told her he cared for her and love didn't exist. It was a word he couldn't wrap his mind around—not until today. Now he understood the meaning and the feelings that went along with the word. And maybe the knowledge didn't happen all at once. Perhaps with the evolution of their relationship, the feelings grew over time.

"I love you, Cat," he whispered, wishing she was awake and could hear him say the words. "You're my duchess, Roc's duchess." The words coming from him never sounded truer. He ran his fingers through her hair, reveling in the silken fire.

Outside the sunlight began to slowly filter through the curtained window. His life was flawless and he hoped Cat felt the same. He guessed he slept for a few hours, but at the moment he was wide-awake and infused with energy.

He knew the moment she began to wake up. Her fingers moved against his chest. "Are you awake, *mon petite chatte*?" he asked enjoying everything about her.

"Caitlin's duke, are you awake?" she asked, the tiny purr arousing him, just those few words made him hard and craving her. "Are you going to make love to me before we eat? I'm famished though. Perhaps we should wait a few minutes."

"Whatever you want," he told her, his voice soft so different from the way he spoke to her even the night before.

She turned in his arms, sitting up and letting the covers slip to her waist, feeling at ease with her nakedness. "What is it? You sound different somehow." Concern filled her and she knew things needed to be said between them, but she had no idea what it was.

"I have changed. The events of the last few months have changed me." He grinned. "But it's nothing you need to be concerned about." Unclothed and seemingly unconcerned about it, he rang for a servant to bring food.

"Pull the covers up," he told her as he slipped his buckskins on. "Don't want anyone to see you without clothes except me."

Seconds later the food was on the table, including hot tea and coffee. Roc dished up food while she watched, enamored of the man she married. Desperately she wanted to tell him how much she loved him, but she didn't want to push him to reciprocate a feeling he told her he didn't understand could exist. She would wait for another time, a time when she thought maybe he could return the sentiment.

"The food is good," she told him as she sipped the hot tea, knowing her conversation was stupid and meaningless. "Do you think your mother will show up?"

"Yes," he agreed, his smile soft but so different from what she was used to. "And it better not be today. I'm mean to keep you all to myself, until the sun rises again tomorrow morning."

"What is it you're not telling me?" she asked. "Did something happen last night that I should know about?" He had her worried now, her stomach rolling and she didn't even know if it was because of the baby or what she didn't know.

"I suppose one could say I realized something," he said, his gaze focused on the window and perhaps something he saw outside.

"Do you want to tell me?" she asked, too curious for words but not wanting to pressure him.

"Someday. Tell me about your da—if you want to that is. I promise whatever you say won't leave this room. What is it you think you know about Sean?" he asked, watching her closely as if he tried to read her mind.

She lifted her shoulders slightly, unable to say words that might condemn the man who raised her as if she was truly his daughter in some people's eyes. "It's just a guess and it's not fair to him for me to spread gossip that might not be true." The unease she felt was tangible and heart wrenching. He could have left her homeless and in the hands of the orphanage in Portrush, but he didn't. Instead he gave his heart and soul to her. He cherished her with all his heart.

"Look at it this way. Would you feel better if you told someone what you're thinking?" He touched her chin, as if he hoped to look into her eyes and read the truth there.

"Yes and no." She laughed softly, leaning into him for comfort. "I don't know how it would make me feel. It's something that never made a difference to me before last night, but to some, I'm sure it darkens their thoughts about the man who I believed was my father."

"It's your decision, although I'm certain you would feel better if you had someone to talk with about it." He leaned back, sipping his coffee then closing his eyes, seeming to give her the time she needed to make a decision.

"I love my da," she said, aching from the inside out for Sean, "And I don't want to hurt him, although I know you won't say anything, but I also don't know how you feel about people like him."

"Is he so different then from other folks?" Roc asked, sitting up straighter and fully alert now it seemed she might shed some light on his situation.

"He is," she paused, tracing the rim of her teacup before setting it on the table. "I think he likes men instead of women."

For a few seconds Roc didn't say anything and she was dreadfully afraid he would condemn her da. "There are more people like that than you would guess. Just like Sean, they hide their feelings. His father must have discovered the truth and forced him to abandon the title."

"I don't think so. He told me a few things, no specifics. He has a scar over his right eye. When I asked him about it, he told me his father beat him nearly to death and he had the scar to remind him about fatherly love and what it shouldn't be."

"A violent father is not enough reason to think he prefers men. Blair is violent also." Roc probed for more information.

"There were never any women in his life. I saw him one time down by the beach with a man but they weren't doing anything except talking. I left before he saw me."

"I wonder if Blair knew and blackmailed him," Roc said, gently stroking her arm.

"Perhaps that was what happened. He told me his father thought the beating would change him but it didn't. Da never spoke of a brother, not even when he promised my hand in marriage to Blair. Why would he do such a thing?"

"I don't know. I always had the feeling he detested Blair—more blackmail," Roc said.

"I still can't believe he would do such a horrible thing." She felt sick to her stomach.

"It might have been a way to make sure you would be taken care of if something happened to him."

"Blair O'Connell is a mean and violent man when he drinks, and he detested anyone who disagreed with him. He would have beaten me every night." Nothing made sense to her anymore.

"So, Sean's father thought the beating changed Sean, but Blair knew different. I suppose Sean didn't want anything to do with what he might have considered as being a disgrace to his family."

"His brother blackmailed him." Cat wasn't too sure how she felt about that. Da was just as he was and just like everyone else, he was not perfect. Now it seemed he thought to sell her to his brother to keep his secret. "I'm not sure I want to see him. Right now, I don't have tender feelings for my da."

"We need to speak of this again later and put something more pleasant in the forefront of your mind. What would you like to do today? We could stay in bed and entertain ourselves or we go for a ride in the park." Roc smoothly changed the subject.

"I'd like to ride again as long as you have a mare like Sweety in this stable." She rose and the sight of her made him gasp.

"I don't think I've ever seen you quite so beautiful. That ride is going to have to wait a little bit." He pulled her down, wrapping her in his arms then rolling so he was over her. "A little bit of Cat is not enough Cat. I don't think I'll ever get enough of you, and the slight swell of your belly seems to make you even more appealing."

Later, they shared a bath and another small meal. Dressed in a riding habit, he'd bought for her before they were married, they started toward Hyde Park.

The day wasn't as sunny as the last few. Clouds covered the sky and only a few rays of sunlight filtered through the blanket of clouds. The wind blowing off the river was crisp and chilling for a summer day. A few drops of rain hit the ground, sending tiny swirls of dust into the air.

"Should we go back?" she asked, looking over her shoulder in the direction of his townhouse. "I'm not sure I'm looking forward to a drenching."

"Me neither." He turned his horse, watching her to make sure she followed. "How fast do you think you can go? The water seems to be falling harder with each second."

Her heart in her throat, "Not very. I don't want to fall off."

"Just keep pace with me and focus on staying in the saddle. You'll do fine." As they rode, the rain changed from a few drops to a downpour. By the time they reached the stables beside his home, they were both soaked through to the skin.

He helped her dismount. "We must look like drowned rats," she laughed, enjoying the moment.

"You're the most beautiful wet rat I've ever seen." He pushed dripping wet hair from her face before kissing her. "Come, we need to get inside the house or would you rather wait out the storm here in the stables."

"We've never made love in this room." She teased him, not expecting Roc to take her subtle challenge.

"Then we need to wait out the storm right here." He looked upward. "Well, up there anyway. Can you climb a ladder with all that fabric around your legs?" he asked.

"I can try. As long as you're right behind me, to catch me if I trip." She loved this man so much and needed to tell him how she felt. When would there ever be a better time?

The trek up the ladder was accomplished easily. When they were in the loft, he tackled her, tickling her first then playfully kissing her. She couldn't stop laughing as his fingers fumbled with the fastenings of her gown and she slid her hands beneath his shirt.

In seconds they were undressed and beneath a blanket he'd found below. "Bloody eyes, but I want you every second of every day *mon petite chatte*. Do you know what you do to me?"

He lay above her, and she loved the way she felt when his big body was over hers. Some of his weight a top her, pressing intimately against her, making her feel protected and wanted. "I think it's the same as you do to me. I've never seen a more beautiful man."

"I'm the only naked man you've seen," he chuckled, "and it's going to stay that way."

245

"I don't hear the water pounding on the roof," she said, realizing they needed to return to the home. Their ride had been cut short but they would find more to do inside.

Epilogue

Little William toddled around the big house Roc's family owned in Portrush. It seemed the tiny man would climb anything and everything and it took both of them to keep him out of trouble.

His cheeks were chubby and his hair was as dark as midnight, but his eyes were the same haunting color as his mother's, a violet blue. For Roc it was a good thing William was not a little girl. All she would have to do is look at him with those eyes and he would give her anything she asked for. If she were as beautiful as his mother, he would have to shoot every suitor she had when she grew of age.

"Are you ready to see Sean?" Roc stood by the door, waiting for her to come to terms with this visit that she'd have too many second thoughts about.

"No, but I want to get this over with."

"You don't have to bring up Blair at all. If the thought of him willingly giving you to him, knowing..."

So like The Duchess, she waved her hand in the air, interrupting him. "Now is no different than in the past. Even before we knew who Sean was, he understood the kind of person Blair is. I don't know why he promised me to him, and I'm not sure I care anymore."

"It was all such a shock when we first heard about who he is. You've probably the right of it, blackmail or whatever, it's in the past," Roc said, understanding how difficult this was.

"Ida told me he spends most of his time at the pub. Should we go there first?" she asked, wrapping her shawl around her shoulders.

With the baby in his arms, they walked to the pub. Bloody eyes, but it was strange to be back. He knew the exact spot where he found Cat, with her black eye and broken ribs thanks to Blair.

On a happier note, they walked by the rock wall where they watched the shooting stars. She took his arm, leaning into him and he knew she remembered.

"I wonder if Sean rented my house," she said as they walked by. Then seeing smoke from the chimney. "I suppose he has."

"Do you have any regrets leaving Portrush with me?" He was suddenly insecure about their marriage and what Cat really wanted. Several times over the last few years, he'd almost blurted out to her how much he loved her.

She stopped, turning to him, "How can you ask such a thing?"

"I just want to be sure you're happy." He lifted his shoulders, shrugging and trying to shake off his escalating nerves.

"I am and after we see Da, I want to do something with you. We can leave William with Ida."

"What do you have in mind?" Roc wanted to go anywhere with her, but he also wanted to visit the beach again and watch the waves roll in.

"Just a picnic on the beach. Maybe Ida will pack a basket. We can always give her a case of Bordeaux for her enjoyment."

"I was thinking the same thing," he said, squeezing her hand. "Here we are. Take a big breath and try to remember Sean as you knew him." Roc set William on the floor.

"There's the little man. Welcome back, Caitlin." He placed two pints of Guinness on the bar. "You two enjoy and I'll take a moment to get to know William."

The time seemed to speed by then, "Why didn't you ever tell me who you really were?" Caitlin asked.

"Because the man you knew, your da, was that person. I didn't think I would ever regain my rightful title. For that matter, didn't care. All I wanted was to make sure you grew up and had a good life."

"That's why you promised me to Blair." She waved her hand, "I told myself I wouldn't ask you that question.

"I promised your hand because I knew you would refuse, but I also understood it would keep my brother respectful to you. If I didn't promise you to him, I don't have a doubt in my mind that he would have forced you."

She inhaled sharply. "That makes sense," she said.

At Sean's words Roc's gut tightened and his respect for Sean grew. "You did the only thing you could."

"It's what I thought was best," Sean replied. "If it wasn't, I apologize from the bottom of my heart."

Caitlin reached out a hand, touching Sean's, "Are you happy in this new role that's been thrust upon you?"

"I am. I've found the folks around here appreciate my efforts to make their lives better."

"What I don't understand is why no one questioned it when you were not named the earl and your brother took over."

"They had no choice or say. They just wanted to take care of their families. What the O'Connell's did or didn't do only concerned them when the taxes were raised. They had no reason to believe I would do anything different."

Questions asked and answered Roc and Caitlin left William with Ida and set off in his carriage for the beach and what he hoped would be a private getaway. But the weather wasn't cooperating. Rain dripped lazily from the sky.

Winston pulled the vehicle to a stop then unhitching the horse, "When do you want me back?" he asked.

"Two hours," Roc said, "don't get too wet. Now, what do we have in the basket?"

"Stop," Cat said, placing her hand on his. "Before we do anything where I can't think or even breathe, something that you do that turns me into a spineless boneless heap. I have to tell you something."

Roc paused, concern sweeping through him, even fear. "What is it?"

She looked down, "Nothing to be too concerned over." She moistened her lips, her hand shaking now. "Roc," she inhaled a long deep breath, "Don't feel you have to respond to me. I'm not expecting anything in return."

"Cat..."

"Hush now, hear me out." She placed a finger on his lips then blurted. "I love you, have always loved you."

The smile growing on his face exploded in his heart. "It's alright. I love you so much sometimes I think I can't breathe. Remember that night in London when we first learned about your father? I realized it then. I was just afraid to tell you."

"I didn't think you were ever afraid of anything?"

"Just of you not loving me." He smiled again. Then, "You played a fiddle in an Irish pub."

"And I fell in love with an English Lord. I love you Richard Oaks Crandall Leighton, Duke of Ravenswood. You're my duke, Caitlin's duke."

"And I love you, *mon petite chatte*, duchess of Ravenswood."

Coming February, 2020
from
Rogue Phoenix Press
by
Christine Young

Piper's Unexpected Infatuation

Chapter One

182

Strolling through Vauxhall, Brett MacLachlan, concentrated on the little brown and white dog with the curly tail that terrorized the visitors of the gardens. No one was immune to his quick feet and even faster nose. In less than a second the dog was able to pick a handkerchief or a small purse from its intended victim's pocket before darting away to safety.

The quick-footed animal snatched something from a young man then scurried into a secluded corner of the park before the victim realized what had been done. Brett laughed at the animal's antics. He'd been watching now for the better part of ten minutes and was sure he knew precisely where the animal disappeared.

The slight pressure to his hip caught his attention. "Bloody Hell! Scoundrel. Demon dog," He sprinted after the animal, having a good idea the direction the dog would take. Dodging through the people, the dog made substantial speed. The small animal was agile and quick on his feet. Brett swore again then watched the mongrel duck down an untraveled and unlighted path.

His frustration kept him from rational thought as he followed the dog into the shifting light of the darkened footpath. A slight scuffling noise to his right brought him to an abrupt halt as he reached for the knife he kept in his boot.

Poising on the balls of his feet, he waited, patience in battle a strong suit. Silence seemed to encompass him, shadows painting an eerie picture in the waning light. All his senses tuned into the tiny area he knew was inhabited by the dog and the boy. What exactly he would do when he trapped them, he wasn't at all sure.

He ran after the unlikely pair because he wanted his purse back, but now he craved something more, an answer to his curiosity perhaps. At the moment he wasn't sure what that was, but he meant to figure it out once he had the young man by the scruff of his neck.

A small noise in the bushes sent his body on edge, muscles tense, all instincts honed, but it seemed to be nothing more than lovers looking for some privacy in the darkness. A male groan then a slight mew, told him he was right to refocus the direction of his task.

Slowly moving forward, he meticulously studied the dancing shadows and listened for any sound. Breathing was hard to conceal. One had to take in air, after all. He supposed the boy could hold his breath, but the dog wouldn't. The couple most likely had experience in hiding and adapted to it. After all, to succeed, he had to win the game more than he lost.

"Show yourself and it will go better for you." The command, he knew, would not be obeyed. In this case the boy stayed alive by outsmarting the opponent, and showing himself would not work to his advantage. He had to try though and perhaps his words would give him some advantage. Didn't know what that might be yet but he was willing to try.

The slight breeze stilled the air. Sultry and hot it seemed stagnant this deep into the forested area, as did the shadows. Attuned to every movement, he froze, ready for whatever the boy would try. If he were the cornered prey, a mad dash might seem the best course, but from experience he knew sitting still would serve the lad well. If he tried to scurry away, he knew he could catch him.

No way in hell, though, would he abandon this quest. Since the boy single handedly put a damper on the evening with his mistress he had planned, the lesson he intended teaching changed dramatically.

"I mean you no harm," he said, hoping his words were believable. Once more he watched for the wild rush to freedom he assumed would eventually materialize. "Come out and we'll talk."

Then...the dog rushed in one direction and the lad in the opposite. He wasn't swayed in his purpose. The animal could go anywhere it pleased. Two strides put him next to the boy. He grabbed him by the collar of his shirt. The boy turned, swinging at him and kicking, connecting more times than Brett wanted to count.

"Oy, governor, le' me go! Bloody eyes but yer hurtin' me." For a second the lad broke free.

"No, don't think I mean to let you go anytime soon. You stole my purse. I could hand you over to the magistrate."

Brett grabbed him by the neck before he could get away, gripping him tightly. "Whether you're agreeable to my plan or not, it's your lucky day. I found you and I do believe I'm going to enjoy taking you off the streets."

"Not lucky in my mind." The lad squirmed, trying to get away again.

"I'm going to give you a chance to improve your lot in life. I'm sure you'll find my home more amenable than what you can find in St. Giles." Brett felt a bit smug at his thought, but he didn't know why he had this sudden feeling of charity. Improving this lad's life would not be an easy feat, especially if the lad fought him every step of the way.

"Like it just the way it is," the lad bit out, taking another swing at his benefactor and connecting.

Brett let out a slight grunt. "Perhaps boxing lessons should be one of your first lessons. That was pretty weak even for a boy of your age. Would think you had a bit more muscle to put into that punch."

"Don't want no boxin' lessons." But he stopped as Brett's fingers tightened around the lad's neck as did the grip on the boy's arm.

"You have a name, lad?" Brett asked, wondering if the boy would give him any information.

"None that I'd tell you."

"That's what I thought." By now they reached one of the better lit and traveled pathways in the park. "I'd like to call you something besides boy or lad.

For some reason the lad stopped fighting him, yet Brett didn't let up, tightening his hold and waiting for an attack from some unknown angle, perhaps the dog. No one appeared to defend the boy or help.

Keeping a watchful eye, Brett looked to other attackers, a friend of the boy, someone who might care what happened to him. For all anyone knew, he was on his way to find a constable.

No one came to the lad's defense.

Brett hailed a cab, keeping his grip tight on the boy's neck and looking over his shoulder for the dog.

"Get inside," he directed the boy, staying close but obviously having to loosen his hold and expecting the lad to duck out the other side. Instead, the boy sat on the middle of the seat, his hands between his legs and his head down, appearing contrite and amenable, something Brett didn't think the boy was capable of pulling off.

"What you plannin' on doin' with me?" he asked without looking up, his defiance seeming to vanish.

"Not too sure at this moment. Depends on how you decide to act." Rubbing his chin, Brett wondered at the lad's sudden question. He could have asked any number of questions. He had ideas, but that's all they were—ideas.

"Don't want to go to Newgate." The boy looked at him, his deep blue eyes shimmering with what Brett could only define as fear.

Brett leaned forward, his arms resting on his legs as he studied the boy. "Don't plan on sending you there. But if you give me any problems..." He didn't want to delude the boy. If he had to, he'd call in the law.

"Not going to give you any problems, governor, but I can't vouch for Jocko and his crew. They'll come lookin' for me and they're mean devils."

"Who's Jocko." This was something new to consider. Jocko was probably his handler, the man who received all the stolen bounty. Bounty he'd forgotten about in his quest to catch this thief. The purse was inconsequential, having only a few coins in it. He never carried anything of value when he visited Vauxhall.

"None of your business. What you don't know won't hurt you more." He squirmed in his seat, looking uncomfortable.

"Perhaps I need to know in order to keep you safe from this man.

You say he's going to come after you. Why?" Brett said, studying the lad whose features seemed too delicate for a boy. And yet... If this boy were unimportant, no one would look for him.

The incessant barking behind and around the carriage brought him to the most immediate present. "What the devil, is that your dog?"

"He won't stop until you let him inside. Rogue, for some reason, wants to protect me. He's loyal to me."

"Rogue, you say. Is that his name?" Brett asked, trying for as much information as possible. He didn't want to take a dog into his home along with this unpredictable lad, yet he saw no other way.

He tapped on the roof and the carriage rolled to a stop. When he opened the door, the dog leapt inside and with a growl, he settled beside the boy. His obvious protective nature gave Brett a reason to smile.

Brett sat back, crossing his arms over his chest, waiting to reach home and not feeling as if anything could be gained from further conversation. Every instinct he possessed told him there was something wrong with this scenario, but he couldn't figure anything out. He didn't dare close his eyes and try to think.

The townhouse he just purchased was his destination, and he decided the first order of business when they arrived would be a bath for both boy and dog. Maybe it would take two dunks in the tub for the lad to really be clean. He didn't dare tell the boy. It might cause him to bolt and Brett didn't have any desire to chase him again.

"You takin' my dog, too?" the boy asked belligerently, hands on his hips.

"If that's what you want," Brett said, hoping to learn more about the boy who now didn't seem to want to leave. "You know you have to give over the handkerchiefs and the purses you and Rouge stole. They will go back to their rightful owners if the constables can locate them."

The boy shrugged and his shoulders pressed against the fabric of his shirt seemed too slender for a boy his age, too thin and delicate. Perhaps he'd not been fed or perhaps this was part of what didn't quite seem right.

"Doesn't make no difference to me. I would've had to give everything to Jocko anyway. He only lets me keep a coin or two."

Curious about this man, "What does this Jocko give to you in exchange for all the risks you take," he paused, "besides a coin or two?

There must be more for you to keep going back to him."

"Protection," he said quickly, perhaps too quickly. "And food. Gives me clothes, too, when these wear out." He plucked at his shirt. "He's training me for when I'm older, too old to pick pockets."

"So," he paused in thought, "you take all the chances and he gives you food, none of the money these things merit. Not even half? What is it he's training you for?"

"Not my place to question what he does and doesn't do. He gives me a safe place to sleep and something to eat. Don't have to look over my shoulder just to stay alive. Know I'm not going to be attacked in the middle of the night."

"I suppose some place to sleep at night is important as well as food," Brett rubbed his chin thoughtfully, understanding there was a lot more to this story and he was going to discover every intricate nuance.

"Then there's the scarred man, even Jocko's afraid of him. He says I've got to be careful of that man and try not to do anything to get on his bad side. Says he knows something about me that could hurt me. He also said if I discovered the truth, he'd kill me. Seems he's keeping me alive only because I'm ignorant."

"The scarred man...why are you telling me all of this when you won't even tell me your name?" This tale grew more interesting with every passing sentence.

"You haven't asked me my name since I've not been scared of you anymore. When you stopped to get my dog, I knew you were nice, and I didn't have any reason to think you'd do something bad."

"What's your name then?" He smiled, wondering if he would continue to give him information.

"Piper. What's yours?" she shot back to him.

"Brett MacLachlan. Do you have a last name?"

"Not that I know of, but Jocko knows, at least I think he does. He once told me that I'd never know what it is because the scarred man would make sure I didn't. If I asked too many questions about my name, he'd kill me."

Hearing those words, a shiver shot down Brett's spine. This lad's truths caught every instinct he possessed and stretched them thin. For some reason, he wanted to solve the growing mystery surrounding Piper.

"We're here," Brett said, wondering how difficult it would be to get this boy into a bath. Confined in the tight quarters of the carriage, his stench was overwhelming.

"This yer home? It's quite the thing. Never been inside one of these." He peered out the window, nose smashed against the glass. "Only been in little houses, ones with a room or two.

"Yes, and now it's yours." He tried to figure out what he was going to do with the boy. Supposed he could be a stable hand if he wasn't afraid of horses.

"Why aren't we goin' in the front door?" the boy asked, watching him with wide eyes. "Isn't that what civilized folks do?"

"Well," Brett didn't know how to answer his questions without giving his attentions away.

"Get on with it. Bloody eyes, just tell me the truth. Not used to hearin' lies except from my enemies and I'm hoping you're not my enemy."

Brett wanted to get him inside before he confronted the lad, Piper, with a bath, figuring the boy might not even know what a bath was. Then there was the dubious thought the lad would work for him and in what capacity exactly.

They stepped inside, Rogue following. "Mrs. Pickery, this is Piper. He's going to work here, and he needs a bath, the dog too."

Rouge settled down in a corner, his chin resting on his paws, seeming to watch the scene enfolding.

"Oy, governor. Don't want or need no bath. What you tryin' to do? Torture me?" Piper asked slowly, moving backward, arms stretched out in front of him as if he could stop Brett.

"No torture intended. Have you ever had a bath?" Brett asked and while they spoke, he watched Mrs. Pickery begin to heat the water. "There's a large tub in the scullery, Mrs. Pickery. We'll use that one."

"Not that I can remember. Never had a bath. Not goin' to take one now."

"Then you've years of dirt to wash off." Brett grinned, watching the delightful and at times horrific play of emotions sweeping across his face.

Piper stood in one corner, pale faced, while he watched the tub as it was brought into the kitchen then the hot water dumped into the large vat.

Brett didn't understand the sudden terror. Piper seemed resolved to what was going on here, even pleased that he would no longer live on the streets, until the bathtub appeared.

"Don't want to wash any dirt off," he mumbled then pushed against the wall as if he wanted to become one with it. "Like me just the way I am."

"You won't know how great a tub of hot water feels until you try it. I'll stay in here with you and Mrs. Pickery will find something to do in another part of the house. You don't need to be shy."

His eyes grew wide and his gaze focused on the door.

Mrs. Pickery nodded, slipping from the scullery. "I'll leave the two of you and I'll put out the word that we need some britches and shirts. Those clothes can't be salvaged."

"There it is. Take your clothes off and get into the tub." Brett watched as Piper started shaking, his face pale as a ghost, his eyes wide.

"If you leave," Piper asked the impossible, yet seeming adamant in his request. "Not taking my clothes off with you in the same room. Can't do that, no siree. Jocko told me never to do anything like that. He'd have my hide if he ever found out as well as the man who saw me."

"You'd rather have Mrs. Pickery stay in here with you?" Brett tossed that out as an afterthought, but when Piper nodded, his misgivings escalated. "Bloody hell, what the devil are you thinking?" He stepped forward, believing he needed to shake a bit of sense into the lad.

When he darted across the room, picking up a butcher knife waving it in front of him, Brett backed up a step. This wasn't something he expected.

"Bloody eyes, governor, don't test me or I'll skewer you through. Don't you ever doubt my intentions. I'll use it. I will." He backed from him, the weapon held in front of him, his hands shaking.

"Put it down, Piper. You don't want to hurt anyone." He searched his mind for the reasons behind this bazaar behavior. "Just hand it over to me and if it's Mrs. Pickery you want, then I'll get her. Problem is, it might make her very uncomfortable to see a young man naked. Do you want to make her uncomfortable?"

"No..." Piper's voice wavered. "No, no I don't but..."

For a moment he looked to the door as if he meant to run. Brett lunged, grabbing his wrist. The knife fell to the floor before he kicked it aside. "I'm not playing anymore games with you. The bath is getting cold while we waste time with this nonsense." He ripped the shirt. "Mrs. Pickery is looking for new clothing as we speak."

The boy seemed to freeze, his arms wrapped around himself. "Now that you got your way." His voice weakened, sounded as if he suddenly gave up. His narrow delicate shoulders were shaking so hard, his breath seemed to catch in his throat.

With the shirt off, without stopping to think, Brett reached for the knife and slit the bindings that were wrapped around his chest from top to bottom. Frustrated and irritated with the boy, he didn't stop to think about the bindings and what they might mean. "Britches off now." He understood the force of his voice and wished he wasn't letting his annoyance get the best of him.

With his back turned to him, the boy stepped from his pants.

The air Brett was holding in his lungs rushed out painfully. It seemed he finally saw the entire picture.

Brett suddenly realized the bindings around the boy's chest and the baggy pants were hiding a girl. Her slender waist, and wide hips without the fabric hiding her curves was obvious. "Mrs. Pickery."

Good God, but he couldn't take his gaze from her perfectly formed figure. Her tight butt was nothing like the women he bedded, his mistresses. In a flash, his body hardened with a desire he couldn't control. "Mrs. Pickery!"

"Yes, sir." His cook poked her head in the door. "What is it?"

"He's a she."

"What did you say?"

"Get her in the bath. If you need anything, ring for me and I'll be here even though she's naked. Don't let her leave." Well, that was stupid. He really didn't think she'd run out the back door stark naked.

His gut rolled. He'd never forcefully disrobed a girl, ripped her shirt. He rubbed his face then roughed his hands through his hair. Trying to make excuses, and attempting to convince himself, "He truly believed Piper was a boy." He inhaled a long deep breath, wishing he could take the last few minutes back and do them over.

"It's alright, Sir. You didn't know. None of us knew. I'll take care of her now," Mrs. Pickery touched him on the back. "Don't you worry about her."

"That's just it. I should have known. Every instinct I possess was telling me there was something wrong, but I didn't listen." He berated himself then before he strode through the kitchen door. "Don't give Mrs. Pickery any grief. You'll rue the day you were born if you do."

"I've already done that too many times to count," she told him looking over her shoulder, her breasts visible to him.

His hands fisted tight, he strode through the house and out the front door. For a few seconds he thought to get his horse. A good ride might ease the tension radiating across his shoulders and throughout the rest of his damn body. The site of her naked evoked a powerful sensation through him.

He stopped himself when he rounded the corner of the house and saw the back door, the entrance to the scullery, reminding him of the girl soaking in his tub. A young lady who'd had one hell of a life. He decided to find out more about her.

Swiveling on a heel, he walked back to the house, entering through the front door. Brandy seemed to call his name. At the sideboard, he poured a full glass and thought to sit down and wait for the outcome of the bath. He didn't hear anything emanating from that direction and decided that was a good thing.

"Ah." He swirled the amber liquid in the glass, mesmerized by the changing colors or thoughts of Piper, he wasn't too sure. What was he going to do with the lass? And what about Jocko and the scarred man? If anything, she said held a hint of truth, her life might be in danger now that she was out of their fold.

The alcohol burned an enjoyable path down his throat. She would need clothing, everything a woman likes as well as a position in the house. The downstairs maid perhaps. He didn't need one but she would have to have some means of employment. The last thing he wanted or needed was gossip surrounding him. She would have to live in his home. There were small servant quarters on the third floor.

Perhaps Mrs. Pickery could help with the clothing. She did have a daughter who he thought was about Piper's age. That was another thing. How old was Piper? Dressed as a boy he guessed her to be about thirteen, now as a girl, he paused in thought. She could be any age. However, he supposed her handler would hand her over to a pimp as soon as possible.

That didn't make sense. Fourteen-year-old girls were sold to whore houses and pimps. By the short glimpse he caught of Piper's curves, she was well past fourteen. He'd guess at least eighteen. If he'd looked closely, he would have seen her hips and even the curve of her breasts beneath the bindings. He'd been intent on one thing, catching her, so he'd lost his concentration.

He caught a side view of her when she looked over her shoulder to give her parting shot. She rued the day she was born too many times to count. He decided he'd be the man to change that.

Smiling to himself, he sipped again closing his eyes and trying to image her naked, all of her, from tips of her toes to the top of her short cut hair. He bolted upright, reminding himself he had no right to do that. Well, something about Piper intrigued him more than he wanted to admit.

He reached over and rang the bell signaling Molly, his scullery maid. A few minutes passed before she appeared.

"Sir," Molly curtsied before stepping back to wait for his order.

"Can you poke your head into the scullery and let me know how it's going in there? If Mrs. Pickery needs any help," he asked, downing the last bit of brandy, wishing he dared look instead.

"Yes, sir." She turned to do his bidding.

Waiting didn't suit him. He stood again, pacing the room, needing to occupy himself. He turned in the direction of the scullery.

"Sir," Angus, his valet, stood in front of him. "I set out clothes for you, for tonight. Are you wanting a bath first?"

"What? Oh, I forgot." Muira, his current mistress would be waiting for him. He'd agreed to take her to the opera tonight. A boring night for him, but she begged. Now the little interest he had in the opera as well as Muira vanished. His only concern now was Piper and what would happen next. He was intrigued and excited to discover more about Miss Piper.

"Sir," It seemed Angus was losing patience with him.

"Send a message to Muira with my apologies, but I've pressing business to attend to tonight. Don't want a bath or a change of clothes."

"Yes, sir."

Brett chuckled slightly, hearing the censure in the man's voice. Angus usually berated him for seeing Muira, a mistress, and now it seemed she was the preferable entertainment.

"Master Brett," Mrs. Pickery stood in front of him. "You should come see Piper. Except for one thing, I think you'll be pleased."

~ * ~

Piper hugged her arms around herself. She couldn't remember the last time she'd been stark naked and humiliated in front of anyone let alone a man. Brett saw her with nothing on, naked. Even when she took a quick swim in the lake, she wore her clothes. Now she stood in the scullery, naked with a man staring at her backside, a man she barely knew. Her long-kept secret was secret no longer.

When she decided to stay with the man, she never thought her identity would be uncovered, never expected a bath, of all the nerve. Over the years she'd taken huge steps to keep people from knowing she was a girl. Jocko helped but it was only because he had something in mind for her, something he said that would make them both rich. Said they'd live a life of luxury. Jocko told her he would train her to be a rich man's mistress and...

"Come on now, get in the water, dear. Let's not be wastin' anytime. Master Brett is going to want to see you when we're all done here, and I want him to be proud. Need to check for lice and make sure you're squeaky clean. After that, we'll give your dog a bath." Mrs. Pickery seemed to chatter nonstop.

Slowly, she turned and feeling as if she walked to her execution, she approached the vat of steaming water. She looked at Mrs. Pickery before accepting her fate. Heaving a huge breath of air, she stepped into the water.

"Ouch!"

"Now Miss Piper, the water is not too hot. Cold water will not soak off the layers of grime covering you. God knows what some of it is, but no one else wants to know. Would you like me to wash you or can you do it yourself?" Mrs. Pickery held out a soapy sponge, eyeing her as if she was a little child.

Catching her bottom lip between her teeth, she started to shake her head. The last thing she wanted was someone else doing something to her.

"Want to do it myself, but not really sure what to do. Never had a bath," she mumbled, swirling the water around with her hand.

"That's easy, dear. Just rub this," she held out the sponge, "with the soap on it all over your body. Don't miss any spot or I'll have to do it myself. While you're doing that, I'm going to wash your hair and make sure there's no little nits in it."

Minutes later the water was a cesspool of filth. Looking down, Piper couldn't see her body for the dirt. Inwardly cringing, "How am I going to get clean when the water is so dirty?"

"Good question lass, that's why I've got more water heating for a second bath in another tub. Angus brought one from upstairs a few minutes ago. Seems Master Brett had the same idea." She nodded toward the kitchen stove and the pails of steaming liquid. "Now let me pour this bucket over your head and rinse out the soap."

To Piper, it seemed an eternity before Mrs. Pickery was finally finished and handing her a towel. "Wrap it around you then we'll get you dressed. Sent Molly out lookin' for a dress that might fit. We'll see how she did."

After the second bath, mindless and confused, Piper followed the cook's directions. She cloaked herself in the towel and waited for what would come next. Mrs. Pickery vanished for a moment then reappeared holding a dress in front of her and what appeared to be underthings.

"You want me to wear that? What is it and how does it work?" she pointed to the garments. "Don't believe I've ever worn one of those things. How does one..." she paused, "put it on?"

"Don't you worry your pretty little self about that. Molly and I will help you then when you're ready, we'll take you to Master Brett."

"Molly?" she thought it had just been the two of them.

"Molly, there you are," Mrs. Pickery said.

"Master Brett wanted me to check on you. Let me just tell him you'll be ready soon and I'll be back." She curtsied and disappeared only to return in a few seconds.

Piper felt pushed and pulled in every direction possible while the maid and the cook laughed and chatted. Finally, she was laced into a contraption she had no idea how she would get out of and clothed in a dress that left her breasts revealed for anyone to see.

She pulled at the top of the bodice, trying to cover herself then looked at Mrs. Pickery, hoping she would have the answer to her problem. "I don't think this is supposed to be this low."

"Oh dear," Mrs. Pickery said, rubbing her hands together, clearly distraught. "Her bubbies are too big for the dress." She wiped her hands on her apron. "Can't show her to Master Brett like this."

Molly whispered, "They're more like kettle drums."

"Master Brett not's going to like this on her but it's the best we have right now. Maybe he'll have a solution."

"We can't present her to him like this," Molly moaned softly, shaking her head as if that would give her some clue as to how to fix this. "Can't just can't. He's a refined gentleman."

"You'll never convince me he's never seen a woman's breasts before," Mrs. Pickery said indignantly.

"No, of course not but it might put wayward thoughts into his head," Molly said with a slight moan of despair.

"I've no doubt he'll make this right. The sooner we show her to him, the sooner we can get back to our regular work. He's not going to ravish her just because he can almost see her nipples. I've not started anything for dinner and as you well know, he's had a change in plans. He's not visiting his mistress tonight. Come along, Miss Piper. Let's show you off."

Mrs. Pickery held open the door and waited.

Piper inhaled a long breath of air before starting forward. Being talked about and around had not been enjoyable. "Why do you have to show me to him?" she asked but her experience with men in her short life told her they always wanted to have all the information.

When she stepped in front of him, she closed her eyes. She didn't know what she expected, not complete silence, but that seemed to be what was happening. Jocko was never silent. She always knew what to expect and what he was thinking simply because he told her.

"Mrs. Pickery?" His voice held a tinge of irritation.

"Yes, sir." She stepped forward, her hands clasped in front of her. "The dress, it's all we could find on such short notice, sir. Didn't expect her to be so..." she looked to Piper then back to Brett.

"So well endowed?" he asked pleasantly, one eyebrow tilted

upward. "Can you find her a small shawl, something to cover herself, privacy you understand? And something to pin it with?"

"Yes, sir, I'll be back soon, sir, but you might not get your dinner until later." She started to leave.

"Forget about dinner. We'll be going on an errand soon. Sit down, Piper. Would you like something to drink?" His smile seemed pleasant enough.

Piper sat down next to him where he patted the seat. "You don't like the way I look?" she asked, not sure if she felt meek or was acting strangely. She wanted to please him simply because she needed him to like her. If he kicked her out, she no longer had her disguise, so she'd be sold to a pimp or a whorehouse. His opinion meant everything to her, meant her life.

"You clean up very nicely. The dress is wonderful on you but shows a bit too much you. I think we can rectify the situation."

He handed her a drink. "Sip it slowly."

His words came too late. She coughed and droplets of brandy splattered in front of her. She covered her mouth with a hand. "So sorry. I didn't know..." Jocko warned her about spirits and the consequence they might have for her. Told her never to drink anything stronger than tea.

"It burns a little, but you can get used to it if you like." He smiled. "Mrs. Pickery could bring you tea if you would rather have that."

The look in his dark brown eyes melted her heart. "I've never had spirits. Jocko says they're the root of all evil, but this is fine."

"Jocko never drinks? For some reason I've trouble believing that. Maybe you should tell me more about this man you've spent a lot of time with."

"Oh, he drinks. It's just what he tells me. Says my mind shouldn't ever be impaired." Yet she sipped again, this time more slowly. "I think I like it. What is it?"

"Brandy." He took the half empty glass from her hand. "Perhaps Jocko has a point."

"I've known Jocko ever since I can remember," she said, recalling the times he played with her on the floor of his apartment.

"How long is that?"

"I might have been two, but I've never known anyone else. He's always taken care of me. He's sort of like a father. What are we going to do now?" She smoothed her skirts and when she did, it seemed the bodice slipped farther down.

He was staring at her and when she looked where his gaze was riveted, she saw the circles that surrounded her nipples. Quickly, she tugged her dress upward. His eyes shimmered with something she'd never seen before. Jocko never looked at her like that.

"Here you go, sir," Mrs. Pickery hurried into the room, holding out a small lace shawl, one that would just cover her bodice.

"Thank you, Mrs. Pickery. You may go home for the night. Piper and I will be at the dress shop. I'm hoping Madame Chantal will have something appropriate for Piper to wear. She can't run around popping out of her dress."

Popping out of my dress. "A dress shop? A place where you buy clothes?" Hands shaking, she picked up her glass of brandy and downed it all before Brett could take it away from her.

"Where else would you get clothes?" He smiled at her, one eyebrow cocked upward. "I hope you don't regret downing your drink. If your head starts feeling a bit hazy, let me know."

She wondered how he did that, lift one eyebrow and not the other. She scrunched her face, trying to do the same thing but to no avail. "Never got any clothes in a dress shop."

"Of course, dress shops are where you get clothes. Where do you get your clothes?" he asked, seeming to watch her intensely.

Unable to help herself, she smoothed her skirts. When his eyes darkened farther, she moved uncomfortably. Jocko warned her about men and the way they looked at women, but she never believed him. Now she understood but she didn't feel dirty, not like Jocko said she would. She liked the way he looked at her.

"Piper?"

"Oh, I was just thinking about your eyes." His gorgeous dark brown eyes that seemed to change color according to his mood.

"You were—my eyes?"

She started to smooth her skirt again then stopped herself. Instead, she moistened her lips before sucking the lower one into her mouth. "You had that look Jocko told me about. The one where men stare at you and make you feel dirty, but I didn't feel that way, dirty."

"Oh," he sat back, his arms across the back of the sofa, grinning. "I love your honesty. How did my looking at you make you feel?"

"Hot."

He ran a finger around his collar before clearing his throat and laughing. "We should leave now. There's Angus. The carriage is ready. You can tell me more about yourself on our ride through town."

"Two rides in a carriage in one day." She stood, feeling as if she was in a brand new world. "Before this I've never set foot in one, a carriage."

"Wait." He stopped her and wrapped the shawl around her shoulders, his finger brushing the tops of her breasts when he fastened it. Then he held out his arm for her, his gaze touching hers, her heart pounding out of control.

She wasn't positive what he wanted her to do, but she placed her hand on his arm and walked with him. It must have been the right thing because he made no comment.

Inside the carriage, she watched him settle back on the seat, his arms spread wide on both sides. "Tell me about yourself."

"Only if you tell me about you," she countered, watching his brows draw together and shrugging her shoulders. "It's only fair."

"Very well, you're right, I suppose it's only fair. In fact, I'll start. I grew up in Scotland. Ran wild and did pretty much what I wanted until I turned fifteen." He stretched his legs, crossing them.

She leaned forward, fascinated by the size of the man, not so much by what he didn't tell her but by the width of his shoulders and the muscles that seemed to stretch his jacket to its limits. "What brought you to London?"

"My turn." He picked up her hand and studied it, tracing tiny circles in the palm, sending shivers of heat through her. "They even got your fingernails clean. What's the first thing you remember?"

Feeling sensations she didn't understand begin to spiral out of control, she pulled her hand from his. "I must have been about two, I think. No one knows how old I am or where I came from. No one but the scarred man and maybe Jocko knows."

"What is it you remember?" He prodded.

"Just Jocko playing with me. I had this little doll. I've always had it until now. I suppose they'll throw it away now that I'm not living with them." She wasn't sure how she felt about that. The doll was her only connection to her past.

"A doll, it might lead us to your mother or father."

"Don't know why you'd want to do that. If there was any family who wanted me, I wouldn't have ended up in the orphanage. Mother and father must be dead, dead for a long time." She heard the bitterness in her voice well up inside her.

"Not sure I understand. If Jocko and the scarred man were taking care of you, why would they put you in the orphanage?"

She was shaking her head, unable to stop the barrage of memories. "I was in the orphanage to learn how to pick pockets, nothing more. I rarely stayed there at night. Jocko started my education for after my pickpocket days last year. He told me I wasn't going to get away with pretending I'm a boy much longer."

He leaned forward, his forearms resting on his thighs. "And what would that be? What are his plans for you?"

"Jocko was training me to be a mistress to some rich gent," she blurted, not really sure of the difference between a whore and a mistress, but Jocko reassured her many times that it was infinitely better to be a mistress than a whore.

"We're here and I hope to continue this conversation when you're finished." He walked her into the dress shop.

"Blimey, never seen anything like this. What do I do now?" she whispered, clutching Brett's arm as if he could protect her from the woman descending on them. Her breath seemed to catch in her throat, and she could barely breathe.

Brett cleared his throat, smiling. "Chantal, how nice to see you. I need some everyday clothing for this young lady. She's going to be my downstairs maid and she has nothing to wear. I'd also like one walking dress."

"I see," Chantal said as if she truly could see through the miniscule scarf Brett wrapped around her for modesty sake. "You have a large problem. Where did you get this dress?"

"My cook's daughter was happy to lend this to Piper. They are approximately the same size except for the bust." Brett said, grinning while he kept his gaze averted from her bosom.

Piper didn't understand anything that was going on or why the size of her breasts was the topic of conversation.

"This will take some time but let me get her measurements while you pick out fabrics," Chantal said, picking up the tape. "We should go into a fitting room."

"I'll need one dress finished by tomorrow morning. I don't mind paying the extra fee to make sure that happens. She does need something decent to wear," Brett called out as they disappeared into the room.

"Now, let's take the shawl off so I can measure you. No need to take everything off. I can get everything I need. I'm assuming you're not wearing a corset and don't want one."

"I..." Piper swallowed hard before clearing her throat. "Never wore one," she managed to mumble. Wasn't too sure what the dressmaker was talking about.

"Never? My dear, where have you been?"

Piper didn't really think the lady should know anything about her, so she chose not to answer. And she didn't appreciate the dressmaker's tone of voice. She stood still for her while she moved the tape from place to place then wrote something on a piece of paper.

"Done, shall we see what Monsieur MacLachlan has picked out for you? She smiled, opening the door for her.

They stepped outside the room. Brett was immersed in the fabrics and fashion plates as if this was a second home to him. The two spoke while she fiddled with the shawl and the pin, unsure of what she should do with them.

When they were finished, "Come here, Piper." Brett reached for the shawl and adeptly fastened the scrap of material. "There you go," he whispered as the backs of his fingers floated across her skin.

She felt the touch to the tips of her toes, saw the look of disapproval on the dressmaker's face. "Can we get out of here? Please?"

"Of course, are you hungry? There are food carts. We can walk if you like since the sun is out and it's not too cold. We could find a pub and get something to eat there."

"I suppose I'd like that, but I don't have any money. You took the purse I stole from you." She shouldn't have said that, somehow knowing Brett wouldn't like to be reminded of this afternoon.

He cleared his throat, seeming to ignore her statement. "Mademoiselle Chantal will have one dress ready for you tomorrow morning as well as underclothes. I've arranged for them to be sent to my home."

"Underclothes? Except for the bindings, I've never worn anything under my clothes. Why would you want to do that?"

Brett roughed his hands through his hair before letting out a bellow of laughter. "Don't know exactly," he frowned. "We just do. I don't think I could get much done if I knew you didn't have anything on under your dresses."

"Do I have to?" she queried, wondering at the ridiculous waste of time of putting on more clothing than what was essential as well as trying to figure out what he just said about getting things done. "Why would it make a difference to you if I wore underthings or not?"

"You should wear them." He laughed softly and the look in his eyes told Piper he was thinking of something pleasant.

"Why?" she persisted.

"It's not important. Let's go inside here," The pub sat on a corner. "This is a nice quiet place to eat and have a pint."

"A pint?" It seemed she didn't know about anything he talked about. She guessed from some of the conversations she'd overheard Jocko and his friends it was something to drink.

"You'll like it." Brett took her hand, leading her into the tavern and finding a spot in the corner of the room where one could see everyone. "Had no idea just how innocent you were. Didn't expect a street lad to be naïve."

"Promise? Will it be like the brandy you gave me?" She laughed, enjoying herself even as she heard her stomach rumbling noisily. "Don't really care about the pint, but I am hungry. Haven't eaten since yesterday morning."

He ordered and it was only a few minutes before they each had a pint of ale and basket of bread on the table, cheese followed.

She watched him, so in his element and here she was, unsure and hesitant. Sipping the ale, she wasn't all that positive she liked it, but with most of the glass gone, she was beginning to feel a bit lightheaded.

"As to your duties, you'll start tomorrow, and I expect you to dust everything every day and sweep the floors."

"Is that all?" she asked. "It's not going to take very long to sweep and dust. What will I do the rest of the time?"

"For now, that's all and you can do anything you want the rest of the day," he told her, leaning forward. "Tell me more about Jocko and this mistress training."

She sighed, letting out a long breath of air. "Shouldn't have told you about his intentions. Doesn't make any difference now that I've a job and a place to live."

"Of course you should. If I'm going to protect you, I need to know everything about the people you used to live with and how they treated you. You did live on the wrong side of the law."

"I didn't really live with anyone. Jocko gave me a room to use, that's all. I never shared it with anyone because he didn't want the fact I was girl to get out. He told me he couldn't protect me if it did."

Brett's brows drew together as if he was muddling over what she said. "Why would he want to protect you? What makes you different than every other pickpocket in London?"

"Not really sure. Think it must have had something to do with scar face. Jocko's afraid of the man, and I think he knows something about me he won't share."

"Think I'll find out everything I can about scar face," Brett mumbled.

"Wouldn't do that if I were you. Jocko says scar face would murder his own mother if he could turn a profit." Suddenly, she didn't feel all that well. "Brett..." she began then closing her eyes, she rested her head on the table.

"What is it?" He reached out, touching her.

She moaned, looking up and licking her lips, which had turned suddenly very dry. "I don't feel well. Can we go home?"

Without answering, he left coin on the table then sweeping her into his arms, he carried her outside. She clung to him, finding comfort in the warmth emanating from his muscled body. Letting her head fall against his shoulder, she let down her guard for the first time since she could remember.

He hailed a cab and set her inside. She leaned back, her head against the back of the coach. "I think it was the drink."

"On no food," he added. "We'll be home in a few minutes, and I'll put you to bed. No, you should eat first. I'll have to see what cook left for us. Then I'll put you to bed," he repeated.

Drowsily, she mumbled. "Never slept on a bed before. How does one put someone else to bed? Seems like something a person can do by themselves."

He laughed. "Only if you know where your bed is. Do you?" He picked up her hands, warming them.

"No, do you?" she countered.

~ * ~

"What happened to Piper?" Jocko paced the two-room apartment in St. Giles he called home. The only place Piper had ever lived. "She can't just vanish. Someone has to have seen something."

"Saw her get into a cab with some man, an aristocrat if my guess is right. He stopped the carriage for the dog too," Bobby told him.

"Saw him too," Billy said, rubbing his jaw as if thinking. "What's goin' to happen' to him? Gentry didn't seem to be takin' him to the constables. Looked like he was headed in the wrong direction for that."

"The two of you are going to find out where he took Piper and bring the lad back to us," Jocko stared out the one window. "Needs to be done before something happens to the boy."

"How we gonna do that?" Bobby asked, cleaning his nails with a knife. "We ain't got no way of finding out who the bloke was."

"You two just sit tight while I put out some feelers. I'll find out the details and get back to you. The two of you can break into his house in the middle of the night, take Piper back and pick up a few valuables in addition." Jocko tried to hide the trepidation he felt. Scar face might just kill him if he didn't get the girl back.

Except for scar face and the man's anger, Jocko thought the plan a fine one, but he had to find out where she was for starters. A trip to scar face was in order. The thought of confessing he lost Piper sent a shiver down his spine. Perhaps it would be best to wait until he got the girl back.

"Not real good at waitin'." Billy said, "Need to be out and about. Don't mind the idea of robbin' the place but don't know if Piper will come with us. If he's got a nice place to settle down, he won't want to come back here."

"Fine then, get out on the streets and see what you can find out. Go to Vauxhall, maybe someone saw him there and knows who took him."

Jocko watched the boys leave before picking up his jacket and setting out to find scar face. The man would be angry he contacted him, but under the circumstances Jocko didn't see another choice. He'd be angrier if he didn't tell him.

With the sun setting, Jocko stood at the back entrance to the townhouse of Viscount Avery Bainbridge. Stepping inside, he waited for someone to realize they had a visitor.

On his way across town, Jocko took every precaution to make sure he wasn't followed. Now he hoped Avery would appreciate the effort and not skewer him through for doing the unthinkable, visiting him at his home.

"Bloody hell, what are you doing here?" Avery stepped through the door from the kitchen into the scullery. "My butler told me I had a visitor. Didn't expect the likes of you. Did anyone see you?"

"Couldn't wait for our next meeting," Jocko said, running a finger around his collar. "Important information. Something that you have to know now."

"It better be." Avery stood back, feet apart, his arms crossed over his chest. "As you know, I've no patience for failure or surprises."

"Piper's gone," Jocko said waiting for the explosion of wrath that was sure to follow the words. What he didn't expect was the calmness of Avery.

"Just where has she gone? A lass or lad, with no means to her name can't go very far. Find her."

"Got a couple of lads workin' on it."

"She's important to my plans, plans that were going to be put in motion in the next year. I don't want any problems."

"You never told me about any plans." Jocko suddenly felt the world he planned falling apart. If Avery wanted her as his mistress, there would be no extra funds coming his way. He remembered the day Avery brought the baby to him. The viscount told him to keep the child alive but nothing else.

"You didn't need to know. Your instructions were to make sure her virginity remained intact. I assume you've done that." His calm seemed to escalate to anger.

"She's still a virgin, but I can't guarantee anything now that she's lost to me. A gent took her and if he knows he's a she, then..." He'd seen her naked, helped her from time to time with her bindings, knew any man would love to get a hold of her tits. They were very pretty and large. He'd been hard pressed to keep his hands to himself for the last several years.

"Make sure you get her back before something happens. It won't go well for you if you don't."

Avery's subtle threat didn't go unnoticed by Jocko. "Have her back in my lair tomorrow. The boys will find her. They're out doin' their jobs right now."

"I'll check in with you tomorrow night. Whatever you do, don't come here again. I'll let you know where to meet me."

Other Books by Christine Young
Available at Rogue Phoenix Press

Catching Meara
Book One in the McKenna Clan Series

Meara Thorton was a feisty, world-class computer hacker—cornered by the FBI and shockingly given the chance to be their newly acquired technical analyst. Brilliant and intuitive, yet aching with the loss of everyone she has cared about, her restless heart led her to discover a love she fought and a world she didn't know could possibly exist.

Sweet Sexy Sadie
Book Two in the McKenna Clan Series

From the first time Sadie's eyes met those of Brody McKenna in the hot Sierra Madre Mountains, theirs was a potent attraction—not gentle, slow, and easy, but hot, hard, and all-consuming. The daughter of a dysfunctional family, Sadie had dreams no man could wrench from her with hot sex and an all-consuming passion. She'd challenge this alpha male with all the strength she possessed. But her red hair, fiery temperament, and indomitable spirit obsessed Brody...and he knew he had to find a way to show her he was more than he appeared and convince her to make a life with him.

Sweet Misbehavin'
Book Three in the McKenna Clan Series

Cast adrift after fleeing the home of Jokul, the ice demon, Atantsi, a firestarter, grew to womanhood as she moved through time to keep the demon from finding her. Though stubborn and courageous, she was ill prepared to use powers she had not been taught. Her first sight of the intoxicating Carr McKenna left her breathless, and her second encounter gave her hope for a future she never thought she had.

A playboy, a second son and a shifter, a man who thought his life would be carefree, Carr McKenna was shocked to discover the woman he'd paid as an escort is a firestarter who is running for her life. He is the leader of all the McKennas around the world and that he has multiple powers. His passion for Margo and the need to defend her might cost him his life as well as hers.

Sweet Talkin' Sugar
Book Four in the McKenna Clan Series

Lyonesse McKenna, was dreaming or was she? From the instant Lyn saw Deacon McClain across a black jack table in a crowed Las Vegas casino the unmistakable attraction sent Lyn's senses flying into overdrive. Her family of shapeshifters believed in soul mates. She'd always been skeptical yet she couldn't help but question the way her heart sped when he looked at her.

When Deacon appeared in Las Vegas he knew his first job was to save Lyn from a Sea Demon, but the next order of business was to convince her he would someday mean more to her than she'd ever expected. But her stubborn nature and unbendable spirit consumed Deacon...and he had to chase away all the demons real and imagined in order to win her heart.

Sweet Surrender
Book Five in the McKenna Clan Series

Ripped from her family at the top of Infinity Cliff, Kimi McKenna finds herself thrust somewhere into the future. Dark elements threaten to destroy the earth unless Kimi can work together with the white witch to stop the destruction. Confused by her mate's role in the conspiracy, she refuses to acknowledge the connection. But amidst raging fire and attacks on the people she is coming to hold dear, she allows Maska O'keefe into her heart.

Maska O'keefe has loved the beautiful shapeshifter for years. Unable to save her life years ago, he vows to watch over her as he is given a second chance to convince her that even though he is a witch and not a shifter, they are indeed soul mates. Kimi's divided loyalties between her family and the cause she is now a part of will determine their relationship. Only the part she plays as the messiah can bring this to a conclusion in the final battle.

Dakota's Bride
The first book in the Lakota/Pinkerton Series

When Emma St. John received her brother's letter imploring her to escape her stepfather's vengeful scheme and to trust Dakota Barringer with her life, she was willing to chance it. But the handsome, brooding riverboat owner Emma found in Natchez a danger of another kind. For Emma soon found herself surrendering to an unrelenting desire.
Raised by the Sioux when his parents were killed, Dakota had been betrayed once before by a white woman. He wasn't about to trust another, especially one claiming that her stepfather, a powerful U.S. senator, had framed her as a murderess. But he couldn't let Emma's intoxicating effect on him. Now Dakota would risk his very life to protect the innocent beauty who had seduced him with her tender love.

My Angel
The second book in the Lakota/Pinkerton Series

A BEAUTY IN BUCKSKINS
When her father decided to send her to a finishing school back East, Angela Chamberlain refused to be confined to stuffy drawing rooms. Instead, the daring spitfire who could shoot like a man and ride like the wind longed for a life of adventure and romance—and she knew exactly who could give it to her. Devil Blackmoor was a hired gun with a dangerous reputation. But Angela was willing to go to the ends of the earth to capture the handsome devil's heart.

A DEVIL IN DISGUISE
He'd come to America looking for excitement, but Devil Blackmoor got more than he bargained for when he encountered a beautiful rebel who answered his kisses with a wild innocence that touched his very soul. Yet standing between them were more obstacles than either ever dreamed. For Devil had strapped on a gun for the wrong man. And that made Angela his enemy. Now he'll have to choose between his duty and the woman he loves more than life.

The Locket
The third book in the Lakota/Pinkerton Series

The year is 1894. Seeking revenge for crimes against his family, Misha Petrovich follows a path that leads straight to Ariel Cameron's boarding house in Mist Harbor, Oregon. A family heirloom in Ariel's possession leads Misha to believe she is guilty. The locket has been handed down to the oldest girl in the Petrovich family for generations. Ariel is innocent of wrong doing, but her father is not. Misha is torn by his feelings for Ariel and his need for restitution against her father. Knowing that the relationship between them is fragile, Misha does everything in his power to protect Ariel's father. His efforts are to no avail when her father is shot. Ariel comes to realize Misha's steadfast courage and determination to protect her and her father despite what has happened to his family. Ariel's love and devotion heals Misha's heart.

The Talisman
The fourth book in the Lakota/Pinkerton Series

Running from a marriage that lasted one night, Dr. Moriah McKeown discovers the land she has settled on is coveted by determined and lawless men. Yet the proud young woman who once vowed never to abandon her home has second thoughts when her adopted children are threatened. Her only recourse is to enlist the aid of a dark, dangerous gun for hire.
Haunted by the past and a betrayal he will never forgive, Ian Civanovich uses his fast gun and his reckless courage to forget the faithlessness of a woman in his past. He will trust no female—nor will he rest until the threat hovering over Moriah McKeown is put to rest.

Forever His
The fifth book in the Lakota/Pinkerton Series

Struggling to come to terms with the part she played in Jacob St. John's death, Etta Barringer resigns from Pinkerton Agency and seeks peace and solace in a Rocky Mountain Cabin.
Jacob has vowed to discover the reason Etta has betrayed him, sold him out to his enemy and left him for dead.
Isolated in their cabin, they discover their love for each other and learn to trust. But the trust is shattered when Jacob learns she is married to his sworn enemy; the man who left him in the desert to die.

Allura's Secret
Twelve Dancing Princesses Book One

Allura McClellan is horrified by her father's decision to take out an ad in the Times awarding her to the man strong enough and smart enough to win her hand and uncover her secrets. She's an intelligent young woman who takes great delight in the freedom allotted to her by her father. She's well aware that marriage would effectively curtail the adventures she's shared with her sisters and cousins.

Hunter Gray is nothing like the other men who've arrived to vie for Allura's hand in marriage and everything that goes along with it. However, he is the first to refuse to concede defeat and pursue her despite her attempts to disguise her true appearance. It's her temperament that is of more concern to him than her looks. Hunter has worked all his life with the hope of someday owning his own land. Now that it looks like there's a very real possibility that everything he's ever wanted is within reach nothing is going to deter him – including Miss Allura's disagreeable disposition.

Amorica's Wager
Twelve Dancing Princesses Book Two

Amorica Hepburn was sent to London to find a husband. Finding a man was the last item on her agenda. With her two cousins, Amorica wagers she can dissuade her suitor before the others. Despite her efforts she discovers a chemistry that cannot be denied. Suddenly she is the arrogant man's wife, pledged to a marriage neither desire. But swept off to his ancestral home above the Dover cliffs and into his strong embrace, Amorica is soon possessed by a raging passion for the husband she had vowed to despise... Damian Andrews couldn't afford to trust the emerald-eyed spitfire who happened upon his secret. Amorica's hatred of all men of his kind only inflames the war that rages between them. Still, he can not control the intense desire his stubborn bride inspires, or make her surrender to his will until he has conquered the headstrong beauty on the battlefield of love...

Ravyn's Marriage of Inconvenience
Twelve Dancing Princesses Book Three

A REGAL BEAUTY
When the duchess decides to wed her to a wastrel and a fop, Ravyn Grahm

takes matters into her own hands and declares her engagement to another man. Instead of fessing up and telling her great aunt what she has done, she goes through with the pretense. Aric Lakeland is the bastard son of an earl and has a dangerous reputation. But Ravyn is willing to do most anything to keep the duchess from discovering the lie.

A DEVIL-MAY-CARE SMUGGLER
He'd bought land in America, looking to put down roots and end his life of adventure, but Aric Lakeland got more than he bargained for when he encountered a beautiful heiress who made a promise she didn't want to keep. But the promise could not be undone and standing between them were more obstacles than either ever dreamed. Aric had made plans to spend the rest of his life in America and that was at odds with Ravyn's plan of living in England and running her father's estate. Now, he'll have to choose between his dreams and the woman he loves more than life.

Christel's Sunrise
Twelve Dancing Princesses Book Four

He Made Her An Offer...

Life has thrown Christel McClellan some experiences that could have devastated a less determined woman. Beautiful, self-assured and fiercely independent, she is trying to forget the loss of her stillborn child. But is the child alive?

She Couldn't Deny...

Life is carefree for Ryder MacLaren who loves to see what is on the other side of the sunrise. Laird of Clan MacLaren, he is wealthy, handsome and happily unencumbered...until stunning Christel McClellan enters his life. When he hears her story, he believes the child she thought dead has been sold to a wealthy buyer.

Storm's Passion
Twelve Dancing Princesses Book Five

SHE MADE A PROPOSAL...

Life strikes Storm Graham a shattering blow when she learns her father has bartered her to a man she detests. Storm is beautiful, self–assured and fiercely independent, and refuses to be a pawn in her father's schemes, yet she can find no way out of this bargain made in hell. Going on the offensive she asks the wealthiest man on the eastern coast of England to marry her, never believing she might fall in love.

HE TRIED TO REFUSE...

For Hadden Johnston life has provided everything he ever wanted, including a sanctuary for homeless children. He is wealthy, handsome and happily unencumbered...until stunning Storm Graham marches into his life and proposes a marriage of convenience. Yet this type of marriage to a woman who inflames his senses is far from acceptable. If he's going to be tied down, he will move heaven and earth to have this woman warming his bed.

Gotta Have Fayth
Twelve Dancing Princesses Book Six

A regal beauty with raven hair and piercing blue eyes, Fayth Graham is unwilling to parade herself in front of the wealthy Lords of England during the season. Seeking a means to dissuade any man wishing to wed her, she seeks a way to ruin herself for marriage. When she unexpectedly meets a man with sparkling gray eyes and an infectious grin, she decides this is the man who will keep her from agreeing to obey.

He returned from six months at sea, looking for a few nights of pleasure with a willing lass, but Jarret Kinsley got more than he bargained for when he met a beautiful debutant who responded to his kisses with a wild innocence that touched his heart. Yet the obstacles looming between them might rip them apart. Both had vowed never to marry, so when consequences of their dalliances got in the way, Jarret would have to choose between the life he's always desired and the woman he loves more than life.

Ella's Pleasure
Twelve Dancing Princesses Book Seven

A WHISPER OF PLEASURE

Ella Hepburn was an auburn haired debutant from the harsh Scottish coastline—a wild innocent to be seduced and tamed. A spirited beauty, she captivated Drake Montgomerie's jaded heart—while succumbing to the smoldering desire she felt for her unyielding suitor.

A WHISPER OF DANGER

In Drake Montgomerie's glittering world of money and privilege, young Ella discovered passion and desire could overcome everything she'd been taught to resist—entangling Drake, the heir apparent, in a lethal coil of aristocratic family intrigue. But grave peril would only nurse the sparks of a love that knew no limits and a magnificent ecstasy that would not be denied.

Eveleen's Seduction
Twelve Dancing Princesses Book Eight

A WHISPER OF SEDUCTION

A brutal attack on Eveleen Hepburn's cherished island off the Scottish coastline leaves her shattered and bewildered. Learning a man she once trusted can kill as easily as he can breathe even though the deed saves her life, creates questions that need answers. An innocent beauty, she enchants

Logan Maxwell's cynical heart—giving in to the raging passion she feels for her mysterious suitor.

A WHISPER OF INTRIGUE

In Logan's Maxwell's world of espionage and privilege, young Eveleen discovers truths about herself she never expected, and a need for passion and love can overcome all her fears if she learns to accept certain truths. She finds herself entangled in a lethal battle for land that was once owned by French nobility, taken from them during the revolution and sold to Maxwell. But grave peril would unleash the flames of love that simmers, creating a magical union that cannot be refuted.

Tavia's Deception
Twelve Dancing Princesses Book Nine

WHISPERS OF DECEPTION

When her father decides to send her to London for her season, Tavia Hepburn resolves to see the world instead. The raven haired beauty decides to disguise herself as a lad and find employment on a ship bound for Barcelona as a cabin boy. But she never bargains on finding passion and love to a red haired sea captain who rescues her from certain death.

WHISPERS OF MURDER

For James Macmurra, the world is black and white until he meets a young debutante, who turns his world upside down. He's unable to deny Tavia's intoxicating effect on him. In a match tense with obstacles, unwillingness to divulge secrets, and unforeseen peril, irresistible desire and passion grows into undeniable love. James would risk his life to shelter and protect the innocent debutante who seduces him with her sweet love.

Larena's Fascination
Twelve Dancing Princesses Book Ten

WHISPERS OF FASCINATION

Fiery, free spirited Larena Graham never wanted to marry a duke. She is thrilled to be in love with the fourth son of an aristocrat, Gavin Broon. But when it seems Gavin ignores her, she set her sights on politics and bettering human life. Unsuspecting intrigue and a plot against her, she continues her dangerous plans despite Gavin's wishes.

WHISPERS OF TRUST

Gavin has every intention of properly courting the beautiful Larena until he must leave the city in order to put his affairs in order. Returning to London, he finds the woman he means to make his own is embroiled in political protests that could lead to a prison ship. Larena must learn to trust the handsome Scotsman whose most pressing mission is to protect her and keep her from harm.

Tira's Eeucation
Twelve Dancing Princesses Book Eleven

WHISPERS OF EDUCATION

Learning how to build ships is Tira Hepburn's only dream until she meets Jamie Lundin and her world is turned upside down. With her raven black hair and vivid green eyes, she tempts Jamie and pushes him to defy his vows. She never bargains on finding an irrevocable love and a passion to a man who cannot fulfill her dreams despite his burning desire for her.

WHISPERS OF A BARGAIN

Arrogant and self-assured Jamie is brought up short when Tira captures his heart. All his carefully made plans are put to the test when he decides to teach her the art of ship building if she will spend a week with him alone on his ship. He is unable to deny Tira's intoxicating effect on him. When Tira leaves him behind unwilling to live with him without the benefit of marriage, he races after her. Jamie will risk everything to shelter and protect the innocent debutante who seduces him with her sweet love.

Tira's Eeucation
Twelve Dancing Princesses Book Twelve
Whispers of Love

Aidan McLellan has loved since she first set eyes on him as a young girl. Spontaneous, wild and eager to grow up, Aidan haunts his waking thoughts day and night, insinuating herself into his life. With her fiery red hair and sparkling sapphire eyes, she seizes Blade's heart even while he tries to resist the innocent child until she becomes a woman.

Whispers of Courage

Blade has waited what seems a lifetime to claim the woman who captures his heart as a little girl. Claiming his inheritance before his younger brother takes what is rightfully his, Blade must convince Aidan of his sincerity after years of avoidance and wed her before his father dies so he can return home, securing his rightful place. Everything is put to the test when his life as well as Aidan's is threatened by the man who once called him brother.

Twelve Days to Love

When Archer Steele shows up at Calanthe Durand's failing plantation with an alligator over his shoulder, Cali thinks she's never seen a more handsome man. During the war she had to defend herself and her servants from both union and confederate soldiers. Independent and self-sufficient, she vows to never marry.

But Archer Steele has different ideas. The first time Archer sees Cali in town, he feels an instant attraction. He decides he will do everything and anything to convince the beautiful Miss Durand he is worthy of her love. During the weeks leading up to Christmas, he gives her twelve gifts in hopes she will fall in love with him. Yet they are faced with challenges they must overcome before Cali can commit to a marriage.

Door to Heaven

Jessica Lawrence is the stepdaughter of a woman born in the twentieth century transported back in time to the year 1868. An acclaimed suffragette, she raises Jessica to believe in the equality of women. Jess Law believes everything she was taught, and when the time is right she becomes a private investigator. Courageous and impetuous, Jess finds danger in her quest to save all women from white slavery. Her passionate mission results in a wedding to Roc Newman, a man she knows can steal her heart...

Roc can't trust the sapphire-eyed spitfire who invades his home in search of secret papers and knocks him flat with her karate moves. Jessica's refusal to obey his wishes serves to inflame the war between them. Still, he cannot control the intense desire his reluctant bride inspires, or make her surrender her independence, until he has conquered the headstrong beauty on the battlefield of love...

Rebel Heart

HER REBEL SPIRIT DEFIED HIS OUTSIDERS SOUL... She was velvet and silk, eyes the color of a summer storm and amber hair. Victoria DeMontville, because of a promise and a codicil to her father's will, was forced to marry one man to protect her from another. She hated Cameron Savage with a fierce passion. But to hold on to her genetic research and find a cure for the deadly Signe virus, she must pretend to love the enemy at her door, come with weapons of fire to melt her icy heart...

HIS OUTSIDERS TOUCH IGNITED RAGING PASSIONS... He wore a

mask, disguised as the Phantom, a true legend come to life. Even as war and debate over new genetic research engulfed them all, he would find his greatest adversary in the beauty who'd branded him an outsider and barbarian, the woman he was born to possess, his soul mate.

Safari Moon

Solo St. John, a wildlife photographer, is preparing for a trip to Alaska. Suddenly, Solo finds women of all sorts invading his privacy, his home and his office, all cooing nonsense words and blatantly throwing themselves at him. Solo doesn't know why, and he has no idea how to rid himself of the persistent women. He finally decides to beg a favor of his best buddy Nyssa Harrington.

In love with Solo for the past ten years and knowing he doesn't return her feelings Nyssa doesn't want to talk to Solo. She knows if she accepts his phone call, she will not be able to resist the temptation to hope again.

Straight to Heaven

Running from demons, Alexandra McMurdie stumbles into Forbidden Ground where up is down and elements of nature are contested. Though a strong independent woman in the twenty-first century' she is unprepared for life in the 1800s. Her first site of the formidable James Lawrence makes her heart skip a beat, giving her cause to reconsider her desperate need to find a way home.

Born with a silver spoon, James' life was torn apart during the War Between the States. Moving west he vows to put the life he once knew in the past. When he discovers a half-frozen woman near Gold Hill, his heart begins to thaw. His love for Alexandra and his need to keep her from a man who has pursued her through time might cost him his life as well as hers.

A Valentine's Anthology

The Lending Library-a fantasy by Christie L. Kraemer

Faeries try to fit into the human world when the forest where they make their home is destroyed by a mysterious enemy.

Chasing Rainbows-a contemporary romance by Genene Valleau

An eccentric aunt, an inventive uncle, a mother who wears poodle skirts, and a brother who wears pearls provide a hilarious backdrop for the courtship of a young woman who yearns for a "normal" family.

The Gift-an historical romance by Christine Young

A man and a woman on opposite sides of the Civil War get a second chance at love after one final battle returns soldiers to their war-torn homes to rebuild their lives.

A St. Patrick's Day Tale
by
Christine Young, C. L. Kraemer, Genene Valleau

Tumble through time…

…to Ireland in 1817, when tensions are high between Protestants and Catholics and faey people guide the fate of villagers. A lovely Catholic lass stumbles upon the weakly ritual fisticuffing between Irish lads. She falls into the lap of a handsome young Protestant. Family ties, grudges, and two conniving faeries threaten their budding love. But the faeries outsmart themselves when they hijack a time machine that has mysteriously appeared in their forest and are whisked to…

…Eugene, Oregon in the 20th century, amid a property feud between the local faeries and night elves. The conniving faeries from Olde Ireland try to stir up more mischief. However, a warrior gnome convinces the magic folk to control their own destiny, and forces the intruding faeries to take refuge in the time machine again, spinning their way toward...

...A modern day castle in western Oregon. An eccentric inventor is determined to reclaim his wayward time machine and save his beloved wife from her latest misadventure. If only they can travel safely past the black hole...

a May Day Anthology
by
Christine Young, C. L. Kraemer, Rosemary Indra, Genene Valleau

Highland Miracle — Christine Young

HURTLED THROUGH TIME, Sean Michael Sterling, landed in the midst of a May Day celebration he didn't understand, assuming the role of Laird Sterling.
ILLIGITAMATE CHILD OF NOBILITY, Reagan Douglas searches for a way out of her half brother's house.

Defying the Odds — C.L. Kraemer

The night elves on the hill aren't happy without their magic. They concoct a plan to punish those who were involved in the act that rendered them almost human. Meanwhile, Uther, the rogue night elf, has returned to woo the Librarian to be his eternal mate.

Love in Bloom — Rosemary Indra

When childhood friends reunite it takes two fairies and a matchmaking daughter to help them admit their true love for each other.

No More Poodle Skirts — Genie Gabriel

After drifting for years in the innocent age of the 1950s, a woman struggles to join today's world by finding a career and a new love, with some help from her zany family.

Once Upon a Christmas Moon
by
Christine Young, C. L. Kraemer, Genene Valleau

TWELVE DAYS TO LOVE

When Archer Steele shows up at Calanthe Durand's failing plantation with an alligator over his shoulder, Cali thinks she's never seen a more handsome man. During the war she had to defend herself and her servants from both union and confederate soldiers. Independent and self-sufficient, she vows to never marry. But Archer Steele has different ideas. The first time Archer sees Cali in town, he feels an instant attraction. He decides he will do everything and anything to convince the beautiful Miss Durand he is worthy of her love. During the weeks leading up to Christmas, he gives her twelve gifts in hopes she will fall in love with him.

BOOTS AND BLADES

An ancient evil from the old country has arrived in the high desert of Oregon. Gnome children are vanishing then re-appearing, showing various stages of traumatization. Tiamoon, warrior gnome, will put her skills to use alongside Killian, a handsome warrior, also in need of a cause.

CHRISTMAS PAWSIBILITIES

With their world destroyed and their space ship malfunctioning, the dogizens of Planet Canid have little choice but to crash land on Earth. They face tortuous experiments at the hands of the Geeks in Green...or they can trust an eccentric inventor and his zany family to deliver the Canine Queen's puppies and help them celebrate new lives.

VISIT OUR WEBSITE

http://www.roguephoenixpress.com

Rogue Phoenix Press

Representing Excellence in Publishing

*Quality trade paperbacks and downloads
in multiple formats,
in genres ranging from historical to contemporary romance,
mystery and science fiction.
Visit the website then bookmark it.
We add new titles each month!*